~p in
~~~~~~ ~~~ ~~~ ~~~~~~ ~~~~~~ and also
married a policeman. After becoming the mother of triplets, she took some time off from her writing whilst she raised her children. Shortlisted for the Romantic Novelists' Association Award in 1993, she has now written twenty-seven hugely successful novels. Lyn Andrews divides her time between Merseyside and Ireland.

lyn
andrews

*Mist Over
The Mersey*

headline

First published in 1994 by Corgi Books
an imprint of Transworld Publishers

First published in this paperback edition in 2008
by HEADLINE PUBLISHING GROUP

2

ISBN 978 0 7553 4187 0

Typeset in Janson by Avon DataSet Ltd,
Bidford-on-Avon, Warwickshire

Printed and bound in Great Britain by
Clays Ltd, St Ives plc

Headline's policy is to use papers that are natural, renewable and
recyclable products and made from wood grown in sustainable
forests. The logging and manufacturing processes are expected to
conform to the environmental regulations of the country of origin.

HEADLINE PUBLISHING GROUP
An Hachette Livre UK Company
338 Euston Road
London NW1 3BH

www.headline.co.uk
www.hachettelivre.co.uk

For Elizabeth Banks,
a new friend but a dear one.

I would like to thank Graham Maddocks, author of *Liverpool Pals*, for allowing me to use extracts and information from his excellent book on the history of the 17th, 18th, 19th and 20th Battalions Kings (Liverpool) Regiment. No factual or indeed fictional work that strives to portray the history of Liverpool could do justice to the subject without the aid of Mr Maddocks's extremely informative book.

Lyn Andrews
Southport, 1993

Part One

Chapter One

1912

'THEY'RE POSH. OUR MAM says they're posh.' Chrissie Burgess's statement, uttered in a tone of smug defiance, broke the silence that had descended at her approach. The three figures grouped around the street lamp by the bridge over the Liverpool to Leeds canal at the bottom of Burlington Street, stared at her with hostility.

The evening was cold and held a promise of rain or sleet. The usually harsh yellow light thrown out by the spluttering gas jet was misty, diffused by the dampness rising from the murky waters of the canal. The two girls in the group pulled their shawls closer to their bodies, a meagre defence against the chill. They had congregated here for as long as they could remember. And as soon as they had been able to climb, the boys had always perched on the stone parapet of the bridge. Winter and summer they'd come here. After school, after chores had been finished, after street games were over and after mass on Sundays.

But this was a special meeting. In three days' time it would be Christmas Eve, and they'd been discussing their hopes and plans for the holiday until Chrissie's arrival had silenced them. This sharing of joys and sorrows, ambitions and disappointments would be the very last one for most of them. Today, Friday 20 December, was the day they ceased to be children. They'd left school that afternoon. Most of them had raced through the doors of Our Lady's in Eldon Street, laughing and cheering. Jerry Harvey was the exception as he'd always gone to a Protestant school. Now they stood on the brink of adulthood: at least, working adulthood.

'Ah, gerroff, Chrissie Burgess! Posh people don't live around 'ere.' Mary Simcock was openly derisive in her disbelief.

Chrissie who, at eleven, was three years younger than anyone else, narrowed her blue eyes and glared at Mary. She'd expected this reaction and had prepared for it. She glanced quickly up the street. She didn't have much time. It was eight o'clock and Mam would be yelling any minute now for her to get inside.

The Burgesses ran the grocery shop on the corner of Burlington Street and Vauxhall Road and were better off than most of their neighbours. 'This is a respectable family and we should set an example,' was her mam's standard reply whenever she complained about having to be in. It was uttered with heavy and deliberate emphasis when some of their more rowdy neighbours came staggering up the street from the Black Dog on their way home.

Chrissie tossed her head, her thick dark ringlets catching the lamplight and gleaming blue-black like a crow's wing. 'They *are* posh! Mam says she heard the woman talking to one of the kids. "Deirdre, stop dawdling and help your father!"' Chrissie mimicked the plummy tones with some accuracy.

'Deirdre! Bloody Deirdre! What kind of a name is that?' Mary screamed aloud with laughter, falling against the shoulder of Chrissie's brother Michael who was grinning broadly.

'A posh one!' Chrissie snapped. 'An' I'll tell Mam you swore, Mary Simcock, and that you laughed at her, our Mike!' Chrissie glared at her brother, stung that her news had been met with such hilarity.

'Oh, shut up! Go home and play shop with your banie mugs. Mam will be looking for you.' Mike was still grinning, but it irritated him beyond endurance to have Chrissie tagging along everywhere he went. She'd never understood that this was *their* place. 'You don't *own* that lamp! You don't *own* this street!' was Chrissie's usual retort, and what was worse, Mam backed her up. 'Take her with you,' was Mam's reply when he complained.

His smile disappeared. She'd have to realize now that he was grown up. He was no longer 'our kid', in fact he was no longer a kid. Tomorrow morning he would don a brown overall coat and stand behind the counter with his dad.

His expression became disgruntled. It wasn't what

he wanted. It wasn't what his mam wanted for him either, but it was better than the docks, which was where Tommy Kerrigan was headed tomorrow, or across the water to the Woodside Lairage and abattoir where Jerry Harvey was headed.

These thoughts had barely formed in his mind when Hilda Burgess's strident voice echoed down the length of the street.

'Chrissie! Chrissie, get in here now!'

Chrissie pursed her lips tightly but held her ground. She had more to tell them about the new family that were moving into number eighty, on the corner of Titchfield Street, and it wasn't often she had such an interested audience despite the laughter.

'Christine Burgess! Do you hear me? It's nearly five past eight. Get in here now!'

'You'll get a belt around the ear if you don't go,' Mike prophesied.

Chrissie knew her moment of glory had passed. She also knew that he was right, her mother's use of her full Christian name was always a sign of annoyance that boded ill for her.

'Well, you just wait and see! There was lots more I could have told you!' She stuck out her tongue and screwed up her nose before turning and running swiftly up the street.

The little group watched her disappear into the gloom. Behind them, where Burlington Street crossed Great Howard Street and beyond, where it converged with the Dock Road, the silos and warehouses of Tate & Lyle's sugar refinery loomed like dark mountains against the sky, and from the river came the deep-throated blast of an outward-bound liner's steam whistle.

Mary drew her shawl tightly to her and crossed her arms over her chest. She was tall and well developed for her age, with dark brown eyes and a mane of unruly reddish-brown hair. She usually wore her old black shawl thrown carelessly around her shoulders. Her calico blouse was tucked tightly into the waistband of her skirt to emphasize the fullness of her breasts. Mary was what was known as 'a bold madam', despite all Lizzie Simcock's attempts to restrain her daughter's flirtatious manner.

'Do you think she's right?' Mary asked of no one in particular.

'With a name like that I bet she is,' Nancy Butterworth answered glumly. 'You should have let her stay until we'd at least found out something more about them.' This rebuke was addressed to Mike. 'No one posh has ever lived here,' she finished.

'Well, I'm fed up with our Chrissie taggin' on all the time. At least Mam keeps her out of the shop, so I'll get some peace and quiet at last.' Chrissie was a pain, a constant torment to him, and she was crafty too. If she didn't get her own way she knew just what to do and say to get him into trouble, but the fact that he would be in the shop all day didn't bring him that much pleasure. 'Mind, I'd liked to have gone to the Mechanics Institute,' he added wistfully.

'Maybe later on, lad,' Mam had said consolingly.

'Times are hard – for everyone,' was what his father had stated firmly, ignoring the look of annoyance his wife had shot at him. Mike balled his fists and thrust them deeper into his pockets. The whole top and bottom of it was that there simply wasn't the money to spare for more education.

Mike smiled ruefully at the girls. They were as different as chalk and cheese, he thought, although both were fatherless, Mrs Simcock and Mrs Butterworth each having been widowed long years ago. There the similarity between the two women ended. Lizzie Simcock was a thin, starchy-looking woman, mean, miserable and narrow-minded. Bridgit, or Bridie Butterworth as she was known, was plump, easy-going, and she liked her drop of gin too. She was always laughing and joking with Red MacClelland at the Black Dog, or so he'd heard. There were other things he'd heard about Bridie Butterworth, but he didn't dwell on them, at least, not when Nancy was around.

He wondered, as he'd done so many times before, did Nancy take after her long dead da? She was a serious girl, unlike her jovial mother in more ways than one. Whereas Bridie was plump, Nancy was thin. Bridie had thick auburn hair, Nancy's was a pale imitation that often straggled untidily. Bridie's green eyes always seemed to sparkle, Nancy's hazel ones seldom did.

His speculations were interrupted by the sounds of laughter and hobnails sparking on the cobbles.

'So you finally got here. What kept you?' Mike asked of the taller of the two lads.

'Ask him.' Tommy Kerrigan jerked his head in his companion's direction.

'Me da an' his sermons!' Jerry Harvey answered irritably, rolling his dark eyes expressively. 'Hard times are sent to test our spiritual strength and how we should praise the Lord that we have gainful employment.'

Mike pulled a face. Times always seemed to be hard around Scotland Road. Mr Kerrigan, Tommy's da, never knew from one day to the next if he had work. It was the system they used down at the docks, and when he did have money most of it was spent before he got home. Then Mrs Kerrigan would get mad and there'd be one of the very public shouting matches that characterized the Kerrigan household. Usually, all the Kerrigan kids joined in, all nine of them. They were what his mam called 'no marks' and she'd never approved of his friendship with Tommy.

Jerry's da was better off. It wasn't a bad job working on the tugs; it was steady and they had the entire house to themselves, even though there were only four of them. Unlike many houses in the street, there weren't two or three families living there. No one lived in their cellar, either. They used it for the purpose it was intended – to store coal – and there weren't many cellars in Burlington Street which could boast that fact.

The Harveys were a cut above many of their neighbours. They were very religious and went to the Mission Hall three times on Sunday. Mike thought that having to go to church once was bad enough, with all the scrubbing and polishing it involved; to say nothing of the nagging from Mam. He knew Jerry hated having to go, but he also knew that Jerry was too afraid of his da to rebel. They were in the minority in Burlington Street, and lived at the top end with the other Protestant families. The middle and bottom of the street was predominantly Catholic. Even amongst their neighbours, most of whom belonged to the Loyal Orange Order, the Harveys kept themselves to themselves.

'Our Chrissie said there's a posh family moved into number eighty.'

'No one posh would come and live here,' Tommy retorted.

'She said the girl's name was Deirdre!' Mary laughed.

'That definitely sounds posh,' Jerry agreed.

'They must be mad or broke, or both,' Tommy added.

'Fallen on hard times maybe?' Nancy said sagely.

'Oh, don't you start an' all!' Jerry retorted, thinking of the time spent listening to his da's moralizing.

'Well, let's go and have a look at them for ourselves. I'm fed up standing here. It's freezing and me feet are numb.' Mary looked down at her feet with disgust. They were encased in worn and broken boots, and she had no stockings. She didn't care what her mam said, when she got her first week's wage from Wilson's Laundry she was going to buy herself a decent pair of boots and thick woollen stockings. Maybe even new ones, something she'd never had in her entire life. She sniffed, thinking of what Lizzie said whenever she complained. There was no man's wage coming into number four Devon Court. Only what she could earn by cleaning. Mary supposed she was lucky to have a pair of boots at all. A lot of kids – herself included more often than not – went barefoot in all weathers.

Nancy's voice interrupted her deliberations.

'We can't just go and stand gawping at them across the street.'

'Why not? It's what your mam does. There's nothing goes on in this street that she doesn't know about. Or your mam, Mary,' Tommy laughed. 'Me mam says she makes a point of waving and calling "Ow do, Lizzie!" whenever she passes your 'ouse, 'cos she knows she's peerin' out of the window.'

Mary grimaced comically. Mary wouldn't mind having Bridie as a mother. You could have a laugh with Bridie and she didn't care what people said to her, or about her. Her own mam did and it was true, Lizzie was always peering through the curtains. She'd often wondered if there had been a mix-up when she and Nancy had been born within hours of one another. Had someone swapped the babies over? These things did happen. She was far more like Bridie than Nancy was.

Their indecision was ended as a slight figure approached them. Jerry sighed heavily.

'It's your Hannah,' Mike needlessly informed him.

'I've to come and tell you you've to come in. Da says you've to be in bed early, 'cos you'll have to be up at five to get the first ferry.' Hannah's words were uttered apologetically.

All the lightness went out of Jerry's mood as his dark eyes searched his sister's face. Why did Da have to make him look like a kid, like Chrissie Burgess, in front of his mates? 'I've only just got here! Tell him I won't be long,' he said curtly.

'He said . . .' Hannah's voice faltered and she stood twisting her thin hands together. She was so pale and nervous-looking.

'Oh, all right, I'll come in a few minutes,' Jerry said reluctantly, and was rewarded by the look of sheer relief that crossed his sister's features.

'Don't forget to bring us a nice bit of beef 'ome termorrer!' Mary laughed.

'Fat chance of that. I'll probably be up to me knees in blood an' guts. That's if I'm not gored or trampled to death first!' Jerry said morosely.

'Sod that for a lark! I wouldn't fancy working there,' Tommy commented.

'It's a job, isn't it? Us five have been dead lucky. More than half our class haven't got any job to go to. Besides, Nance and me will be stuck in that stinking, sweaty laundry all day.' Mary linked her arm through Nancy's. 'Come on, Nance, let's go and see what this "posh" lot are like. I've never heard of anyone called Deirdre before, have you?'

After deliberating for a moment, Nancy shook her head and the two walked across the bridge in the direction Hannah Harvey had taken.

The three lads hesitated, each searching the others' faces for a decisive sign until Mike shrugged and began to follow the girls. Tommy fell into step beside him. They both found their curiosity hard to overcome and besides, there was nothing more interesting on offer. It was too late and too cold for just hanging around street corners, hoping a better diversion would turn up.

The door of number eighty was open, and on the pavement stood a battered cabin trunk and a hatbox.

Mary nudged her companion and pointed to the hatbox. 'Looks like Chrissie was right, no one round here has one of those.'

'Well, why have they come here? If I had money I wouldn't come to live in this street. I wouldn't want to live around here at all.'

The two boys had caught up.

'Go on, knock on the door,' Tommy urged.

Nancy looked horrified. 'We can't do that!'

'Why not? It's half open. Ask if there's anything we can do ter help, like.'

Mary thought it odd that there were no neighbours around, no one moving the things off the street and into the house. People always helped each other, and usually there were at least one or two women standing at their doors: the only place available in overcrowded households for a bit of peace and quiet and a breath of fresh air. 'You knock then,' she challenged.

Tommy shrugged. 'Wasn't me who wanted to come up here.'

'Oh, shut up, you're as nosey as the rest of us,' Mary answered scornfully, boldly going up the four narrow steps and raising her hand to the tarnished knocker.

Like most of the houses in the street and in the dark, fetid courts that led off it, number eighty was badly in need of repair. The paintwork on the door and the tall sash windows was peeling and cracked. The stone steps were worn and flaking but, unlike all the other houses, the windows were streaked with dirt, no curtains hung at any of them. No donkey stone had been used to whiten the steps or window-sills, and no plume of smoke issued from the chimney.

Before Mary could bring down the knocker, a dim figure emerged from the narrow lobby.

'Er, can I help you?' The voice was quiet and there was no heavy nasal inflection, no trace of the local 'Scouse' dialect.

Mary hastily retreated down the steps and the others moved backwards as the girl came out onto the top step, looking nervous.

Mary quickly eyed her up and down. She looked to be about the same age as Nancy and herself. Her dress had once been a warm shade of deep pink and was quite fashionable, but it was now shabby and stained. Her light brown hair was straight and drawn severely away from her face. Her eyes were a pale, watery blue and on the bridge of her nose, balanced lopsidedly, was a pair of spectacles. One of the arms had been mended with rows of black thread.

Mary pointed at the trunk. 'We wondered if there was anythin' we could do to, er, help.'

'Oh, I see.' The girl glanced nervously over her shoulder towards the back of the house.

'The lads can carry those in, if you want them to,' Nancy offered. 'Are you . . . are you Deirdre?'

The girl smiled. 'Yes. How did you know?'

Nancy hesitated. It would be rude to say their arrival had caused a stir. 'Oh, er . . . someone told me, so we've come . . . well, to say hello.'

They all stood staring at each other in awkward silence, until Mike spoke up.

'Do you want them shifting or not?'

The girl bit her lip and glanced over her shoulder again. 'Well, you see, my mother's not well, and my father's gone to the little shop, up there, to see what he can get for her.'

'Ma Burgess will have a field day!' Mary muttered to Nancy. She'd probably have his entire life story out of him in ten minutes flat and then that Chrissie would be unbearable. Mother and daughter had at least one thing in common, a mouth like a parish oven. Well she wasn't going to be outdone by them. 'What's the matter with her?'

'She . . . she hasn't really got over having Rose, my sister. She's not been well . . . since then.'

Again there was an embarrassed silence.

'Have you got any brothers? Will they be moving that lot, is that it?' Tommy asked.

The girl came down the steps after pulling the door behind her. 'Mother says we've not to be telling all and sundry our business but, well, I've got two brothers and a sister. I'm the eldest. Philip and David are trying to sort out the bedrooms. Or at least one room. Mother says this place should be condemned, it's not fit for human habitation, and there's hardly any furniture at all and they said there would be.'

'Oh, is that what she said? What did she come here for then if it's not fit to live in?' Mary's tone was harsh and the friends drew closer at this outspoken condemnation of their street, their homes. All the

15

houses were in the same dilapidated condition, but no one complained much. They made the best of things, for there were far worse places than Burlington Street.

'There was nowhere else. We just couldn't afford anywhere else.'

There was no trace of arrogance, regret or self-pity in the girl's voice, and suddenly Nancy felt sorry for her. She'd obviously been used to better things. 'Why? I . . . I mean I don't want to be nosey, Deirdre . . .'

The girl smiled again. 'Dee, call me, Dee, it's better than Deirdre. I hate my name!' This was uttered with conviction. 'I'm Dee Chatterton.'

Nancy smiled back shyly. 'I'm Nancy. Nancy Butterworth. This is Mary Simcock, Tommy Kerrigan and Mike Burgess, his mam and dad have the shop your dad's gone to.'

Dee nodded at them in turn. They were the first friendly faces she'd seen all day. And it had been a long, weary, confusing day. Father had been hopeless. She'd automatically looked to him for help, organization and some stability. That's what fathers were for. They were supposed to be the ones who made the important decisions and made sure their orders were carried out. It upset her dreadfully to realize that her father was as confused as she was. He just didn't know how to cope with anything; the smallest decision seemed beyond him. It had been at her insistence that he'd gone to the shop. Mother had screamed at him for most of the afternoon. The same accusations, the same vituperative slurs on his character that were now all too familiar, but which still had the power to wound and destroy what little self-confidence he had. Little Rose had cried and screamed, and both boys had been sullen and stubbornly uncooperative. The burden of coping with everything had fallen on herself, and she was too young, too inexperienced.

'Right then, we'll move this first.' Mike grinned at Dee and indicated to Tommy that he take the other handle of the trunk.

Dee stepped aside and pushed open the door, then the smile was wiped from her face and she bit her lip. Her mother was standing in the doorway and despite her obvious thinness and exhaustion, Dee could see she was angry.

'Just what do you think you're doing with that trunk?'

The two lads looked at each other, taken aback by the curt, hostile tone.

'Er . . . we're just moving it, Missus, 'elpin' yer, like,' Tommy answered.

'Well, you can just put it down again. You're moving it nowhere and I'll thank you not to call me "Missus". Deirdre, come inside, please . . .'

Nancy and Mary both looked at Dee pityingly, as she ducked her head and went up the steps.

'I've told you, I don't want any of you associating with these . . . these people.' Gwendoline Chatterton's icy gaze swept over the little group on her doorstep with distaste.

'Mother, they only wanted to help.'

'I'm sure, but your father and the boys will manage.

Come inside, please, and see to Rose. I'm too tired to cope with any more of her tantrums.'

Before she followed her mother, Dee cast an imploring look at Nancy and Mary. 'It's her nerves and she *is* very tired,' she whispered.

'That's all right. Perhaps we'll see you tomorrow,' Nancy whispered back.

'Perhaps,' Dee replied, closing the door with a heavy sigh.

'Well, isn't she a stuck-up owld bitch!' Mary stated loudly, as they began to walk up the street.

'Oh, take no notice of her. She'll soon come down off her high horse. Toffee-nosed old biddy,' Tommy concurred.

'God, fancy having a mam like that, it must be terrible.' Nancy felt very sorry for Dee Chatterton. She knew what it was like to have a mother that everyone talked about, and if Mrs Chatterton intended to carry on as though she owned the street and call her neighbours 'people', which in that tone of voice meant she considered them scum, then tongues would certainly be wagging.

As she bade goodbye to Mary, then Mike and Tommy, Nancy wondered why the Chattertons had come to Burlington Street. They were obviously used to much better neighbourhoods, so why could they only afford four-and-six a week rent for a supposedly furnished house? Why didn't they have any furniture of their own? Maybe she'd find out tomorrow. She'd try to see Dee again, for she'd warmed to the plain, quiet girl in whom she sensed a kindred spirit.

Chapter Two

————◆————

Dee FOLLOWED HER MOTHER down the dismal, dirty lobby with its bare boards and tattered remnants of wallpaper. Her back and shoulders were aching and her eyes smarted with unshed tears of humiliation. They'd only been trying to help, they were about her age and they'd seemed friendly enough. Just like the other people who had come to the door when they'd first arrived in Burlington Street, seven hours ago.

Father had wanted to accept their offers of assistance and to the first man he'd even said, 'Thank you very much, it's so kind of you,' before Mother had interrupted with words of icy, contemptuous dismissal. Words that were just the right side of politeness, but only just. Dee hadn't seen any of their new neighbours, she'd only heard the short conversations before the door had been firmly closed. She had been too busy trying to control her younger brothers and little Rose, and overcome her own feelings of horror and wretchedness at their predicament. She didn't know quite what she had expected, but it certainly hadn't been this.

Had it really only been seven hours since they'd got out of the taxicab, which had been sheer extravagance as the driver had muttered acidly as he'd helped pile their few belongings on the pavement. She had stared down the street with its rows of tall, soot-blackened houses crowded together. There were barefoot urchins who seemed to be everywhere and women standing on their doorsteps or in small knots, dressed in long dark skirts and voluminous black shawls which covered their heads. She'd seen no one wearing a hat, except her mother. She'd caught a glimpse of the even more dismal courts that dissected the street like rabbit warrens, and the huge buildings that dominated the bottom end of it. Her numbed and shocked mind had refused to believe that this was where they were now to live.

As soon as they reached the kitchen Gwendoline Chatterton turned on her daughter. 'Deirdre, I forbid you to speak to anyone in this street. I don't want them hanging around the door either, do I make myself clear?' She was bone weary. Her pain-wracked body cried out for the comfort of a soft bed, clean sheets and warmth, but there were none of those things to be had and she, too, was in a state of exhausted shock. She hated her husband for what he'd done to her, to them all. He was the weakest, stupidest, most improvident man she'd ever met. If she'd had some money of her own she would have walked out and left him. She'd have left them all without a backward glance because she was sick of them with their constant demands on her. With fury and resentment burning in her, her once beautiful face contorted with these emotions, she sank slowly into the battered chair, the only chair in the room, and indicated that Dee pass her her handbag: a scuffed remnant of better days.

Silently Dee watched her mother open the bag, rummage around and draw out a small enamelled pillbox. 'Shall I get you some water?' she asked hesitantly.

Gwendoline nodded and watched as her daughter went into the tiny scullery. There was no light in the room, for there were no windows at all in the back of the house. Dee suppressed a cry as she heard the quick scuffling and felt something run over her foot. She knew where the few cracked and chipped dishes were, for she'd got to know this room quickly. There was no running water and she'd gone to the standpipe around the corner to fill the kettle and the only pan, both of which now stood on the stained wooden drainingboard. As she clutched the kettle and the cup to her, two tears ran down her cheeks. This was surely a nightmare. It had to be. She'd wake up soon, she *had* to.

Dashing the tears away with the back of her hand, she returned to the kitchen and handed the cup to her mother, ignoring the look of disgust on Gwendoline's face at the sight of the vessel.

'For heaven's sake, isn't there a better cup than that?'

'You know there isn't, I showed you . . . out there . . .' Dee's voice trailed off. Couldn't Mother see she was trying to do her best? She poured the water from the kettle, her hands shaking with fatigue.

Gwendoline gulped down the pills and water quickly. 'Has your father sorted out those dreadful rooms up there?'

'I . . . I think the boys were supposed to do that.'

'How can he expect children to move furniture around? And where is he? He's been gone simply hours!'

It was on the tip of Dee's tongue to say there was only a packing case and an old lumpy mattress upstairs, but she bit back the words. To stem the torrent of abuse that she could see forming, Dee lifted little Rose from her mother's lap. Rose had exhausted herself, and her head drooped on Dee's shoulder.

'It's all right, Rosie, go to sleep,' Dee soothed. Rose was little more than a baby, and because she'd been born so long after David, she'd been thoroughly spoiled. She threw terrible temper tantrums and couldn't understand why all the things she'd been used to had suddenly disappeared. Mother's way of dealing with Rose's tantrums was to either ignore them or slap her hard, which only made three-year-old Rose worse.

'I'll take Rose and see what they're doing up there. Father won't be long now. You rest.' With those words, and clutching Rose tightly to her, Dee fled in the direction of the staircase.

The light from the street lamp on the corner filtered in through the grimy window of the front bedroom, and she could see Philip sitting on the edge of what looked like a large board. David was scrabbling around on the floor.

'What's he doing and why haven't you done something . . . anything?'

Philip stared at her morosely but didn't answer. Life was getting worse by the hour. He was still upset and shocked by the catastrophic events that had overtaken him. He'd had to leave his boarding school hastily, not that he'd minded that too much. He did miss his friends, and home had become a battlefield, the air electric with tension and hostility. He realized that Dee was still talking.

'You're twelve, Phil, you're old enough to try to help me!'

'Help you to do what, Dee? It's awful here. There are no beds, just a smelly old mattress and a tea-chest in there.' He jerked his head in the direction of the back of the house where the other bedroom was situated. 'There's nothing.' He kicked the edge of the piece of wood at his feet, and Dee now saw that it was an old door.

'Then we'll just have to make do with what there is!' she snapped. If she began to think about how little there was of anything in this so-called furnished house, she would just break down. 'David, stop doing that!'

David Chatterton, possessed of an easy-going nature and with all the cheerfulness of a nine-year-old who had had little in the way of parental restraint over the last weeks, grinned up at his sister. 'There are hundreds of spiders, Dee. I've got a pocket full of them.'

Dee uttered a shriek. 'You little monster! Stamp on them, quickly!'

'It's bad luck to kill a spider, they eat all the bugs. I've got some bugs, too.'

Dee felt hysteria rising up in her and she clutched Rose so tightly that the child cried out. 'Hush, Rosie. Oh, Phil, do something with him, please! Anything. I don't think I can stand much more. I feel dizzy.'

Philip moved quickly and, grabbing his brother, began to shake him. David started yelling at the top of his voice.

Dee swayed and groaned aloud. This was only getting worse and she was so tired, so very, very tired. Putting Rose down gently, she reached out and slapped David hard. 'Get downstairs this minute and go and empty your pockets in the street! And don't go crying to Mother, she's already cross and tired.'

Stifling a sob, David ran out and they heard his boots clattering on the bare boards of the stairs. Dee picked up her sister and sagged against the window-sill. It was so cold in here that she could see her breath.

'Oh Phil, what are we going to do? Mother's ill, and Father just can't cope. He looks so . . . so lost.'

'Lost is the right word, Dee,' Philip said spitefully. 'He "lost" all his money and that's why we're stuck in this . . . this dump!'

'Don't you start, Philip Chatterton! I'm sick and tired of hearing about it. It's all Mother goes on and on about.'

Philip was unrepentant. 'Well it's true, it's all his fault.'

Dee's remaining resolve snapped and, burying her face in Rose's hair, she cried, her body shaking with deep, racking sobs. She wanted to go home. To their lovely house in Highgate. She wanted her own bedroom with its rose-patterned wallpaper and pink carpet, a cheerful fire burning in the fireplace and Nanny tucking her up in her bed. A bed with crisp white sheets and soft, satin-covered eiderdown. She missed Nanny desperately. It was no use Father telling her she was grown-up now and she didn't need a nanny. She didn't want to be grown-up, not if it entailed all the terrible things that now faced her in this dreadful house. She was only fourteen, still a child, as both her mother and Nanny had so often reminded her in the past. Now she desperately wanted to remind both her parents of this fact, but was afraid to. Things were bad enough without causing more trouble, or throwing a tantrum like Rose.

Philip, too, was near to tears but he fought them back manfully. All his life it had been impressed upon him that boys and men didn't cry. It was cowardly and just not 'done'. 'I'm sorry, Dee, I didn't mean to make you cry.'

Dee sniffed. 'I know, but I keep thinking it's all a dream, that I'm going to wake up at . . . at home.'

Philip placed his arm around her thin, shaking shoulders. 'It's not our home any more. The bailiffs came, don't you remember, Dee?'

She could only nod. She wished she didn't remember that awful day. They'd taken everything. All they had been allowed to keep were the clothes they stood up in, some spare clothes and a couple of blankets that were now in the trunk which was still out on the front step. Her father had stood as though turned to stone. Her mother had wept, clinging to his arm, while they'd all huddled together, watching, unable to believe what was happening.

Then they'd had to leave the house. Apparently it now belonged to the bank. They'd gone to a seedy hotel until they'd come here. That decision had been taken without any reference to them. Their opinions didn't matter. They were only children.

When she looked back she realized that, one by one, things had begun to disappear. Pieces of her mother's jewellery, the silver tea-set, the big silver punch bowl from the dining-room, even the cruet sets.

Tradesmen had come to demand money, and then pieces of furniture, too, disappeared. There had been loud complaints about unpaid wages, and some of the servants had left. Then Mrs Whelan, the cook, and finally Nanny. She'd cried and cried that day and Nanny had wept too.

It had been explained that Father had made a great number of bad investments. He'd had a very good position in the City, in a merchant bank, but he'd gambled unwisely on the stock-market. And then there were the other forms of gambling; there were large sums of money owing. Gentlemen always had to honour such debts. Under such circumstances the bank had demanded his resignation, and the house had to be sold. Mother had been very extravagant with her clothes and jewels, and the grand parties they'd always given. Mother's friends had drifted away and the house had become very quiet. Both her mother and father's parents were dead. She'd never known them, nor did she have any aunts or uncles, so there was no one to help them out.

That's why they'd come to Liverpool. It was a thriving port and Father had what her mother had called 'contacts' here. It was supposed to be a new start in a city where no one knew about them, where no one could look down their aristocratic noses or sneer at their disgrace. And it was a terrible disgrace, so she'd gathered from the frequent arguments. Despite each shock she had had to contend with over the last weeks, today had been the worst day of all.

No one had realized how desperate life had really become until they had tried to find affordable accommodation. Oh, they'd looked at some very nice houses and rooms in quiet, prosperous areas of the city, but they couldn't afford the rent. Nor were landlords prepared to take four children. Miserably they'd trailed after their parents as they'd moved around the city, until Mother had been so exhausted that she'd taken them all back to the Ladies' Waiting Room at Exchange Station. Through teeth gritted with pain and anger she'd instructed Father to 'just find *somewhere*, for God's sake! Do you want us to sleep in the street?' He'd come back an hour later and ushered them all into the taxicab which had brought them here.

She tried to fight down the sobs, to check the tears. 'I'm all right now. You and David bring the trunk in. We can empty it, and Rose can sleep in it. Mother and Father will have to have the mattress in there.' She was feeling a bit calmer now. The hysteria was fading. 'I saw a pile of old newspapers in the corner of the front room; they're supposed to be quite good to lie on. I read that somewhere.'

'Will we have to sleep on the floor?' Philip sounded incredulous.

'I suppose we can sleep on that,' she pointed to the door. 'We can roll up some papers for pillows. We'll have to sleep in our clothes and put our coats over us. There's only two blankets.'

'It's freezing in here. Can't we light a fire, Dee?'

'What with? Father's gone to get something to eat, and some candles and matches, and maybe some coal or wood, but there won't be enough for two fires. We'll have to use the range to boil water.'

From downstairs came the sound of angry voices, and they both looked at each other with trepidation.

'Father's back,' Philip stated. 'I'm sick of them rowing all the time, Dee.'

'Hush, I hate it too, but things are bad enough. Don't let them hear you saying things like that.'

Wearily she dragged herself down the stairs and into the kitchen where her parents were yelling at each other. At the entrance of Dee and Philip the shouting stopped.

Edward Chatterton was a fair-haired man in his early forties, usually mild-mannered and easy-going, but now harassed and prematurely aged, his shoulders a little stooped. His suit was crumpled and his shirt grubby. He had placed his few purchases on the square deal table. His wife studiously looked at the floor.

'There are some candles, matches, a loaf, a bit of tea

28

and sugar and some margarine. The woman in the shop was very helpful. A pleasant sort, I thought. She said the dairy was closed but she gave me this: it's a sort of milk. And she let me have some bundles of wood – "chips" she called them. I left them in the hallway. At least we can all have a cup of tea. That should cheer us up.'

Dee could have cried again. He was trying. He was trying so hard to be cheerful, for he'd never had to buy food or candles or wood in his entire life.

'And what are we supposed to make it in, or drink it out of?' Gwendoline snapped. 'Did that "pleasant sort of woman" tell you that?'

Edward Chatterton looked so deflated and beaten that Dee wanted to throw her arms around him and tell him they'd manage just fine. She'd often sat in the kitchen and watched Mrs Whelan. She would do the cooking. She also wanted to slap her mother hard. She knew she shouldn't feel like that. Mother was ill, she was cold, exhausted and in a state of shock, like everyone else.

'There are cups and a kettle. Phil will light the fire in the range, and we can boil the water in the kettle and put the tea in it. It will be nice and hot and we can all have a sandwich.' She tried to imitate her father's forced cheerfulness and received a look of gratitude from him.

Unceremoniously she dumped the still-sleeping Rose on her mother's lap as the two boys noisily dragged in the trunk, Phil explaining that, empty, it could be used as a bed for Rose. Dee busied herself with the kettle of water, the tea and the bread and margarine. There was no meat or cheese to go with it, but that didn't matter. She was faint with hunger and cold.

Edward Chatterton took charge of the fire, blowing on the pieces of screwed-up newspaper and wood until a small blaze was kindled on which Dee set the kettle. David had lit two of the candles and had stuck them at either end of the mantel.

The meagre rations hadn't filled six empty stomachs, and Rose complained bitterly that she was hungry and cold and that she'd wet her knickers. But Dee was thankful that at least her mother looked a little better.

'Things will be better tomorrow. I've got some people to see and we'll get some furniture and maybe Mrs Burgess at the shop will let us have groceries on credit. I explained that we were only temporarily short of money. I'll have a job in no time at all.'

Dee didn't miss the quick, scornful glance her mother shot in her father's direction. 'I met a boy called Burgess, Mike Burgess. He called with some of his friends. They wanted to know if they could help.'

'And did they?' her father asked.

Dee shook her head and gave her father a rueful little smile that was half a grimace.

'No, I sent them away. I don't intend to associate with anyone in this . . . this dreadful place, and I won't have the children mixing with those . . . those street urchins.'

Dee's lips were set in a thin tight line as anger and

resentment rose in her. Beggars – and that's what they were, whether Mother liked it or no – couldn't be choosers. They desperately needed anyone's help, just to survive, and if she saw them again she wasn't going to poke her nose in the air and ignore them.

'Come on, let's get those newspapers,' she urged her brothers. 'I'm so tired I don't think I'll even mind the bugs.' It was a brave statement and one she didn't mean. She knew she would lie awake all night, in terror of everything that crawled and scuttled up there. She was rewarded with another grateful glance from her father.

Chapter Three

DEE AWOKE NEXT MORNING cold and stiff. Her head felt as though it were bursting, her throat was on fire and she could hardly swallow. Despite everything she'd slept fitfully, tossing and turning on the hard, makeshift bed. She had never slept fully-dressed before, and she felt dirty and unkempt.

As she entered the kitchen her mother barely raised her eyes, and there was no sign of her father. Rose was crying.

'I'm hungry! I'm hungry, Dee, I want my breakfast. I want an egg and soldiers.'

Dee was in no mood for tantrums this early. 'Shut up, Rose,' she croaked. 'We're all hungry, and there's no eggs or bread. Where's Father?'

Gwendoline had spent what she considered to be the worst night of her entire life. She'd lain awake shivering with despair, revulsion and pain beneath the thin blanket. She had sobbed quietly for hours, wishing she were dead. Anything would be better than this predicament. Edward, the cause of all her distress, had snored beside her as though he hadn't a worry in the world. Now her dress was creased and dirty. She felt as though she reeked with stale perspiration, her once shining blond hair was dull and straggling. The pain in her abdomen was worse.

'I don't know. He went out, he didn't tell me where he was going. I just hope it's to find one of these "contacts" and get us out of here, or at least get us some furniture and linen and food.'

Dee passed her hand across her aching forehead. It was going to be another day like yesterday, she just knew it. 'I'll go and get some water, then we can all have a wash,' she said flatly.

'Then you can start to clean this disgusting pigsty up or we'll all contract some terrible disease. Get the boys to help you,' Gwendoline ordered.

Dee thought she had already caught something horrible. 'There's nothing to clean it up with,' she answered quietly, before going into the scullery for the pan and the kettle.

Nancy and Mary had met up on the corner of Limekiln Lane at six that morning. Sleet was lashing against the walls of the houses, driven by a strong north wind coming off the river. The roofs gleamed dully and the cobbles underfoot were slippery with sodden rubbish. The pall of thick yellowish-grey smoke, emitted by hundreds of chimneys, was being quickly dispersed by the gale. With heads bent and shawls wrapped tightly around them, they'd made their way to Walker's

Laundry that comprised a series of cavernous rooms wreathed in steam of varying density.

They'd both been sent to the huge boiler-room where the rows of coppers stood like shiny metal sentinels. It was hot and heavy work. With long wooden tongs they had to push and pull the wet linen. Then it had to be lifted and passed in metal trucks to the room that held the troughs of cold rinsing water. Betty Napier the overseer had told them it would be years before they got to work in the pressing-room and then finally the packing-room, which was considered to be the 'cushiest' job in the place.

By the time the whistle went for lunch, Nancy felt as though her arms were coming from their sockets. Her back ached and she was soaked with sweat and water. They were only allowed twenty minutes for their lunch, but she decided she would go home. Mary had quickly become very pally with two older girls and had been persuaded by them to go to Ma Bullen's pie shop. She had cajoled twopence from Lizzie, as a sub on her wages.

On reaching home, Nancy plumped herself down in the old rocker by the fire. Bridie was sitting reading a copy of yesterday's *Echo*.

'I'm worn out, Mam, and I'm that hungry my stomach thinks my throat has been cut.'

Bridie didn't raise her eyes. 'Well, you knew it wasn't going to be a bed of roses, Nance, didn't you?'

'What's for dinner, then?'

'You'll have to go down to Burgess's. I haven't had time yet.'

Nancy looked around the untidy room and wondered what her mam had been doing all morning. Then she sighed. Bridie had probably only just got up.

'Go and look in the press, luv, see what we're short of and then ask Hilda to put it on the slate. I'll get me wages tonight.'

Bridie worked as a barmaid at the Green Man on the corner of Vauxhall Road and Green Street. She went in at lunch time and stayed until six, then she went up to the Black Dog to start her second stint of the day. It was often late when she got home, and she'd usually had quite a few drinks as well.

Wearily Nancy went and looked without much pleasure in the wooden, mesh-fronted food press. Tea, sugar, marge, bread, a tin of 'Conny Onny', as condensed milk was known; mentally she ticked off their requirements. She'd get a bit of back bacon and some potatoes, too. That would do for tea, and some ribs and dripping from Mr Rawlinson at the butcher's, that would do for tomorrow. Food was always bought on a day-to-day basis. Hardly anyone had enough money to stock up for a week.

'I'll see you later, Mam,' she called as she closed the door, just catching the faint response from Bridie. If she'd known there was nothing in, she'd have gone to Burgess's first and not wasted precious minutes, she thought impatiently as she walked down the street.

On the corner of Vauxhall Road she almost collided with Dee.

'Hello! Where are you off to then?'

'The shop.'

Nancy grinned. 'Me, too. There's not enough for the damned mice to eat in our house; they've moved next door.'

Dee smiled at her. She hadn't been looking forward to going to the shop because she was going to have to ask for credit and wasn't sure how this request would be greeted. 'It's like that in our house too, only the mice haven't gone yet. Nancy, do you know . . . do you know if Mr Burgess will let you have things and pay for them . . . later?'

'Of course he will. They'd all be in the workhouse if they didn't. Everyone around here puts things on the slate, then they pay up when they've got the money.'

Nancy's brow furrowed as they entered the shop. It was crowded and she instantly picked out at least three women who came for a gossip as well as their groceries. She might not have time to wait. 'God, we're going to be here until the cows come home.'

Dee looked around at the food stored on the shelves. Packets of tea. Big square tins of Crawford's biscuits. Tins of Fry's Cocoa, big glass jars of dried beans, peas and lentils. On the floor stood sacks of potatoes, bundles of 'chips' and other assorted hardware. Sides of bacon and hams hung from hooks above the counter. She was so hungry she could have cried.

Even though Nancy was impatient to get served, she couldn't overcome her curiosity. 'Can I ask you something, Dee?'

'What?'

'Why have you come here, like? To live here I mean.

If you don't want to tell me it's all right,' she added hastily.

'Father lost all his money and then his job. He worked in a bank, a merchant bank. We lived in London, in a nice big house in Highgate.' Dee swallowed hard. She didn't want to think about the home she'd lost.

'Oh, how did he lose his money then?' He must have been awfully careless, she thought.

'It was all to do with bad investments, and gambling debts and Mother's clothes . . . and other things.'

Nancy didn't know what an investment was, but gambling she understood. She knew of more than one family who had been evicted because the rent had been lost on a horse or a game of pitch and toss.

'So you came all the way up here? Will he get a job, do you think?'

'I hope so. He has some "contacts", but I don't know just how well he knows them, or if they can help.' Dee really didn't hold out much hope that these people could be of assistance. Father had come to Liverpool to be anonymous, so they couldn't possibly be friends or even acquaintances. 'I think he could do something in an office.' She fervently hoped her prediction was right.

Nancy wasn't optimistic. 'He might. Work, any kind of work, is hard to get. Don't be too disappointed if he doesn't. But I'm sure he will,' she added, disturbed to see that Dee's eyes had filled with tears. The thought of work also reminded her that if she didn't get back to her job smartish she'd be out of the door. 'I can't wait any longer, I'll have to go back to work. I started in the

Laundry this morning, Mary did too. You stay and don't be frightened to ask for tick. Look, Mike's serving. He was with us last night, remember?'

'I remember,' Dee answered. She was sorry that Nancy couldn't stay with her, she would have liked her support.

'Look, come down to our house tonight. It's number forty-two. Mam will be out at work, we can have a bit of a natter then. Get to know each other, like.'

'Oh, I don't know if I can.'

'Oh, go on! They'll not miss you. Come about seven. I'll get some chips.'

The day suddenly looked brighter to Dee. She didn't know how she was going to get out later on, but she was determined she was going to try.

When her turn came it wasn't Mike who served her but his father. Dee hesitated. 'Er, can I have the groceries er, on credit, please?' She thought there would be less embarrassment all round if she asked first, rather than have everything weighed out and then be refused.

'What's your name, luv? I haven't seen you in here before.' Frank Burgess looked at her kindly. She must belong to those new people Hilda had been going on about last night.

'Dee Chatterton, we moved into number eighty yesterday.' She was very relieved when she saw Mr Burgess take a book from beneath the counter and turn to a fresh page. Nancy had been right, she thought, the book was nearly full. She watched him write down 'Chatterton. No. 80' at the top of the page, aware of the curious glances she was attracting, the colour rising in her cheeks. 'Father will pay when he gets his wages,' she said, to cover her awkwardness.

'When will that be then, luv?' Hilda asked, glancing over her husband's shoulder while measuring out sugar, pouring it into a blue bag and expertly twisting the corners.

Dee felt her cheeks burning for all eyes were on her now. 'Oh, before Christmas . . . I think.'

'Right, what do you want?' Frank Burgess was brusque. He wanted his dinner and if he stood jangling to this girl, as he suspected most of his customers would like him to do, he wouldn't be getting it until nearly tea-time.

'Bread, tea, sugar, cheese, bacon, soap—' Dee reeled them off.

'Aye, luv, but how much of each?'

Dee blushed again. She'd never shopped for food before and had no idea of the quantities she'd need. She looked imploringly at Frank.

'How many of you are there, Dee?'

'Six. Mother and Father, David and Philip, me and Rose. She's the baby. She's three.'

'Right then, leave it to me.' Frank Burgess began to weigh out the sugar.

'Put some washing soda and Jeyes Fluid in, too, Frank,' Hilda advised, then nodded to Dee. 'Your mam will have her work cut out with that place. Nice mess the last lot left it in, so I heard.'

Dee couldn't bring herself to say that it would be left to herself to try to clean up their new home; she just smiled thankfully instead.

The buzz of conversation resumed as her purchases were measured out, wrapped and the amount and price entered into the book. As Frank Burgess deftly placed them in her outstretched arms, Mike grinned at her.

'Tarrah, Dee!' he called as she struggled through the crush.

'Poor little thing, used to better things, she is. You could see that she didn't even know how to shop. She's probably never had to worry her head about buying food in her life.' Hilda addressed her comments to Lizzie Simcock who stood clutching a hemp bag and a battered purse, the usual sour expression etched on her thin features.

'Aye, well, that mother of hers has certainly got airs and graces! Nasty piece of work she is, too, so Emily O'Brien told me. Her Harry went to see if he could help and she sent him off with a flea in his ear. Told them they needed no help, and Em said that the bloke and the kids were just standing around, doing nothing, like fish out of water, an' all their stuff on the street till all hours. And our Mary said they got the same treatment when they called. Only trying to be helpful and neighbourly they were. She said that Dee wasn't to mix with us "people", our Mary told me.'

Hilda sliced away at a shoulder of bacon, cutting off wafer-thin slices. She knew Lizzie's request of 'not too thick' really meant slices you could almost see daylight through.

'Well, he seemed nice enough when he was in here last night. A proper gentleman he was. Please and thank you, Mrs Burgess. "Very grateful for your advice.

We're in a bit of a fix and I'm not used to shopping but my wife's ill." And he paid cash last night. Had the decency to show he could pay up without being asked to and before sending her in asking for tick.'

Lizzie sniffed and peered closely at the strips of bacon that Hilda held out on a sheet of greaseproof paper. 'Well, I'm only saying what Emily and our Mary told me, that's all.'

'Speak as you find, I always say,' Hilda retorted, reaching for the condensed milk that was the universal stand-by for fresh milk and which kept longer, especially in summer.

After waiting her turn and taking it all in, Sal Kerrigan had at last reached the counter beside Lizzie. She was a big, blowsy woman who always smelled faintly of stale sweat and cooking. She rubbed her fat, grimy hands together in anticipation of what she was about to announce.

'I'll 'ave me usual, Frank, but I'll be wanting a big order just after Christmas.'

'Oh, aye, you going to have a "do" then, Sal? Your Pat been made a blockerman then, or 'ave you come into money?' Frank joked with her. He liked Sal. You always knew where you were with her. She wasn't moody or vindictive, and she had a lot to put up with. Pat was a bit of a drunkard, but then those kids would drive a man to drink.

'God, I hope not,' Hilda muttered as Lizzie counted out the coppers for her purchases, stung by Hilda's remarks about paying up.

Lizzie pursed her lips and nodded her agreement.

The last time the Kerrigans had had a 'do' the whole street had been up, and in the end the scuffers had had to be called when the brawling had got completely out of hand. Half of the 'guests' had ended up in Rose Hill Police Station.

'Our Joan's getting wed. The last Saturday in January,' Sal announced proudly to everyone. Joan was the eldest of the Kerrigan brood and had miraculously, or so it seemed to Sal, found herself a lad who had a good steady job and lived with his mam in Everton. A lovely, clean and comfortable place, Joan said. She wouldn't mind living with her future ma-in-law at all. It was a palace compared to Burlington Street.

A buzz of surprise ran around the shop.

'Well, that's a turn up. It's a bit quick though, isn't it?' Hilda was openly speculative.

'She's not in the club, if that's what you're getting at, Hilda Burgess,' Sal shot back. 'She's going to live with him and his ma in Priory Road. He works on the railway. It's a good steady job, with a regular wage. I'm made up for 'er, we all are, so we've got to put on a bit of a "do" for them, haven't we? Got to do things proper, like.'

There was a stunned silence while this piece of news was thoroughly digested. Joan Kerrigan had certainly done well for herself, Hilda thought. She'd always been quiet, had Joan, not like the rest of them.

Frank was the first to recover. 'Well good luck to them both, Sal. It'll be boiled ham, tongue and fancy cakes, will it?'

Sal nodded.

'Where is it then – Our Lady's?' Hilda asked, this was one wedding she wasn't going to miss seeing, Saturday or no Saturday.

'Where else? They went to see Father Fitz yesterday an' she's going to Blacklers for her frock. Mind, she's not havin' the rest of them as bridesmaids. She wants it quiet, like. She said she won't 'ave it turned into a May procession with that lot trailing after her. Thank God, I said to Pat. We can't afford frocks for our Monica, Abbie and Ginny too. Mind you, if I could get those three off me hands I'd put me soul in hock.'

With this sentiment Lizzie silently concurred. That Monica Kerrigan was a bold piece and headed for trouble with the carry-on out of her, that was certain. But then her Mary was no angel either, and caused her many a sleepless night wondering where she had gone wrong. In this respect she knew how Sal felt.

The shop bell shrilled loudly and the waiting women drew back a little as the rotund figure of Father Fitzpatrick, the parish priest, entered the shop, his soutane flapping around his legs in the fierce draught blowing in from the door.

'Frank, I know it's not the best of times, but I'd like a quick word.' He waved a piece of paper that looked like a letter towards Frank and Hilda.

Hilda raised her eyes to the ceiling. 'Get our Chrissie out here for a few minutes, she can wrap,' she instructed Frank, who was beckoning the priest towards the back room.

'Not bad news, Hilda?' Sal probed.

'How would I know what it is when I'm standing

here serving? It's probably something to do with food for Christmas.'

'Oh, aye, they eat like kings round there, even though Lily Gillan burns everything black. Neither use nor ornament as a priest's housekeeper that one. I don't know why they keep her on,' Sal commented tartly.

'They keep her on because the poor old soul's nowhere else to go and they've got to keep their strength up, haven't they? Can't have the clergy taking to their beds morning noon and night!' Hilda snapped, annoyed at being left to deal with the steady flow of customers, and consumed with curiosity as to the reason for the priest's visit.

'It's turning into Fred Carno's Circus, what with one thing and another, isn't it?' Sal replied without rancour. She loved a good jangle, and what with her own news, the new family in the street, and now a mysterious visit and letter from the priest, things were certainly looking up.

Hilda Burgess concentrated on the next grocery list that had been handed to her and wondered if she dare put up the 'closed' sign on the door for half an hour, while she had a quick cup of tea and she found out the reason for Father Fitzpatrick's visit. She decided she couldn't. There would be a riot and besides, they needed the money.

Chapter Four

———— ✦ ————

IT WAS SIX O'CLOCK WHEN Hilda at last drew down the blind on the shop door. Pressing her hands into the small of her aching back, she went through into the back room where Chrissie had made a pot of tea and had toasted some potato cakes. Frank's conversation with Father Fitzpatrick hadn't been long, but there had been no chance to ask him what it was all about, for she certainly didn't want to broadcast any news throughout the entire neighbourhood.

'I know I shouldn't complain, business is business, but I'm dead on my feet.' She sank down on a chair by the table. 'Chrissie, luv, ease my boots off, will you. Well, what did he want then? What's the mystery? Couldn't it have waited until now?'

Frank bit into a hot potato cake, swimming with butter. He was just as tired and hungry as his wife. 'He'd had a letter from Kevin Doyle's missus, Kitty. You remember them?'

Hilda did. They were distant cousins of Frank's – at

least Kevin was – and they lived in Dublin. In the slums of Dublin. 'What do they want?'

'Poor Kev's dead. Consumption it was, and Kitty's bad with it, too. She's not got much longer. She got her parish priest to write to Father Fitz. She didn't have our address.'

Hilda sipped her tea thoughtfully. She'd not particularly liked either of them on the one and only occasion she'd met them, ten or more years ago, at another cousin's wedding.

'Kitty wants us to take her youngest lad, Sean. Then she'll rest easy. All the others have left now anyway.'

'Take him – what does she mean by that?'

'Take the lad in, give him a home, a job, I suppose.'

'Why the hell should we do that? We don't know him. He could be a right hooligan for all we know. How old is he?'

'Sixteen.'

'Then he's old enough to fend for himself. And what about the rest of them? Can't they take him in?' Just who did Kitty Doyle think she was, asking people who were almost complete strangers to take in her kids, when they were old enough to work and find digs?

'They're all scattered. America, Australia, Canada. And don't be like that Hilda, they're family.'

'Only just. Cousin, half a dozen times removed.'

'But still family. How would you feel if it was you dying and our Mike and Chrissie were going to be left to fend for themselves? And it is Christmas,' he added, hoping this would appeal to her sense of Christian duty.

He'd known all afternoon that she wouldn't take kindly to the idea.

'What's Christmas got to do with it?'

'Well, it's Christ's birthday: love thy neighbour—'

'Will he talk like Mr Kerrigan?' Chrissie asked. She had been very interested in this news and wanted to know more about this cousin she'd never met.

Hilda glared at her daughter. 'You mind your own business, miss. Go out into the yard and get our Michael to help you bring more potatoes in.'

When Chrissie had flounced out, Hilda turned on her husband. 'You've got it all worked out, haven't you? You want him here.'

'Why not? Why can't we give the lad a home?'

'And what will he do for a job, where will he sleep and what if he robs us blind?'

'He can sleep with Mike, and I'll get him something, and don't go judging the lad before you've even met him.'

Frank had that familiar stubborn look on his face. Usually he was easy-going. 'Anything for peace' was his motto, but his chin jutted forward and Hilda knew that he would dig his heels in over this. He set great store by 'family'. She was tired, dog-tired, and she still had plenty to do in the house. Chrissie was inclined to be lazy if she didn't keep on at her. And there would still be customers coming in until nine o'clock.

'Oh, have it your own way. I want nothing to do with it. And if he turns out to be a criminal, you can deal with him! I wash my hands of the whole thing.'

Frank placed a hand on her shoulder. 'I'll write to

Kitty, make arrangements. You sit there for a bit, I'll go and open up when I've had my tea.'

Hilda thought about Sal Kerrigan's remarks and sighed. Yes, with one thing and another Burlington Street was getting to be a bloody circus.

Dee walked into another row. She heard the raised voices as she went up the steps, and her heart sank.

She ignored both her parents and placed the parcels down on the draining-board in the scullery. Apparently, from what she could gather, Father hadn't had any luck at all. She sighed heavily. It didn't surprise her. He'd been unable to see anyone and had been told by various officious clerks to come back on Monday.

He was hurt by the humiliation he'd suffered. Her mother's response was to call him a useless, idle waster and a criminal for bringing them to this slum.

Dee had heard it all before. Mother sounded like a gramophone record that had stuck. As she rolled up her sleeves and prepared to do her best with the washing soda and disinfectant, she was determined that as soon as she could escape she was going to Nancy's house. In the meantime she'd better organize Phil and David, and try to get some of the dirt dealt with, for her mother certainly wasn't going to.

She jumped nervously as the shouting stopped and the front door slammed, the sound echoing through the empty house. Father had obviously stormed out. Gnawing her lip with anxiety, she fervently hoped he would come back. She wouldn't blame him if he didn't. Ill though she was, Mother could surely try to do something and stop blaming him for everything. For she'd played no small part in the disaster with her extravagance.

Dee eventually decided she was not going to ask if she could go out. There would be another argument, for she knew her mother would forbid her to go. To her relief Father had returned after an hour and had helped her to remove some of the rubbish into the back yard. The privy was so disgusting that she had retched the whole time she was trying to clean it, even though she had one of her father's handkerchiefs tied over her nose and mouth. It had to be done if there was to be any hygiene in the house, and no one else was going to do it. 'Cleanliness is next to Godliness,' Nanny had always said. She was glad that Nanny couldn't see what she had been reduced to, she thought, as the tears slid down her cheeks. Her resentment against her mother had been building up all day.

After the meagre meal she'd washed the few dishes, wrapped Rose up in her own coat and a blanket, and settled her in the trunk by the spluttering fire. She'd left her father staring morosely into space, puffing on a Woodbine, which she thought was a shocking waste of money. Her mother was dozing and the boys were half-heartedly playing 'I spy', when she had let herself quietly out.

The wind instantly cut through her thin dress and she shivered uncontrollably, wishing she hadn't left her coat covering Rose. With her head well down, she ran down the street, counting the houses.

She paused outside Nancy's house, for there were

lights in every window, even the cellar. The door was ajar so she pushed it open and stood uncertainly in the lobby. All the doors that she could see were closed tightly, but she could hear the sound of voices, a lot of voices. She was certain that Nancy had said her mother would be out.

She decided to knock on the nearest door.

'I wondered if you'd come; if your mam would let you. Come in. I got the chips.' Nancy's smile was genuine as she ushered her new friend into the room which she had tidied up a bit after Bridie had gone.

Dee glanced around. The room was warm and stuffy and clothes steamed gently from a rack suspended from the ceiling by an intricate pulley system. After the coldness of the street and number eighty it looked cosy. There were thick curtains at the window. The range shone with blacklead, and on the mantel above it was a collection of cheap ornaments and bric-a-brac. In the middle was a statue of a man in a red cloak pointing to his open and wounded heart.

She sat on the horsehair sofa beside Nancy.

'Who's he?'

'The Sacred Heart. Jesus. Our Lord,' Nancy explained. 'Oh, I didn't think. You're Protestant, aren't you?'

'I'm Church of England. Does that matter?'

'No. Not to me, anyway. It's . . . it's just that people here are a bit touchy.' Nancy knew this was a serious understatement. People in this city regularly half killed each other on St Patrick's Day and the 'Glorious Twelfth' of July, the anniversary of the Battle of the Boyne.

'Is your mother out?'

Nancy nodded. 'She works in the pub, the Black Dog.'

'I could hear other people . . .' Dee wasn't sure if she should mention this, but Nancy laughed.

'Oh, there's not just Mam and me here. Mam lets the other rooms for a few coppers a week, but no one else is supposed to know that she charges. There's Mr and Mrs O'Hare and their lot upstairs, and the Flynns down in the cellar. They all have to scarper next door when the Inspector comes around. Everyone leaves their back doors open 'cos you never know when they'll just arrive. It's a bit of a laugh, everyone running from house to house. Dead funny it is, just seeing the look on his face. He knows what's going on, but he can never catch them.'

Dee smiled, relaxing for the first time in days in the warmth of the room and Nancy's friendship. 'It's nice in here.'

'It's not too bad. I'll get the chips. You can make a butty with them.' Nancy was being the soul of hospitality.

Dee was puzzled. 'What's that?'

'Two pieces of bread with some chips in the middle. Don't they have butties in London?'

'Yes, it's just I've never heard a sandwich called that before. Yes, please, could I have one?'

Nancy was practical. She took the parcel, wrapped in greasy newspaper, from the oven, unwrapped it and divided the chips into two small parcels. 'Have you had anything to eat today?'

'Just a bit of bread and a cup of tea. I haven't really had much time. I've been trying to clean.'

Nancy was sawing away at the loaf. 'It's a bit of a dump, but you and your mam will soon sort it out. There are worse places, believe me.'

Dee thought of the hours she'd spent scrubbing the dirty linoleum and wooden boards. Her hands were raw and chapped with the soda. She thought of the privy and of her mother sitting, staring into the fire, offering no help or encouragement, and the resentment, hopelessness and misery welled up and she burst into tears.

Nancy dropped the knife and ran to Dee's side, putting her arm around her.

'Aw, come on, Dee. It's not that bad. I know it must be hard, but you've got me and Mary; we'll help out, we're your friends.' Nancy pulled the shaking shoulders to her and held Dee until her sobs subsided.

'Mother . . . Mother's too ill to help me – or she says she is – but she could at least try!' She was too upset to try to hide this betrayal.

Nancy looked horrified. 'You don't mean you've had to do it all yourself?'

'Yes, and I don't really know how to clean and there's no furniture or sheets or towels and we've no money.'

Nancy looked at her pityingly. 'Come on, let's eat, you'll feel better and then we can see if we can sort it out.'

Dee wiped her eyes and followed her friend's example, piling the chips between the doorsteps of bread and cramming it into her mouth. Nothing had ever tasted so good.

When they'd finished Nancy leant back against the sofa. 'Right, let's think. You can get orange boxes from Rooney's, the greengrocer's, for nothing; you can use them to sit on, put things in or for the fire, they're very useful. Send your brothers out to pick up paper, bits of wood, any old rubbish that will burn and I'll look and see what we have for towels and stuff like that.'

Dee was feeling calmer now. 'I . . . I couldn't take your things—'

'Why not? That's what friends are for, to help out. Isn't there any money at all?' Nancy probed.

'I think Father's got about five pounds left. He paid the rent for two weeks and spent some on food last night.'

'We'll go and see Solly Indigo at the pawnshop. He's got lots of things and they're dead cheap.

'He's Jewish an' they have their Sunday on a Saturday, but it doesn't stop him opening until nine o'clock. It's his busiest day. Shall I tell you how he got his name? It's not his proper one. His proper name is Bloomfeld.'

Dee was amazed at Nancy's common sense, and was very relieved by her capable attitude.

'Everyone takes their best clothes in to him, men's Sunday suits, like, "In d' go on Monday, Out d' go on Friday." It's a joke, like.'

Dee laughed, but there was no hint of hysteria in her laughter, just sheer mirth and relief. She was so glad she'd come. So glad she'd found Nancy. 'Will I go and ask Father for the money now?'

'No. Let's go and see what he's got first. Then your da can go down and pay him and Solly will fetch it up on the handcart. Haven't you got a coat?'

'No. I wrapped Rose up in it, but I'm not cold now.'

'You soon will be.' Nancy handed Dee her thick black shawl. 'Here have this. I'll use Mam's old one.'

Dee was surprised how heavy and warm it was as she wrapped it around her, covering her head with it, too.

'Right, let's get you sorted out, Dee Chatterton.' Nancy grinned at the sight of her new friend's pale, bespectacled face peeping from the folds of the shawl.

'How can I ever thank you, Nancy?'

Nancy was embarrassed. 'Aw, shurrup. You're my friend,' she said, pushing Dee into the street.

Chapter Five

———◆———

BETWEEN THEM THEY'D EARMARKED buckets, pans and dishes; towels and blankets were added, and an old sheet that Nancy said could be torn up and used as cloths for a variety of purposes. A horsehair sofa was also chosen, and a big wooden food press that could act as a sideboard as well. None of the brass or iron bedsteads were affordable, but Dee said that a large and fairly clean flock mattress and two bolsters would do until such times as beds could be bought. A couple of not-too-threadbare rugs were added, and Nancy promised to teach Dee how to make peg rugs with a sugar sack and cut-up strips of old rags that could be got from Paddy's Market for a penny a bundle. They did wonders to brighten the place up. They could also be washed in summer and given a vigorous beating against the yard wall in winter.

'There now, a nice furnished house and all for the bargain price of five guineas.' Solly grinned at them expansively, showing gold-filled teeth.

'Oh, I think all of it might be too dear, perhaps we could leave some things out.' Dee's gaze scanned the prospective purchases, wondering just what could be left out. They seemed to need everything.

'You tell your da to come and see me, we'll strike a deal, and don't forget there's free transport.' He indicated a sturdy-looking handcart outside on the pavement.

Both girls thanked him and left, but as they drew nearer number eighty some of Dee's euphoria began to disappear. What would Mother say about it all? She decided not to dwell on that, after all neither Mother nor Father had made any effort to make the house more livable. They'd left everything to her.

'Come in with me?' she urged Nancy, who was hanging back, remembering the reception she'd received last night. Dee didn't want to face them on her own, and she needed them to see how helpful Nancy had been.

Phil and David were wrestling on the floor of the lobby.

'Get up, both of you,' Dee hissed.

'Where've you been? Mother's furious,' Phil said, brushing himself down.

David seemed careless of his mother's mood. 'Who's she?'

'It's Nancy, my friend. I've been to her house and she's helped me get some things,' Dee whispered. She ignored the odd looks that both her brothers were giving her and went into the kitchen.

'Just where do you think you've been and what . . .

what on earth is that . . . that garment?' Gwendoline's voice rose to a shriek.

Dee had forgotten she was still wearing Nancy's shawl. 'It's Nancy's shawl. She lent it to me, Rose had my coat.' Dee decided she would have to brave it out, so before her mother could speak she plunged on. 'Nancy took me to the pawnshop and Mr Indi— Mr Bloomfeld can let us have practically enough things to furnish the whole place for just five guineas and he'll bring them up on his handcart.' Her cheeks were flaming hot and she was quaking inside, but she held on tightly to Nancy's arm for support and courage.

'That's right, it's the God's truth. He said if you would go down and see him . . . er . . . Mr Chatterton—' Nancy, too, was ignoring the look of fury on Gwendoline Chatterton's face. She riveted her gaze on Dee's father and tried to smile confidently.

David decided to help them out. 'Are there blankets and pillows and a sofa, Dee?'

Dee nodded enthusiastically. 'And a mattress and towels and pans and buckets. Everything we need.'

To her relief she saw her father get to his feet, a broad smile on his face. 'Well, thank you Nancy. It's very kind of you to help like this.'

'That's all right, er, sir. Dee's my friend, and I asked her to come to our house tonight an' we had a bit of supper, like.'

Gwendoline was so furious she was speechless.

'Right. I'll go and see this Mr Bloomfeld. You two can come with me.'

David and Phil danced out of the door ahead of

their father, leaving just Dee, Nancy and Gwendoline. Rose had slept through everything.

Reluctantly Dee took off the shawl and handed it back to Nancy. 'Thanks, Nancy. It was very warm,' she said quietly.

'We can go to Paddy's Market on Monday and get you one.' Nancy was ignoring Dee's mother.

Gwendoline was furious. 'I'll see you dead before I'll let you wear one of those . . . those common things!' Her cheeks burned with two bright spots of red and her pale blue eyes held pinpoints of fire.

Nancy felt Dee's grip tighten and decided that Gwendoline Chatterton was a lazy bully. There were plenty of them in the street and she'd seen her mam deal with them often enough. Dee was obviously terrified of her mother, but Nancy wasn't. Not now. It had been different last night when she'd not known much about them. Now she saw things more clearly. There was a strong sense of fair play and a streak of stubbornness in Nancy that she had inherited from her da. If it hadn't been for herself they would still be wondering how they would manage, with no beds or even a sofa to sit on. It seemed to her that only Dee had any common sense at all. The rest of them were just plain stupid.

'That's a stupid thing to say. If she goes on running around with no coat in this weather she will be dead and buried with pneumonia—' she paused for effect, glancing around the bare room, 'in a pauper's grave an' all!'

Gwendoline got to her feet and when she spoke her

voice was cuttingly cold. 'How dare you speak to me like that, you insolent child. Remove yourself from my house this instant!'

Dee shrank visibly and Nancy wondered had she gone too far. 'Yes, it is "your" house Mrs Chatterton, but it's me who's got the nous to show you how to furnish it on the cheap. And you can't expect Dee to do everything, especially when she doesn't know how to. But at least she tried. You should be grateful to me and to Dee.'

Gwendoline compressed her lips tightly and took a step forward, but Dee pushed herself between Nancy and her mother, gaining courage from Nancy's stand. 'She's my friend and she's right. We need help. We just don't know how things are done.' Dee pushed Nancy towards the door as her mother, shaking with the force of her emotions, sank back into the chair.

'It'll be all right now, Nancy. It will be all right when Father gets back with the stuff. She'll calm down then, but thanks,' she said quietly, her voice shaking a little.

'Well if she starts on you again, Dee, you know where I live. I'll see you tomorrow, some time.' Feeling rather shaky at her outspokenness, but satisfied with the outcome of it, Nancy let herself out.

Dee was so reluctant to return to the kitchen that she waited, shivering on the top step until she heard the sound of voices and the rumbling of the iron wheels of the handcart on the cobbles. She even managed a smile as the odd quartet came into view: Phil and David staggering under the weight of pots, pans, buckets and blankets while her father and Mr Indigo, as she was always to call him, sweated and strained with the handcart and its burden of precariously balanced furniture.

In the excitement of moving their things in and finding places for everything, she managed to ignore her mother, but she was thankful when, tired but satisfied, she went up to join David and Phil in the bedroom that now at least had a mattress and bedding. Her mother hadn't spoken a word of either reprimand or encouragement, but neither had she forbidden her to see Nancy again.

By Sunday morning the sky had cleared and was a pale, whitewashed blue. During the night the wind had dropped and the temperature had fallen. A mantle of white hoar-frost covered everything, gleaming and sparkling on roofs, covering window panes with exquisite lace patterns.

Nancy, Mary, Mike and Tommy had managed to make their way to the lamp; they knew that Jerry would follow as soon as he could.

Mike stamped his feet and blew on his fingers. 'It's still freezing. Our Chrissie slipped on some ice outside church, she didn't half come a cropper, and she didn't half yell until Mam boxed her ears for making a show of us all.' Making a Show of Yourself was high up on the list of unforgiveable sins in Hilda's eyes. It rated third after drunkenness and brawling. 'I hear your Joan's got herself a husband?' he said to Tommy.

Tommy grinned. 'Oh, aye, me mam's made up with him. It's Terry this and Terry that, all day long it's bloody Terry. I'm fed up hearing about him and so is me da. What's more, he don't drink, not even a half of shandy! That's really upset me owld feller. He goes round mutterin' about bloody Temperance Societies. Me mam said our Joan's got her head screwed on, at least she won't be led the dance she has had with me da! It should be a good "do" though. She's ordered ham and stuff and Da's bound to get the ale in, even if old "Teetotal Terry" won't have a drop. You can come round to our house – all of you,' he offered generously.

Mary grinned. 'Thanks.'

'I'll be lucky if I can get out anywhere. We're having some cousin called Sean to live with us,' Mike announced gloomily.

'Go on. When?' Tommy was very interested in this piece of news.

'He's coming over on the ferry from Dublin on Christmas Eve. I've got to go and meet him and he's got to share my room.'

Tommy was unsympathetic. 'Oh, tough. You don't know you're born having a room to yourself.' He had always had to share his room with his three brothers.

'What's he like?' Mary was always interested in any new male in the street.

'I don't know, I've never met him. He's sixteen and Mam reckons he should fend for himself, but his da's just died and his mam is dying, so he's coming to live with us. Da says he'll get him a job. He can have mine, I hate that shop. You should hear all those old biddies jangling and moaning all day, it's dead boring.'

Jerry arrived breathless, his cheeks glowing with his exertions and the cold air. 'It's supposed to be Christmas! Glad Tidings of Great Joy and all that, but you'd never think so to hear old Misery Guts Jones. Hellfire and brimstone and the evils of drink. He went on for hours!'

'We were just talkin' about drink,' Tommy said.

'Or the lack of it in some houses in Everton,' Mike added.

'Me da's a hypocrite. He said he'll leave me black and blue if he catches me in a pub,' Tommy complained. By his reckoning, if he was old enough to pull his guts out down at the docks, he was old enough to have a pint, but his da thought otherwise.

'Listen to him, swallowed the dictionary then? They must all be dead clever them dockers, if they use words like hypocrite,' Mary jeered. She was sick of hearing about drink, she wanted to know more about this cousin of Mike's. 'So, when will we get to see your new relation then, Mike?'

'At mass on Christmas Day, 'cos as soon as I've got him home it's down to the grind for me.'

'Christmas Eve is always a dead busy time,' Nancy put in. Dee hadn't come knocking on the door last night, so she assumed things weren't too bad at number eighty.

'We know,' Mary concurred sourly. 'All the damned laundry has to be done and out before five o'clock. We won't be fit for anything, Nance.' She turned to Jerry. 'How was work in the cattle yards then?'

Jerry grimaced. He wasn't going to tell them that

the noise, the smell and the sheer volume of manure had made him blanch. He'd been shown around the huge pens on the other side of the river, where the cattle and sheep from Ireland, America and Argentina were unloaded and penned, awaiting fattening or slaughter and transportation.

He'd also been shown the huge chill rooms where the carcasses were kept before being loaded onto carts. His initial job had been working, with many other lads, to clear the tons of manure that was loaded onto barges which took it out to sea to be dumped. He certainly had no intention of telling them that on his visit to the slaughterhouse he had vomited. The cattle were poleaxed, none too expertly. The sheep and pigs had their throats cut and were then hung up. The whole place was awash with blood. His retching had been greeted with laughter by the slaughtermen.

He wondered if he would ever get used to the sounds, the sights and the smells. He didn't think so, but after listening to his father's half-hour-long lecture on the benefits to the soul of hard work and earning an honest crust, he'd vowed not to utter a word of complaint. Besides, his wages helped his mam out, for Abe Harvey was renowned for his meanness.

'Was it that bad?' Mike prodded.

'Yeah, but I expect I'll get used to it.'

'You could always look for something else,' Nancy said, for she sensed Jerry's distaste.

'Like what?' he asked morosely.

'Cheer up, at least it'll be Christmas soon and you'll get your wages,' Tommy said.

'It won't be much of a Christmas at number eighty,' Nancy said darkly.

'I saw that feller and those kids with Solly Indigo last night,' Mary suddenly remembered.

'I took Dee down to his shop. She came to our house, too.' Nancy knew she now had a very interested audience.

'I'm surprised that old bat let her,' Mary sniffed.

'She didn't tell her, well not until later, anyway. There was a right row, too! You should have heard the way she spoke to me, and I'm sure she wanted to belt me, honest!' Nancy cried, seeing the look of disbelief on all their faces. 'She's awful! She's a real bitch!'

Mary was curious. 'So, what else did you find out?'

'It's a cryin' shame, Mary. They don't know nothin'. Dee's never even learned how to wash clothes or cook. They had a great big house in London, in Highgate, and they had servants. Lots of them.'

'Gerroff!' Mary was scornful.

'They did. They had maids to do all the work and a woman to cook.'

'I don't believe a word of it, Nance, you're having us on!'

'I'm not. You can ask her yourself! She even had a woman to look after her and the other kids.'

'Why couldn't her mam do that?' Jerry asked.

'She was too busy going out to see her posh friends and going to posh places, but it's all right, Dee said everyone she knew had a nanny.'

Mary pealed with laughter. 'You mean it was her granny? Her nan?'

'No, they're all dead. She wasn't related at all. She was paid, when they had money. They had special rooms too, at the top of the house, called nurseries. All the kids lived up there. Their mam and dad came up to see them at night and sometimes in the day, too, and Dee sometimes had her dinner downstairs with them, 'cos she's the oldest.'

All this was so fantastic, so utterly alien to them that Nancy could have been describing the lifestyle of Red Indians for all they knew.

'I wouldn't have minded that,' Mike said, thinking of how Hilda watched him morning, noon and night. He certainly wouldn't have minded a nanny if she had kept Chrissie locked upstairs all the time.

'It sounds awful to me. What kind of a mam is she if she only goes and sees her kids for a few minutes a day?' Tommy was outraged. He'd never known a time when his mam hadn't been at home to give advice or comfort and sometimes a clip around the ear.

'I'm only telling you what Dee told me. Anyway, they haven't got any money now and Dee has to do everything, her mam's bone idle. She says she's sick but she didn't look that sick to me. Her da gave Solly five quid for all the stuff, all the money he had, so they're skint now, so it won't be much fun in their house at Christmas.'

'Won't they get a parcel from the "Welldoers"?' Tommy asked. They'd often had one and they were great. Full of things they never had in their house. Oranges and cake and a piece of pork or ham.

'I never thought of that, Tommy. I suppose they

could have one.' Nancy was thoughtful. 'They're poor enough.' They'd had one a few years ago. In fact most families had had one at some time or other.

'You have to let them know who needs them,' Jerry advised.

'So who do we tell?' Mary asked. She was curious to know more about the Chattertons and if she got the chance she was going to ask Dee about all the things Nancy had mentioned, just to make sure Nancy wasn't making it all up.

'Dad will know. We'll ask him.' Mike jerked his head in the direction of the shop and they all moved off together.

'I don't know that they'll take kindly to you poking your noses in, folk have pride, even if they've got little else,' Hilda remarked as they all crowded into her kitchen and enlightened Frank as to the purpose of their visit.

'It won't be much of a Christmas for them, Mrs Burgess, honest. They're skint,' Nancy urged.

'I heard that she didn't take kindly to people interfering.' Hilda reminded them all of what they already knew.

Nancy wasn't to be put off now. She'd faced Gwendoline Chatterton's wrath once and she wasn't afraid to do it again, for she knew she had the rest of the family on her side now. 'Oh, you don't take any notice of her,' she said cuttingly.

'She couldn't even be bothered to look after her kids, she paid someone to do it. They had a nanny,' Mary said, still hoping to prove Nancy wrong. Hilda

Burgess was sure to know all about nannies.

Hilda raised her eyebrows at Frank. 'Good Lord, they must have had a few bob then.'

Mary looked a little crestfallen, but Frank looked concerned.

'It must be terrible for them then, having to come here. I'll go up and see them at the League of Welldoers and put their names down. They deserve a bit of help.' He reached for his cap and overcoat.

'I could do with a bit of help myself around here,' Hilda remarked acidly, but Mike and his friends had already disappeared out of the door.

'Will we go and tell them?' Mary enquired.

'Well, I don't know. It could be a surprise,' Nancy answered.

'Oh, you just want to be contrary.'

Tommy poked Mary in the ribs. 'Look who's talking, Mary, Mary quite contrary!'

'Oh, ha, ha! Very clever, Tommy Kerrigan! Grow up!'

'All right, we'll go and see Dee,' Nancy agreed.

'If we get the same treatment as we got yesterday, I'm not hanging around,' Jerry muttered darkly. He didn't get much time to himself on a Sunday and he certainly wasn't going to spend it being insulted, but he followed the little group along the street.

To Nancy's consternation it was Mr Chatterton who answered their knock.

'Oh, er, we ... can we see Dee, please?' she stammered.

'It's Nancy, isn't it? She's with her mother. I'm afraid

my wife really isn't well, she should have a doctor.' He looked worried. Grey and worried, Nancy thought.

Mary nudged her in the back and she felt guilty, remembering what she'd said about Dee's mam.

'Shall I go for Doctor Wallace?' Jerry asked hopefully. His da couldn't blame him for missing the afternoon service if he was on an errand of mercy, he thought.

Edward Chatterton looked perturbed. 'I . . . we . . . haven't—'

'He won't come out until he sees the colour of your money,' Mary stated. 'Miserable old git!' she added.

'I could go and fetch mam, she'll know what to do,' Nancy offered.

'Oh, I don't know if—' Edward faltered.

'Or we could get Ma Ollerenshaw, she's the midwife an' she does the laying out,' Tommy added helpfully, he thought.

Dee appeared behind her father, her brow furrowed, her eyes anxious.

'It's your friends,' Edward explained.

'Oh, Nancy, I'm glad you've come. Mother's in terrible pain and I don't know what to do!'

It seemed only polite to usher them all into the house, Edward thought. They trooped into the kitchen, their quick, furtive glances taking in the drab bareness of the room, for there were still no curtains and there was a very obvious lack of the bric-a-brac and clutter that characterized their own humble homes.

Mike looked at the two boys and their bewildered father, and at the little girl who was sucking her thumb and clinging to Dee's skirt and decided to take charge of things. 'I think we'd better leave the girls to it. Tommy, Jerry and me will take the lads out for a bit, if that's all right. We'll go to the Pierhead and see all the ships.' He addressed himself to Edward, who nodded gratefully, while Phil and David looked eagerly at this new friend of Dee's.

'Tommy, you take the little girl up to your house, your mam will know what to do with her. She can play with your Seb and Ginny.'

'Come on, Mam'll give you a sugar butty,' Tommy promised as he took Rose's hand. He'd had plenty of experience dealing with children.

Mary had rolled up her sleeves. 'Have you got any Indian brandy or peppermint?' she asked Dee. They were her mam's tried and tested remedies for pain, taken with hot water.

'No. No.'

'I'll ask Mike's mam for some. I won't be long.' Mary followed the boys who, with David, Philip and Rose, were already out in the street.

'I'll go and get Mam,' Nancy said firmly to Dee, who looked very relieved.

Edward Chatterton sat down heavily on the sofa as both his daughter and her friend disappeared. Gwendoline might not think much of these people, but he was beginning to see just how good, how generous and helpful they were. He might not have made such a terrible mistake in coming here after all.

Chapter Six

———◆———

'I'M NANCY'S MOTHER,' BRIDIE announced, looking down at the thin, haggard features of Gwendoline Chatterton.

Gwendoline was too ill, too wracked with pain to care any longer about any invasion of privacy.

Bridie squatted down beside the mattress. 'It's bad, I can see that by your face, luv. What is it?'

Even a day or two ago Gwendoline would have been aghast at the very idea of telling a complete stranger such intimate details. Now circumstances were very different and haltingly she told of the difficult birth of Rose, of the pain, weakness and heavy bleeding that had followed. She recounted details of her long convalescence, the continued fatigue and the terrible black moods, when she would cry for hours or be consumed with irrational anger that she would vent upon her husband, children and, in better days, the servants. And finally, with tears wetting her cheeks, she told Bridie of the excruciating pain in her abdomen and the wretchedness and utter despair that now engulfed her.

Bridie was sympathetic but businesslike. 'This place is enough to give anyone a fit of the miseries. Have you had anything for the pain?'

'Some pills the doctor in London gave me. I took the last one yesterday morning.' Gwendoline indicated the empty enamelled pillbox on the floor.

'I'll go and get you something for it. I won't be long, but you really should see a doctor.' Bridie had come across the symptoms before. They followed a set pattern after a woman had had a few children. The outcome was usually a horrendous operation to 'take everything away' or, in some cases an even worse fate.

'There's . . . no . . . money.' It still cost Gwendoline dearly to have to say those words to this common-looking woman.

Bridie's gaze alighted on the pillbox. 'You could get your Dee to take that little bit of nonsense to Solly Indigo tomorrow. It would pay Doctor Wallace's fees.'

Gwendoline didn't reply, so Bridie stood up and left the room.

In the kitchen, Nancy and Dee were huddled together. Mary was mixing something in a cup while Edward looked on.

'What's that, Mary?' Bridie asked.

'Indian brandy. What's up with her then?'

'"Women's trouble." Nance, go and get that bottle I keep in the back of the food press. Dee, go and find a brick, a big stone or anything like that and shove it in the fire, then get a bit of an old towel and wrap it up.

71

Then take it up to her.' Bridie delved into her pocket and drew out some coins. 'Mary, luv, go up and ask Red MacClelland for a drop of gin. If he starts getting stroppy, tell him I sent you and that it's for medicinal purposes.'

All three girls disappeared hurriedly to carry out these instructions.

When they'd gone Bridie looked at the man sitting on the sofa, twisting his hands together. Anxiety and bewilderment were stamped on his face. He wasn't a bad-looking man she thought. Yes, had the suit been clean and pressed, the shirt pristine instead of grubby, he would be considered quite handsome. You could see by his soft hands and clean fingernails that he'd never done a day's manual work in his life. It was all too obvious that he was completely out of his depth in the predicament he now faced.

'She really should have Doctor Wallace to see her. Oh, I know money's tight, but she's got a nice little box up there that Solly would give you a few bob for. Get it down to him in the morning and then get the doctor out. It's women's trouble like I said, and I don't suppose any of this has helped.' She gestured with her hand to indicate the still cheerless room. 'Still, we'll do what we can.'

'It's very kind of you, Mrs . . .'

'Bridie. Call me Bridie, everyone does.'

'I really don't know how I can repay you, Bridie.'

She was about to ask him about his job prospects when the door opened and Lizzie walked in, her face a mask of disapproval.

'What's our Mary doing walking into the Black Dog bold as brass and on a Sunday?' she demanded. She had shouted to her daughter, but Mary had either not heard her or ignored her.

'I sent her for a drop of gin, Lizzie, an' it's not for me, so don't go getting all airyated! Mrs Chatterton's bad.'

'I know that. I came to see if I could do anything.'

'I've sent Nance for my laudanum and Dee to find a brick to heat up. Hilda sent down some Indian brandy, so with all that inside her she should get some sleep. Mr Chatterton here is going to get the doctor out tomorrow. I doubt he'd come out today, even if we could afford his higher rate.'

'Oh, he costs,' Lizzie said flatly.

'We all know that, Lizzie. Don't worry, Mr Chatterton has the money, or he will have.'

Having rapidly taken note of the poor, sparse furnishings, Lizzie wondered just where the money was coming from. Before she could comment on it, Mary and Nancy arrived back together. Dee had already returned and had poked the half brick in the fire and stood watching it, the remains of a towel over her arm ready to wrap it up.

Bridie added half the gin and a few drops of laudanum to the cup of Indian brandy, then handed it to Dee. 'You take it up to her, luv, she won't want half the street up there in her bedroom. I'll see to the brick, your da can take it up when it's ready,' Bridie advised. She felt certain that when Gwendoline Chatterton hed recovered a little, she wouldn't take kindly to having had her bedroom full of women. Nor would she give

Lizzie Simcock the satisfaction of seeing that poor bare room and then jangling about it to all and sundry.

Dee did as she was bid. Bridie was about to pluck the brick from the embers. 'God Almighty! It's getting like Lime Street Station in here!' she exclaimed as Frank and Hilda Burgess appeared in the doorway.

'Afternoon, Lizzie, and that's a nice way to greet someone, Bridie Butterworth,' Hilda remarked caustically. 'I've brought a few things and Frank's brought some coal and you can stop poking at that, you'll burn yourself.'

Frank put down the small sack he'd been carrying, while Hilda placed a basket containing some groceries and a stone hot water bottle down on the table.

'That's great, Hilda, thanks.' Bridie pointed to the hot water bottle.

'Frank, make that fire up, it's damned cold in here,' Hilda instructed, then, turning to Edward, her expression softened. 'Is there a fireplace up there?'

He looked perplexed. 'No, I'm afraid not; should there be?'

'Pity. How much is that robber charging you for all this, if you don't mind me asking?'

'Hilda, it's not the time or the place,' Frank remonstrated. He had piled on more coal and had set a sheet of newspaper across the opening of the grate to create a draught from the flue to 'draw' the fire.

'I wish you wouldn't do that, Frank! God knows how long it is since that chimney's been swept. You'll set it on fire and choke us all and we'll have the fire bobbies down on us!' Hilda shot back.

Frank ignored her, concentrating on judging the exact moment to whip the paper away before it caught fire and caused a blaze and proved his wife's prediction accurate.

Edward Chatterton seemed overwhelmed. 'I . . . I don't know what to say. This is all so generous.'

'There's no need to say anything. We'd do the same for anyone,' Frank said, smiling.

'Try to keep her warm and get Dee to make her some of this Bovril. It'll build her up,' Hilda advised. 'I've told our Michael to bring the lads back to our house. I'll give them some tea, and Sal Kerrigan said she'll keep the little one overnight, if that's all right. She's a bit "come day, go day" is Sal, so one more added to that lot won't make any difference,' she added. 'Well, I think we'd all best get off and leave this poor man in peace,' she finished.

Bridie was the last to leave, shooing Nancy out ahead of her. She paused in the lobby and handed Edward the small dark bottle. 'Here, just give her a few drops at a time with the rest of the gin if you think she needs it.'

'I couldn't take it. You've already been kindness itself, Mrs . . . er, Bridie.'

'We may not have much round here and we may be rough an' ready, but we won't see anyone in trouble and not try to help. What she needs is rest, warmth and some nourishing food. She's not been really well for a long time, so she told me. And recently she's had one shock after another.'

Edward ran his hand through his hair, astounded

that Gwendoline appeared to have confided in Bridie. 'I know, but I don't know how I'm going to manage to give her all those things.'

Bridie felt so sorry for him that she laid a hand on his arm. 'Look, things aren't too bad now. You'll manage. Dee can nurse her, she's a sensible girl. You'll find work and she'll be up and around in no time and you'll soon get organized.'

Edward would have liked to believe her comforting words but even when Gwendoline was well enough, he knew she would never try to make this house into a home for them all. She'd never had to cook or clean or wash. Oh, she'd been good at selecting furnishings and colour schemes, but this was totally different. This was all so basic that she'd just go on complaining, and in all honesty he couldn't blame her. He'd failed her. He'd failed them all. That fact was the worst thing he'd ever had to admit to himself.

'Edward, can I call you that?' Bridie asked. He nodded. 'Look, why don't you go up to the pub for an hour tonight? You need a bit of a break from all this. I'm not saying spend the whole night there getting plastered, just have a pint. I'll stand you one. Meet the other blokes, Pat Kerrigan, Bert Soames, Mo Cowley, Harry O'Brien. They might be able to help you out with work or getting money from "the parish". They know all about being skint. Most people around here do. Come on, it will do you good.'

Edward looked down at his rumpled suit.

Bridie read his mind. 'Look, you don't need to be all dressed up.'

He smiled at her. It was such a tempting offer. 'People might think—'

'Oh, to hell with what people might think! Anyway they won't think anything. Women's ailments are best left to women, that's their opinion, every man jack of them.'

'All right, I'll come for an hour. I'll look forward to it, er, Bridie.'

She smiled at him, her green eyes lighting up. 'Right then, I'll see you later, and if you want me to be here for the doctor, just let me know.'

He had enjoyed it far more than he thought he would. Bridie seemed to have paved the way, for there were no awkward or embarrassing questions. Everyone was very friendly and he'd been offered help and advice on just about everything, for in these poor neighbourhoods people banded together in times of adversity. The alternative was the workhouse.

Bridie had been cheerful and companionable and he thought what a difference there was between her and Gwendoline. She'd told him something of her life history and he'd marvelled at how well she'd managed all these years by herself. She'd had a hard life, she'd told him. As, to be fair, had Lizzie Simcock, yet there seemed to be no bitterness or resentment in Bridie.

'Well, you just have to make the best of things, don't you?' she laughed.

He'd left Dee and Nancy to see to Gwendoline should she wake, which he doubted. She seemed to be in a deep, coma-like sleep which, when he thought about it, was only to be expected from mixing alcohol and drugs. He'd left the two girls sitting in the kitchen engaged in making something with an old sack, a large wooden peg and bits of brightly coloured material.

The two boys, having been fed like kings by Hilda, had been treated by Frank to their first ever moving picture show, with Mike and Tommy as minders. Sal Kerrigan had called to say that Rose was a little luv, happy as a sandboy she was, playing with Ginny and being spoiled rotten by Monica and Abbie, who were very taken with her 'posh' accent. He was not to worry about her.

With all his children in responsible hands, he felt more at ease than he had done for quite a while.

Red MacClelland, so-called because of his shock of carroty hair, placed another pint down in front of him. 'Get that down yer, lad. I'm not known for me charity, as it would be abused by some I could mention, but you look as though you need a bit of bucking up, like.'

'Thank you, I'll just have this then I really must get back to Gwendoline.'

'Ah, leave the women to see to things, don't they just love to be in charge? Sure it makes them feel important,' Pat Kerrigan advised, shoving his greasy cap further to the back of his head and draining his glass.

'Oh, so that's why you're in here mornin', noon an' night. So Sal can be on her own to make her feel important! I'll be sure and tell her that. I'll tell her what a generous feller she married. She'll be delighted with you, Pat.'

'Oh, the divil away with yez Bridie! You'd not be causing trouble between man and wife, would yez?'

'Try me,' Bridie laughed.

Edward had finished his drink and to a chorus of 'Good night! Don't be shy to come in again', and 'Good luck, mate', he left the warm, fuggy, convivial atmosphere and stepped out into the cold street, much cheered.

Gwendoline had slept very heavily and awoke feeling drugged and disorientated. Dee was standing beside her with a cup of something hot in her hand.

'Doctor Wallace will be here soon. How are you feeling, Mother?'

Gwendoline raised herself on one elbow and took the cup. 'We haven't got money for doctors.'

'I went to the pawnshop earlier on.' Dee had been up at six, and on Nancy's advice had been outside Solly Indigo's shop at half-past. Even at that early hour there was a queue forming. Women and girls stood patiently with oddly-shaped parcels and bundles under their arms, and Dee was forcefully reminded how the pawnbroker had got his name.

Gwendoline sipped the beefy liquid.

'Mrs Kerrigan had Rose to stay overnight, and Mike Burgess took Philip and David to the moving picture show. Nancy and I stayed in, making a peg rug.' She thought it best not to say that her father had spent part of the evening in the Black Dog. 'People have been very kind. Mrs Butterworth, Mrs Simcock and Mr and Mrs Burgess came yesterday with . . . things.'

Gwendoline felt as though she were standing on the brink of a yawning black chasm of despair. It seemed as though the entire neighbourhood had descended, en masse, to take over their lives. What was to become of them all? she thought wildly. 'Has your father gone to see those people?'

'Not yet. He wanted to wait until the doctor has been.'

'And what use will he be? Go down and tell him to go and look for work, that's more important to me than anything this doctor has to say.' She handed Dee the empty cup and lay down. Her head was thudding and she felt very woozy. Trust Edward to think his presence was more important than seeking work. He could never do the right thing.

Doctor Wallace was extremely surprised to find that his newest patient was a woman of his own class. He listened to Gwendoline's medical history. The birth of Rose, the depression, the lassitude; the visits to a Harley Street man, then the sequence of recent events: the pain, the intermittent bleeding, the worry, despair and her shattered nerves. Then he examined her.

'And your youngest daughter is now three?'

'Yes.'

'This must all be a terrible shock to you.'

'I can't tell you how much of a shock. I am at my wits' end! Oh, I despair, Doctor, I really do!' The tears slipped slowly down her cheeks.

He nodded slowly. He was almost certain of his

diagnosis but he was also certain that in her present state of mind, he couldn't enlighten her as to the cause of her illness. 'I'll leave you something for the pain. You must have rest, plenty of rest. Now don't worry, I'll speak to your husband.'

Downstairs Edward Chatterton, Bridie and Dee waited apprehensively. Bridie had sent the boys out to play in the street and Rose had again been sent up to Sal Kerrigan's house.

Doctor Wallace turned to Dee. 'Go up and make your mother as comfortable as you can, child.'

Bridie knew instantly that there was something seriously wrong, but she was torn between leaving them to talk in privacy and staying to be of assistance. 'Well, I'll be off, too.'

'No. Please . . . I'd like you to stay.' Edward, too, felt very uneasy.

Doctor Wallace took a bottle from his bag. 'I'll leave you this, give it to her for the pain. I'm afraid . . . I'm afraid it's not good news. Maybe you'd better sit down.'

Edward sat on the sofa, but Bridie just folded her arms over her bosom.

'I intend to get a second opinion, but I'm certain that your wife has cancer of the uterus and, quite frankly, I'm at a loss as to why the Harley Street man, who probably charged you a small fortune, didn't diagnose it.'

'She hasn't seen him for, well, for quite a while,' Edward informed him.

Doctor Wallace nodded. That would explain it.

Bridie looked at Edward Chatterton with real pity.

Her Mick had died of lung cancer and it was a slow, terrible, undignified death. It was she who spoke.

'So, how long does she have then?'

Doctor Wallace remembered Mick Butterworth and the then plump young widow and small child he'd left. 'Not long, I'd say. Three months, six at most. All that can be done is to try to make her as comfortable as possible. You know that, Mrs Butterworth.'

'Aye, I do,' Bridie said, holding out the money Edward had given her. She was taken aback when Doctor Wallace shook his head. 'Getting soft in your old age, then?' she remarked tartly, thinking that never once had he refused the money she'd given him.

'Use it to get him a stiff drink. He needs it.'

Edward was unable to take it in. It just wasn't possible. There must be a mistake. Gwendoline couldn't be . . . dying!

'Look, go and see this man, he might be able to help out.' The doctor was scribbling something down on a piece of paper, but as Edward made no move to take it he passed it to Bridie, who ushered him to the front door.

'He needs a job and she'll need nursing. I wish I could get her into a proper nursing home.'

Bridie stared at him, thinking bitterly what a difference an accent made.

'But I'm afraid that is just not possible,' the doctor continued. 'It's beyond their means. Is there anyone who can help?'

'There's Dee, his eldest girl and we'll all rally round, you know we all help each other. No one else does,' Bridie said curtly as she opened the front door.

When she returned to the kitchen Edward was still sitting on the sofa, looking dazed. She sat down beside him.

'I'm so sorry, I really mean that. My Mick died of lung cancer.'

'I can't believe it. I just can't believe it. I didn't know – I just didn't realize she was so ill. What will we do? How will I cope?'

'I'll go and get us a drop of whisky – or brandy if you prefer?'

To her surprise he reached out and caught her arm. 'No, not yet, please, don't . . . don't leave me.'

'All right. I'll make us a nice cup of strong tea.' When faced with such shattering news, men often found it difficult to cope, she thought. Yet they were supposed to be the strong ones. At the prospect of becoming a widower Edward Chatterton looked as though he was going to fall apart. That his brain was incapable of a single coherent thought. When she'd been told she'd be a widow, her thoughts were of the pain of losing Mick and a fierce determination that neither she nor Nancy would end up in the workhouse. She busied herself with the tea while he just stared into space, slowly shaking his head.

Nancy called in her dinner break and found Dee and her father and Bridie sitting in the kitchen. Her mother nodded quickly at her and she knew instinctively to take Dee over to their house. When they got there Nancy pushed Dee into the old rocker by the range.

'Is your mam bad, Dee?'

Dee nodded. Her throat felt as though it had closed over.

'I thought so by the look on Mam's face.'

'She's— Oh, Nancy, she's going to die!'

The scalding tears that Dee had fought back could no longer be checked. She'd thought that things couldn't possibly get any worse. She'd forgotten all the anger and resentment that had been directed against Gwendoline. Her mother was dying. 'Oh, what will we do without her?' she sobbed.

Nancy held her in her arms. 'Oh, Dee. I know how you feel, really I do. I can still remember my da and how it felt when . . . when he'd gone.'

Dee clung to her, sobbing as though her heart would break, and Nancy held her, knowing it was best to let her cry out her shock and sorrow.

Bridie had quickly organized a conference of all her neighbours. In fact, when she'd finally left Edward Chatterton and gone to tell Hilda, it was Hilda who sent Chrissie to fetch Lizzie, Sal and Emily O'Brien. She had a pot of tea on the table when they arrived and sent Chrissie out of the room.

'He's absolutely demented! He doesn't know where to start,' Bridie informed them.

'She'll need nursing and you can't expect that child to do that *and* run a home, not on her own,' Hilda stated.

'Aye, it would be different if it were our Nancy,' Bridie replied thoughtfully. 'But the poor kid hasn't got a clue, even though she's a real little tryer.'

'Right then, we'll have to help out or they'll finish up in the workhouse.'

Hilda and her neighbours viewed that as a fate worse than death.

'I could go and see to her in the mornings,' Bridie offered. 'Dee can get the lads out to school.'

'I'll have the little one, she's not a lot of trouble and she's got lovely manners. She doesn't snatch, like my lot,' Sal offered.

'Our Nancy said she'll go over after work.'

'So will our Mary,' Lizzie volunteered. 'And I'll see to her in the afternoon, if you can give me a hand, Hilda?'

Hilda nodded. She had precious few hours to herself, but it wouldn't be for ever.

'I'll do the washing,' Emily O'Brien offered. 'There'll be plenty of it.'

'The best thing for him to do is find a job,' Hilda mused. 'Keep his mind occupied. He doesn't look the sort who'll take it well.'

'Doctor Wallace gave him the name of someone to go and see, but he's not up to going anywhere today.'

'You seem to know all there is to know,' Lizzie sniffed, but everyone ignored her.

'Right then, it's all sorted. Bridie, you best go and tell him the arrangements, seeing as how he seems to find you easy to get on with.' Hilda had heard of the visit to the Black Dog.

'What about the funeral?' Lizzie asked bluntly.

'For God's sake, Lizzie! It's a bit soon to be thinking like that, and what's more it's bloody morbid!' Bridie cried.

'All I meant was, he won't want her in a pauper's grave, will he? Especially with her being, well, posh and all.'

'She's got a point,' Emily O'Brien agreed.

'Well, I'm not starting on about that. The poor bloke's cut up enough as it is,' Bridie stated firmly.

'Leave it a few days or until he's got a job, then he can start putting something away in the Club,' Hilda advised. A pauper's burial was the worst thing that could happen to anyone. The disgrace hung over the entire family for years and so everyone put a penny a week away in the Burial Club, even if it meant more hardship.

'Of course, she might get all airyated about everything. She might chuck us all out,' Lizzie said grimly.

'She's in no position to complain about anything or chuck anyone out. Does she know, Bridie?' Hilda asked.

'Doctor Wallace didn't tell her and I don't know if he . . . her husband's going to, when he's up to it, like. Dee knows, but I don't think the other kids should be told, not yet anyway.'

'A fine bloody Christmas it's going to be for them,' Sal said, shaking her head sadly.

Chapter Seven

———◆———

IT WAS WEDNESDAY, CHRISTMAS EVE, before Edward Chatterton found the courage and the strength to tell Gwendoline that she was very ill, but not that she was dying. He couldn't bring himself to tell her that. He tried to ease the terrible blow by telling her of the kindness of their neighbours, who wanted to make the coming months more comfortable, more bearable.

All the arrangements had been conveyed to him by Bridie Butterworth. She'd sought his consent, but he hadn't been able to utter a single word and his eyes had filled with tears of gratitude and relief. The nursing of his dying wife and the running of his household were things he couldn't bring himself to face just yet. Events had all happened too quickly, they were jumbled together in his mind like a kaleidoscope. And when he did try to think about it all rationally, he knew he would never have survived, let alone face the months ahead, without help. He was pathetically grateful, overwhelmed, Bridie thought.

Dee, too, felt as though everything was unreal. Like her father she leaned heavily on those who offered support, particularly Nancy. Mary and even Mike, Tommy and Jerry had called, anxious to help in any way. The boys were a little self-conscious, but Dee didn't notice. Terrible though each day was, she drew comfort and strength from them all. Now, when she needed friends desperately, they were there. A small, tightly-knit circle, offering the only things they had: time, compassion and support.

It was the arrival of the parcel from the League of Welldoers that brought the situation to a head. Philip had opened the door and had staggered down the lobby under the weight of the cardboard box, which he set on the table, having informed his father, sister and brother that a man had brought it and wished them all a Happy Christmas.

'But how did he know our situation?' Edward asked as the boys delved into the box, drawing out apples, oranges, biscuits and tea, while Dee exclaimed over a plump capon, her mouth watering at the thought of roast chicken. 'Mr Burgess went and told them that we . . . we were very poor. It was all Mike Burgess's idea, Nancy told me,' Dee answered.

'Maybe this will make Mother feel better,' Phil cried, clutching two oranges and darting upstairs before either Edward or Dee could stop him.

Father and daughter looked at each other with trepidation.

'I'll go if you want me to,' Dee offered bravely, yet terrified that her father would accept the offer.

Edward shook his head. 'No, Dee. It's my duty. This is one thing I have to do alone, you understand.'

Dee nodded, fighting back the tears.

He found Gwendoline sitting up, staring with astonishment at the oranges which Phil had placed on the bed. She looked grey and drawn. 'He says they came in a parcel.'

'They did, with a lot of other things to eat.'

'But who sent it? Was it Doctor Wallace?' She had been very reassured and comforted by the way the doctor had treated her and by the fact that he'd given Edward the name and address and a personal recommendation, to someone who could maybe offer employment.

Edward turned to his son. 'Go down and stop your brother from eating all those biscuits.' This was probably the hardest thing he'd ever had to do in his life, he thought. Far harder than losing his money, his position and his home. Far worse than having to tell Gwendoline that they were destitute, far worse than trying to come to terms with the knowledge that he was a complete failure.

'No. The parcel came from our neighbours. They wanted us to have a . . . a happier Christmas than my . . . circumstances could afford. They don't have much themselves, it's very kind of them.'

Gwendoline's expression clouded at his words. They reminded her, as if she needed reminding, of their circumstances. She also remembered how many of her neighbours had been in and out of the house for the past few days.

'You have to agree, it is kind.'

'Yes, I suppose it is.' The words were spoken tiredly. 'Have you been to see anyone about work?' she asked.

'Not yet. I'll go after Christmas. Things have been rather . . . hectic.'

She felt very weary. 'Edward, you're so lackadaisical! Dee can cope with the house and the children, she's proved to be very sensible. Work is a priority! Don't you understand that it's absolutely vital that you get a job? A job that will enable us to get away from here. To have a decent house in a decent neighbourhood. I can't stand it here. I just can't stand it!'

He fiddled awkwardly with the edge of his waistcoat and refused to meet her eyes. 'Work and . . . and all that will wait, Gwen dear.'

'Why? What is so important? What can possibly take precedence over a job and getting away from this slum?'

He took her hand gently and swallowed hard. 'Doctor Wallace said—'

'What exactly did he say to you? I need rest and good food, that's what he said to me.'

He swallowed again, his throat and mouth felt like sandpaper, and beads of sweat stood out on his forehead, despite the chill of the room. 'You're too ill to be moved, my dear. You'll need constant nursing.'

She gripped his hand tightly as fear began to rise in her. 'I'm not that ill. I won't stay here, Edward, I won't! I'll be back on my feet in no time, once I get away from here.'

He felt as though someone was twisting a knife in his gut.

'Gwendoline, my dear, there's no question of us – you moving from here for quite a while.'

Suddenly he saw the fear in her eyes but he knew he had to go on. 'It's a complicated diagnosis. Lots of long medical terms. You will get better, but it will take a long time, I'm afraid. And you must have total bed rest. I'm so sorry, so terribly sorry, my darling.'

She stared at him her eyes wide, the pupils dilated with shock. 'But I can't stay in bed for months! Mr Forsythe never said anything about being totally confined to bed!'

He took her in his arms. 'It's a long time since you last saw him, Gwendoline. Please believe me, my darling, I've failed you so miserably and now . . . now this. Oh, I'm so sorry!'

He felt the shudder run through her and then came the tears. He held her tightly. Never in his life had he felt so helpless or so guilty. If he had known about her condition earlier, then somehow he'd have managed to find a way to keep the house. He'd have sold his soul to let her have these last months in comfort in the home she'd loved. She would leave this house, this street she so detested, but it would be in a coffin.

'At least we have friends, good friends. We are surrounded by people who just want to help. Who are willing to give up their time to help, with no thought of inconvenience or payment.' He tried desperately to soothe her.

She raised a tear-stained face. 'What friends? What people?'

He explained that Bridie, Lizzie and Hilda would

91

nurse her. He told her of Emily O'Brien and Sal Kerrigan's kindness, and that of Nancy and Mary, and in that instant Gwendoline knew beyond the shadow of a doubt that he was telling her the truth. The terrible, terrible truth, that she was going to have to stay in this dreadful house, in this terrible place, for a long time, maybe even for ever. Her children would grow up here to become – what? All the anger and resentment were washed away by the tide of hopelessness and fear that engulfed her, and she clung to Edward.

Earlier that morning Mike had stood in the rain-washed darkness of the landing stage, watching the Dublin ferry ploughing its way through the choppy waters of the Mersey. He had been reluctant to leave his warm bed, but Hilda had poked and prodded him, reminding him that they all had a long, hectic day ahead of them, not least herself.

He'd caught the first tram and had sat huddled on the wooden seat while the icy rain sluiced down the windows and the trolley sparked and flashed overhead. He'd pulled his cap further down and turned the collar of his coat up, as he'd walked down the floating roadway. A row of carts, the huge Clydesdales waiting patiently with heads bowed, lined the road. They were waiting for the cargo to come ashore.

He stood under the awning of the Riverside Station, watching the ferry edge closer. He wondered what this new cousin would be like. Would he even like him? Kitty had written, or at least a priest had written, to say that the boy was tall, thin, dark-haired and would be carrying a cardboard suitcase provided by the priest himself.

Mike walked up and down impatiently. How long did it take to get an old tub like the *Munster* alongside? At last the hawsers were secured, creaking and groaning in protest as the grey, foam-flecked swell tried to pull the ship away from the stage.

The gangway was at last raised and people started to crowd down it. Mike began to search the crowds, some of whom had obviously been celebrating Christmas rather early and were the worse for wear with drink, or maybe it had been a rough crossing, he mused. It frequently was. There were quite a lot of people carrying suitcases, but none of them were young, dark-haired lads travelling alone. He began to wonder if this Sean Doyle was on the boat at all. Maybe he'd missed it. Then he saw the tall gangly lad with a shock of dark, curly hair protruding from beneath his cap. His clothes were shabby and thin, and he carried a small brown case. He had no overcoat, just an old tweed jacket, and he was shivering.

Mike pushed his way through the throng. 'Are you Sean Doyle?'

'That I am. Are you Michael Burgess?'

'Yes.'

They stared at each other with open curiosity until Mike remembered Hilda's admonition of not to stand dawdling all day, there was work to be done. 'Right, we'd better get going.'

Sean was taking in the sights and sounds of this city where he'd heard there was work to be had and all manner of diversions. He noted Mike's warm overcoat, stout boots and the woollen muffler wrapped around his neck. His own shirt was collarless and patched, his boots worn, the soles lined with cardboard that was becoming wet and soggy. By the looks of this boyo here he'd fallen on his feet. It was three square meals a day at least and maybe even good clothes from now on, he thought.

At first he hadn't wanted to come. Things had become very confused. The pattern of his life had changed with first his da dying, then his mam getting sick. Being the youngest he'd always had to stand up for himself, and in their neighbourhood he'd soon learned to steal and to fight for what few possessions he'd obtained. He wasn't stupid; even at school they'd known that. 'Crafty as a cartload of monkeys' was the way Brother Francis had described him. Well, you needed to live by your wits in Emerald Square. He had quickly realized that when his mam had gone to her reward, and God knew she deserved it, it would be the streets of Dublin for him.

As they boarded the number twenty-one tram and settled themselves Mike asked him how his mother was, more for something to break the strained silence than out of genuine concern. He didn't know Kitty Doyle.

'Ah, now, she's not good, not good at all.'

'I'm sorry. I'm sorry about your da, too.'

Sean thought of his da, always on the jar when he had a bit of money, cursing, swearing and belting his mammy too if she opened her mouth or looked sideways at him. She had told him that it was for the best to go to Liverpool. She'd begged him go and make something of himself for her sake. Then she'd feel that her efforts hadn't been totally in vain. The more he thought about it, the more determined he became that that was just what he intended to do. Firstly, he intended to find out the set-up, the lie of the land. 'So, you're after following your da then, in the shop I mean.'

Mike grimaced. 'It's a job, but I hate it. It's not what I want.'

'You hate it. Working in a nice warm place all day. With a wage an' all at the end of it.' This cousin of his was a fool, he thought. But Mike Burgess had had more of the good things of life than himself, and obviously his expectations were higher because of that.

Mike felt guilty. He supposed Sean was right. He was being ungrateful and he was lucky. He had his mam and dad and Chrissie.

'It's not that bad. What I really meant was I wanted to go on and get some training. Be an engineer or something.'

Sean didn't reply, he was watching a train lumbering along on the overhead railway. It was something he'd never seen before. Trains that ran up in the air. Who would have believed it?

'Is there something you really wanted to do?' Mike probed.

'I wanted to go to America or Australia, like me brothers did.'

'Oh, aye, that would be great. But Liverpool is not so bad, there's plenty to do if you have the money.'

So, Mike had big ideas about being an engineer, he didn't want the shop. Now there was something to think about for the future, Sean mused.

They travelled in silence as the tram trundled down Lord Street and Church Street with its fine shops, then through Clayton Square and Lime Street with its imposing municipal buildings, and along Byrom Street towards Scotland Road.

It was a grand city, Sean thought. There was plenty of money here. From the deck of the ferry he'd seen the forest of masts and spars and the funnels of the steamships in the docks. Aye, plenty of money if you knew where to look for it.

Frank was just about to open up when he saw them walking down Burlington Street. Sean looked around him distastefully and thought that there really wasn't much difference between Burlington Street and the miserable streets he'd left in Dublin, but he brightened as Frank came out to greet him.

'Sean, so you've arrived safely, lad. Come on in and get something to eat, you look starved.'

Sean took the outstretched hand and shook it firmly. Start as you mean to go on, boyo, he told himself. 'It's very good of you, that it is, to take me in. What will I call you?'

'Frank will do.'

'Ah, no, I couldn't, it's not respectful.'

'Well, Uncle then?'

Sean smiled and nodded as Frank ushered both boys into the back room where Hilda was just clearing the table.

'So you've arrived then,' she said, eyeing him up and down. He looked none too clean and his clothes were a disgrace, but then, having travelled all night on that cattle boat didn't help.

Sean was quick to notice the difference in her attitude to the open friendliness of her husband's. 'I have that and it was a dreadful crossing. I never want to do that again. I'm very thankful to you both.'

'Well, we'll get everything sorted out later on. It's our busiest day of the year.' Hilda put on her shop coat. 'Chrissie will get your breakfast from the oven and then, when you've eaten, Michael will show you where you're to sleep and you can unpack your things and get a wash. You'll feel better.'

Sean nodded. She didn't like him, that was evident, although she was trying to hide it.

'How are you at figures, Sean?' Frank asked as his wife disappeared into the shop. Chrissie had taken a plate from the oven and had put it on the table, glancing from beneath her long dark lashes at Sean who, at Mike's indication, had seated himself.

'Great. I'm great at figures, not much with the reading and writing, though.'

'Good, then you can give a hand in the shop later on, when you've unpacked.' Frank smiled at the lad as he went to join Hilda.

Sean tucked into the bacon and egg and black pudding. He was starving. 'It's a grand place you have here, Michael,' he said, his mouth full of food. His quick gaze had taken in the homely comfort of the warm kitchen.

'It's Mike. Only Mam insists on calling me Michael.'

'It's rude to talk with your mouth full,' Chrissie interrupted. She didn't like the look of him. He was rough and she'd noticed his eyes darting around the room.

'Shut up, Chrissie. He's hungry and he's been travelling all night!' Mike snapped.

Ah, a sharp little rossi that one, Sean thought. Like her ma, but he'd fallen on his feet all right. A warm, comfortable home with as much as he wanted to eat. He didn't mind helping in the shop today. It would give him a chance to meet the customers. He'd soon get a job; with all those ships in the docks it shouldn't be too hard. Yes, things were definitely on the up for poor sleveen Sean Doyle from Emerald Square. He'd have to be careful with Hilda, she was distrustful of him. Perhaps she didn't want a stranger in her home, maybe that was it. Still, his mam had always said he could charm the birds off the trees when he wanted to. He'd work at it.

Hilda greeted her first customer briskly. 'Morning, Lizzie, the usual? Don't forget we're closed for two days.'

'I scc your new lodger has arrived,' Lizzie said.

'You don't miss much, do you? He's only just off the boat.'

'He looks a bit rough an' ready. Give me a pound of extra potatoes and a bit more tea and marge and I'll have four ounces of that ham.'

'We're really pushing the boat out, aren't we?' Hilda remarked caustically, angered by Lizzie's remark.

'You'd look a bit worse for wear yourself if you'd made that crossing. It's a nightmare, I can tell you that from experience.'

The shop was filling up and she had little time to converse further with Lizzie Simcock. But the woman was right. She'd have to get him some decent clothes and soon. She wasn't going to have half the parish nudging each other at mass on Christmas morning and whispering about the Burgesses' poor relation. More expense, and she hadn't taken to the lad either. She seldom took an instant dislike to anyone, but it was just something about him. It was his attitude, oh, on the surface respectful enough, yet cocky . . . or perhaps she was just imagining it; she was harassed, it being Christmas.

Winifred Harvey was next in line. She was a timid-looking woman with a perpetually worried look.

'Everything all right, Winnie?' Hilda asked.

'Yes, thanks. It's a busy time for everyone, isn't it?'

'Oh, it is. How's Jerry getting on with his job?'

'Fine. You know Jerry, he doesn't say much.'

Hilda wondered were they talking about the same person. Jerry was always very chatty whenever she saw him. Perhaps he never got the chance at home. There was far too much bible reading in that house. In fact it was a very silent house from what little she'd gleaned, and that wasn't natural in her book.

'Happy Christmas then, Winnie.' She smiled as she took the woman's money. The Harveys were one of the very few families who paid in full.

Sal Kerrigan surprised her by passing over a list.

This was very unusual, for Sal was never very organized.

'That's what I like to see, Sal. A bit of organization,' Frank joked.

'Aye, well, I've a lot on me plate just now.'

Hilda noticed little Sebastian, the name being one of Sal's flights of fancy always shortened to Seb, and Rose Chatterton hanging on to Sal's skirt. 'I see you've still got the little one, then.'

'Aye, she's not much trouble, got a bit of a paddy though, but she's taken to our Seb, and our Joan's taken a real shine to her. Calls her a proper little lady. "Don't she talk nice, Mam?" she keeps saying.' Sal shook her head, her eyes full of foreboding.

'So why the face?' Hilda asked.

'Because I've got a feeling she's thinking about having the little 'un as a bridesmaid, that's why.'

Hilda pursed her lips and nodded. That would put the cat amongst the pigeons, Joan having refused to entertain the idea of her sisters as bridesmaids.

'How is she at number eighty?' Hilda asked.

Sal sucked in her breath and shook her head. 'Not good. Our Tommy said Nancy told him that they haven't told her about "you know what". They're not going to at all. But he'll have to tell her something.'

'How's he going to explain Bridie, Lizzie and me trooping in and out all day and the little one there virtually living with you?'

'I don't know, I feel so sorry for him. I saw them delivering a parcel, so that should buck them all up a bit. Do you know Hilda, I'll be glad when Christmas is over, I will! What with Pat falling in drunk every night. Oh, he believes in celebrating early, he does, any excuse! Our Joan turning her nose up at everything, like lady bloody muck. I tell you Hilda, the sooner she takes herself off to Everton the better. And then there's the rest of them mitherin' me about Christmas presents an' me with hardly a penny to bless meself. Go and ask yer da about Christmas presents, I keep saying! I'm worn out.'

'I know the feeling. God knows what time I'll get finished today, and then I'll have to start again in there.' Hilda jerked her head in the direction of the back room.

'Never mind, you'll have Sean and Mike to help,' Frank said.

Hilda pursed her lips and wondered whether they would be any help. Mike was slow and was more interested in what was going on in the street outside, and could she trust that Sean? She was inclined to agree with Sal, it was an awful lot of work and expense just for a couple of days.

Chapter Eight

———— ✦ ————

THE NEW YEAR OF 1913 came in accompanied by heavy snowfalls and freezing temperatures. Many of the residents of Burlington Street suffered extreme hardship, for the old houses were damp and draughty. Often there was a frosting of ice on the inside of window panes, and any water kept in the house froze solid overnight. Even the water in the standpipe was sometimes frozen.

Edward Chatterton had got a job as a clerk in one of the many shipping offices in the city. Dee was delighted, until her father told her that his wage was a very small one compared to the salary he'd commanded in London. It would still be a struggle to make ends meet. Added to her anxiety for her mother was the constant worry of how to balance the household budget. She often felt as though she'd been pitched headlong into a sucking quagmire of debt, insecurity and harassment. Both Philip and David had been enrolled at the local Church of England school and

Rose spent her time with the Kerrigans, reluctantly returning home each night. So reluctantly that Dee often had to drag her screaming and kicking all the way. Rose, being a self-centred child, wasn't particularly bothered about seeing her mother. Sal made an excellent surrogate, and the entire Kerrigan clan indulged her shamelessly, but Gwendoline wanted to see her youngest daughter. True to their word, Bridie, Lizzie, Hilda and Emily O'Brien came in each day, their presence a blessed relief for Dee in an otherwise lonely and fraught day.

Sean Doyle had settled in very quickly and made friends easily. Even Lizzie Simcock could find very little fault with him.

'Ah, good mornin' to you, Mrs Simcock. You're looking very well today, ma'am, if I may be so bold as to say so,' was how he'd greeted Lizzie one morning.

She had eyed him with suspicion. 'Well, you've the gift of the gab, I'll give you that, lad.'

Sean had smiled ruefully. 'Ah, I hope you won't be holding me being Irish against me. I was just being pleasant.'

'She'd have a job doing that, lad. Wasn't her man born in County Cork?' Sal had interrupted, grinning. He was a nice enough lad, she thought, until she remembered that she'd first heard that comment from Monica, and hadn't that bold piece rolled her eyes expressively?

'I wasn't putting him down, Sal,' Lizzie had answered tersely. 'Not at all. Isn't it nice to see a youngster with manners and consideration?'

Lizzie was nearly smiling at the lad, which was unusual. If that grimace could be called a smile, Sal thought. Lizzie hardly smiled at anyone.

'Let's hope you still feel that way when your Mary starts bringing him home for tea,' Sal laughed, winking at Sean. 'He's made a big impression on our Monica and Abbie, I can tell you.'

Lizzie pursed her lips, determined to say nothing about Monica Kerrigan who was far worse, in her opinion, for chasing the lads than was her Mary.

'You'll have them all running in and out of here on any excuse, Hilda. He'll charm the birds off the trees. The girls will be flocking here from miles around,' Sal laughed.

'Oh, now stop that, Mrs Kerrigan, ma'am, you're making me blush and you're giving me a reputation I don't deserve, so you are,' Sean had laughed bashfully.

'Aye, well, I'm having none of that nonsense. He'll be going out to work soon,' Hilda had replied grimly, making a mental note to keep her eyes open for any unusually frequent visits from Monica Kerrigan or Mary Simcock. She'd soon put a stop to anything like that. This was a place of business, not a public park.

Sean did make himself available and useful at every opportunity. Mainly, this was to ingratiate himself with Hilda, but it was also because he was truly grateful for a roof over his head, food in his belly and decent clothes on his back. He accompanied Tommy and Pat Kerrigan each day to the docks, where sometimes he got work and sometimes he didn't. But it didn't matter.

What wages he got he gave to Hilda, who gave him back at least sixpence for himself.

He had watched carefully and had been quick to note that a lot of pilfering went on at the docks, the results of which were sold in the back entries, away from the prying eyes of the scuffers. Men and women with families to feed and clothe didn't ask questions as to where such bargains originated. He was surprised that Pat Kerrigan didn't take advantage of such opportunities as a half box of tinned peaches or a few cans of corned beef. Especially with the forthcoming wedding. But Pat was lazy and Tommy was too scared of the blockermen and the Paddy Kellys – otherwise known as the dock police – who knew what went on and often caught the culprits, with dire consequences.

The forthcoming wedding of Joan Kerrigan was the main topic of interest in the street. As Sal had prophesied, Joan intended to have little Rose as her only bridesmaid.

'Oh, that's very nice, I must say! You won't have your own sisters but you'll have a stranger,' Sal said, acidly. She couldn't afford dresses for her three girls, but that wasn't the point.

'She's not a stranger, not now, Mam. She practically lives here. I said I wanted it quiet and with one small bridesmaid, it will keep it that way. I'm not having it turned into a bloody circus!'

'You watch your mouth, girl! Or it'll be the back of me hand you'll be getting, never mind a "do", quiet or otherwise!' Pat shouted over the top of his paper.

'You want. That's all I've heard from you for weeks!

Want! Want! Want! You're all the bloody same. Well, if your sisters refuse to go, I'm not going to make them.' Sal folded her arms over her ample bosom and glared at her eldest daughter.

'What's up now?' Monica Kerrigan bounced into the room. At seventeen she was a cocky, cheeky girl and was a sore torment to her mother with her bold ways.

'She wants little Rose as a bridesmaid,' Sal stated.

'I thought you weren't having any bridesmaids!' Monica was put out and didn't try to hide it.

'She won't have you lot, if that's what you mean. She won't 'ave it turned into a bloody circus.'

'She's ashamed of us, Mam. She is! If she had her way none of us would go to the wedding at all.'

Joan was stung. 'I'm not ashamed of you!'

'You bloody are! Your face would stop the Liver clock sometimes, when he's here especially. If looks could kill we'd all be dead an' buried. And the gob on your "fiancé" when me da offers to stand him a pint! I tell you she's ashamed of us, Mam.'

Pat lowered his paper again. All he wanted was some peace and quiet, it wasn't much to ask after a man had been working all day. 'Will you all shut up and let me have a bit of peace. You've got mouths like sewers, "bloody" this and "bloody" that. I'll not have it!'

'You swear,' Monica shot back.

'I'm bloody entitled to, it's my house and you lot would make St Peter swear!'

Sal returned to the fray. 'Well, who's going to pay for the dress?'

'I will. I'm not asking you to put your hand in your pocket, nor me dad either,' Joan said stubbornly.

'I'm glad about that because there's nothing in it!' Sal retorted.

'Well, if she's having that snotty-nosed little madam, I'm not going! It's not going to be much of a "do" anyway, not with misery guts and his sour-faced old ma looking down their noses at us. And I'm going to tell our Abbie and Ginny.' Monica flounced out.

Sal turned on Joan. 'Now see what you've done! I suppose you're happy now you've upset everyone!'

Pat threw down his paper in disgust. 'That's it! I've had enough. I'm off to the alehouse for some peace, and I wish to God you'd pack up and move to bloody Everton tomorrow, girl!' he roared at Joan.

When he'd gone Sal sat down in his vacated chair. 'He doesn't need much of an excuse to go off boozing, you know that. How the hell I'm going to manage to pay Frank Burgess for all the stuff I've ordered I don't know, with him drinking every bloody halfpenny he gets his mitts on!'

Joan was contrite. 'I'm sorry, Mam, I really am.'

Sal sighed heavily. 'I wish you'd eloped, it would have been a damned sight easier and less expensive. How's it going to look, Joan, slighting yer sisters like that?'

'Mam, I don't care how it looks. God, now I wish I had eloped.'

'You'd better go and ask Rose's da then, if you're set on it. Don't go mithering Mrs Chatterton, she's too ill.'

'I'll put the kettle on, Mam. You put your feet up for

half an hour, I'll clean up.' Having got her own way, Joan was being very conciliatory, but she was beginning to think that the sooner it was all over, the better for everyone.

There were no hired carriages, and the bridal party walked the short distance to the church. Joan was resplendent, but cold, in a cream dress trimmed at the high-collared neck and tight leg-o'-mutton sleeves with blue ribbon. She held the skirt well clear of the grey-coloured slush that still clung to the pavements. Pat wore his Sunday suit, and the starched wing collar of his shirt cut uncomfortably into his neck. The rest of the family followed, also in their Sunday best, Sal wearing a hat she'd borrowed from Hilda. Monica, Abbie and Ginny all looked sullenly at Rose, who shivered in a pale blue muslin dress obtained from a small shop in Islington. If it was kept in pristine condition it could be taken back and half the purchase price would be refunded, Joan had informed her mother. Sal had been horrified at the cost.

'Then I suppose they'll sell it again for three quarters of what you paid. That's a good way to line your pockets!' Sal had retorted scornfully. 'They must have seen you coming!'

'It's a good idea though, isn't it?' Chrissie Burgess had remarked with great interest. She'd been sent up with the borrowed hat. Joan and Sal had both glared at her, so she'd gone home.

The whole street turned out to watch Joan's triumphal procession, and Dee stood with Nancy and

Mary who pointed at Tommy, resplendent in his first suit and looking very smart.

'Oh, get him! Done up like a dog's dinner!' Mary called.

'Can't you keep your mouth shut and behave decently for once in your life?' Lizzie hissed at her.

Everyone had been invited to the house that evening, for only the wedding party were having a tea at the Kerrigans that afternoon. Then the festivities would really get under way after six.

Dee hadn't wanted to go. She felt it would be wrong with her mother so ill.

'No one will think like that,' Mary had protested.

'It will do you good to get out for a few hours,' Nancy had urged.

'I've never been to a party – a proper party – and I won't know anyone and they might think I'm imposing on them.' Dee was still unsure.

'I wish you wouldn't use words like that,' Mary had said looking pained.

'It means—'

'I know what it means. You think they'll think they are being put on. Well, they won't. They wouldn't have asked you otherwise.'

'And you know lots of people, you know us and our mams, the Burgesses, Mrs Kerrigan, Mrs O'Brien.' Nancy wasn't going to give up.

In the end Dee had agreed.

'I hope it doesn't end up like the last do they had,' Nancy said, as she walked round to the church with Dee and Mary, followed by a group of neighbours.

'Don't be such a misery, Nance, I'm looking forward to it,' Mary chided. It was the best bit of excitement she'd had for ages and she just might get to know Sean Doyle a bit better.

'Well, I don't want to end up in the nick like half of them did last time.'

Dee was fascinated. 'What happened?'

'They had the street up, that's what happened. They all started fighting and someone called the scuffers in the end.'

To change the subject and because Dee was now looking very apprehensive, Mary changed tack. 'Didn't she look lovely, though? I wonder how much the frock cost.'

'An arm and a leg, by the look of it. She got it in Blacklers, so I heard. I wonder, did he pay for it?'

'She didn't have a veil,' Dee commented. 'I thought she would have.'

'You don't have to have a veil. That hat was very nice,' Mary replied. Obviously the only weddings Dee had seen were big posh ones where the bride wore yards of satin and lace. 'What are you going to wear, Nance?'

'My dark blue skirt and white blouse, what else?'

'I've borrowed a dress from Madge, she's got hundreds.' Mary always exaggerated. Madge was a girl she worked with. She was a year older than herself and always dressed up a lot. Mary envied her. 'It's green and all trimmed with black braid and rows of little buttons. It's gorgeous.'

'You can't wear green to a wedding, it's unlucky!' Nancy cried.

'Don't be daft, Nance, that's an old wives' tale. Anyway it's hanging up at home now, so I'm not going to ask to borrow something else. What are you wearing, Dee?'

'My pink dress, it's all I've got, except for these.' She indicated the dark grey lindsey skirt and calico blouse she was wearing beneath her shawl, all of which had come from Paddy's Market. She tried not to think of all the beautiful dresses she'd once owned. A whole wardrobe of them to choose from for special occasions. She realized that Mary was speaking to her.

'You shouldn't pull your hair back so tightly,' Mary advised.

'Why not? It's the only way it stays tidy.'

'It's tidy, but that's all. You'd suit it better if you wore it like mine.' Mary's hair was swept up in a loose roll that framed her face. 'I'll come over and do it for you, if you like,' she offered.

'Dee's coming to our house to get ready. Mam said we weren't to be tripping in and out, upsetting Mrs Chatterton,' Nancy stated.

Mary wasn't put out. 'All right, I'll come over to your house. At least then I won't have Mam nagging me about everything. If she had her way I'd be wearing sackcloth and ashes, or at least something that covered me from head to toe.'

By the time they were all ready, Mary looking very grown-up in the borrowed green dress, Nancy in her white high-necked blouse that had been carefully starched and ironed, and Dee in the pink dress that had been sponged and pressed and with her hair styled like Mary's, which Nancy said really suited her, they were looking forward to a pleasant evening.

The door to the Kerrigans' house stood wide open and every room was crowded with people; a few had even spilled out onto the street.

Tommy made a beeline for them. 'God, it's murder in 'ere, you can't move, and me da's been on the ale since we got back from church.'

'Who else is here?' Mary asked, her eyes darting around at familiar faces, searching for the dark, curly hair of Sean Doyle.

'Mike and Jerry are in there somewhere and so is Sean. Will I get you all a drink?'

Nancy and Dee were not too sure, but Mary said she'd have a drop of sherry or stout.

'The sherry's long gone, Mam and Bridie polished that off between them, so it will have to be stout.'

'Where's the new ma-in-law?' Nancy asked.

'She's in the kitchen with our Joan and Terry, and the three of them have got right gobs on! I wish they'd all just go. Joan said I was to try and keep me mam sober, that's a laugh! She said she's done enough worrying over this wedding that now she's bloody well going to enjoy it, an' if our Joan doesn't, that's her look-out.'

Mary decided she would try to find Sean, so Dee and Nancy sat on the stairs, which gave them a good view of almost everything that was going on.

Tommy eventually arrived back with the drinks in mugs, and with Mike and Jerry in tow, too. Both looked hot and flushed. Dee sipped the dark-coloured beer politely and tried not to pull a face, for it tasted sour.

Nancy had no such qualms. 'God, it's horrible!' she cried after taking a mouthful.

'Well if you don't want it I'll have it,' Mike said. 'Can't let it go to waste. Where's Mary?'

'Gone to find your cousin,' Nancy answered, grinning at Mike who looked as though he'd already sampled the stout, or maybe it was only the press of people.

'The dancing will start soon, as soon as they can get "Mine's a half" Cowley to the piano.' Tommy laughed at the nickname Mo Cowley from number twenty-four had earned himself by his habit of always trying to cadge a drink.

'Since when have you had a piano?' Nancy was incredulous.

'It's not ours, it's from the priest's house. Father Fitz lent it to us. He's supposed to be dropping in for a drink some time.'

'That'll put the mockers on things,' Mike said.

'No, it won't. He won't stay long, he never does. It's just to make sure we all turn up at mass in the morning and if we don't then he can read us the riot act!'

'I don't see your mam and dad, Jerry,' Nancy said.

'That's 'cos they're not here. Can you imagine them coming to something like this, especially if your Father What's 'is Name is here. He'd have a blue fit. He's always going on about "Popish idols", you know what he's like.'

'That's a bit off, isn't it?' Mike said, thinking the Harveys' behaviour was downright rude.

'Naw, my da came up last night to see Tommy's da. To apologize, like, for not being able to come. Our Hannah would have liked to, though.'

Nancy felt sorry for Hannah Harvey. She was a bit younger than the rest of them, but she was hardly ever allowed out of the house. It had always been that way, even when they'd been younger. She'd never been let out to play in the street.

'She never goes anywhere, does she, your Hannah? Is there something wrong with her?' Nancy probed.

'No, she's just quiet and shy, like.'

'She's never had the chance to be anything else,' Nancy whispered to Dee. 'Can't set foot over the doorstep, except for school and church. So what did they say as to why they couldn't come?'

Jerry shrugged. 'I don't know. I never asked.'

'He said they had a prayer meeting,' Tommy informed them.

'Oh, aye, there's always a prayer meeting going on.' Jerry didn't want to be reminded of his father's words before he'd left the house. It had only been at his mother's and his own pleading that he'd been able to come at all. That and the promise to behave himself, like a Christian person.

The strains of 'There is a Tavern in the Town', played with more gusto than accuracy, suddenly rose above the din.

'Come on Nance, let's have a bit of a twirl.' Mike

caught Nancy's arm and pulled her in the direction of the front room.

'There won't be much jigging about, not in here!' she replied as they joined the crush. The mats had been taken up and the furniture shoved against the wall, what there was of it.

'Come on, Dee,' Tommy urged. He really liked Dee, even though she was a bit prim and a bit plain.

'I've . . . I don't know,' she stammered, not wishing to draw attention to herself. She was quite content to sit and watch.

'It doesn't matter, I can't dance either and besides, none of that lot will even notice.'

She had had dancing lessons and could execute a waltz, a polka and a mazurka quite well, but she'd never done it in public or with a boy; but her protests went unheeded as Tommy led her down the stairs.

It wasn't much of a heady or exhilarating experience, she thought, as there was hardly room to move and besides, Mo Cowley played everything in the same tempo which the other dancers ignored, moving at their own chosen pace. She caught sight of Mary looking very attractive and laughing up into Sean Doyle's eyes, and Nancy and Mike twirling around quite energetically, considering the lack of space. She also caught a glimpse of Pat Kerrigan, now totally unconscious in the corner, a grin fixed on his face and an empty pint mug clutched in his hand. Judging by the way Mrs Kerrigan was hanging on to the neck of Kenneth, her eldest son, it wouldn't be long before she became oblivious too.

When she got the chance, Mary managed to extricate herself from the crush, pulling Sean with her. She couldn't hope for much privacy but she was determined to get a few minutes alone with him. The scullery was empty. It was also dark and a bit smelly, but it was so tiny that they had to stand very close together.

'It's a bit cooler out here. I couldn't stand that crush for much longer,' she said, by way of an explanation.

'Didn't you like me holding you, Mary?' Sean asked, his tone serious but his eyes dancing with laughter.

'I didn't mean that! I only meant—'

Sean drew her closer. 'And will you be tossing your head and pulling away if I try to kiss you?'

'I don't want you to think I'm forward.'

'I don't.'

'I'm not *that* sort of a girl.' She ducked her head but her heart was beating faster.

'Did I say you were?' He lifted her chin gently. 'I just don't see the point of wasting time, do you? I want to kiss you and you want me to kiss you.'

He fell silent as her arms slid around his neck. He pulled her warm, softly rounded body closer and felt the shiver of pleasure course through her.

'There's another keg of ale in here!' a voice yelled and their increasingly passionate embrace was interrupted by Ken Kerrigan.

'No there isn't, you can't swing a cat in here!' Mary snapped, angry at being so sharply brought down from the cloud she'd been floating on.

'There is. A little one. I purrit under the sink meself!'

Sean bent down and yanked out a small keg from under the stone sink. 'Is this it?'

'That's it.' Ken picked it up and grinned slyly at Sean. 'Sorry if I interrupted.'

'You didn't,' Mary shot back. The spell was broken.

'Don't get all airyated with me, you should 'ave found somewhere else to do yer courtin.' Anyway, yer mam's lookin' for yer, Mary.'

'Oh, God, isn't that all I need!'

'Come on, let's be getting back to the party then.' Sean kissed her on the forehead. 'Will you come out with me one night, Mary?'

'Of course, Sean. There's other nights and other places.' She smiled in what she hoped was a seductive way, but her expression hardened as she caught sight of Lizzie in the kitchen.

'I've been looking for you.'

'Well, I'm here, Mam. I've just been getting a breath of air.'

'In the scullery?' Lizzie peered closely at her daughter, noting the high colour in her cheeks. 'I don't want you drinking and making a show of yourself.'

'I have had one drink, Mam,' Mary lied, wishing Lizzie would leave her alone and not embarrass her in front of Sean.

'And that's enough and stay where I can see you, too.'

'Oh, Mam, stop it!' Mary cried, in an agony of resentment.

'Well, I think it's time to go and see how the dancin' is doing. Would you do me the honour, Mrs Simcock?'

Sean held out his arm and smiled at Lizzie. He didn't want to dance, but if it would keep the miserable old biddy quiet, then he'd suffer it.

Lizzie became more amiable. 'That's kind of you, Sean, but I'm a bit old. I'd be glad of a drop of stout and maybe a few ribs, if there's any left.'

Sean went off in search of the requested items, winking at Mary from behind Lizzie's back.

Mary could have killed them both. What was he playing at? When he came back her mam would monopolize him, moaning about everything and everyone, herself included. It would be awful and they'd not get another minute alone, her mam would see to that all right. She decided to have another drink herself and to hell with Mam, then she'd see what the others were up to.

As the evening progressed, Nancy had managed to find some ginger beer, and their little group moved into the back yard where at least you could get a breath of air and it wasn't quite so noisy. Mary and Tommy were looking rather green and Mary said her head was beginning to spin.

'You're drunk, you shouldn't have had all that stout. Your mam will kill you,' Nancy prophesied.

'She'll have to find me first,' Mary answered, her words a little slurred.

Jerry, who hadn't taken part in the dancing but had had his mug filled up regularly by Norman Kerrigan, swayed slightly. He shook his head to try to clear his vision. Being able to hold your drink was a sign of maturity and counted for a lot in this neighbourhood.

'I don't think this fresh . . . fresh air is doin' me any good.' Tommy's words were slurred and Nancy giggled at him.

'I can't see any of you lot being able to get to mass in the morning, and then you'll have Father Fitz down on you like a ton of bricks.'

'Oh, shurrup, Nance, don't be such a misery,' Mary groaned. She felt bad enough now, and tomorrow morning just didn't bear thinking about. Nor did she care any longer where Sean Doyle had got to.

The sound of raised voices and the words 'Miserable Proddy git!' came quite clearly from inside the house.

'Oh, that's done it now! I knew it. I just bloody knew it. Someone's insulted someone and now they'll all be at it!' Nancy cried, getting to her feet, for the sound of shouting now issued from the kitchen.

'I'm going home before they start belting each other,' Mary announced, staggering towards the back door and the entry beyond.

Before either Mike, Tommy or Jerry could make out what was going on inside, the tall figure of Abe Harvey charged through the doorway.

Jerry stepped back at the sight of his father's face. Abe had come to find out why his son was not at home, as he had promised he would be, instead of lingering at this disgusting, drunken orgy.

'Blasphemy! Drunkenness and evil and I let you come into this den . . . this lair of Satan!' Abe shouted at his son.

Frank Burgess and Harry O'Brien had followed him out.

'Oh, come on Abe, it's a wedding,' Frank said, trying to calm him down. The man was a lay preacher and was bordering on fanaticism in his opinion. To call him a mean, narrow-minded, Protestant bible-puncher was not one of Ken Kerrigan's better decisions. Any more than Norman Kerrigan calling him an Orange bastard had been.

Abe had caught Jerry by the shoulder and he'd smelled the drink on his son's breath. 'You're drunk! Drunk like the rest of these debauched sots!' He lashed out and caught Jerry a blow which sent him reeling. 'I'll teach you to flout me, to flout the teachings of God!' He yanked Jerry to his feet and began to hit him.

'Abe, Abe, for God's sake leave the lad alone!' Frank cried.

'It's for God's sake that I'm going to teach him a lesson he'll not forget!' Abe roared.

Dee and Nancy clung together. Dee began to tremble, for she'd never seen anything like this before. Even Mike and Tommy stood as though petrified, for Abe seemed like a man possessed.

Frank's temper rose, there was no need to carry on like this, but Jerry wasn't his son. He had no right to interfere. Jerry was yelling, begging his father not to hit him any more, but Abe had taken off his thick leather belt with its heavy buckle. The first blow struck Jerry across the face, leaving a livid wheal.

Nancy screamed in terror for Jerry and then the tiny yard seemed to erupt. Mike caught Jerry and pulled him out of Abe's reach, while Frank and Harry O'Brien were both shouting and trying to pin Abe Harvey's arms to his side. Abe was denouncing them all as fiends and criminals.

'That's enough, Abe, you'll kill the lad. Do you want that on your conscience?' Frank yelled.

Abe seemed to quieten down.

'That's better. All right, I know the lad did wrong, they all did, they're too young to drink, but he meant no harm, no one did. They meant no disrespect to you or your beliefs,' Frank reasoned, wishing to God that the two oldest Kerrigan lads had kept their mouths shut.

Jerry stood with his hand against his cheek. His eyes were filled with fear and yet there was something else in their depths. Resentment and the stirrings of hatred. One day, one day, Da would hit him once too often and then he'd find out what it was like to be beaten.

Abe shook himself and seemed to regain his composure. 'I'm the one to judge whether he meant harm or not. I should never have let him come here.'

'It's a wedding, man, don't spoil it,' Harry O'Brien urged.

'Well, it's over for him, anyway. Get home to your mother, she's worried about you,' Abe instructed his son coldly.

For an instant Jerry didn't move and everyone held their breath, then he walked slowly towards the yard door. His father followed.

'I wouldn't like to be him when he gets home,' Mike said quietly. The whole episode had had a sobering effect on them all. Frank and Harry O'Brien went back inside.

All signs of joviality had disappeared and the friends stood silently in the yard until Mike said, 'That's put the damper on it all, I think I'll go home.'

Nancy and Dee followed him, leaving Tommy to wonder where he was going to find a corner to sleep in a house still crowded with his rowdy relations and half of Burlington Street.

Chapter Nine

———◆———

GWENDOLINE CHATTERTON DIED ON 16 September. It was a day that Dee was to remember all her life. Over the months a routine had been established that had lulled her into a false sense of security. Life was ordered and there were actually times during the day when she forgot that her mother was dying. She was now used to seeing Lizzie, Hilda, Emily and Bridie in the house. Their presence seemed to blur the stark reality. They made it easier for her, for them all, to believe that life would go on like this, not indefinitely, but at least for next week, next month, maybe even the rest of the year. Dee's days were spent doing the chores, the shopping, the cooking and sitting with her mother in the late afternoons until Nancy called on her way home from work and her father came in at the end of the day.

During the night, when sometimes she found it hard to sleep, her thoughts did turn to the future. She would tell herself over and over that when it came she would be prepared. She had grown up so much that she often looked back with sheer disbelief at the child she had been before they'd come to Liverpool. Her mother's death would be a blessed relief, as Hilda often said. But on that warm, golden September afternoon she wasn't prepared, and the full realization hit her like a heavy, physical blow. It didn't matter how many times Hilda and Lizzie told her that Gwendoline was now out of pain and in a better place than Burlington Street, she had sobbed uncontrollably.

That night her father had got morosely drunk, for Pat Kerrigan had acquired a bottle of whisky from a shipment that had come into the docks, and had come to offer his condolences.

For the sake of her bewildered and grieving brothers, Dee had finally pulled herself together. Rose had only been told by Sal that her mam had gone to heaven where it was warm and lovely and there was no pain. Rose, accustomed now to life in the rumbustious Kerrigan household, her mother a frail, unreal figure in a hushed and subdued house, hadn't uttered a single word. Instead she'd gone off to play with Seb and the other tots, and Sal was glad that she'd taken it so well. Little ones were very resilient, she thought.

It had been Bridie, with the help of Dee and Nancy, who had got Edward upstairs and onto the bed that Dee and her brothers still shared.

Ma Ollerenshaw had been in earlier and Gwendoline was laid out in the other bedroom.

'Where will you all sleep?' Nancy asked, concerned.

'She can sleep on the sofa, the lads can go in with

their da,' Bridie had answered, sweeping up the newspapers and dirty dishes and taking them into the scullery.

They'd both sat down on the sagging sofa and Nancy had put her arm around Dee.

'I know it's not much use, and you've probably heard it a dozen times today, but at least she's in no more pain, Dee.'

'I know. I keep telling myself that. Oh, Nancy, it was awful to see her. It wasn't my mother lying there at all. It was someone . . . different.'

Bridie came through and handed her a cup of strong, sweet tea. Dee sipped it politely; she'd lost count of the cups of tea she'd had that day. Her insides were awash with it.

'You're not to worry about anything, Dee. We won't just disappear now that she's . . . she's gone. If there isn't enough in the Club for the funeral, we'll all chip in.'

Dee hadn't even thought about the funeral.

'Your da will be all right in the morning, and you'll all be better once the funeral is over. It sort of marks the end of a part of your life. I know that's how I felt when Nancy's da was buried.'

Her words had done nothing to comfort Dee. Yes, a part of her life was over. Until a year ago it had been happy and carefree. The very last remnants of her childhood years had gone with her mother.

Bridie wanted to give Dee something to think about. Something to occupy her thoughts. 'What will you do now?'

Dee had just stared at her blankly. 'Now?' she'd asked.

'You can get a job. The boys will be at school all day and Rose will be with Sal. It will do you good to get out of this house. You've got to think of yourself now, Dee, and you'll all be better off, money-wise.'

'But . . . but what can I do? I've no training. I didn't even finish school. I've no Leaving Certificate.'

This was better, Bridie thought, seeing the spark of interest in Dee's eyes. 'You're better educated than anyone around here, you speak well, you'd be wasted in a factory, although you'd earn better money.'

'What about the Laundry, with Mary and me?' Nancy interrupted. 'They might take her in the packing room. Your writing is so neat, Dee.'

'What about an office job, like your da?' Bridie suggested. Dee's quiet, serious demeanour would certainly fit well into an office.

Dee didn't think she would like that and wondered why Bridie was going on about jobs now, when she really couldn't concentrate.

'What about one of the posh shops in town?' Bridie was relentlessly pursuing the subject.

'Mam, she hasn't got the right clothes,' Nancy pointed out.

'She doesn't need a wardrobe full of clothes. They all wear black dresses with white collars.'

'I mean, when she goes to ask for a job, she hasn't got the right clothes to go in.'

'Then we'll borrow some. She's only slight, about the same size as Chrissie Burgess, I'd say. Chrissie's got a nice blue coat and hat that Hilda bought in Sturla's, on tick, well, on the cheque.' Chrissie had grown so much that Hilda had been forced to buy her new clothes and she'd been moaning about the fact for the past few weeks.

Despite everything Dee still looked interested and Bridie knew her strategy had worked. At least now the girl wouldn't be awake all night crying for her mam. Oh, she'd cry all right, that was natural, but she'd also have something to look forward to, and God knew they needed the extra money a job would provide.

The funeral was terrible, Dee thought. It was like looking through a window, watching other people moving from place to place, slowly and silently. There was no reality to it at all. The whole street had turned out, all those who possessed mourning clothes wore them, and those who didn't wore black armbands. As the horse-drawn hearse passed, men doffed their caps and women crossed themselves. Edward had walked behind the hearse, comforted by the lines of silent neighbours. Dee held tightly to her brothers' hands and Rose, who had refused to be parted from Sal, walked behind them with little Seb Kerrigan clinging to his mother's skirt, too, neither of them knowing properly what was going on.

When the service was over and they stood in the graveyard, Dee had marvelled that the sun could shine and that birds still sang. The sound of the first clods of earth falling on the coffin was the most final sound she'd ever heard.

The rest of the day had passed with the same sense of unreality. The women who had nursed Gwendoline, along with Nancy and Mary, came back to the house and laid out the plates of ham sandwiches and gave cups of tea to the neighbours who called to pay their respects. When at last everyone had gone and the dishes (many of which had been borrowed) had been washed and dried, Nancy and Dee sat on the back step in the golden light of the early autumn sunset. The last roseate rays just penetrated the gloomy corners of the yard.

'I'm glad today is all over.'

Nancy sighed. 'Yes, it's horrible, all that standing around the grave.'

'I'll miss going into the room and seeing her there, Nancy. I don't know if I'll ever be able to go . . . in there.'

'I know. Things will be a bit strange for a while. At least you've got something to look forward to.'

Dee nodded.

The day after Gwendoline's death, and while her father and Frank Burgess had been arranging the funeral, Hilda had provided some writing paper and envelopes, and Dee had written to some of the better class shops in the city centre. Her father had delivered them by hand the next day in his lunch break. She'd had replies to them all, but only one calling her for an interview, from George Henry Lee in Basnett Street. The interview was in two days' time.

She still didn't feel as though things were even approaching normal when, with Chrissie's coat covering her black skirt and blouse that had been purchased for the funeral, and with the blue hat covering her neatly brushed hair, she got off the tram in Church Street. She didn't stop to look in the windows of the Bon Marché that was on the corner of Basnett Street, nor in the windows of George Henry Lee's, she was too nervous. Instead, she handed the letter to the uniformed commissionaire on the door.

He scanned it and then directed her to Miss Purvess's office on the second floor, just beyond Ladies' Gowns.

She was shaking inside as she was ushered into a tiny cluttered office by the buxom, well corseted figure of Miss Purvess. She knew she at least looked presentable, although she had no gloves and her hands were red and chapped from housework. She tried to hide them by tucking them tightly together, palms upwards, and holding them closely against her.

Miss Purvess's attitude was brisk. 'You have no experience, there are no references from school?'

'No, ma'am, you see I didn't finish school in London. We moved here and I . . . I was needed to nurse my mother. She died last week.'

'I'm sorry to hear that, Miss Chatterton.'

The sympathy seemed genuine. 'Thank you,' Dee replied.

'And have you carefully considered this step? Is it just a job you are seeking, or is it something more?'

Dee hadn't carefully considered anything, but she felt that to say so would be wrong. She was flustered and very nervous. 'I . . . I hope that, in time, I may be able to achieve—'

'What?'

Dee felt as though her stomach was awash with ice water. 'A career,' she ventured timidly. Father had told her to say she was interested in a career.

'You have no intention of marrying then, Miss Chatterton?'

'Er, no, ma'am.' She thought it a strange question to ask someone who had only just had her fifteenth birthday, but it seemed to have been the right answer.

'I can start you as a junior on Haberdashery, at three shillings a week. You will work Monday to Saturday, from eight o'clock until six.'

Dee could have cried with sheer relief. 'Oh, thank you, ma'am.'

'We will provide your working dresses, which must be kept clean and pressed at all times.'

Dee nodded again. She was mentally working out how much difference her wages would make to the household budget. Miss Purvess was informing her that she would be entitled to a discount on everything she purchased, but Dee knew it would be a long time, if ever, before she could afford to buy anything here.

She found that she enjoyed the work and she also enjoyed the company of the other girls and the daily contact with the customers she served, although she was very shy to start with. She was allocated buttons, which were a popular item and she was kept busy, but managed to keep the small wooden boxes tidy and note when stocks were getting low. She was sometimes asked for her opinion or advice, and this, once she had overcome her shyness, she really enjoyed. She had a good substantial meal at lunch time in the staff canteen, and began to fill out. Life still wasn't easy. She was up very early and it was nearly eleven o'clock when she got to bed, for there were still the household chores to see to. But the house had gradually begun to look brighter and more homely, even though most of the furnishings were bought second- or even third-hand.

The boys were quite happy at school, although Philip had initially come in for some teasing and bullying because of his accent, but once he'd shown he could stand up for himself the torments ceased. David had quickly slipped into the local idiom and they were allowed to play out with their friends until seven o'clock, providing homework was done.

Edward seemed to have adjusted well to their new lifestyle, much better than Dee had envisaged he would. During her mother's illness she'd often thought he looked like a fish out of water, but perhaps he'd been maintaining the veneer of a stiffly formal gentleman for Gwendoline's sake. Some evenings he went up to the Black Dog for an hour or two, sometimes he went for solitary walks and once he'd been invited to the home of one of his colleagues for supper. Bridie always seemed to be popping in and out and Dee thought that it was good for Father to have friends again, even though they weren't of the class he'd formerly mingled with.

It was Rose who was causing the most worry, Dee thought as, one evening in mid November, she walked home from the tram stop. Rose was running wild and she knew her mother would be turning in her grave. Rose had quickly picked up the nasal accent and now fought and argued like the rest of the Kerrigan family, and because Sal was easy-going and laboured under the delusion that Rose might possibly be missing Gwendoline, she did little or nothing to chastise the child. Every night it was a battle to get her home and Dee was tired and certainly not looking forward to another tantrum.

When she got in she found Phil poking the fire, trying to encourage it to draw. She had strictly forbidden Frank Burgess's method after the night the chimney had caught fire. Thankfully there had been no damage. David was laboriously writing on a piece of loose and rather grubby paper. Homework, obviously. Her father would be in shortly, so she set a pan of scouse on the range; she'd prepared it all last night. She decided to get the battle with Rose over early; she might then get some peace for the rest of the evening.

'Just watch that pan will you, Phil? I won't be long. I'm going for Rose.'

Philip nodded but raised his eyes to the ceiling, thinking that occasionally a good hiding wouldn't do Rose any harm. She was becoming a horrible, spoiled brat.

Sal's door stood wide open, it was never closed winter or summer, and Ginny was sitting on the top step, a wedge of bread and dripping in her hand.

'I wouldn't go in there, Dee,' she said darkly.

'I've come for Rose. What's the matter?'

Ginny grimaced. 'Our Monica's in dead lumber.'

That was nothing new, Dee thought. Monica Kerrigan was always outraging the sensibilities of her family in one way or another.

'Where's Rose?'

Ginny jerked her head towards the lobby. 'In the kitchen.'

Dee took a deep breath. Maybe with an argument in progress, she could get Rose out quickly and with the minimum of fuss.

The kitchen was untidy as usual. Rose and Seb, each with a crust covered in dripping, were sitting under the table which was cluttered with dirty dishes and a pile of damp washing. Abigail Kerrigan stood with her back to the scullery door, her hand to her mouth, her eyes wide, while Monica sat slumped in a chair near the range. She'd never seen Monica so quiet but, glancing at the faces of Sal and Pat, she sensed that the girl's latest escapade was very serious.

'I'm sorry to interrupt. I've come for Rose.'

The air was electric and no one spoke. So she bent down and reached out under the table.

Rose backed away. 'Rose, don't start. Can't you see that everyone's upset? Come out from under there now!' Dee hissed fiercely.

'Shan't,' came the defiant answer.

Dee looked imploringly at Abbie for help, but there was none to be gained from that quarter.

'Rose, I'll smack you hard if you don't come out this minute!' Dee was getting very cross and embarrassed.

'I won't! Yer can't make me!'

Dee turned to Pat in desperation, her cheeks burning. 'I'm so sorry, could you . . .?'

'Get out from there, now!' Pat bawled.

Rose didn't move, she was used to Pat shouting. Everyone yelled in this house, it was the only way you got noticed.

'Oh, bloody leave her there. I've got enough on me plate with this . . . this tart!' Pat cried.

Dee looked at Sal and saw the tears running down her weathered cheeks. 'Aunty Sal, what's the matter?' she asked, stricken. She'd never seen Sal cry before, no matter what the provocation.

Abbie covered her face with her hands. 'Oh, tell her Mam! Everyone's going to know soon enough.'

Sal wiped her face with the edge of her grubby apron. 'It's her . . . that . . . that trollop!' She wagged a stubby finger at Monica who shrank further into the chair.

'Up the bloody spout, she is, the little whore, and she won't say who the father is – if she bloody well even knows!' Pat stormed.

Dee felt sick. Monica Kerrigan was pregnant. It was the very worst fate that could befall any young girl. She forgot all about Rose and went and put her arm around Sal. 'Oh, I'm so sorry, Aunty Sal.'

'I'll not be able to hold me head up around here! I'm mortified. And what's Father Fitz going to say?' Sal's face was again wet with tears. 'I've tried. God knows I've tried with her!'

'Then you should have tried bloody harder, she's

been running wild for months. I've never 'ad this much trouble with the lads!' Pat roared.

Dee thought that was very unfair, Monica was his daughter too, but she said nothing.

'What about me?' Abbie wailed. 'I'll get tarred with the same brush, her being me twin and all! Oh, Mam, I'll get skitted something terrible. Me name will be ruined!'

'What's our Joan going to say, and her so respectable now!' Sal sobbed. 'And Terry's ma. Oh, Jesus, Mary an' Joseph!'

'Never mind our bloody Joan or that owld biddy! What about us? The disgrace on us all, on me, her da!'

Dee again thought that Pat was being very selfish and she tried to think of something comforting but couldn't. 'What will happen . . .?' She nodded in Monica's direction. Monica, too, was in tears.

'She'll have to go to a home for fallen women. I'm not having her here, under me nose, reminding everyone what a whore she is!' Pat paced up and down, glaring at Monica.

Sal began to think more practically. 'I'll get me shawl an' go and see Father Fitz now, it's got to be sorted out and the sooner the better. Her next door will have had her ear glued to the wall, half the street will know in ten minutes.'

Pat grabbed Monica by the shoulder and yanked her to her feet. 'An' you can go with her, you dirty little bitch and be thankful that I haven't taken me belt to you! It's a bloody good hiding you deserve!'

Monica was ashen but grateful for small mercies. She'd fully expected a thrashing.

Dee remembered the supper and without ceremony she bent down again and yanked Rose bodily from under the table. 'One word from you and I'll give you the hiding you deserve, Rose! Aunty Sal is very upset. Everyone is upset, so you're coming home now!' Rose had never seen her sister so grim or determined, and she'd never seen Aunty Sal cry either, so she submitted to being shoved down the lobby and out into the street.

The news spread like wildfire. The women were sympathetic to Sal to her face, but said they'd all seen it coming, and Monica Kerrigan should have been chastised severely before this. The men took a more charitable attitude. It wasn't spoken of at all in the Black Dog.

Lizzie said to Mary let it be a warning. After the initial shock had worn off, Mary wondered like everyone who the father was. It couldn't be Sean for she'd been seeing him quite a lot. But she'd have to be more resolute. He'd been trying to get her to go 'all the way' and so far she had refused, but she had been weakening. Well, now he wouldn't find her quite so willing to indulge in heavy petting. Monica was still refusing to tell even the parish priest who the father was, and that took a lot of courage. There was even a rumour that it was a married man and that's why Monica was so silent. Mary didn't believe that for a second.

'Isn't it awful?' Nancy said to Dee.

'It's poor Aunty Sal I feel sorry for.'

'Oh, aye, nice as pie they are to her face, but you should hear what everyone's saying behind her back.'

'Mrs Burgess said Monica's going to a convent in the country somewhere and that the nuns will look after her and find the baby a good home. Uncle Pat said he won't have it in the house and Aunty Sal agreed. She said it would remind them all the time.'

'She's ruined,' Nancy said solemnly. 'No one will ever marry her now.'

Bridie entered, catching the last words of her daughter's prediction. 'Aye, she's really done it this time. You mind you two take notice and don't go letting any lad take advantage of you.'

Nancy was scandalized. 'Oh, Mam, I'd never do anything like that!'

'Well, I hope not. But let it be a warning, that's all.'

Nancy decided to change the subject. 'Where are you off to then?'

'Oh, just for a drink with your da, Dee. Red has given me a few hours off, so we've decided to go into town, for a change.'

Nancy glanced at Dee. Bridie was spending a lot of time with Edward Chatterton lately, and before Monica Kerrigan's disgrace, she'd heard it commented on. She hoped Dee didn't mind.

'It does Father good to get out, otherwise he just sits and broods about . . . things,' Dee said.

Bridie smiled at her. 'You're a good girl, Dee.'

Nancy silently agreed: Dee was very thoughtful, but she also thought her friend was being very naïve.

Part Two

Chapter Ten

D EE COULD HARDLY BELIEVE that they had been in Burlington Street a year. It had gone so quickly and she had changed so much. The years of her childhood seemed to belong to a totally different age and to a very different person. She still felt a sense of loss at her mother's death, yet if she was honest with herself she would say that life was better than it had been six months ago.

She had her job, which she enjoyed, despite the fact that the run up to Christmas had been hectic and she was exhausted when she arrived home each night. Her wage meant that there was plain but wholesome food on the table and good second-hand clothes for them all. David had proved to be very resourceful, being possessed, like herself, of a practical streak. Young Bertie Kerrigan had shown him how valuable extra money could be earned. On Saturdays they hung around the stalls at the Great Homer Street Market, particularly those who sold rolls of linoleum. Then they would offer to carry home anything the customers had purchased. This often meant a long and wearying trek, but gained them up to threepence a journey.

They also went to Paddy's Market where, at the end of the day, stallholders who hadn't managed to sell their tattiest items dumped them in a skip which was emptied by the local bin men. The next morning, very early, they were up at the yard in Bevington Hill and grabbed as many rags as they could carry and sold them to the 'Raggies'. Raggy Billy in particular. They eventually made a cart from two planks of wood and some old pram wheels; this way they could carry more. They also used the cart for bringing home the 'fades' they filched from the fruit market in Great Nelson Street. All welcome additions to the household budget.

Sometimes she worried about her father. Oh, usually he tried to be cheerful, but there were times – fewer now – when she caught him staring morosely into the fire. Once she'd asked him why he was so silent.

'I was just thinking, Deirdre.'

'What about?'

'Oh, the days when I had so much more in life. Money, position, friends.'

She'd nodded her understanding. 'Sometimes I think like that too. I wonder what I'd be doing, where I would be going and what I'd be wearing if—'

'I don't want you to be unhappy, Deirdre.'

'I'm not, truly I'm not. Are you unhappy, Father?'

'No, I don't suppose I am. Sometimes I do find it hard to fit in. To feel as though I belong. I suppose I'll always feel like that to a degree.'

'But everyone is so kind. We have so many friends.'

'I'm not complaining, my dear, I was just stating a fact. I suppose I'll never fit in properly; it's all to do with roots, background, class. But I'm not unhappy.'

He had smiled and patted her hand, and she thought she understood. Sometimes she got confused or she said something that Nancy or Mary or Mrs Burgess didn't understand, usually with reference to her days in London, and she'd have to explain. Then she felt awkward and embarrassed. Three times a week her father did go up to the Black Dog, and occasionally on a Sunday evening he and Bridie would go to the music hall – the Hippodrome or the Lyric.

Dee was looking forward to Christmas Night, for Hilda had been coerced into having a party. It was a joint effort on the part of Frank, Mike and Chrissie, but the deciding factor had really been the fact that Mrs Rooney from the greengrocer's was giving a party on Boxing Night to which only a very select few had been invited. She'd been given an old and tatty copy of the *Illustrated London News* which had given her the idea.

'The airs and graces of her! It's not a "do", it's a soirée! A soirée, round here. No one knows what the word means. I had to ask Father Fitz,' Hilda had cried with derision. 'She doesn't know how to give a good "do", doesn't that one. Sherry and bits of cheese from Coopers if you please. Fancy inviting people round and only offering them bloody bits of cheese!'

This outburst indicated to the other members of the family how outraged she was. Hilda had appointed herself the doyenne of social etiquette (such as it was) and prided herself on never swearing.

'We should show her what a really good "do" is,' Frank had said, not too enthusiastically. It didn't do to be too enthusiastic or she suspected that she was being manipulated. It had worked. She had even foregone the usual form of invitation, by word of mouth. She had written out little cards and sent Chrissie to deliver them.

Frank had begun to regret the suggestion in a way, for it looked as though he was going to have to provide a slap-up buffet and beer for almost the entire street. He had put his foot down over asking all the Kerrigans. Sal and Pat, Tommy, Abbie and Norman only were invited. Norman wasn't too bad without the influence of Ken, who had gone off to Manchester to look for work after a row with his da. Monica had been packed off to the tender mercies of the Sisters of Charity in a distant part of Lancashire. 'Not that she'd get much charity out of them!' Bridie had remarked.

The Harveys had of course refused, politely. Only by Frank going personally to see Abe and Winnie and promising on the Bible that not a drop of alcohol would pass Jerry's lips had the lad been allowed to accept.

Mary had been saving up for a dress for Christmas anyway, she told Dee. There was a tontine at work. A sort of savings scheme, where you paid up to threepence a week (if you could afford it) for a year and at the end of that time you had a fair bit to spend.

'I've been to every shop in town, well, not your shop or Hendersons and the like, and I've seen a gorgeous one in Frisby Dyke's in Lord Street. It's pink, bright pink!' Mary's eyes became misty when she thought of it. The first brand new, really stylish dress she'd ever had or had ever dreamed of. Lizzie said it was a scandalous waste of money, it wasn't in the least bit practical, but it was her money. She'd worked damned hard for it in that laundry all year.

'Is this to impress Sean?' Dee asked.

Mary laughed and tossed her head. 'Him! I wouldn't be caught dead with him.' When she'd refused his increasingly insistent demands, he'd called her a tease and they'd argued, but in the end they'd both laughed. You couldn't stay angry with Sean for long.

'Well, you can't blame me for trying, Mary,' he'd said.

'Lads! You're all the same,' she'd replied and had admitted to herself that it was better to part, in fact his kisses and embraces had become less exciting of late. She wasn't a bad girl, she just liked a bit of fun and excitment in her otherwise dreary life, but she wasn't going to *have* to marry someone she felt she couldn't really love for ever. Nor was she going to end up like Monica Kerrigan.

'That wasn't what you were saying a couple of weeks ago,' Dee laughed.

'I can change my mind if I want to, it's my per . . . per . . . Oh, you know what I mean, Dee.'

Nancy said nothing. In her opinion Mary had pursued him shamelessly, obviously now he had either grown tired of her or it was the other way around. But Mary was flighty and seemed to fall in and out of love very easily.

'No, I've got my eye on someone else.'

'Who?' Dee demanded.

'Wait and see,' Mary teased, and no amount of coaxing could persuade her to divulge the new object of her desires.

Nancy, too, had been saving with the tontine, but being more prudent she had bought a pair of boots, a jacket and a new blouse. She'd fallen in love with the boots, they made her feet look so small and dainty. They were shiny and were fastened up the side with tiny black buttons. The blouse was cream, a colour that suited her and the front was pintucked and edged with cotton lace, which also trimmed the cuffs and neck. She had adopted the same hairstyle as Mary and Dee, and Bridie had remarked that at last she was trying to make something of herself, instead of looking like a 'plain Jane and no nonsense'. A sentiment which Nancy didn't take too kindly to.

One of the girls Dee worked with was very handy with a needle and Dee had bought some royal blue gabardine, marked down as soiled stock. With her discount off she was now the proud possessor of a new, if rather plain, dress.

'You could brighten it up with a bit of braid or even a flower pinned at the neck,' Mary had suggested helpfully, when Dee had shown it her.

'I like it plain. I don't want to offend you, Mary, but I don't suit frills and flowers, like you do.'

146

Mary wasn't a bit offended. 'Oh, suit yourself. It was just a thought.'

Hilda had moved most of the furniture next door, along with all her precious ornaments and china. She had been baking for days, Chrissie informed everyone, and apart from the sandwiches, pies, cakes and jellies, there were to be sheets and sheets of ribs and pigs' trotters and tripe, all considered to be great delicacies. Frank had been heard to mutter that he was sorry he'd ever opened his mouth and that the whole thing was getting out of hand and was threatening to put him in the workhouse. The piano from the presbytery had again been borrowed and Chrissie and Ginny Kerrigan had spent hours and hours making chains from coloured paper and blowing up balloons. All these preparations were carefully noted and it was unanimously decided that Hilda Burgess's Christmas party was going to far outshine Maggie Rooney's tea party, as it was being called – mainly by those who had not been invited. Maggie had been heard to remark that it was useless trying to raise the tone of the place, some people actually enjoyed being ignorant. Mr Rooney had been heard to reply that if his wife didn't keep her opinions to herself, they'd have no customers – genteel or otherwise.

There were many cries of 'See you tonight!' after mass that morning and Hilda positively glowed with pride and satisfaction as she walked home, having seen the look of chagrin on Maggie Rooney's face.

Bridie and Nancy came to call for Edward and Dee. Phil, who was considered to be very sensible, was to be left in charge of David, Rose, Bertie, Ginny and Seb Kerrigan, although he was none too pleased with this role and would have preferred to have gone to the party. But when pressed, he admitted he was too young anyway.

Bridie looked very handsome in a black skirt and an emerald green blouse edged with black, her hair swept up into a loose chignon, and Nancy did look far more attractive than usual.

'Well, don't we all look grand!' Bridie exclaimed at the sight of Dee in her new dress and Edward in a white shirt with a winged collar, a narrow black bow tie, borrowed from a colleague, and his dark office suit obtained from Solly, freshly pressed and brushed by Dee.

'I hope Mary doesn't get drunk and disgrace herself – again,' Nancy said to Dee as they walked behind their parents.

'She won't. It's going to be nothing like Joan's wedding – Mrs Burgess will see to that. Mike said he's fed up, hearing about how she's having nothing that comes under the heading of "Bad Behaviour". If anyone even mentions religion then Mr Burgess is to throw them out personally. She said she doesn't care who starts it – out they go!'

'Is Jerry coming?' Nancy asked, for there had been some doubt about it even at this late stage.

'I think so, providing he doesn't drink.'

'That won't be much fun for him.'

'You and I don't drink, well, not beer anyway, and it won't stop us from having a good time.'

'If there's any sherry or madeira wine, I'm having some.'

Dee nodded her approval. 'I might try a glass, as long as it doesn't taste like stout.'

'Look at the style of everyone!' Nancy exclaimed, as they entered Hilda's front room to a chorus of greetings.

Dee had to agree. It looked as if everyone had begged, borrowed or stolen to look their best, and she suspected it was to cock a snook at Mrs Rooney, who had cast aspersions (albeit unspoken ones) on their wardrobes and manners by a marked lack of invitations.

'Dee, look at Abbie Kerrigan! Where did she get that dress?' Nancy cried, too astonished to whisper.

The lilac coloured bombazine dress had been chosen and bought by Joan from T J Hughes. It was demure but very stylish. Sal thought it far too stylish for someone of Abbie's age, but refrained from saying so, seeing as she wasn't paying for it. Seventeen-year-old Abbie looked very pleased with the result. The dress had been a present from Joan, but she had included Sal's name to give the purpose of the dress more weight. It was by way of a bribe, an implied promise that if Abbie did not follow the path her twin sister had trodden, she could expect to be rewarded.

Monica's disgrace had had a very sobering effect on Abbie, so she'd told Joan in one of the tête-à-têtes they'd taken to having recently.

'I want more, Joan. More than Mam's got anyway.' Abbie had looked at her sister's neat and polished parlour with a twinge of envy.

'I swore to myself that I'd never put up with everything Mam's been faced with all her life.' Joan wiped an imaginary smut from a pot dog with the corner of her apron. 'Da's boozing, him in and out of work, us lot. She's been nothing but a skivvy all her life.'

Abbie had nodded. 'And she hasn't got much to show for it either. I want . . . I want something like this.' Abbie had flung out a hand to encompass Joan's home.

'Then don't go chucking yourself at the first lad that comes along.'

'I'm not like our Monica!' Abbie had protested.

'I know. I didn't mean to upset you.'

'I'm fed up with being tarred with the same brush as her, just because she's me twin.'

'Well, the only thing you can do is to show everyone that you are a quiet, respectable girl.'

'How can I do that?'

'I'll help you. I've learned a lot from Terry's mam,' Joan said proudly. 'Now, this do of Hilda's is the perfect chance for you to show them how different you are. Oh, they'll all say they are going to let their hair down and most of them will, but you can be sure Hilda and Lizzie Simcock will be watching everyone like hawks!'

A gleam of determination had entered Joan's eye. Abbie had looked eager and hopeful. She envied Joan, who was always neat and nicely dressed. She kept a good table, and the little house was spotless. Terry's mam hardly had to lift a finger, a fact that increased her approval of Joan. Yes, Abbie would love a house like Joan's, and she realized that there was a fair chance of making a silk purse out of a sow's ear. Joan hadn't done too badly at all. Her elder sister had encouraged this view and had even done Abbie's hair and given advice on the small amount of etiquette that she'd picked up from Terry's ma.

'She looks like a picture from a magazine,' Mary commented enviously. It made her dress look cheap and tawdry. Still, she didn't worry about that after Norman Kerrigan had brought her a drink and was looking at her with undisguised admiration. She fluttered her eyelashes seductively, she hoped. Tacky-looking her dress might be beside Abbie's finery, but it was having the desired effect.

'He's far too old for her,' Nancy said disapprovingly as she and Dee were yet again relegated to the stairs. Bridie had steered Edward into the kitchen after he'd insisted on greeting everyone cordially and complimenting Hilda on her appearance and culinary talents.

'I wondered who Mary was trying to impress,' Dee added.

Chrissie had perched on the stair above them. 'Our Mike's looking at Abbie Kerrigan like a big soppy kid. Look at him, the soft dope! She's two years older than him.'

It was true, Mike was staring at Abbie with a mixture of astonishment and adoration.

'You'd think he'd never seen her before in his life!' Chrissie jeered.

'Why don't you go and blow up some more balloons, or better still, take a walk off the Pierhead,' Nancy said cuttingly.

Chrissie ignored her but then, changing her mind, went downstairs in search of her mam. Mam didn't approve of the Kerrigans and she should know that Mike was making sheep's eyes at Abbie who was all done up in a very posh frock.

'That one's a nasty little cat,' Nancy said, thankful that Chrissie had departed.

Dee was searching the faces below. 'I can't see Jerry anywhere. Or Tommy for that matter.'

Nancy brightened. 'Here's Tommy now.'

'And Sean Doyle,' Dee added as the two boys came towards the stairs.

'Didn't I say they'd be here, lording it over us all, sitting up there like the Pope.' Sean laughed at his own wit.

'Shurrup! No one's to mention religion!' Tommy hissed.

Dee smiled. She liked Sean with his friendly manner, and he was always ready with a witty remark. He was sporting a new suit.

'I suppose that fell off the back of a wagon,' Nancy said.

'It did not! It's bought and paid for. I've been lucky these last weeks.'

'Well, you look very smart, Sean,' Dee complimented him.

Tommy wished he'd had a new suit and looked as sharp as Sean Doyle. He'd had work himself, for the docks were busy, but unlike Nancy, Dee, Hilda or Frank, he knew where Sean made his extra money. The money he didn't tell Hilda about. Buying and selling, was how Sean explained it, but he took terrible risks, or so Tommy thought. If he got caught he'd be spending next Christmas in Walton Jail.

'Will I get you ladies a drink?' Sean was being very gallant. He could afford to be, he felt on top of the world. He had money in his pocket and his first new suit on his back. Hilda could find no complaint with him, though she tried hard enough. He'd enjoyed a few dalliances, the last being Mary Simcock who he'd tired of, fortunately at the same time as she'd tired of him, so he couldn't be accused of throwing her over. He'd misjudged Mary, or maybe the plight of Monica Kerrigan had something to do with her suddenly prudish attitude.

'If there's any sherry or madeira wine we'll have some,' Nancy replied.

'But no stout or beer of any kind, thank you,' Dee finished.

'And it's a pint for yourself, Tommy?' Sean asked.

Tommy nodded, settling himself on the stair above the girls.

'Mike's making a fool of himself with your Abbie.'

Tommy laughed at Nancy. 'Ah leave him alone. I know she's me sister but she looks smashing, and she's all right is our Abbie, not like—' he didn't finish, and Dee hastily interrupted.

'She looks really grown-up and very elegant.'

Tommy looked pleased. 'She does, doesn't she? Mam says she hopes she'll be proud of her, she needs to be proud of one of us. Our Joan bought the dress. They're very pally those two.'

'Is Jerry coming or not?' Nancy asked.

'Yes. He can't have a bevvy though!'

'Well, don't you go getting in that state again,' Nancy scolded.

'No fear.' Tommy could still remember how bad he'd felt the morning after Joan's wedding.

'They had both, so I brought a glass of each,' Sean announced. 'You can swap your glasses over if you want to.' He carefully handed the two glasses to Nancy and Dee and joined Tommy on the stair.

Dee sipped the sherry. 'It's nice. It's sweet. Taste, Nancy.'

Nancy sipped it and nodded. 'Taste mine, Dee.'

Dee obliged. 'I like that better.'

'So swap,' Sean urged. So they did.

'Have you seen Jerry Harvey, Sean?' Dee asked.

'No. Maybe auld misery has changed his mind.'

'Hush. Remember Mrs Burgess said if anyone mentions religion they're to be thrown out, and that includes you.'

'Oh, he'll be here. Come on Nancy, Mo's in fine form tonight and don't tell me you can't dance, didn't I see you kicking up your heels with Mike at the Kerrigan wedding?'

Nancy passed her glass to Dee and let Sean lead her down the stairs and into the front room, where Mo Cowley was yet again pounding the piano unmercifully.

'You look different tonight, Nancy,' Sean said, holding her closer than was deemed proper. He meant it. Usually she looked so pale, so timid. Tonight she looked older, more confident and definitely attractive.

'It's probably my hair, I've done it differently.' Nancy felt awkward, she wasn't used to being complimented, nor was she used to being held so closely, and Sean Doyle was handsome and very charming when he wanted to be.

'And that colour makes your skin look like buttermilk.' He ran a finger around the collar of her blouse.

'Ah, stop giving me that blarney,' she replied blushing.

'It's not blarney, Nancy. It really suits you. Shall I tell you something?'

'What?' she asked cautiously.

'I've always thought you looked – well – delightful.'

It was a strange thing to say, she thought, but then he often used flowery words.

'Yes, that's it: "delightful". I'm delighted with you.' He repeated the word for she seemed to like it. Her cheeks flushed prettily and her hazel eyes were like pools of leaf-tinted water.

'Oh, stop it, you're making me feel silly.'

'Good. Everyone should feel "silly" now and then, in a nice way. Not stupid or dumb but—' he searched for the right word. He picked things up quickly and by listening to Frank and Chrissie, and by improving his reading, he'd increased his vocabulary. Big words always seemed to impress people. 'Frivolous. That's the word.'

Nancy didn't know what he meant but she wasn't going to let him know that. 'Oh, stop it Sean!'

'All right, I won't say another word,' he laughed, his dark eyes dancing with merriment. She was a demure little thing, which was a change after Mary's brash, bold ways.

'What's he saying to her? She's blushing,' Dee said to Tommy, who had moved down and now sat beside her.

'He's kissed the blarney stone, he has. He's the same at work, always using long, fancy words. He's got a way with him, that's why he gets so much work. He charms the blockerman, he does,' Tommy said grudgingly.

Dee nodded, she could see that Tommy had a point. 'He's nice, but well, a bit too . . .'

'Flashy?' Tommy supplied.

'I would have said glib.'

Tommy suddenly remembered his manners. 'Do you want to dance, Dee?'

'No, truly, I'm fine. I like just watching and besides, I've got to mind the drinks.'

'That's all right,' Tommy said affably; he was quite content to just sit and let everyone else get all hot and sweaty and besides, Dee was the sort of girl you could talk to easily. She had a way of encouraging you, not interrupting or trying to be smart. Of course she was much cleverer than any of them, but she never made you feel small or ignorant and he liked her a great deal.

'It's hard to think you've been here a year, Dee.'

'I know.'

'But you've all fitted in now, haven't you? I mean—' Tommy suddenly thought that perhaps he shouldn't have made any reference to her past.

'It's all right. I'm happy here, Tommy. I am.'

'And your da seems to be settled; does he miss his posh friends?'

'I think sometimes he does, but he's making the best of things now, and Bridie cheers him up no end.'

Tommy didn't comment. Dee could be very shortsighted at times, he thought, and it had nothing to do with her having to wear glasses. Tongues were beginning to wag about how much time Dee's da and Nancy's mam spent together.

'Yeah, she's a good skin is Nancy's mam. Me da likes her, a lot of the fellers do; she speaks her mind. You always know where you are with her, me da says.' He was trying to tell Dee in a roundabout way that Bridie was what his mam considered to be a flirt, although Sal had used a more derogatory expression. 'It looks as though everyone's turning into "Love's Young Dream".'

'What?'

'Look at Mike and Abbie, and Nancy and Sean, like sick calves the four of them.'

Dee saw he was right. Mike was gazing down at Abbie as though she were a vision from heaven and was holding her as though she were a rare and precious object. Nancy's face positively glowed, she'd never seen Nancy looking so . . . so . . . lovely. That was indeed the word, for her friend had blossomed. She hoped Sean wasn't just flirting, she didn't want Nancy to be hurt. 'That just leaves you and me a pair of wallflowers,' she laughed.

Tommy laughed too. He liked Dee more than she realized but he felt that even though her circumstances were almost the same as his own, she was too intelligent and lady-like for someone as ignorant as himself. 'Well, here's another one for the bunch!'

Jerry had finally arrived, but he looked far from happy and his right hand was heavily bandaged.

'What's up with you?' Tommy asked.

'I've been to Stanley Hospital.'

Dee looked concerned. 'What for? What's the matter?'

'It's my hand.'

'We can see that,' Tommy said shortly.

'It's been throbbing for days. I couldn't stand it any more.'

'What is it? Did you fall?' Dee asked.

'No. I'm always getting cuts and scratches. I got a deep cut a month ago at work, I was hanging carcasses, and the hook slipped. It's all swollen up now.'

'Did they put anything on it?' Tommy asked, for Jerry's face showed the ravages of pain.

'No, they cut it open to let the badness out. It's supposed to be some kind of a boil, so they said.'

Dee shuddered. 'You poor thing.'

'Oh, well, look at it like this, it'll probably be better in the morning.'

'I hope so, but they said to come back if it's not. They asked me where I worked, and when I told them the doctor stared at me hard, in a queer sort of way.'

'Probably he was thinking what a bloody fool you were to stick a meat hook in your hand. Oh, I'm sorry Dee, I didn't mean to swear.' Tommy looked abashed.

'And I can't even have a drink,' Jerry said mournfully.

'Don't get a cob on about that. I don't intend to get bevvied.'

'And Nancy and I certainly don't either, and Mary said she had enough last time. She'd never felt so ill, so you're in good company,' Dee consoled.

'Nancy looks as if she's swigged a bottle already,' Jerry remarked.

'No, she's gone all soft over Lover Boy Doyle! What with those two, Mike and Abbie and your da and Bridie Butterworth—' Tommy could have bitten his tongue, seeing Dee's eyebrows shoot up in surprise.

'I suppose you two will be at it next,' Jerry said hastily to cover Tommy's gaffe.

'Don't be daft, Jerry. We're friends, all of us,' Dee replied, a little too quietly. Tommy's words about her father and Bridie had disturbed her and she didn't like to think that they were all being paired off either.

'Oh, take no notice of me, I'm just miserable with my hand, that's all.'

Chapter Eleven

———◆———

Dee couldn't get Tommy's words out of her mind. The more she thought about Bridie and her father the more perturbed she became. She began to take people's remarks as double edged. She'd tried to talk to Nancy about it, but Nancy was used to people talking about her mam, and she was too wrapped up in Sean Doyle, for she'd seen him nearly every night since the party and felt as though she were floating in the clouds for most of the time. Dee finally decided to try to bring the subject up with her father.

She'd waited until the boys had gone to bed, then she'd made a fresh pot of tea.

'Father, can I talk to you?' she asked hesitantly as she handed him his cup.

'What's the matter, Deirdre? Has David been causing more trouble at school?' David was always in some kind of a scrape. 'No. nothing like that.' This was very hard she thought.

'Then what is it?'

'It's . . . it's . . . about you and . . . and Nancy's mother. People, well . . .' she was blushing furiously and she couldn't look at him.

Edward sighed. 'Bridie and I . . . we're friends, very good friends, like you and Nancy.'

She nodded.

'Bridie's very good to me, to us all. From the day we arrived here she's given us moral support, and no one could have been kinder.' Edward hadn't known the extent of speculation about his increasing fondness for Bridie Butterworth; Deirdre was obviously quite upset. 'She's helped me to get over your poor mother's death. She's helped me to keep my sanity in these changed circumstances.'

'I know. I didn't mean—'

'I know what you meant, Deirdre, but I don't want you to worry about gossip and rumour. It doesn't worry me and it doesn't worry Bridie; she says while people are talking about her they're leaving someone else alone.' He smiled.

Dee felt better, although not completely happy with the explanation. It might not bother them, but it did bother her.

'Everything all right now?' Edward probed.

Dee nodded. 'It's just me being stupid. I'm going to bed now.'

'You're not to worry, my dear,' Edward called after her.

She tried hard not to think about it, but it wasn't easy, particularly when Bridie seemed to be forever popping in.

*

She tried again to pin Nancy down on Saturday evening when she knew Bridie was out. Unfortunately Mary arrived on the doorstep at the same time.

'Hello, Dee, come to see Nance?'

'Yes.' She had really wanted to see Nancy alone, but Mary was also a close friend and maybe she'd help her to get Nancy's mind off Sean Doyle for a few minutes.

'Mary, will you help me? I can't get Nancy to take anything seriously and I need to talk to her.'

'That won't be easy, she's full of Sean Doyle, and he's no good for her, Dee. I know him, he'll break her heart, she's too trusting, too serious, like, is Nance.'

Dee felt ominously that Mary had a point, but she didn't have time to dwell on that now.

'What's this then? A formal visit? Are the rest of them coming down too?'

'Don't be sarcastic, Nance, it doesn't suit you,' Mary said good-naturedly. 'I've come to borrow your grey jacket, if you don't mind, and if you're not wearing it tonight, and Dee's come for – what have you come for Dee? You never told me.'

All three of them had settled themselves in the kitchen, close to the range.

'Nancy, I want to talk to you about your mother and . . . my father.'

Mary's eyebrows shot up, although she wasn't surprised. The only thing that surprised her was that Dee hadn't heard the gossip sooner.

'Oh, you're not going to start on about that again, Dee. I've told you people have always jangled about

Mam.' Nancy was more interested in what she was going to wear to go to the Rotunda with Sean.

'You should hear what they say about my mam,' Mary said pulling a face, 'but that's not the point. Nance, will you stop dreaming about Lover Boy for a few minutes and concentrate.'

Nancy frowned, remembering that Mary had been out with Sean, although he would never talk about Mary, except to say she was a 'bold rossi'.

'It's really upsetting me, Nancy, people are all talking. I know they are. Whenever I walk into a shop they stop and stare at me.'

Nancy sighed. 'Well, what do you want me to do?'

'I don't know. I . . . I did try to tell Father.'

'What did he say?' Mary asked, thinking Dee had been quite brave to broach the subject.

'He just said they were friends. Good friends, the way we are.'

'And he's right. They are friends, so just ignore the old biddies, Dee. I do. Now can we change the subject?'

Dee smiled but she didn't feel any better.

'Are you off out tonight, Mary?' Nancy asked.

'Yes. Norman's taking me to the Hippy; there's some good turns on. He's been saving up so we can have good seats. Well, not right up in the gods anyway. That's why I was wondering if you could lend me your jacket, it will go nicely with my red skirt.'

Nancy agreed. 'Sean's taking me to the Rotunda,' her eyes became dreamy as she thought of him. She tingled all over when he held her and kissed her and told her she was a sweet little darling. No one really knew her, he said, people said she was serious and shy, but he knew otherwise. She was just like a violet, beautiful in a quiet sort of way. You had to look closely to find that beauty. He used such lovely words, she thought, and he was so generous. He always had plenty of money and bought her sweets, and even on two occasions a bunch of violets, telling her they were her 'special' flower. He'd wanted to buy her a beautiful shawl she'd admired in Lewis's window, but she'd had to be very firm about that. Mam would have killed her. Gifts of clothing could only be accepted when you were married, or at least engaged.

'We might as well go home, Dee, she's not even in the same room with us, she's away with Sean Doyle somewhere.' Mary shook her head. Nancy had got it badly. She thought she was in love with Sean Doyle and she thought he was in love with her. Privately, Mary thought the only person Sean really cared about was himself. She really didn't want Nancy to be hurt but she knew if she voiced such sentiments, Nancy would get mad with her and say she was jealous.

'At least her mam isn't going mad with her for walking out with him,' Mary said as she walked up the street with Dee. She thought this was a little strange. If anyone knew about men it was Bridie Butterworth. Surely she must be able to see through Sean Doyle, but maybe she was too preoccupied with Dee's da to notice.

'No,' Dee mused. She felt left out. Mary was walking out with Norman Kerrigan, Nancy had Sean and Mike was smitten with Abbie Kerrigan. 'At least she's not been forbidden to see him again,' she said, thinking of Mike.

Mary knew what she meant. They'd all heard of the row that had followed the Christmas party. Hilda had been annoyed that Mike was so set on Abbie and she'd said so. She'd forbidden him to speak to Abbie. Frank had told her privately that she was being too harsh, that she was judging the girl by her sister, which wasn't fair. He'd also received the sharp edge of Hilda's tongue.

'He's still seeing her. They have to meet on the sly, like. Usually in town somewhere, and they have to go in on different trams. I think Ma Burgess knows, though, but she can't catch him out,' Mary said with satisfaction.

'How does she know?'

'Because that little snitch Chrissie followed Mike!'

Dee was outraged that a sister could do something like that to her own brother. 'Oh, how could she do such a thing?'

'Oh, don't worry, Mike didn't half belt her and made her promise to keep her big mouth shut or he'd break her neck!'

Dee felt that Chrissie Burgess deserved what she'd got.

'She went and told her da though.'

'She didn't!'

Mary nodded. 'She got no change out of him. She got another belt for being a snitch and a sneak and he told her to leave Mike alone.'

'Good for him.' Dee had a great deal of affection for Frank Burgess.

'Oh, that Chrissie's a sly madam. She'd buy and sell us all, Sean Doyle included.'

Dee sighed, for they'd reached number eighty and she had an evening of housework ahead of her. 'Enjoy yourself tonight, Mary.'

'I will and don't worry, Dee. Tarrah,' Mary called.

Mary passed Jerry and his father before she reached the corner of Devon Court. She smiled and nodded to Jerry and ignored the look of contempt on Abe's face. She knew he thought of her as a 'harlot', but she didn't care. He thought every unattached young girl was a 'harlot', her mam said. The man was mad. She was concerned because instead of the usual cheery way Jerry always greeted her, regardless of his father, he had just nodded, and he looked upset. She'd try to see him later on. Perhaps she'd call at the house when Abe and Winnie went off to the Mission Hall for a prayer meeting. A prayer meeting on a Saturday night, she thought. What kind of night out was that after a week's hard slog? She'd have to find an excuse, of course, for Hannah was bound to say she'd called. She was sure that Hannah had been made to promise to report on everything. Mam had half a skein of wool somewhere, she'd take that up. Winnie Harvey was a great knitter.

When she was ready to go out with Norman she found the wool and ran quickly to the top of the street.

It was Jerry who opened the door.

'I've come to give this to your mam,' she held out the wool then lowered her voice. 'What's up with you? You looked pig sick this afternoon.'

To her astonishment Jerry asked her to step into the lobby. No one was ever invited into the Harveys' house, not even into the lobby. She looked around with interest. Everywhere was painted a dark chocolate brown. On the walls were embroidered samplers with quotations from the Bible, and the more familiar 'Bless This House'. The lino was highly polished and the peg rugs were clean. It smelled of beeswax. 'Jerry, what's up?' she pressed, for Jerry looked awful.

'It's my hand. I went back. The pain is terrible, Mary, I can't sleep or eat hardly. It's making me sick!'

Mary was now very concerned. 'What did they say?'

'They've got to cut into it and put some kind of acid stuff on it.'

Mary was aghast. That sounded like torture. 'What for?'

'They said I've caught tuberculosis,' he pronounced the strange word slowly, 'from the cows, and it's got into the bone on my thumb.'

His words rendered Mary speechless. She didn't know what to say. Consumption, as tuberculosis was called, was a chest illness, a bad one, and there was no cure for it. But she'd never heard of anyone getting it in a hand. 'They might have made a mistake, Jerry.'

'No, they said it's quite common if people work with cattle. It's to do with diseased blood, it's called "bovine tuberculosis".' They were words he would never forget, they'd be imprinted on his mind for the rest of his life.

'Will the acid stuff cure it?'

'They don't know.' Jerry felt faint even thinking about it.

'What about work?'

'I can't work, not with my hand like this, and it's my right hand, too.'

Mary was shocked to the core. Jerry had had a rotten life as it was without having this, and not being able to work either. There had been precious little laughter or fun in here. It might be cleaner, less crowded and more comfortable than most homes in the street, but there was a gloomy, even sinister air about the place.

'I'm sorry, Jerry, I really am.' She cast around for something to say to try to cheer him up. 'Look, Norman and me are going to the Hippodrome tonight. Come with us? Norman won't mind, not when I tell him.'

'I can't. Da doesn't approve of the music hall.'

'He doesn't bloody approve of anything, but you need cheering up, so tell him you're going to go for a long walk, maybe even a trip on the ferry, to . . . well . . . to think about your hand and what they said. He can't moan about that, can he?'

Jerry managed a smile. 'Thanks, Mary, I'll do that.'

'Great, get yourself ready. I'm on my way to Norman's now. Tell your Hannah you're going for a long walk, then follow me down to Sal's.'

She was half way down the street when the full impact of what Jerry had said hit her. It didn't matter what they called it, Jerry had consumption, and you died from consumption.

As the news spread everyone felt sorry for Jerry Harvey. Frank had known someone who'd had bovine tuberculosis years ago, and he'd died before he was thirty.

'It spreads into all the bones. It's slow, not like in the chest,' he told Hilda. He didn't say it could turn you into a lunatic if it got to the brain.

'Oh, the poor lad.'

'Of course that was years ago, they might be able to do something now; maybe this acid will work.'

'That sounds terrible. I can't even think about it without feeling faint. Winnie was telling me they'll cut the flesh away, scrape the bone and pour this mixture of acids onto it.'

Frank winced visibly.

'She's heartbroken is Winnie. She's so clean, always scrubbing and polishing and he goes and picks that up at work. Do you know what that madman, that bloody lunatic said? It's God's way of testing Jerry's strength, his faith! Have you ever heard the like! Not a word of sympathy!'

Frank shook his head. Hilda was right, the man was a lunatic. The poor lad needed comfort and support, not religious rantings and ravings about faith being tested.

Jerry's plight cast a shadow over Nancy's romance, and she and Dee were trying to think of a way to boost Jerry's spirits when Bridie arrived at Dee's and Edward called both girls into the front room. It was a room that was never used as there was no furniture in it, and never a fire. In a few other houses in the street, those like the Harveys that didn't house an entire family, it had a special status. It was a parlour, to be used only on very rare occasions. Nancy glanced at Dee in alarm.

'Now what have we done?' she hissed.

Dee couldn't think of any misdemeanour.

They stood looking awkward until Edward spoke.

'We thought you two should be the very first to know. I have asked Bridie to marry me and she's accepted.' He looked rather shyly at the two girls.

'I've . . . I'm very fond of Edward,' Bridie added.

Nancy and Dee moved closer together, although neither of them were conscious of the movement. 'Oh,' Dee managed to mutter at length. Nancy was still too stunned to speak.

'Is that all you can say, Deirdre?'

'I . . . I'm . . . very glad,' Dee stammered.

Bridie laughed. 'They're shocked. I told you they would be. I think we'd better leave them to get used to it.'

Edward smiled. As usual she was right. He'd given a lot of thought to the matter before proposing. He was very fond of Bridie, she was good for him, she made him laugh, she put things into perspective. Oh, she wasn't his class, but somehow that didn't seem to matter so much here, in Liverpool. At least not the way it did in London – or maybe it wasn't as important to him now. He didn't brood on the past quite so often these days. She didn't have the breeding or the gentility of Gwendoline, but she had humour, common sense, and warmth. He'd looked ahead to the future, a future that looked empty and lonely for Deirdre, the boys, and eventually Rose, would all get married and leave him.

Bridie could offer him affection and companionship and he could offer her his name. The status of a married woman and perhaps a better standard of living.

Dee and Nancy stood staring blankly at each other; all thoughts of Sean had fled from Nancy's mind. At last Dee took her hand and they went back to the warmth of the kitchen.

'I don't know what to say, I honestly don't, Dee.'

'Nor I.'

They sat for a few seconds in silence, each trying to digest the news and all its implications.

'I suppose it'll be all right,' Nancy said hesitantly. 'I mean, we're all friends.'

'Will you be moving in here?' Dee was at last thinking of the practicalities.

'There's no room for you to come and live with us. There's five of you.'

Again there was silence.

Nancy was thinking that at least now everyone would stop talking about her mam, when the shock of this wedding was over. Dee was wondering where everyone would sleep. Then the thought of her father and Bridie sharing the same bed brought the blood rushing to her cheeks.

'Do you think they'll . . . get on?' Dee was remembering the terrible arguments between her mother and father when they'd first come here.

'I think so. Mam's very easy going.'

Dee thought that it would be a bonus to have help with the housework, she wouldn't be so tired. Then she thought how terribly overcrowded they would be and wondered would there be any point at all in trying to keep the place tidy.

'We'll be sisters, Dee. Stepsisters, but sisters just the same.' Nancy at last smiled.

This cheered Dee up. 'Oh, Nancy, that's great isn't it? I hadn't thought about it like that.'

'And with your da's wage, Mam's, yours and mine, things will be a lot easier. We'll have more money for ourselves; won't that be great, too?'

'Will your mother still go to work?'

Nancy shrugged. Married women in this neighbourhood worked more often than not. They all did something. Even Sal Kerrigan did a bit of office cleaning in the evenings, when she could get it. 'She might give up going to the Black Dog. I mean, it won't look right her serving her husband, will it? People will talk.'

'Nancy, there's going to be a lot of talk when this news gets out.'

'Oh God, Dee, I know! It's going to be awful for a few days, but it'll be a nine-day wonder. We'll just have to put up with it. I can just see Lizzie Simcock's face, she's going to be the worst. I think she had designs on your da herself.'

Dee grimaced. 'I'd much sooner have your mother.'

Nancy smiled. 'At least we can face them together, Dee.'

Chapter Twelve

———◆———

THE NEWS OF THE forthcoming wedding almost divided the street. There were those like Emily O'Brien and Sal Kerrigan who said they were glad for both Bridie and Edward. There were those like Hilda Burgess and Lizzie Simcock who said it was a scandal, especially with that poor woman barely in her grave. This sentiment was voiced often and loudly by Lizzie.

'You've certainly changed your tune. You said she was a snob and didn't have a good word for any of us, even though we wore ourselves out seeing to her and the kids. You'll be talkin' about her as though she were a bloody saint next, Lizzie!' Sal had exploded one day when there were just herself, Lizzie and Hilda in the shop.

'Well, I don't know what's got into him. A gentleman like that stooping to Bridie's level. And no matter what his circumstances are, he'll always be a gentleman. He'll never change,' Hilda put in.

'All men are the same, Hilda. Gentlemen or

dockers. They're selfish and wanting their beds warming. And I bet he didn't get much in the way of bed warming out of her, God rest her; too cold by far I'd say.'

'Oh, so you're the expert on the marriage bed now,' Lizzie retorted.

'I bloody well should be after nine kids! Good luck to them both. I would have thought you'd be glad for Bridie, Lizzie Simcock, you being a widow an' all.'

This was far too close to the truth for Lizzie's liking, so she stormed out.

'Hit the nail on the head there, didn't I?' Sal remarked smugly.

'I still don't think it's right. But only time will tell as to how it works out,' Hilda had replied.

The customers of the Black Dog were unanimously in favour of the union. Bridie was well liked, and because Edward was always grateful for any advice and gracious in giving it when it was requested of him and stood his round, he was congratulated.

The wedding itself had proved to be a difficult obstacle to overcome. Bridie was a Catholic and Edward Chatterton was not. Nor did he really want to convert to Catholicism. Bridie had respected his wishes, not being a devout Catholic, but Father Fitzpatrick had not. He refused point-blank to marry them. It was absolutely impossible to marry a Catholic and a non-Catholic. Totally and utterly out of the question. Uncharacteristically, Bridie had lost her temper and told him that she would be married at

Brougham Terrace, the Registry Office, and she didn't care whether he approved or not. She was reminded that in the eyes of the church it would not be a binding marriage, to which she had replied that in the eyes of the law it would be and that was that. Father Fitzpatrick countered that for the sake of Nancy's soul he would stop short of excommunication, but Bridie would not be welcome in his church. Bridie had retorted that Nancy's soul was in no danger and that she herself wouldn't darken his door ever again and that if he felt he must damn her soul for eternity and inform every other priest in the area about it, then she would join the Loyal Orange Order and to hell with them all. This outburst had rendered the parish priest speechless with fury. Despite her anger, his attitude hurt Bridie deeply.

'Oh, Mam, you didn't say that you'd join the Lodge!' Nancy cried when the exact words of the argument had been relayed to the two girls.

'I did. I don't mean it but I was so mad, so hurt; I knew he wouldn't be very happy about it, but there was no need to take that attitude.'

'If it's going to upset you so much, perhaps I should consider changing,' Edward offered.

For a minute Dee thought Bridie was going to encourage him and wondered would she, too, have to convert to the Church of Rome.

Bridie shook her head. 'No. It's different when you're born into it or even brought up with it, but if you don't believe, or you believe in something else, it's not right. No, but thanks.'

'Brougham Terrace then?' Nancy asked.

'It's not that bad. I had the church bit and everything with your da.'

When it got out that it was to be a Registry Office wedding it caused more gossip, and Dee and Nancy began to wonder would the controversy go on for ever. They had both been hoping it would have lost momentum after a week.

It was far from a fancy 'do', Nancy thought as they walked up the steps to the Registry Office, a sombre, soot-blackened building. It wasn't much better inside either. Dark brown paint, a table and a few hard wooden chairs.

'It's very gloomy,' Dee whispered to Nancy.

'It's downright miserable,' Nancy whispered back. When she got married she wanted a white dress and maybe a veil, with Dee as bridesmaid, and flowers and hymns. It would be a day she would remember for the rest of her life. The day she changed her name to . . . Doyle? At least there would be no problems with religion there.

There was no reception as such. Just a family tea, but Sean and Mike, Tommy and Jerry had been invited, as had Mary and Abbie Kerrigan. This had caused a major row in the Simcock house, but Mary had had the last word, saying that both Dee and Nancy were her friends and that her mam could lump it. Jerry didn't come as he was feeling very under the weather. The treatment seemed to be worse than the disease. Mike was in the doghouse at home because Abbie was going and Hilda was annoyed with Bridie for inviting her and with Sal for letting her go.

Dee thought sadly that this wedding seemed to have caused an awful lot of trouble and heartache. She hoped it was worth it. Everything had been sorted out in the previous weeks. The furniture from each house had been critically appraised and decisions were made as to what was to be kept and what was to be sold. There had been a long discussion about moving to a bigger house in a better area – after all, money wasn't as tight now. Edward, the boys and at first Dee had been in favour of it. Bridie and Nancy had said that while it would be great to have more room, neither of them could leave all their friends and neighbours of such long standing. Burlington Street was their life, Bridie had said tearfully and in the end, and with Dee's change of heart, their views had been accepted. Philip and David were to move into what had been Edward and Gwendoline's bedroom. Dee, Nancy and Rose would share the other room and Bridie and Edward would use the parlour as a bedroom and occasionally as a sitting-room, too. Besides the brass bedstead, which was Bridie's, a wardrobe and two easy chairs were crowded into the small room. The kitchen would be used by the entire family and Dee tried to imagine seven people in it and decided that it couldn't be much more crowded than when there had been five of them. Rose spent more time at Sal's than she did at home anyway, and in the summer the boys were out playing. It wouldn't be too bad.

After the meal was over, the girls washed up,

laughingly scolding Bridie that she couldn't do housework on her wedding day.

When Nancy and Dee's friends arrived, Bridie produced a small bottle of sherry that Red had provided, and Edward had sent Sean up to the pub with two big jugs to be filled with beer.

'It's a shame you can't go away for a few days,' Abbie ventured.

Bridie laughed. 'A honeymoon, Abbie! I didn't have a honeymoon the first time around, luv. There was no money to spare for things like that.'

Abbie looked a little embarrassed.

'Now don't go thinking you're upsetting people, Abbie. Mick Butterworth and Gwendoline Chatterton aren't names that have to be forgotten, are they Edward?' Edward shook his head, smiling at his new wife. 'No. We're not going to try to pretend they never existed. Where did you and Gwendoline go for your honeymoon?'

'Nice, in the South of France. It was very beautiful,' Edward answered, his eyes misting a little.

'I remember Mother telling me about it once. She said everyone was very fashionably dressed and strolled along the *Promenade des Anglais* in the evening,' Dee said quietly.

Abbie thought this was very romantic and smiled at Mike.

Edward thought it better to change the subject or this could get out of hand. 'I hear there's been a mutiny at the Curragh, Sean. It's a bit of a slap in the face for the Government.'

Sean had only just begun to take an interest in the politics of his country. He nodded solemnly. 'Aye, I suppose it is. There's a big army barracks at the Curragh,' he informed the others knowledgeably, although he'd never been to the place. He remembered his older brothers ranting and raving about the British and Home Rule, and how Parnell had dragged the Irish cause in the mud and lost them the chance of freedom. Even his da had joined in sometimes, but he'd been too young to understand all the intricacies, and at that time he hadn't cared much about any of it. 'I suppose Home Rule for Ireland will have to take a back seat now,' he continued.

'No, it might just help. There is a Home Rule Bill in the pipeline.'

'Ah, give over with all that talk of politics, we don't want to spoil the evening, and I don't understand any of it,' Bridie interrupted.

'I think that we should all get out from under your feet. Give you a bit of peace . . . on your own, like,' Mike said.

'That's not very sociable of you, Mike Burgess,' Bridie said.

'I didn't mean it like that. What I thought was, it's not a bad night for March, we could all go down to the Pierhead, maybe take a trip on the ferry.' Mike didn't intend to waste precious time sitting in the Chattertons' crowded kitchen when he could spend it with Abbie somewhere where there were not so many people.

'That's a grand idea, Mike!' Sean concurred,

noticing the look of encouragement Nancy was giving him.

Nancy thought that once they got to the Landing Stage they could pair off, but she wondered about Dee and glanced at her quizzically.

Dee smiled back. She didn't mind being with Tommy and Mary, they got on well; Rose wanted to go back to Sal's and with some prompting David and Phil were encouraged to go as well. David and Bertie Kerrigan were great pals, and Phil liked listening to Pat's tall stories.

'Oh, it's foggy, we won't be able to see anything!' Dee exclaimed as they alighted from the tram and crossed the cobbled expanse of Mann Island.

'That's not fog, Dee, it's just mist. It's been a nice day today, warm for March, so now it's misty. You should know the difference between this and a real fog by now,' Nancy laughed.

'If it was real fog we'd be deafened with all the fog-horns,' Tommy added as they walked down the floating roadway.

'If we hurry up we'll just make it. Look, the *Woodchurch* is ready to go!' Mike cried, grasping Abbie's hand and breaking into a run.

They all followed suit and, out of breath and laughing, they climbed the stairs to the ferry's open upper deck.

'How many times shall we cross?' Mike asked.

'How much money have you got? We can't dodge the deck-hands all night,' Tommy replied.

They pooled their resources and found they had enough to cross back and forth twice.

'I'll have had enough by then anyway,' Tommy commented to Dee as the others wandered off. 'It looks as though you girls are stuck with me.'

Dee laughed at him. 'I don't mind.'

'Nor me,' Mary added.

'Just as long as you don't talk about frocks and things all night.'

'Just as long as you don't start on about Liverpool Football Club,' Mary rejoined.

'I always think it's sort of romantic, when it's misty like this on the river,' Nancy said, snuggling into Sean's shoulder as they leaned on the rail at the stern, and watched the dirty, foamy wake of the ferry.

'Mist over the Mersey,' Sean said.

Nancy smiled up at him. 'That's just like you, Sean Doyle, with your flowery words.'

He bent and kissed her forehead.

'I felt sorry for Mam today, Sean.'

'Sorry? Now why did you feel like that? Wasn't it her wedding day? She looked happy enough to me.'

'I know, but it was awful in that place. Dead miserable.'

'Don't forget they register deaths there as well.'

'I know. I kept thinking about that. It was all dark, there wasn't even a flower in sight. It wouldn't hurt them to put a few flowers in a vase.'

'Ah, well, that's the authorities for you.'

'When I get married I want it to be beautiful. In a

church with music and flowers and a proper wedding dress and bridesmaids . . .' She sighed.

Her words alarmed Sean and he had to stop himself from moving away from her. He was very fond of Nancy, he really was, but weddings, churches and flowers were definitely not things he was contemplating. He had no intention of saddling himself with a wife, then kids, and then debts for the rest of his life. No, indeed, Sean Doyle was enjoying life and he had plans and they didn't include a wife. 'I'm sure you'll have all that, Nancy, when the time comes. But why are we wasting precious time talking? I thought we'd never get to be on our own.' He gathered her in his arms and kissed her passionately; he wasn't going to give her another opportunity to start on about weddings. Not tonight.

Nancy felt as though she were made of thistledown as she clung to his lips. She loved him so much and he loved her. He didn't want to waste a single precious moment of their time alone and he'd said he was sure she'd have the wedding of her dreams, when the time came. He loved her and he would give her everything. She didn't mind waiting. Someday they would be married. He'd said 'when the time comes', and that was all that mattered.

Life settled into the familiar pattern again as spring turned to summer. People said it was amazing how well they all got on at number eighty, and it was true, they did. Life was much easier for everyone, too. Bridie still worked in the Green Man, but she, Nancy and Dee shared the chores and the girls had far more money to spend on themselves. Although their wardrobes were not extensive and their pleasures few and relatively cheap, they considered themselves very lucky.

June 28 was pleasantly warm. The sky was a bowl of deep azure blue with a fine tracery of wispy white clouds. The sunlight was dazzling, as yet devoid of the fiery brassiness of late summer. It was the day that Monica Kerrigan returned home and the Archduke Ferdinand was shot dead in Sarajevo. Both events received equal attention in the Black Dog that evening.

'Well, the black sheep's come home,' Pat announced to everyone in the saloon bar before anyone else could convey the news.

'So I heard. What was it, the baby I mean?' Red said laconically, filling up a pint glass for Pat. Nothing much surprised him these days.

'A boy. Fine healthy child, an' he's gone to a good, Catholic home. He'll be better off. He'll have a better life than we could give him.' Pat tried to sound resolute. He didn't want to dwell on the fact that his first grandson would grow up not knowing him. The decision had been made and it was the best decision for everyone concerned.

'And how are things at home, then?' Frank asked cautiously.

Pat took the pint from Red and gulped it down thirstily. 'Sure, Sal was pleased enough to see her, but our Abbie wasn't.'

Remembering how much Hilda disapproved of Abbie Kerrigan, Frank could understand the girl's reluctance to be overjoyed at her sister's return. 'That I can understand,' he said aloud.

'Aye, well, she's changed has our Monica.'

'She's bound to have done,' Red concurred.

'Not ten minutes in the house and she informs us that she wants to be a nun.'

'That's a bit drastic, isn't it?'

'That's what I said Frank, but she's really changed, gone very quiet and determined like, from what I could see. "Da," she says, "I've done my penance. I've seen the error of my ways. I want to devote my life to God."'

Frank raised his eyebrows. It certainly didn't sound like the Monica Kerrigan he knew.

Pat lowered his voice a tone. 'I think she's been "got at".'

'You mean she's been coerced into making this decision?' Edward asked. He knew very little about Catholic convents, but the change in Monica Kerrigan had to be attributed to something.

'Dead right. Coerced.' Pat pronounced the word slowly so he would remember it for future reference.

'It might be the making of her, Pat.'

'It could be, Harry, she's not got much choice of anything else has she? I mean, I'll never get her wed now, will I? Who'd 'ave her?' Pat certainly did not relish the thought of Monica at home for ever, slowly turning into a religious maniac like Abe Harvey, forever running round to church or worse, reverting back to what she had been.

'If that's what she wants, it might be best to encourage her,' Edward put in.

'Eddy, I think I'll do that. Save a lot of trouble all round it will.'

'I never thought I'd see the day, Pat, when you'd have a nun in your family.'

'Aye, Frank. Sal always had a bit of a hankering for one of the lads to go into the priesthood, but we couldn't afford it and besides, can you see any one of those hooligans as a priest? All they ever think of is beer, women and a bit of excitement.'

'There might be more excitement than they bargained for soon,' Edward said grimly. 'It's getting very serious in the Balkans, especially with Franz Ferdinand being assassinated.'

'Who the hell is he anyway?' Pat asked.

'The heir to the Hapsburg Empire. It could have very serious complications.'

'Ah, what's it to do with us? They're always murderin' one another over there.' Pat, like most of the other men in the bar, considered the continent of Europe to be very remote. It could have been at the other end of the world for all they cared. None of them could see what it had to do with Great Britain when foreign royalty got themselves shot at and killed.

'We've pledged to support the freedom of small nations. France, Germany and Russia could become involved. Germany sides with Austria and her empire, we have to side with Belgium and France.'

Frank was trying to concentrate. 'But we've always fought the French. For hundreds of years we've fought them.' Vaguely, from his far-off school days, he remembered names like Crécy and Agincourt.

'I know, but things have changed and if you ask me, the Kaiser is just spoiling for a fight. Why else would he have increased his army and his navy? The German fleet is almost as big as ours now.'

'It'll take more than a few extra dreadnoughts to worry our lads!' Mo Cowley put in. The British Navy had ruled the seas with supremacy since Nelson's day. It was invincible. To think otherwise was ludicrous.

'So you think there could be a war?' Frank asked.

Edward nodded. 'There very well could be.'

'If there is there'll be no holding that lot of mine,' Pat said, feeling disgruntled that he would be too old for any such excitement.

'It's been a momentous day all round,' Edward said sagely, nodding for Red to fill up everyone's glass. It was his round. But the news had had a sobering effect on him. War wasn't all fancy uniforms, bugles and bravery.

Chapter Thirteen

———— ✦ ————

AS THE SUMMER WORE ON the clouds of war loomed ever larger. The young men who at first thought the events taking place in Europe did not concern them, eventually began to view the situation with growing interest and excitement.

August bank holiday that year was stiflingly hot, but everyone was looking forward to a couple of days' rest.

Nancy and Sean were going to the Hippodrome to see Jimmy Learman, the inimitable comedian, who was very popular. Mary and Norman were going for a day trip to New Brighton, 'probably with most of Liverpool,' Mary commented, thinking of the cloudless blue skies and burning sun of the last couple of days. For Mike and Abbie there was little chance of a day together. The most they would get was a few hours. A walk by the river maybe, or a stroll in Sefton Park. Dee had promised herself a rest. She had a book to read and had treated herself to a whole quarter of Everton Mints.

When Sean came to collect Nancy he found Edward reading the *Daily Post & Mercury*, looking very grim.

'What is it that has you looking like you'd found a penny and lost sixpence?' he asked good-naturedly.

'This.' Edward pointed to a boldly printed notice stating that all workers at the Cammel Laird shipyard should report to work the following morning, their annual week's holiday was cancelled due to 'important work'.

'So?' Sean saw nothing ominous about it.

'I think it means that war is imminent. The bank rate has shot up and last night you couldn't move on Lime Street station for Navy Reservists. There were three special trains in for Portsmouth, Falmouth and Chatham.'

'Oh, Uncle Edward, don't spoil things, we're looking forward to the show,' Nancy cried.

'Aye, don't take the shine off the evening for them,' Bridie said laughingly, but beneath the smile she was anxious. Edward was an educated man and she implicitly believed everything he told her.

After the show Sean and Nancy decided to walk part of the way home as it was still very warm.

'Do you think Uncle Edward is right about the war?' Nancy asked.

Sean put his arm around her waist and drew her closer to him. 'He's no fool, Nancy. He's an educated man and he understands these things. I think he's right.'

'Oh, I hope not. Everyone will have to go.'

Sean didn't answer, he was deep in thought. He was

enjoying life and life was very comfortable, so why change it? Why swap it for the hardships that joining the army would certainly bring? Less money, harder work, danger and no Nancy. Besides, he was Irish, why should he go? What had Britain ever done for Ireland or the Irish? Very little, according to what he'd been reading lately. All the British had ever done was to let them starve, force them to emigrate, exact terrible retribution after each attempt to win freedom. He'd read all about it and he'd gone to hear Jim Larkin speak. Why should he go and fight for the freedom of Belgium when his own country was under British rule?

'What's the matter, Sean? You've gone very quiet,' Nancy asked.

'I was just thinking, Nancy.' He smiled down at her.

'Will you go, Sean, if there is a war?'

'Would you want me to?'

'No. I wouldn't want you to leave me. I wouldn't want you to go and fight.'

He drew her into a shop doorway and bent and kissed her. 'Then I won't go,' he said. Let her think it was because he didn't want to leave her, that suited him fine.

'Do you love me, Sean?' she asked, drawing away from him.

'Of course I do, Nancy. Do you love me?' He caressed the nape of her neck gently. Girls were always asking questions like this. Even the girls he'd had a brief fling with since he'd been going out with Nancy had asked had he loved them. It did no harm to tell them a few lies. It made them give their favours more readily.

Nancy was different of course. She wasn't flighty or bold and he was quite fond of her. Also Hilda couldn't find fault with her as he was certain she would do with some of the others. Nancy was 'respectable', so respectable that he didn't hold out much hope of her surrendering herself without a very good reason, more's the pity he thought, letting his fingers move to her breast, his kisses becoming more passionate.

Nancy was feeling light-headed and was trembling with the force of emotion his lips were evoking, but she pulled away. 'No, Sean, please . . . not here.'

'Nancy, why do you pull away? I love you, you know that.'

'I can't, Sean. Nice girls . . . don't.' She wished nice girls did. She wanted him so much, so very much.

He kissed her on the forehead. 'I know. I'm sorry, it's just that I want you, Nancy.'

'I want you, too, Sean, but not—' she had been going to say 'not until we're married', but she felt that that was being very forward.

'Come on, we'd better go home. We'll get the next tram that comes along.'

Nancy returned his smile and squeezed his hand. He still loved her, his smile told her that.

They had all enjoyed the holiday, but on Tuesday 5 August war was declared. Posters proclaiming 'Your King and Country Need You', 'A Call to Arms', appeared overnight and thousands rushed to join up. Amongst them the young men of Burlington Street, including Ken and Norman Kerrigan.

It was a long time since they'd all congregated

around the lamp, but circumstances seemed to warrant a meeting. On the wall near the lamp was one of the new recruiting posters.

Mary was disgruntled. Her romance with Norman Kerrigan was progressing well. She had a genuine, deepening affection for him which at times surprised her. When she thought about it she always became confused. Was it really love? Was it because he was older and more experienced than she was? Usually boys lost their appeal, the excitement died after a week or two. This time it hadn't and she felt that it was Norman and not herself who was in charge of the situation. And so she followed where he led and had done for the past months. Only once had he 'tried it on' and when she'd refused he hadn't got angry or abusive. He was so different from all the other boys she'd been out with, maybe that was where his charm lay.

'I don't know why Norman had to go rushing off like that,' she said.

'It's exciting. Really exciting. He didn't want to miss it. It'll be all over by Christmas, anyway.' Tommy defended his brother.

'Father says it's not going to be a picnic,' Dee said.

'Oh, all the old fellers are saying that. It's been years and years since the Boer War and the Crimea; they've got crabby.'

'Uncle Edward isn't that old!' Nancy sprang to the defence of her stepfather. She had chosen to call him Uncle. She could never have thought of him as her da, she'd told Bridie, and she couldn't call him Stepfather, it sounded awful. Dee had agreed with her and Dee called Bridie Aunty, as did the rest of the family.

'Well, I don't think it's fair. We're going to miss out and we'll never get the chance of anything like this again,' Mike said.

Tommy pointed to the poster. 'It says nineteen to thirty. We're too young.'

'They wouldn't take me anyway, not with this.' Jerry was nursing his heavily bandaged hand and looked very miserable.

'Don't get upset Jerry, they won't take these two either.' Dee as usual tried to cheer Jerry. He had changed so much, she thought. He was now very withdrawn, but that was only natural. He'd taken to going for solitary walks, although sometimes on a Sunday afternoon she would accompany him. She knew how it felt to be different and she knew, as the others did not, how bleak his life had become.

'It says five foot three and over and with a chest measurement of thirty-four inches.' Tommy drew back his shoulders and pushed out his chest. 'Would you say I was thirty-six, Mike?'

'Oh, will you two stop it! At least I don't get all this nonsense from Sean!' Nancy cried.

'Well, you wouldn't. He's nearly nineteen, but I've not heard him talk about joining up.'

Nancy glared at Mike. 'Why should he? It's not compulsory.'

'He's been reading up on all the trouble that's been going on in Ireland and he's been listening to that Jim Larkin – the one who is always going on about Home Rule. I don't think he'll join up at all. I don't think he agrees with this war. He thinks because he's Irish it's nothing to do with him.'

'So what? Me da's Irish,' Tommy reminded Mike. 'An' our Ken and Norm were off like a shot to join up!'

'Well, it's different for them, they were born here. He wasn't.'

'If we're going to stand here all night arguing about being Irish, then I'm off,' Nancy stated.

'Where is the man himself tonight, Nance?'

'He's gone to see someone. A bit of business it is, that's all. He often has to see people.'

Tommy and Mike looked knowingly at each other. Sean was off selling what he'd managed to pinch from the docks. He was sailing very close to the wind in their opinion. Mike knew that if his mam found out there'd be murder; but Sean was careful enough not to rouse her suspicions. He told her he saved hard and did extra jobs for the blockermen, and although he had a good suit and a couple of decent shirts, he'd been careful not to appear too well-off or flashy. He was like Chrissie, he had a natural cunning, but maybe it came from having to more or less fend for yourself in the back streets of Dublin.

'It's a lovely night, let's go to Stanley Park,' Mary suggested. Norman and Ken were with their da in the Black Dog where there was no other topic of conversation but the war. She was annoyed because Norman had dismissed her complaints airily and had elected to go to the pub instead of taking her out. They had been walking out for eight months now, an incredible time for her, as Lizzie often remarked acidly.

Jerry didn't want to go and Mike and Tommy decided against it, too, so the girls went off on their own.

After ten minutes of idle chat, Jerry said he felt so rotten he was going home to bed, which left the other two lads sitting on the parapet of the bridge, swinging their legs idly. Mike stared morosely at the recruiting poster. 'I wish I could join up. At least Mam couldn't object to that like she does Abbie.'

'Yeah, it's not going to be much fun in our house, either. Our Joan's Terry has joined up, our Abbie's as miserable as sin most of the time 'cos of your mam, and our Monica's round the bloody bend. We have to have Grace now before and after meals. She even took our Seb's plate away from him the other day, because he'd started eating. She's round to the church morning, noon and night. Even me mam says she'll be glad when she goes.' Monica Kerrigan was going to be a postulate nun and would be leaving Liverpool at the end of the month.

Mike was staring hard at his friend.

'What's up, have I grown another head?'

'We could lie about our ages.'

'Gerroff, they'd never believe us.'

'Why not? We don't look all that young, not when we're all done up.'

'Do you really think they'd take us?' Tommy was becoming very interested.

'We can only try. We'll never get another chance. It's going to be dead boring around here with half the men gone, and I'm not going to miss out on the best excitement since the Strike.'

'Great. When will we go?'

Mike thought for a few minutes. 'Give it a few days. Let them all think we've got over the disappointment of being too young. Just act normal, like, because if they get any idea Mam will lock me up and throw away the key.'

'Can't I even tell my brothers?'

'No, they might let something slip and they might even tell your da.'

'All right, me lips are sealed. What about Jerry?'

Mike shook his head. 'No, we can't tell him either. It would just make him feel even worse. No use upsetting him just yet.'

Tommy nodded. It was tough for Jerry, and life would get even tougher if they managed to lie their way into the army and go off to war, leaving him behind.

Ten days later an article appeared in the press calling for all men who wished to serve their country to assemble at the headquarters of the King's (Liverpool) Regiment in St Anne Street at 7.30 p.m. the following day. It was just what Mike and Tommy had been waiting for. They'd told no one, not even the girls, of their plans. True, it did state 'businessmen' but Mike said wasn't his da in business and they could say Tommy's da was in the import business.

'How are we going to get out in our best suits?' Tommy wanted to know.

'We could say we're going to church, to a novena or a retreat.'

'Don't be so bloody daft, they'd never believe that!'

'It's not so bad for you, you can always tell your mam you're taking a girl out. I can't.'

Tommy had a sudden flash of inspiration. 'Yes, you can.'

'She'd never let me out of the door, there'd be murder!'

'Tell her it's another girl, not our Abbie.'

'She'd want to know who it was, where she lives, what her da does, you know what she's like. It's like the Spanish Inquisition.'

'Make it up, say it's someone you met coming out of the Men's Club.' Both boys belonged to the club for young Catholic men attached to St Anthony's church.

'I could, but you will tell Abbie that it's all a lie?'

'You can tell her yourself, after we've joined up. I'll back you up.'

It seemed a perfect plan, but Mike knew he would get a grilling before he left the house, and they wanted to get there early.

It was fortunate that St Anne Street was quite close, for by the time Mike had invented a girlfriend and had answered all his mother's questions it was seven o'clock.

'I thought I'd never get out. Come on, let's get a move on,' he urged Tommy. Tommy had managed to escape without much trouble. All his mam had said was, 'I hope she's worth all this scrubbing and polishing.'

They got off the tram on the corner of Rose Place and walked up.

'There's a queue already,' Mike said in dismay as they crossed the road and approached the building.

Tommy looked along the line of men. 'There's a few here who aren't nineteen. There's Vinny Burke, he was in our class.' He winked at Vinny who winked back conspiratorially.

The line moved slowly and Mike was terrified that someone on a passing tram would see them, so they kept their heads well down. But at last they were inside the drill hall. Before half past seven the room was packed to capacity and another room in the basement had been opened up.

There were quite a few men in uniform already on the platform, but when the stocky figure of the Earl of Derby joined them the cheers were deafening. Mike and Tommy joined in, enthusiastically, throwing their caps in the air like everyone else, the blood pounding in their veins.

'I'm not going to make you a speech of heroics. You've given me your answer and I can telegraph Lord Kitchener tonight to say our second battalion is formed. This will be a battalion of pals, a battalion in which friends who work together will fight shoulder to shoulder for the honour of Britain and the credit of Liverpool.' The Earl's words were drowned in a fresh wave of cheers that went on until he held up his hand and silence again descended.

'I don't attempt to minimize to you the hardships you will suffer, the risks you will run. I don't ask that you uphold Liverpool's honour, it would be an insult to think you could do anything but that. But I do thank you from the bottom of my heart for coming here tonight and showing what is the spirit of Liverpool, a spirit that ought to spread through every city and town in the kingdom!'

Tommy and Mike cheered themselves hoarse, buoyed up by the highly charged atmosphere. Then they were ordered to form lines. Separate tables for attestation had been set up for all the different areas of commerce. The Cotton Association, the Corn Trade, Stock Exchange, the Sugar Trade and the Cunard, White Star and other steamship companies. Both lads joined the queue for the Provision Brokers.

'This lot are all office wallahs,' Tommy whispered.

'So what? We work in Provisions,' Mike whispered back, pulling his cap further down over his face and praying he didn't look sixteen. His turn arrived.

'Name?'

'Michael Joseph Burgess.'

'Address?'

'One hundred and twenty-four Burlington Street.'

'Age?'

He took a deep breath. 'Nineteen.'

The recruiting officer paused and scrutinized him. Mike kept his head up.

'Religion?'

Mike felt his knees go weak with relief. 'Roman Catholic, sir.'

'Right, repeat after me, "I, Michael Joseph Burgess, do swear . . ."'

Mike repeated the words with what he hoped was a steady voice and great solemnity.

'Go over to the Medical Officers. Good luck, lad, in

joining the 18th Battalion, the King's Liverpool Regiment. Don't ever disgrace it.'

Pride surged through him. He'd made it. He was in. He was a soldier. He couldn't hear what Tommy was saying as he was shepherded to the area set aside for the Medical Examination where he was told to strip to his underwear.

When the brief inspection was complete, to Mike's delight, Tommy appeared beside him.

'You made it then,' Mike hissed.

Tommy nodded, his eyes bright with excitement.

It was a bit of a let-down when they were told to go home, that they would be sent for when arrangements had been made for training.

'I wonder how long we'll have to wait?'

Mike paid the tram fare. 'Not long, I shouldn't think.'

'Move along there, lads, an' don't be blocking the aisle!' the conductor yelled.

'Hang on there, mate, you're talking to soldiers! 18th Battalion King's Liverpool Pals!' Tommy shouted back.

The lower deck of the tram erupted in a cheer and both lads grinned, their faces flushed. It felt good to be someone, to be part of the big adventure.

That glow of euphoria had faded somewhat as they walked up the street towards home.

'We're in for it now!' Mike stated.

'Well, there's nothing they can do about it, is there? We've sworn on the oath.' Tommy was more optimistic. Ken and Norm would give him support, he hoped, if they were in. They had two days' leave before they left for Grantham, but he suspected that Norman would be out with Mary Simcock. She'd been getting rather stroppy with Norman lately.

'Will we tell them together, like?'

Tommy considered this and at last nodded. 'It might be the best way.'

When they walked into Hilda's kitchen she looked at them in surprise. 'What's to do with you two? I thought you'd taken that Florence Coyne out.'

Frank could see by the look on their faces that they'd been up to something. 'All right, spit it out the pair of you.'

'We've joined up, Da. Tommy and me have joined the King's Liverpool Pals, like it said in the paper.'

Hilda sat down suddenly, gripping the edge of the table. 'You . . . you can't have!'

'We have, Mam.'

'You bloody fools, you're too young!' Frank shouted.

'We told them we were nineteen.'

Hilda was staring at her son with incredulity. 'You lied to them and they . . . they believed you?'

'There were a lot of lads down there who weren't nineteen.'

'Frank, you've got to do something about this. Go and tell them that they lied, that they can't take them, they're too young!'

'It's too late, Hilda. If they've taken the oath there's nothing that can be done. God in heaven, what possessed the pair of you?'

'Don't go on, Da. We didn't want to be left out. We didn't want to be left here when everyone else was going off to fight the Hun.'

Despite his annoyance Frank could understand that.

Hilda couldn't. 'You fools! You bloody little fools!'

Mike reached out and touched her shoulder. 'Mam.'

'Don't you Mam me! You little liar!'

'We'd best go and tell me mam,' Tommy interrupted.

'Aye, lad, you'd better,' Frank agreed.

'You're not going anywhere!' Hilda informed her son.

'Leave him, luv. Let him go.' Frank laid a firm restraining hand on his wife's shoulder.

Neither of the boys spoke as they walked the short distance to the Kerrigan house. It was Abbie they met in the lobby.

'Mike, you said you were going to Saint Anthony's tonight.'

'I'm sorry, Abbie, I didn't want to lie to you but—'

'But what?'

'Tommy and me have joined up.'

Abbie's cry brought Sal to the kitchen door. 'Now what's up? Oh, it's you two.' She addressed her son. 'Have you been stood up then, lad?'

They all followed Sal into the kitchen but it was Abbie who announced the news.

'Mam, they've gone and joined the army.'

Pat lowered his paper. 'Gerroff, they're not old enough.'

'We . . . we told them we were nineteen.' Tommy waited for the explosion that was bound to follow.

'And they believed you? They believed you were nineteen?' Pat was incredulous.

Mike nodded. 'We've taken the oath and had the medical.'

'Oh, my God! Aren't two sons in the army enough!' Sal cried.

'Well, I think it's great. I'm proud of them . . . both.' Abbie looked at Mike with shining eyes. Mike, her Mike, was a soldier. He was going off to fight the Hun for King and Country.

Mike's smile was of pure pleasure.

Pat shook his head. 'If you're fool enough to join and they're fool enough to take you, then you'd better get on with it.'

'Is that all you can say, Pat Kerrigan!' Sal's voice rose an octave. 'He's sixteen years of age. A boy! And you, me girl, encouraging them!' Sal took off her apron. 'Oh, I'm off to see Hilda, to see what we can do about this.'

'Da says there's nothing can be done. They can't chuck us out, we've sworn the oath,' Mike said, but Sal ignored him and stormed down the lobby with determination.

Chapter Fourteen

———◆———

NEWS CAME THROUGH OF the retreat from Mons and was received with shocked disbelief. The great British Army in retreat, so soon; it just wasn't possible. People told each other it was just a temporary setback. It made all the new recruits more impatient to get on with the job.

Each day Mike and Tommy reported to Sefton Park for training. They had no uniforms and no rifles, but they were paid a 'Living Out' allowance as well as the shilling a day Army pay. They had been told that the Earl of Derby had gone to extraordinary lengths to try to get the uniforms and weapons through. Lady Derby had been instructed to purchase all the khaki cloth she could get her hands on and have it made up.

This prolonged period of training, without uniforms or weapons, had lulled Hilda's initial anger and fear. While it continued it was possible not to think of Mike going to France and yet, if the war went on any longer than Christmas, there was a good possibility that he would actually get to the front line. It didn't deter her from joining everyone else going into town and crowding Lime Street on 5 September, when the newly formed 'Pals' Battalions marched from Aigburth to St George's Hall.

The sight of crowds of cheering people, so many of them wives, mothers and sisters, couldn't help but diminish her anxiety and affect her opinions. For the first time she felt a glow of pride and she smiled up at Frank, who was cheering like everyone else.

Mary, Nancy, Dee, Bridie and Edward had all gone, but Nancy was disappointed that Sean had refused to accompany them.

'I'll stay and try to cheer Jerry up; someone's got to. He's in a right state that he can't go with them,' Sean had replied when she'd asked him to go with them.

She couldn't find any fault with that excuse. Jerry was desolate. He'd thought about trying to enlist. Taking the bandages off and keeping his hand in his pocket until the last minute. But Sean had pointed out that he would have to place his hand on the Bible and sign his name and then the open wound would be seen and questions would be asked.

Desperately, Jerry had tried to practise writing with his left hand, he could swear he was left-handed, but the writing was so spidery and uneven and he held the pen so awkwardly that it was obvious that the ploy wouldn't work and besides, he wasn't as tall as Mike or Tommy and definitely looked younger.

'Give it up, Jerry, it's no use,' Sean had implored.

Mike and Tommy could have wept to see the expression in Jerry's eyes.

'Maybe if I keep practising?' Jerry had said doggedly.

Again it had been left to Sean to speak. 'And even if you managed to get it to look half-way reasonable, how long do you think it would be before the medical men saw your hand? They'd know what it was straight off.'

Jerry had been so wretched that, heedless of Abe's views on drink, the lads had taken him to the Golden Fleece where Billy Baldwin wasn't as particular as Red MacClelland and would serve them, providing they sat out in the back and didn't draw attention to themselves.

Neither of them were thinking of poor Jerry that gloriously sunny autumn afternoon as they marched shoulder to shoulder along Lime Street. It was a great feeling. Amongst the throng of cheering people were their parents, brothers, sisters, friends and in Mike's case, Abbie, who'd be shouting for both her brother and her sweetheart. He hoped she could see him.

They were a little disappointed that the Earl wasn't on the platform on St George's Plateau, where the statues of Victoria and Albert on high-stepping mounts gazed down at them, and the huge, crouching bronze lions seemed to view the multitude with proud approval. The Earl's brother, wife and daughter were there and General Sir Henry McKinnon.

It was again deflating to be dismissed at the end of the march past and told to go home, but it didn't spoil the day. So exhilarated was she by the infectious patriotic fervour that Hilda didn't even object when Abbie joined them on the tram ride home, although she didn't speak to the girl. Abbie had decided her best course of action was not to obviously ignore Hilda, that would be downright rude, but just to remain at Mike's side. To talk quietly and appear submissive and demure. That way Hilda couldn't fault her.

There was a carnival atmosphere in the street as they all walked home, calling their goodbyes to each other. When the Chattertons reached number eighty Nancy stopped. 'I wonder how Sean got on with poor Jerry?'

'That was a fine excuse of his, he couldn't face going and seeing all the lads,' Bridie remarked acidly.

'Bridie, don't be too hard on the boy. He doesn't see it as his war.'

'Oh, isn't Ireland part of the British Empire then?' she retorted.

'If the Republicans had their way, it wouldn't be. Now don't go upsetting yourself, dear.'

Dee sighed. Father had always had this habit of trying to see things from everyone's point of view and quite often it annoyed people. She thought that in this case he was wrong. There were thousands of Irishmen who had enlisted, they were just as patriotic as everyone else. She didn't understand Sean at all. Hilda and Frank had given him everything. He earned his living, he had his home in England, so why wouldn't he join up? At the least it was ingratitude, at worst some would call it cowardice, although she didn't voice these thoughts to Nancy. She didn't want to upset her.

Rose had gone home with Sal, and Phil and David were hanging around Tommy and Mike, gazing at them with hero-like worship, so as soon as they got in the house Dee put the kettle on and Nancy began to set the table. Edward was fussing unnecessarily around her mam, Nancy thought, as she got the loaf, margarine and ham for their tea. She wondered how long it would be before Sean came to see how the afternoon's events had gone.

'I think we'd all better have the cup of tea first; leave that ham, Nance,' Bridie instructed.

Nancy looked at her mother with concern. There was something different about Mam and it wasn't just the headiness of the march past.

Dee looked at her father who was smiling in a way that made him appear almost boyish.

'We've got something to tell you and now seems like a good time, the rest of them being out,' Bridie announced.

Dee felt her stomach turn over, although she had no idea why she should feel so apprehensive.

'You've got a better job and we're going to move?' Nancy ventured, addressing Edward.

'No, Nancy, nothing like that.'

'I'm . . . we're going to have a baby,' Bridie announced shyly. Suddenly she felt very young and rather coy. She hadn't taken any notice when she'd missed the first two months. At her age what could she expect? It was the change. But when she had seen nothing on the third month and had started to feel faint and sickly, she'd been astounded. She'd even gone to Dr Wallace for confirmation, she was so amazed.

She'd wondered how Edward would take the news, but she needn't have feared, he'd been delighted; but she could see by the faces of both Dee and Nancy that they were far from happy.

'You can't be!' Nancy cried. 'Mam, you can't be, you're too—'

'Too old, Nance? Well, I did think that myself at first.'

Dee was looking at her father with undisguised horror. It couldn't be true, and why was he looking so pleased with himself?

'Aren't you going to say anything, Deirdre?' he prompted.

She couldn't bring herself to speak. It was . . . it was obscene, she thought.

'That's upset the apple-cart, hasn't it?' Bridie said tersely. 'If looks could kill we'd both be dead.' She didn't know what she had expected, but it hadn't been Dee's silent disgust or Nancy's undisguised condemnation.

Dee placed the teapot carefully down on its cork stand – very carefully, for her hands were shaking. Nancy had already snatched up both their jackets from the peg behind the door where they had so recently been hung.

Dee finally found her voice. 'If you don't mind . . . I think we'll go and . . . think about it,' Dee said, for she felt that some explanation of their reactions was required.

There seemed only one place to go that was appropriate – the lamp by the bridge – and they walked there in silence.

Nancy leaned on the parapet and stared down into the sluggish grey water, shaking her head. 'Dee, I can't believe it. It can't be true, she's too old. It's . . . it's disgusting!'

'I know, Nancy. Maybe it's a mistake.'

'No, she wouldn't tell us unless she was sure. Oh, Dee, can you imagine her, like the side of a house she'll be. My mam!' Nancy shuddered. She thought suddenly of Sean, and Bridie's pregnancy became even more repugnant. 'What's Sean going to think? Oh, Dee, it's . . . it's a disgrace.'

'What's everyone going to think, Nancy?' Dee remembered vaguely that before Rose had been born there had been a lot of arguments and a tenseness between her parents. There had been lowered voices and nudges from the servants, and that had been five years ago. Even Sal Kerrigan had stopped having babies after Seb.

'This is going to be worse than when they got married. Oh, Dee, I wish we could get away from here.'

'No you don't, not really, you'd have to leave Sean.' Dee managed a smile, but wished there was some possibility of avoiding the storm of controversy that would soon break.

'I'm not going to be able to look him in the face, Dee. Why did she . . . they have to go and do this to us? It's awful. It's so . . . so embarrassing. Oh, everyone will be winking and nudging each other and making snide remarks.'

As usual, now the initial shock was passing, Dee began to think of practicalities. 'It's going to mean more work for us, she'll get tired easily.' Dee remembered that her mother had seemed to be permanently resting when she'd been carrying Rose, but there was no army of servants to run number eighty Burlington Street. Just Nancy and herself. 'And even after . . . well, she'll still be tired.'

'And it'll have us all up all night, yelling and the whole place will stink of babies!' The future to Nancy looked worse by the minute.

'You don't have to have babies if you don't want to. Mary was telling me that her friend Madge went to this woman who—' Nancy shook her head. 'No, Mam wouldn't do anything like that. Even though she fell out with Father Fitz, she wouldn't do that. They could have done something to stop it, though.'

'What?' Dee asked.

'I don't know. There are things, men know about them, or they should do.' She felt her annoyance with Edward rising. It wasn't all her mam's fault. He should have known. Or maybe it was only the men of their class who knew these things. She hadn't realized she'd spoken aloud.

'I don't think so, Nancy. After all, most well-off families don't have a lot of children, it's just the poor ones who do.'

'Or posh families have the money to look after them. Mam won't be able to work any more now and we'll have to turn up more each week.' It was yet another reason to feel aggrieved by the situation.

'Maybe it won't be so bad, not with the war and everything. People will have other things to think about,' Dee said hopefully, although she held out little hope that the war, at this stage, would eclipse this situation.

The war was on everyone's mind, but not to the extent the two girls had hoped. Nancy had actually burst into tears as she'd told Sean, saying she'd never been so mortified in her entire life. He'd laughed and tried to cheer her up by telling her a long and complicated tale about three of the women who lived in the same Dublin street, all older than Bridie, who had kept on having children. It hadn't cheered her at all. In fact it had opened her eyes to the even worse fact that her mam could also go on having more children.

Dee had faced the disapproval of Hilda, Lizzie, Emily O'Brien and the other neighbours with grim silence. Sal had put the whole thing into perspective, Dee thought.

'She must be stark, raving, bloody mad! She's almost got Nancy off her hands and you and the lads are no trouble and I have Rose, and she goes and gets caught again! She should be like me, with Seb at school now and the kids reared, I've got more time to myself and more money, with Pat in work every day, all the lads in the army, our Monica away and Abbie turning up her wages good as gold. I've never been so well-off in me life. She's mad, off her bloody trolley!'

Abbie was sympathetic. 'I know what it's like, Dee. It wasn't so bad when our Ginny was born, then she had a break and then she went and had our Seb. I know what they're all saying and it's awful. I could have died when she was carrying our Seb, I was thirteen and our Monica told me – well she told me things, and I could have died of shame. Try to take no notice of them, especially that old bat, Hilda Burgess.' Abbie's dislike of Mike's mother hadn't diminished.

The clientele of the Black Dog were of divided opinions. Some congratulated Edward, others thought he was mad to saddle himself at his age with a baby. Another mouth to feed, another set of worries to contend with, when he should be easing up on life. The matter didn't occupy their thoughts for long, though, for the war was prominent in most of their minds. In September Ghent and Lille had fallen to the Germans, on 4 October the first bomb had fallen on London: an attack which had sent a wave of outrage throughout the country and had a sobering effect on many people. It was very unnerving to realize that the enemy could strike from so far away. By 14 October the Allies had occupied Ypres, and Ken and Norman Kerrigan had sailed for France.

The 18th Battalion had at last been issued with uniforms and some old Lee Metford rifles. They had all been summoned to Knowsley Hall, the home of the Earl of Derby, and had been presented by the Earl himself with a solid silver cap badge, depicting the family crest of an eagle standing on an eyrie that contained a young child. There were dozens of pubs in the area called The Eagle and Child, so the device was well known.

Mike had experienced a moment of panic when the Earl had stood in front of him and had scrutinized him.

'How old are you?' The question was asked in a precise, clipped tone.

'Nineteen, sir!' Mike again repeated the lie that had become so familiar that he often half believed it.

The badge had been pressed into his hand. 'You liar – but best of luck son!' The Earl had smiled.

Mike had never felt so proud in all his life.

'It's solid silver, Mam, made by Elkington's, and we all got one. They must have cost him a fortune.'

Hilda turned it over in her hand. 'You take care you don't lose it then.'

'Oh, we won't be wearing them, they've given us brass ones.'

'That was a good decision, you'd get them pinched otherwise,' Frank said sagely.

Mike grinned. 'Some of the lads have already christened it "Derby's Duck".' Some had called it 'The Bird and Bastard', 'The Ruptured Duck', 'The Constipated Duck', and worse, but he didn't tell them that.

Hilda was not amused. 'Some people have got no respect for anything! And him standing the cost of it all!'

'Well, I'm glad all this messing about is nearly over. We're going to Knowsley Park next week. His Lordship's had huts built, proper quarters, and we're all going, 17th, us and the 19th. We'll get proper training then and proper rifles. The new Lee Enfields.'

This news Hilda digested in silence. It was one step nearer to the war for Mike, the real war. Nor did she care that the Earl of Derby had known he had lied about his age but wished him luck just the same. The uneasy feeling crept over her again. She watched him getting ready to go out and knew he was going to tell Abbie Kerrigan the news.

'Mind you take care of Derby's Duck when you go!' Frank laughed at him, and Hilda wondered were all men the same? Did they all jump at the chance of 'excitement' as they called it, or to be wounded and maybe killed as she saw it. If they did, then they were all fools from His Lordship down to her husband and son.

Chapter Fifteen

———◆———

IT WASN'T OVER BY CHRISTMAS. The great British army wasn't victorious, nor were the Germans sausage-eating, inefficient buffoons as they'd been portrayed by the press. It was known that an efficient system of trenches had been constructed, a completely different kind of warfare being fought.

Mike had been one of the lucky ones to get a pass home for Christmas Day. Tommy hadn't, but Mike duly went up to Sal's to report on his friend's health and progress.

'It's great there, it is. Snug as bugs in a rug we are in those huts. No having to doss in tents. It's laid out just like a proper camp, and the food's good, too.'

Abbie was staring at Mike with adoration. He looked older, fitter and even more handsome.

'So what do you do all day then?' Pat enquired.

'We drill, have bayonet practice, route marches and we dig.'

'Dig?' Sal echoed.

'Trenches, we practise digging trenches.' Mike had begun to feel that all this practising seemed to have no end. Like everyone else, he wanted to get on with the job. 'There's a huge bank of clay, and we're digging it out and moving it.'

'Sounds like a waste of time to me,' Pat commented.

'Some of us feel like that too. The lads have made up this song to the tune of "Moonlight Bay":

"We were digging all day, on Derby's clay
The picks and shovels ringing, they seemed to say,
If you don't do any work, you'll get no pay.
So we dug, dug, dug, like hell, for a bob a day."'

'No sign of you going over there?' Sal asked. She worried daily for her two eldest sons, who had never been much good as letter writers. She'd had a couple of postcards with a few lines scrawled on the back, that's all.

'They don't tell you things like that.' Mike was impatient to take Abbie out, his time was very limited. 'Well, we're all fine, so I'd best get going.'

Abbie snatched up her mother's shawl from the back of the chair. She wasn't going to waste precious seconds by going upstairs for her smart new jacket, and she didn't care what Hilda Burgess thought of her.

Mike took her hand and slipped it through his arm. 'I really miss, you, Abbie.'

'I miss you, too. You will keep writing, won't you? Mam doesn't say anything, but I know she's upset that our Ken and Norman don't write.'

'I won't stop, Abbie, I promise. Not even when I get over there.'

'Especially when you get over there,' she pleaded with her eyes, before the soft light disappeared from them at the sight of Nancy and Sean Doyle walking towards them. 'He's a coward, that Sean Doyle,' she hissed. 'I wonder she's got the gall to walk out with him.'

Mike didn't have time to reply for Nancy was waving at them both.

'You got home then? Did Tommy?'

'No, just me and just for the day. I've to be back by eight o'clock.'

'How's it going then, Mike?' Sean asked genially, thinking, as Abbie had, that Mike looked well on it.

'It's OK.' He had no intention of telling Sean about moving clay. Sean had made no attempt to join up. He was selfish, he didn't want to give up his soft life and his extra money, or Nancy, and he still had that stupid idea that because he was Irish it had nothing to do with him. Yet there were thousands of Irishmen who had joined the army.

'If you'd join up, you'd know for yourself,' Abbie remarked caustically.

'Don't be like that, Abbie. Sean's work is just as important. Someone's got to load and unload the ships.' Nancy was stung.

'Aye, my da and the rest of them that are too old for the army or the navy.'

'Ah, come on, Abbie, it's Christmas Day,' Sean chided.

Mike decided to change the subject. 'How's your mam, Nance?'

'She's fine.'

'Getting bigger by the day,' Sean laughed.

'She gets tired easily,' Nancy said, wishing Sean wouldn't make a joke of it, especially not in front of Abbie who was getting very touchy these days.

'And Dee?'

'She's thinking of leaving her job.'

'Has she got something better lined up?' Mike asked.

'No, she keeps saying she's thinking of being a nurse. Joining the Voluntary Aid Detachment.'

'Is she?' Mike was very interested in this news.

Abbie was even more interested. 'I didn't know that, I've been thinking about it myself,' she announced. She had been thinking of it. It would be her contribution to the war effort.

Nancy wasn't at all keen on this latest idea of Dee's. If Dee went away, it would mean more work for herself and she had no intention of becoming a nurse. She didn't have the stomach for it.

'I'll come down and see her tonight, when Mike's gone back,' said Abbie.

Nancy didn't reply. She didn't need Abbie Kerrigan encouraging Dee. Now it meant that she'd have to try to persuade Dee before Abbie put her spoke in. It was turning into a miserable Christmas.

Mike had suddenly spotted Jerry Harvey at the bottom of the street. He wanted to talk to Jerry, yet at the same time he felt awkward about it, especially as he was in uniform. Then he noticed something unusual about Jerry.

'Bloody hell, Jerry's drunk!' he blurted out.

They all turned and watched as Jerry staggered from kerb to lamppost.

'His da will kill him! And on Christmas Day, too!' Nancy cried, her annoyance with Abbie forgotten.

'Mike, we've got to stop him getting home, try and sober him up a bit at least,' Sean urged.

'Where did he get the ale from?' Abbie asked, annoyed that her few hours with Mike would be interrupted.

'Let's go and ask him,' Mike said grimly.

'Who the hell let you get in this state, mate?' Mike asked when they reached Jerry, who was hanging on to a lamp for support.

'What's it to you?' Jerry's speech was slurred and he glared at Mike.

'You're my mate and getting like this isn't going to do you any good and if your da catches you . . .'

Sean caught one of Jerry's arms and draped it around his neck, Mike took the other one.

'Where are you going to take him?' Nancy asked.

'Mam will kill me – us – if we take him to our house,' Mike said.

'Mam's having a lie down and Dee and Uncle Edward and the lads have all gone out, to give her a bit of peace, like,' said Nancy.

'It will have to be our house then,' Abbie said sharply, turning on her heel and walking ahead of the little group, knowing they were probably being watched from behind every curtain in the street.

It was a slow journey, for Jerry was reluctant to go anywhere, and they didn't get as far as Sal's. They'd just passed the shop when Abbie turned and said, 'Oh, hell! It's too late. Here's Mr Harvey.'

Abe's worried expression turned to anger as he drew closer. Jerry had ignored his mother's pleas and had gone out straight after they'd come home from the Mission Hall. He'd understood, or thought he had, and had shown compassion by telling Winnie that the lad needed some time to reflect on the sermon that morning. When he'd been gone for three hours and his meal was ruined he decided it was time to find his son.

'So I see you're up to your old tricks!' he barked at Mike and Sean.

'Sure, it was nothing to do with us. He managed to get like this all by himself,' Sean answered. He couldn't stand Abe Harvey.

'He couldn't have.'

'He did and if I had to put up with you lot, I'd get blind drunk as well.'

Nancy clutched at Sean's arm, remembering Abe Harvey's violent temper.

'That's about what I'd expect from a Popish, Irish coward! Not even man enough to enlist and you, Mike Burgess, disgracing the King's uniform.'

Nancy was holding Sean back and Abbie was now helping to keep Jerry upright as Mike, his face grim, turned to the older man.

'I'm disgracing no one! I've not had a drink all day, and Sean's right. You should give Jerry some help . . . some hope.'

'The Lord has sent him this affliction to bear—'

'Oh, for God's sake, don't talk such bloody rubbish!' Sean yelled.

'You'll be struck down for your blasphemy!' Abe roared back.

'Sod you! Sod bloody God!' Jerry suddenly yelled.

Abe looked as though he'd been struck. He stepped back, the colour draining from his face.

Jerry managed to wrench himself from the grip of Sean and Abbie and lurched towards his father. 'Did you hear me, I said sod bloody God!' he shouted at Abe.

Abe recovered his wits, caught his son by the collar of his jacket and raised his arm.

'Go on, belt me! Beat me like you've always done! I don't care! Go on, kill me, I'm going to bloody well die anyway!' Jerry yelled.

Abe let his arm fall and the little group shrank together in horror. It had never been spoken aloud, not by Jerry, not by anyone, that the tuberculosis would kill him. It was Mike who recovered first.

'I'd go home, Mr Harvey. He didn't mean it. It's the drink. We'll see to him. We'll sober him up and then we'll bring him home, when he's in a fit state for his mam to see him.'

Abe nodded. He was profoundly shaken, not because his son had voiced the inevitable, but by his denunciation of God.

Sal, who was more than experienced in dealing with drunks, was outraged at the whole episode, and saddened too. She and Pat undressed Jerry and put him to bed in Ken's bed.

'I'll go up and see Winnie myself. He can't go home until he's slept it off, but she'll need to be told where he is. God help her, hasn't she enough on her plate without this?'

'Abe Harvey's mad! He should be locked up,' Abbie added.

'I'd best go with you, Sal; if he starts I'll bloody well sort him out.'

'No, Pat, it's best I go on me own. There's no point causing any more trouble and if you start on him, you'll have that lot up there all out and there'll be murder. No, not on Christmas Day.'

'I'll walk you home, Nance,' Sean said and Nancy nodded. All the shine had gone off the day. She felt desperately sorry for poor Jerry and she wanted to talk to Dee, before Abbie could recover her wits to remember that, when Mike had gone back, she was going to come and quiz Dee about nursing.

Nancy related the afternoon's events to them all when they returned, and they all agreed that life for poor Jerry Harvey must be a living hell.

When the tea dishes had been washed and the kitchen tidied, Nancy had told Dee she wanted to talk to her. They went up to the bedroom they shared with Rose.

'It must have been awful for you,' Dee said sitting down on the bed, thinking it was Jerry that Nancy wanted to talk about.

'It was, but it's not that, Dee.'

'What then?'

'Abbie Kerrigan said she'd come down, when Mike's gone, to talk about nursing.'

222

'Is she thinking of joining, too?'

'So she says. I wish I'd kept me mouth shut. Oh, Dee, I know I'm being selfish, but I don't want you to do it.'

'I haven't really made up my mind yet,' Dee answered. She'd not seen Nancy so concerned since the day Bridie's pregnancy had been announced.

'I keep thinking of how I'll be left to see to everything when Mam has the baby. I know it's selfish, but I'll miss you, too, Dee.'

This was the very thing that had made Dee hesitate to enrol. She didn't think Nancy was being selfish. It would be unfair to leave her with all the extra work. They managed it between them so it wasn't too bad, but they were both tired when they got home from work and sometimes she thought that Bridie was using her pregnancy as an excuse. Her father was no use at all, he fussed around Bridie like a mother hen. But Bridie, she'd noted, was often well enough to take a short walk or tram ride. She smiled at Nancy.

'I haven't definitely said I'd go, have I? And if you don't want me to, I won't. It wouldn't be fair on you. You're not selfish, Nancy. It's a lot of work keeping up with the washing, ironing, cleaning, cooking, shopping and everything else.'

Nancy was very relieved. 'Oh, thanks, Dee. I've felt so bad about it. I know Mam does get tired, but I think sometimes she's codding on she's worse than she really is.'

'Don't say things like that, even if they might be true,' Dee smiled. 'We'll manage.'

223

'What will you tell Abbie?'

'That I wasn't that serious about it, she'd better go and find out for herself.'

'She's being all patriotic, like; not that I'm saying she's wrong.'

'I suppose she is, after all she's got three brothers in the army, and Mike.'

Nancy didn't want to follow this line of conversation so she just nodded and went to the door. 'Come on, let's try and enjoy what's left of Christmas.'

When Hilda opened up the shop after the holiday it was usually packed with customers whose large families had devoured everything. She looked forward to a brisk day's business, and she was not disappointed.

When it was nearing lunch time she was surprised to see Sean come in. He just grinned at her and took the spare overall coat from the back of the door.

'Have they given you the push then?' she asked.

'No, nothing like that. There's a bit of a lull down there, so I thought I'd nip home and help you out. I knew you'd be busy.'

Hilda nodded but wondered what ulterior motive he had.

Sean, serving Emily O'Brien with his usual good-natured grin, didn't betray the fact that he'd only just got through the dock gate without being nicked. Someone had grassed on him – something that would have been unheard of before the war. If they came looking for him, he was innocently helping out his aunt. Maybe he'd better lay off for a while, he thought. Keep things strictly legitimate.

'How did you get on up there?' Hilda asked Sal, jerking her head in the general direction of the top end of the street.

Sal knew what she meant. 'The poor boy didn't want to go back and I don't blame the lad. It was Winnie I saw, no sign of "Holyitis"; I think he'd gone off praying.'

'It's his own sould he should be praying for, he's got a damned cheek to call himself a Christian, the way he treats that lad,' Emily put in.

Both women agreed as Hilda weighed out Sal's quarter of tea.

'What's up with you? What are you doing here, are you sick?' Sal suddenly asked, catching sight of Abbie who was pushing her way towards her. Abbie looked very pale, yet her eyes were over bright. Sal hoped she wasn't feverish.

'I'm all right, Mam. I'm not sick. It's Sean Doyle I've come to see,' Abbie announced.

Hilda looked surprised, but Sal shrugged, seemingly mystified.

Sean grinned at Abbie engagingly. 'I can't help it, it's me charm, you see,' he quipped.

The grin disappeared and his eyes became hard as Abbie Kerrigan, her head held high, thrust a single white feather into his hand, then after having let her gaze wander over the shocked faces of the other customers, she turned and walked out.

*

Nancy vowed she would never speak to Abbie Kerrigan ever again, but there was no relief to be gained from her decision. She still had to keep up the appearance that she really didn't care that Sean hadn't joined up. A small part of her did care – very much. Even though she tried hard to convince herself that it was because he loved her and didn't want to leave her, sometimes she couldn't quite believe that, and then Mike's words would come back to her.

On Monday 8 March a stab of pain woke Bridie. This was it, she thought. It might be seventeen years since she'd had Nancy, but she remembered the pain. It was still very early, so she didn't wake Edward, but as the severity of the contractions increased she couldn't quite stifle her cries.

'What is it, dear?' Edward asked sleepily.

'I've started.'

Edward was wide awake now. 'I'll go and get Mrs Ollerenshaw.'

'No, not yet, it's too soon. Just make me a nice cup of tea for now, please, there's a love.' Bridie grimaced as she felt the onslaught of the next contraction.

Edward woke both the girls. Dee made the tea while Nancy went to get Ma Ollerenshaw.

The stout midwife went straight into the front room. Nancy followed with the tea.

Bridie managed a smile. 'Thanks, Nance.'

Nancy thought her mam looked awful. 'Is everything all right?'

'I'll know that in a few minutes. Go and start boiling up the water, Nancy, and bring me all the newspaper you can find, and towels or old cloths, clean ones mind.'

'I've been saving the papers, Nance, they're under the sink in the scullery, and there's some old towels in there, too.' Bridie lay back.

'Go on, get off,' Ma Ollerenshaw instructed.

Dee was busy getting David and Rose organized for school and Phil ready for work. Edward was not going, and neither were the two girls.

'How is she?' Dee asked.

'I don't know. They want hot water and newspaper and old towels.'

Phil swallowed the last of his tea. 'I'm off,' he announced. He had no wish to remain at all.

'Take David and Rose up to Aunty Sal's, will you? They can go from there,' Dee instructed.

The morning wore on and they were all on edge. Bridie's cries had brought Sal down and she was helping the midwife. Lizzie and Emily O'Brien had both called in. Edward smoked and paced the kitchen floor, Dee and Nancy just wished it was all over.

'I'm never going to have any children,' Dee said fearfully. Bridie sounded as though she were being tortured.

When it was nearly lunch time, Ma Ollerenshaw appeared, looking flustered.

Edward caught hold of her arm. 'How is she? How long?'

'She's no slip of a girl. It's hard, but then I expected that. At her age it's always harder.'

'She is all right, isn't she?' Nancy cried.

'She will be but I think we're going to need Doctor Wallace.'

Nancy leapt to her feet. 'I'll go for him.'

'Good girl. Dee, boil up some more water and—' The rest of her words were drowned by Bridie's screams. Nancy fled and Edward looked very anxious.

'Don't worry, you'd yell too if it were you. Men! I don't think you'd be able to stand it. You have your little bit of pleasure and it's us women who pay for it. Oh, you'll be in the pub tonight celebrating as if it were you who'd done all the work. Don't worry about her.'

It was nearly three o'clock before Bridie's agony was over. Doctor Wallace came into the kitchen and slapped Edward on the back.

'Congratulations, you've a lovely, healthy six pound baby daughter.'

'And Bridie?'

'Tired out. She's not a young woman, it's been an ordeal, but with rest she'll be up and about in two or three weeks.'

They all crowded into the small room where Bridie lay, exhausted but happy. Sal and Ma Ollerenshaw had tidied up and Doctor Wallace was washing his hands in the scullery.

'Isn't she tiny!' Dee exclaimed in wonder.

'Indeed she's not. Six pounds is a good weight,' Sal replied indignantly.

'Oh, look at her tiny little fingers.' Nancy touched the minute fingernails gently.

'So, what are you going to call her then, Bridie?' Sal asked.

'Elizabeth, after Edward's mother. And it's not to be shortened to Liz or Lizzie or anything else,' Bridie replied.

'Elizabeth,' Dee repeated. 'It's nice. Elizabeth Chatterton, doesn't that sound lovely?'

Everyone laughed before Sal shooed them all out, saying Bridie needed to sleep.

Chapter Sixteen

———◆———

DEE AND NANCY WERE run off their feet and Nancy had pushed Abbie's open hostility to the back of her mind, until it was announced that on 20 March there was to be a march past of all the Pals Battalions at which no other person than General Kitchener himself would take the salute. More recruits were needed.

'I'm not going, I've too much to do, seeing to Mam and little Elizabeth. You can all go,' Nancy said to Dee.

Dee accepted her excuse. It was valid, after all, but she felt so sorry for Nancy. The white feather Abbie had presented to Sean, that now universal symbol of cowardice, had been the first, but not the last. She'd heard how he was treated down at the docks and she knew Hilda felt she could hardly hold her head up. It wasn't as if he was even objecting because of religion or conscience, as some were. No, she could see why Nancy couldn't go and stand with all their friends and neighbours in Lime Street and cheer herself hoarse.

They'd all gone and she'd tidied up, taken Bridie up a cup of tea and put the nappies in to soak when Sean walked into the kitchen.

'So, you did stay at home.'

'Didn't I tell you I would. I've more things to do than go off down town. Do you want a cup of tea? I've just taken Mam one.'

'No, thanks.'

She could see by his face that there was something wrong. 'What's the matter?'

'I've made up my mind, Nancy, I'm going to join up.'

Part of her wanted to shout that she was glad, the other part wanted to tell him not to go. 'You haven't, Sean. Why?'

'Because maybe they're all right and I'm wrong. And maybe because I'm fed up with the likes of Abbie Kerrigan and Aunty Hilda; she hasn't a civil word to say to me now.'

Nancy threw her arms around his neck. 'Oh, Sean. I know it's been hard for you.'

He held her tightly. She didn't know just how hard a time he'd been getting lately. It had got so bad that joining up looked appealing. Did it really make any difference to Home Rule for Ireland if he stayed away? No, thousands of Irishmen had joined up. Home Rule was a pipe dream, it always would be.

'When . . . when will you go?' she asked, burying her face against his shoulder.

'Tonight. They'll have places open, especially after this march past.'

'Tonight!' It was all so sudden.

'Hilda will pack me things up so fast it will make your head spin,' he laughed.

'Oh, Sean. I can't think what it's going to be like here without you.'

'So will you miss me, Nancy?'

'How can you even ask! You know I will.'

He gathered her closely to him. 'I'll miss you, too. I can't see them keeping us here much longer. Things aren't as rosy as they've made out. They need more men over there.'

Nancy felt cold. Until now 'over there' had been a distant, almost mythical place. Somewhere where things happened that didn't really affect her. She clung to his lips, thinking this may be the last time they would be alone.

His kisses became more passionate and his hands explored her breasts. She didn't draw away from him as she'd done in the past, for added to her own tumultuous feelings was the knowledge of his imminent departure.

'Nancy, my sweet Nancy,' he murmured, as he drew her gently down onto the sofa.

The blood was singing in her veins like wine, she felt as though she were on fire. He was lifting her skirt when she dragged herself back to reality.

'No, Sean! No!'

'Nancy, please! I love you!'

'I – I can't, Sean.'

'Nancy, I'll be going tonight. They'll send me off for training. It might be months before I see you again.'

She was weakening. It was true.

'I don't want to say this, but Nancy, we may never . . . I may not come back.'

'No! No! Sean, don't say that, please!'

'Nancy, I love you so much.'

An image of him lying cold and dead flashed through her mind and sent caution and reason to the winds. She didn't care. He loved her and in a few hours he would be gone – maybe for ever.

Afterwards she didn't feel ashamed as she'd always thought she would do. She felt loved and cherished. Nothing mattered now, she was truly his and they would get married when this war was over, he had more or less said so.

It had hurt – actually physically hurt – but not much. It hurt more when he'd left her. Gone to get his things ready so he could inform Hilda the minute she walked through the door. She had said she would go with him, at least as far as Lime Street. She wanted to be seen on his arm as they walked down Burlington Street. She could hold her head up now, she told Bridie.

'It's about time, too,' Bridie had replied, stroking the downy head of little Elizabeth. This little one would never know the hardships of life the way Nancy had. She'd want for nothing, Edward had promised her that. He'd been promoted, for all the young men had gone off to war. Elizabeth would never have second-hand things and she would grow up pretty and admired and loved. Bridie was too engrossed to see the new light in her daughter's eyes, a glow that illuminated Nancy's face.

'You are glad, Nancy, I can see it in your face,' Dee said when Nancy told her.

'Yes, I am, Dee.'

Dee hugged her. 'I know it's been hard for you, Nancy, you've tried to be so loyal to him.'

'I love him, Dee. I love him even more now.' Close though they were, Nancy couldn't bring herself to share with Dee her experiences.

Dee hugged her again, thinking only that she meant that Sean's enlistment had increased that love.

'Go and get yourself ready. Wear your best things, but be prepared for a wait. There were queues when we left. You really should have come, Nancy, it was a wonderful sight and they were all there. The General, the Earl and his family, the Mayor and Mayoress and the Aldermen.'

Nancy didn't mind having missed the parade, for she'd experienced something far more wonderful that late spring afternoon.

A month later Nancy accompanied Dee, Edward, the boys, the Kerrigans, the Burgesses and the O'Briens to Lime Street Station. The time had flown past, there had been so much to do. She'd missed Sean terribly, but knowing that she was now in the same predicament as everyone else had made up for it a little. She'd had letters from Prescot where he was training, and she read them over and over to herself whenever there was a spare moment. But on this glorious April morning the Battalions were moving out at last. They were going to Grantham in Lincolnshire, and then on to France.

The trees in St John's Gardens, at the back of St George's Hall, were full of blossom, and the spring flowers nodded their heads in the breeze, as if giving their approval to all that was going on around them. The city centre was packed, the traffic at a standstill, and police were working hard to control the crowds.

'We'll never get near the station,' Nancy cried to Dee as they alighted from the tram outside the Empire.

'We'll really have to push hard,' Dee answered. Every shop and office in the city had come to a standstill. 'Look, there's Abbie.'

Dee called out and Abbie turned and smiled at them both. Nancy smiled back, forgetting her former vow. Things were different now. They managed to reach Abbie, but the closest they could get to the station was the Washington Hotel, the police stood two deep at the station approach.

'We'll not even see them from here,' Abbie wailed.

'There's nothing else we can do, we can't get through the police line, can we?' Dee said impatiently.

They resigned themselves to the wait, Nancy knowing that Sean's 21st Battalion wouldn't be with them, for they were still training. But she felt she now had the right to be here.

The crowd was good-humoured, there were the lively wags who kept them entertained with their remarks, until at last they heard the sound of the regimental band and the crowd erupted into a cheering, waving mass as the first line of khaki-clad soldiers from the 17th swung into Lime Street, their Battalion Colonel at their head. A token force of twelve men from the newly formed County Palatine Artillery marched behind them, the white horse of Hanover on their cap badges. The irony was lost to almost everyone in the crowd.

They were all young, strong, fresh-faced and smart in their uniforms. They all looked so proud and handsome, Dee thought as she searched the passing ranks for faces that were familiar. Who could doubt they would win? These were 'Derby's Own', Liverpool's finest. She found herself clinging tightly to Nancy and cheering, although the crowds were now joining in with the band that was playing the Boer War song 'Dolly Gray'.

Dee and Nancy's voices soared with the rest,

'Goodbye Dolly I must leave you,
Tho' it breaks my heart to go,
But you know that I am needed,
At the front to fight the foe,
See the soldier boys are marching,
I can no longer stay,
Hark, I hear the bugles calling,
Goodbye Dolly Gray.'

As the lines passed Dee she suddenly caught sight of Mike and Tommy, and began to shout and wave to them. How smart and grown-up Tommy looked in his uniform, she thought. Her cries were joined by those of Abbie, Hilda and Sal, all differences for the moment forgotten. They were all shouting and laughing and yet Dee knew that the tears were coursing down her cheeks and those of Nancy.

'It's silly, Nancy,' she laughed, dashing her hand

across her wet cheeks. 'Everyone's so cheerful, so why are we all crying like babies?'

Nancy wiped her own eyes. 'Because we're daft, that's why. We're proud of them and they look so . . . so fine and grand.'

'It won't be long now, Nancy, before your Sean will be going,' Abbie said, her blue eyes swimming with tears of pride.

Her Sean. Nancy repeated the words in her mind. Yes, he was her Sean. In that moment she felt sorry for Dee. Oh, Mike, Tommy and Sean were Dee's friends, but none of them was her sweetheart, and she couldn't feel the same depth of emotions that she and Abbie were feeling. The glow of euphoria was fading and Dee suddenly felt bereft. She'd miss them, but she would miss Tommy most of all. She hadn't even asked him to write to her, and now she regretted that fact.

The Harveys hadn't gone to see the boys off. Abe was working, someone needed to, he said grimly. There were still ships to be guided into dock. Winnie had managed to find a shop that was open for a few hours, to do her shopping, and Hannah was in the yard with the dolly tub and mangle, doing the washing. Jerry sat in his bedroom, close to tears.

Now his whole arm felt as though it were on fire. The pain made him feel ill, but it was nothing compared to the pain in his heart. They'd all be marching along Lime Street now. Mike, Tommy and all the lads he'd played with, gone to school with, worked with, too. Even Sean Doyle had joined up. They were all going to fight for God, King and Country. Everyone except him. All their families and friends would be there, cheering them on.

He was useless, no good to anyone any more. He'd never look smart in a khaki uniform like Mike had on Christmas Day. All he had to look forward to was pain and misery and in the end . . . He'd always managed to blot out the eventuality in the past, but not now. He was ill and depressed. Life was all pain and hopelessness. He hated his da, he could barely bring himself to speak to him. He'd seen his mam grow older, more careworn by the day. That, too, was his fault. They'd all be better off without him.

He got up and took the length of rope from the bottom of the wardrobe where he'd hidden it. It was better like this – for everyone. He had nothing to live for, his mam and Hannah would be free from worry. His da wouldn't care, except for the shame. Suicide was a sin. It was also a crime. The thought gave him some satisfaction. His hands were shaking, it took courage, he thought as he moved the stool, but it would be over soon. No more pain, no more despair, no more humiliation.

The street was deserted, but it wasn't a day they could celebrate in their house, Winnie thought bitterly. God had given her a heavy burden to shoulder. She wasn't foolish enough to think that all those boys marching out today would come home. No, some would die, but she would lose her son, too. There was no element of chance about that. One day, how long in the future she didn't know, her son would die and there would be no glory in it for her – for any of them.

She was weary when she got home and unwrapped the parcels and stored them. The house was quiet, but it always was, except when Abe was in one of his moods. She went to the back door and opened it.

'Hannah, Hannah, have you nearly finished, luv? I'll make us a nice cup of tea.'

There was no answer and there was no sign of Hannah. A pile of washing was still in the dolly tub, another pile was thrown over the mangle. She called her daughter again, and again there was no reply.

She went back inside and then she heard noises upstairs, then Hannah's screams and she flew along the lobby and up the stairs.

In Jerry's bedroom Hannah was supporting the weight of her brother. 'Mam, oh, Mam help me! We've got to get him to the hospital! Get the police, Mam, quick!'

Winnie clutched the door frame for support as she saw the piece of rope around Jerry's neck and the blue-black lips. Then she was beside him, dragging the rope over his head with hands that shook. 'Is he . . .?'

'No, I don't think so, Mam.'

Winnie held him against her, willing him to breathe, and at last she felt the faint whisper of breath against her cheek.

'I'll get the police, Mam, they'll get an ambulance.'

'No, Hannah!' Winnie cried. 'No, Hannah, it's a crime! A crime against God and man to try to . . . ! He's going to be all right now. Thank God you were here and got to him in time.' Winnie was so relieved that

Jerry was still alive, yet later she was to wonder if it would have been better to let him go.

Hannah had gone for Doctor Wallace, after pleading with her mother, for Jerry didn't seem to be recovering and she was afraid for him. She hadn't told the doctor the full story, she'd just begged him to come quickly.

'What happened?' Doctor Wallace said gently to Winnie, after he'd examined Jerry and they'd got him into bed.

'Oh, Doctor, I . . .' Winnie glanced pleadingly at Hannah.

'He . . . he tried to . . . hang . . . himself.' Hannah got the words out with great difficulty.

The room was silent except for Jerry's laboured breathing. Doctor Wallace shook his head sadly. He should report it.

'Please . . . please Doctor, don't . . . don't say anything, he's suffering enough,' Winnie begged, the tears bright in her eyes.

Of that latter fact he was convinced and he wasn't a harsh man. 'Very well, but there must be no reference at all to this, you understand that. If it should happen again.'

'It won't! I'll see to it, I promise! Thank you, may God bless you for your kindness.' Winnie choked out the words.

Hannah was crying too as she led the way down the stairs and as she closed the door behind Doctor Wallace, she leaned her cheek against the wood and sobbed.

Chapter Seventeen

———◆———

NANCY FELT THAT THE training camp at Prescot
might as well have been at the other end of the
country. Sean seldom got a pass to come home, and
when he did it was only for a few hours, and they were
seldom alone. The training seemed endless, so he
wrote, and they'd heard that the battalion was to be
held in reserve as a feeder for those who had gone to
France and Belgium.

Women were taking over the men's jobs to release
the men for the army. They worked on the trams, in the
Post Office, offices and railways, factories and on the
land. Some were even offering to work on the docks.
She, Mary and Abbie now worked in munitions and
they earned thirty-two shillings a week – a small
fortune compared to what they'd earned in the
Laundry. Dee had a responsible, well-paid job in the
main Post Office in Victoria Street. A job that under
normal circumstances she would not have even been
considered for. There were many houses in Burlington

Street and the surrounding area, where the standard of living had risen incredibly.

The news through 1915 seemed to be all bad. At the end of April had come the terrible news from Gallipoli. The British and ANZAC forces who'd landed there had been slaughtered on the beaches by Turkish machine gun fire. Thousands had died on the barbed wire. Homes throughout the country were devastated, for the Lancashire Fusiliers had formed part of that ill-fated expedition.

There had been riots in the city in May when the *Lusitania* had been sunk and, due to the increase in the U-boat menace, imported food was getting scarcer. Sal proclaimed loudly that now, when she had more in her purse than ever before, there was very little to buy.

Throughout the summer there had been rumours and counter-rumours that soon it would be compulsory to join the armed forces. Men would be 'conscripted'. The Government denied claims of 'forced labour', but the rumours persisted.

Dee had volunteered to do a couple of hours a week auxiliary nursing after work and Abbie joined her, when her shifts permitted. They, like everyone else, had read with shock and outrage of the execution in October of Nurse Edith Cavell for helping French and English soldiers to escape to Holland.

'I don't want to hear any more about you going nursing full time, miss. Not when those . . . those fiends are shooting defenceless women!' had been Sal's instructions to her daughter. Abbie had ignored her outburst.

Christmas of 1915 was miserable for everyone, Abbie thought. People were worried. More and more women were appearing in the black of mourning, and the rumour that conscription was imminent was again rife.

As the first full year of war ended, Hilda received a telegram. Abbie had been on her way to the shop on an errand for Sal and she stopped, frozen with fear, as the boy leaned his bicycle against the wall and went in. The sound of the door closing galvanized Abbie and she'd run the rest of the way. She'd pushed past the few customers and a white-faced Chrissie who had been serving, and burst into the kitchen, just as Frank was opening the buff-coloured envelope.

'Oh, my God! He's . . . he's not . . .?' she'd cried.

'No. No, he's just wounded.' Frank had passed the piece of paper to Hilda who had scanned it and then sat down, suddenly unsteady on her feet.

'How badly?' Abbie had pressed Frank.

'It said a flesh wound.'

Abbie was so relieved she'd begun to cry.

Frank put his arm around her. 'There now, luv, it's not too bad.'

'I suppose we'll get a letter . . . soon,' Hilda had said shakily.

'We're bound to. Even if he can't write he'll get someone to do it for him,' Frank said firmly.

Abbie had pulled herself together. 'I'm sorry for barging in like that. I saw the lad and—'

'No need to apologize, Abbie.' Frank had taken the telegram from Hilda and had passed it to Chrissie, who had been standing in the doorway.

'That settles it! I don't care what Mam says, I'm going to join the VAD and I'm going tonight!' Abbie had announced.

Frank had nodded his approval and Hilda looked at Abbie with respect.

The war was dragging on and on. Conscription had been introduced in January, and in February the wealthy families had been urged to release their servants to work for the war effort.

Mike Burgess had been wounded in the shoulder at Fonquevillers. He had not been repatriated, but was sent to a French hospital to recover. It had been a graze, a flesh wound and he'd rejoined his unit within two weeks. Abbie had gone to Queen Mary's Military Hospital in Whalley, near Clitheroe.

In April Sean had managed to get a day's leave. The weather was warm for the time of year, and he and Nancy had gone over to Thurstaston Common. They'd taken the ferry, then an omnibus.

'I got leave because we're going off to Larkhill,' Sean said as they sat with their backs to a large boulder and looked over the expanse of gentle heath, blossoming with yellow broom, that stretched to Thor's Stone and Thurstaston Hill. It was possible to believe there wasn't even a war going on, Sean thought. It was so peaceful here.

'And then it will be "over there"?' Nancy remembered that this was the familiar pattern, the path taken by Ken and Norman Kerrigan, then Mike and

Tommy, and it was as though a cloud had blotted out the sun.

'Oh, Sean, I know I shouldn't say it, but I'll be so miserable.'

'Don't say that, Nancy. Try and look on the bright side. With me over there the Hun won't stand a chance!' he said flippantly. He wasn't looking forward to it at all. It had begun to dawn on a lot of people now that it wasn't a picnic or the big adventure they'd all thought it would be. There were men in graves in France and men in hospitals all over the country who could testify to that. Except that dead men couldn't speak. He gathered her to him.

'Sean, you will keep writing to me?' she begged.

'Every spare minute I get, but let's not think about it, time's too precious for speculating about the future. It's now we have to think about, and now you're in my arms.'

Nancy surrendered to his embrace, his need for her. The sun warmed her face, the smell of new, sweet grass filled her nostrils and above them a skylark sang as though the world was a joyous place. She forgot there was a war, that somewhere men were suffering and dying. Sean loved her and needed her, that was all that she could think of.

Sean had continued to write, though not frequently, but she put this down to additional training and preparations at Larkhill Camp in Lincolnshire.

June was hot and sultry. Even though it was six o'clock, it was still very warm as Nancy walked from the tram stop. She was weary, for it was heavy work. Dirty and dangerous too, and she was looking forward to a quiet night at home.

She really had to admit that Elizabeth was very little trouble. She was a good baby who slept all night, and now she was livelier, managing to toddle around, clutching each piece of furniture as she went. She knew there would be no more babies because Bridie had told her she was too old to go through all that again.

'There's a letter for you, Nancy, from Sean,' Bridie informed her as she walked in.

Nancy smiled and picked it up. 'I'll take it up to read. Is Dee in yet?'

'No, you've the room all to yourself; Rose is with Sal.'

The bedroom was stifling and she pushed the sash window up as far as it would go, then sat down on the bed and opened the letter. Scanning the lines, she gave a little cry, her hand going to her mouth. He was going. He was off to France next week and she wouldn't see him again before then. She remembered the sweet smell of new grass, the feeling of his lips on hers, his cries of endearment. She'd known then he would be going soon, that being parted was bad, but she'd not reckoned on this feeling of desolation.

'You look almost as bad as I feel,' Dee announced as she entered the room.

'Oh, it's Sean. He's going – next week.'

'I'm sorry, but you knew it had to come soon, Nancy, and . . . Oh!' Dee suddenly doubled over in pain.

'What's the matter?' Nancy cried, getting to her feet.

Dee sat down on the edge of the bed clutching her abdomen. 'It's just the usual, the "curse", but it's been really bad today. I didn't think I was going to be able to stick it until the end of the day. I've had some aspirin, but it hasn't made much difference.'

Nancy felt sorry for Dee, she suffered terrible cramps. 'I'll go and get you something for it. Get into bed, I'll bring you a hot water bottle, too.'

Nancy was halfway down the stairs when she stopped. She hadn't seen anything herself last month, and now it was nearly the end of June and she was ten days late!

At first Nancy refused to believe it. She made excuses. It was the upset of Sean going overseas. She was tired and worn out. The news brought one shock after another. Each day she prayed for the start of her period, but at the same time she realized that it wasn't much use asking God to forgive her, she hadn't been sorry, she hadn't even gone to confession. It had all seemed so right. Love made it right. She tried all the remedies. Gin, hot baths, violent exercise, but nothing worked, and in the first days of July she was forced to face the fact that she was pregnant.

She had been lying on the bed, trying to think of what she would say to her mam, when Dee found her.

'What are you doing up here in the dark?' she asked, reaching to light the lamp.

'Don't, Dee. Don't light the lamp.'

'Have you got a headache? You've been very pale

and quiet these last few days. Are you worried about Sean?'

'No, at least not in that way. Oh, Dee, I've got to tell someone.'

Dee had sensed there was something wrong, for Nancy had been quiet and out of sorts lately. 'What's the matter?'

'Promise you won't tell anyone . . . not yet.'

'What is it?'

'Promise first!' Nancy begged, her eyes full of tears.

'All right, I promise.'

'I'm . . . I'm having a baby, Dee.'

Dee couldn't see her face but she was sure Nancy was crying. She was stunned. 'Oh, my God! Are you sure?' she gasped.

'Almost. It's been over two months.'

'Was it . . .?'

'Sean. Yes, it must have been the last time he was home in April.'

'What will you do?'

'I don't know, Dee. I just don't know. I've tried everything. I was trying to think of what to say to Mam, just now.'

'Will he marry you?'

'Yes, I'm certain of that. We love each other Dee, but he's gone. I don't know when he'll be back.'

Or if he'll be back, Dee thought. She always remembered all the boys in her prayers, especially Tommy. She'd had two misspelt letters from him, but at least he had written and she knew he was alive and well. 'You'll have to write and tell him, Nancy.'

'I know, but I'm going to have to tell Mam, Dee, I can't keep it a secret. Sooner or later it will have to be told.'

Dee knew she was right, but this was terrible. It shouldn't have happened to Nancy, she was too serious, so quiet and trusting. She knew of girls who were bold and flighty and had reputations, but they didn't seem to get caught. Maybe it was just the good girls who did. She prayed for Nancy's sake that nothing would happen to Sean Doyle.

'Let's calm down and think, Nancy. You've missed two months. It's early days yet, so maybe you should leave telling your mam until after you've written to Sean.'

Nancy was distraught. 'Why?'

'Won't it look better if you have a letter from him, saying he'll marry you as soon as he can get home? It would be a sort of engagement, it might make it seem, well, less . . . terrible.'

There was a lot of sense in what Dee said, and Nancy grasped at this straw. 'You're right, Dee. It won't look half as bad, will it? Everyone will know that we intended to get married. It was just, well, he got sent abroad before we could do anything.' She'd already begun to believe this herself.

'It's a pity you didn't realize sooner, when he was still at Prescot; you could have been married now.'

'I didn't think, Dee, and when I did, I just kept praying I was wrong, that something would happen. I wish I was as quick as you to grasp things and sort them out. But I feel much better now.' She hugged Dee tightly, wondering how she had ever managed without her stepsister's quick mind and caring nature.

The 18th Battalion were dug into assembly trenches east of Talus Boise, below the German-held village of Montauban and the Glatz Redoubt.

Mike was back with his mates, but he had changed. They had all changed from the cocky, carefree, ebullient young lads who'd left Lime Street Station that day just over fifteen months ago. They'd left their youth behind in the trenches around Fonquevillers. He'd left many of his mates there too – permanently.

For a whole week now the earth had trembled and shaken with the constant heavy artillery bombardment. The air reeked with acrid smoke. It hung in clouds everywhere, burning the throat and stinging the eyes. At night the flashes lit up the sky, searing the darkness with red and orange. The continuous noise had nearly driven him mad. Each shell seemed to explode in his head, and his ears ached. But at least the waiting was nearly over now. Tomorrow morning they would begin the attack. He sincerely hoped the artillery barrage had had the desired effect on the enemy lines. It was sheer drudgery, carting trench supplies up and down the lines. There was constant movement, so sleep was impossible; but they were too keyed-up to sleep anyway.

'What's this?' he asked Tommy, who was passing equipment along the line.

'Waterproof sheet, iron rations, ammo, two Mills grenades, sandbags, entrenching tools, field dressings,' Tommy rattled off.

'What the hell for? We won't be able to move carrying all this!' Mike shouted.

'Stop bloody moaning!' Tommy yelled back.

The first streaks of dawn were already snaking across the sky. By half-past four it was daylight, but the sun was obscured by the smoke from the shells. The time dragged, but at twenty-five-past six the bombardment increased.

Mike felt his guts tighten into a knot of fear. He felt sick and prayed he wouldn't vomit as he'd done before Fonquevillers. It couldn't be long now. He tried to pray, but he couldn't concentrate on the words. He gripped his rifle tightly, so tightly that his knuckles were white, and still his hands shook. He would never, never get used to this feeling. There were no coherent thoughts, just brief images, disjointed phrases flashing in and out of his mind. He couldn't think of what the next hour would bring. He dare not think about it or he'd start yelling.

Tommy was standing on the fire step, his head pressed against the damp earth of the wall of the trench. He was fighting down the rising waves of panic and terror. He wanted it all to be over. He wanted to be a hundred miles away from here, he wanted to be at home safe and sound, with Mam and Da and all the kids. And Dee. Oh, how he wanted to see Dee again. Maybe he'd even find the courage to tell her how he felt about her. He swore he'd never complain about anything again, if he got home. If he came through this in one piece.

This was the worst part. Once you were on the

move, it didn't seem so bad. Out there was No Man's Land, he could see it in his mind's eye: five hundred yards of untouched land. The racecourse, they called it, for apparently that's what it looked like from the air. A wide strip of greenery unmarked by the shells, but covered with the ugly murderous coils of barbed wire. He prayed that the week-long bombardment had blown that bloody wire to bits. He remembered seeing men caught on it, dying on it. He tried to say the Rosary but he couldn't seem to get beyond 'Hail Mary, Full of Grace'. He couldn't remember what came next. Words of a prayer he'd learned and used since he'd been five years old escaped him.

At seven twenty-five the scaling ladders were in place, at seven thirty the flag fell, the waiting was over and they jerked into action.

The gun smoke still swirled around them, and all Mike could see ahead of him were flashes and columns of smoke erupting like small volcanoes. He was bent double with the weight of the kit he carried, and running was impossible. There were smaller flashes and he knew it was machine gun fire. He heard men screaming as they fell. He tripped over the wounded, but stumbled on, his face a mask of frozen fear. He had to keep going, he had to, there could be no turning back. He stumbled again and this time fell into a shell crater, landing awkwardly, the breath knocked out of him by someone falling on him.

When he had regained his wind he pushed the man aside and instantly recognized him. It was Lieutenant Herdman, and he'd been shot through the head. He closed the man's eyes and uttered a short prayer. Somewhere, quite near, someone was screaming in pain. Mike tried amidst that inferno of noise and smoke to gather his wits. Gingerly he raised his head and saw the figure sprawled just behind the edge of the crater. He leaned forward and found he could just reach the man. Slowly he dragged him towards him, the man screaming all the time. It was Tommy.

'It's me leg! Oh, God! me leg. Is that you, Mike?'

'It's me.' Mike was ripping away Tommy's trouser leg with his entrenching tool.

'Jesus, Mary and Joseph!' Tommy yelled.

'Keep still for God's sake!'

The leg was mangled below the knee and the bone was exposed, gleaming horribly white against the shredded flesh. Mike tied a tourniquet tightly around Tommy's thigh and raised his head again and yelled as loud as he could for a stretcher bearer. He kept on yelling until at last someone arrived.

'Get him back to the field station. His leg's a mess.'

'We'll do our best, but there's no guarantees. It's a massacre. We're down to half strength now. It'll be hours before we can get to everyone. Maybe even days if they carry on blasting at us.'

Mike gripped Tommy's hand tightly and tried to grin. 'Go on you lucky bugger, it's Blighty for you! Give Abbie my love!' he yelled as Tommy was carted away.

He slid back into the shell hole and crouched down, undecided what to do. He should go on. If he stayed cringing here it would be seen as an act of cowardice under fire and he would be shot for it. But he would probably be shot if he carried on. It wasn't much of a choice. The noise had gone on unabated, so it wasn't over yet. He crawled out and slowly got to his feet. Men were still passing him, and some were still falling, but not as many as before. He staggered a few more feet and then stopped, his eyes widening in horror at the sight before him. The bodies were piled two and three high, arms twisted at odd angles, legs broken and bleeding, snapped like matchwood. Some were still moving, others were still. He recognized a lad from Sylvester Street, but could do nothing to help him. He was too tired, too drained to care any more what happened. That sight had totally unnerved him. He walked the rest of the way through the smoke to what was left of Montauban that had been occupied by the remnants of the 18th.

He stared around with smarting, bloodshot eyes along the line of half-obliterated trenches. Debris and abandoned German equipment lay everywhere, bits of paper burned and fluttered, there were mutilated bodies, some still on fire. The stench was nauseating.

Wearily he sank down on his haunches as another soldier came towards him. He recognized Vinny Burke beneath the grime.

'The rest of the lads have gone "souveniring". The Manchesters and the Scotties have gone after the Hun.'

Mike wondered how anyone could have the energy, strength or interest to go looking for souvenirs amongst this carnage. 'How many of us are there left, Vinny?'

'About one hundred and fifty.'

'Jesus Christ! Is that all?' He suddenly thought of his mam and what she would say hearing him take the Lord's name in vain and the tears coursed down his cheeks. He dropped his head in his hands so that Vinny wouldn't see his tears, but he couldn't stop them. He cried like a baby for all the lads he'd grown up with who'd never see their native city again.

Five hundred telegrams were delivered to the families of the battalions of the King's Liverpool 'Pals'. They paid dearly for Montauban, but that was only the first day of the Somme Offensive. The day that plunged sixty thousand families into mourning.

Chapter Eighteen

———•———

THERE HAD BEEN NO letter from Sean, and Nancy was sick with worry, but her anxiety went unnoticed once the dreaded telegrams started to arrive.

Dee had brought Rose home, for the Kerrigan household was plunged into grief. Tommy had been wounded; Ken, Norman and Joan's husband Terry had all been killed.

'Oh, Nancy, I couldn't stay, I just couldn't, I didn't know what to say. Uncle Pat's just sitting staring into space and Aunty Sal's just . . . just fallen apart. Abbie's come home and she's sent for Doctor Wallace. But Abbie's out of her mind with worry for Tommy and Mike.' She bit her lip. She, too, was worried about Tommy, although she hadn't voiced that fear.

'At least Mike's all right. I mean, his mam hasn't had a telegram, has she?' Nancy asked.

'No. Not that I know of.'

Bridie was just shaking her head as though unable to

take it all in. 'Three of them! Three of them!' she repeated. 'Does anyone know how bad Tommy is?'

'No, I wish I did!' Dee answered.

'I'd better go up now and see Sal,' said Bridie.

'Maybe you'd better leave her, dear, the doctor may have given her a sedative,' Edward advised.

'No, I have to go. I've known those lads since they were born. Oh, and poor Joan. Left on her own; I know what that's like.' Bridie looked sorrowfully at Nancy who ducked her head so as not to have to meet her mother's gaze.

Time was running out, Nancy thought, feeling hysteria rising in her. Why, oh why hadn't he answered her letter? Was he wounded or missing or captured? She had no way of knowing, but Hilda hadn't heard, so he must be all right; then why didn't he write? It seemed selfish to be so wrapped up in herself when there was so much tragedy. In nearly every street in the neighbourhood, someone had lost a son, a husband, a brother, a sweetheart.

Dee was very quiet that night, they all were, even Rose who didn't really understand.

'Oh, Nancy, when I look back and think of the way we cheered them on, the day they left Liverpool. We were fools, all of us. I can't believe we were such fools.' Dee's eyes were bright with unshed tears.

'We never expected anything like this to happen Dee; everyone said it would be over and that we'd easily win.'

'I can't believe it. Tommy, always laughing and joking, and we don't know how badly he's hurt! I keep seeing them at Joan's wedding and at that Christmas party. Terry, Ken, Norman. Oh, poor, poor Joan and Mary.' Dee bowed her head.

It was too much for Nancy to bear, and she burst into tears. 'Oh, Dee. I can't stand it! I've not heard from Sean. I don't know where he is. What am I going to do?'

Dee had forgotten about Sean Doyle. 'I'm sorry, Nancy, I didn't know. Oh, why didn't you tell me?'

'Because I kept hoping that a letter would come in the next post. Dee, what am I going to do?'

'Give them a day or so to get over all this and then if there's still no news, you're going to have to tell them.'

'I can't, Dee! I just can't! I keep thinking of all the things I said about Mam when she got pregnant with Elizabeth. I can't disgrace them all, Dee. I can't. And don't you remember how everyone carried on when Monica Kerrigan got caught? I don't think I can face it. I don't think I can go through it all, like Monica did.'

'You'll be all right with the nuns. Abbie said Monica told her they weren't that bad.'

'Only because she promised to join them. I don't want to be a nun. I only want to marry Sean, but he doesn't want me.' She fell against Dee's shoulder sobbing.

'You don't know that for certain,' Dee comforted her.

'It must be that, it can't be anything else.'

'He might not have got your letter. It might still be on the way to him.' Dee tried to sound convincing, but she'd heard Hilda telling Lizzie Simcock that she'd had a postcard from Sean. She'd been complaining that that was all she ever got from him. That had been yesterday.

'No, it's ages since I wrote, Dee, you know it is! I can't face them. I can't go through with it. There's only one thing I can do, Dee.'

'What?'

'That woman that Mary mentioned once.'

Dee was horrified. 'No, Nancy, you can't do that!'

'Dee, I can't go through with all this! I can't. It will kill Mam!'

'She'd get used to it, you know she would. She would.'

'No. I can't, Dee. I can't. I'm ruined. No one will ever want me. I'll be an old maid. A plain, disgraced spinster!'

Dee wished with all her heart that she could get her hands on Sean Doyle, just for a few minutes. She'd kill him, she would, if the Hun didn't do it for her first, she thought grimly.

The whole street was in mourning and Dee insisted that they wait at least a week before asking Mary. A few more days wouldn't matter, she'd said. Mary appeared to be brokenhearted over Norman's death, it wasn't fair to go upsetting her even further, just yet. She had hoped against hope that a letter would arrive from Sean Doyle that would make their visit unnecessary, but by the weekend she knew she couldn't put Nancy off any longer.

Lizzie let them in. 'She's taken it badly,' she said sourly, 'although it's all self-pity.'

'We know. We're very sorry, Mrs Simcock. We're sorry for everyone,' Dee answered quietly.

Mary was red-eyed and looked pale and tired. She'd spent a lot of time at Sal's the past week, until Lizzie had lost patience with her and demanded she try to pull herself together. She'd known what it was like to lose a man, she'd said. Mary was younger than she'd been when she'd been left a widow. She'd had to get on with her life and so must Mary.

'You're just thinking of yourself, as usual. What about poor Sal, aye and what about the poor lad himself?'

'Oh, shut up, Mam, for God's sake!' Mary had cried. She was shocked. She couldn't take it in. She really must have loved him, she thought sadly, because she felt so awful. She felt the same as Joan did, she'd sat for hours listening to Joan and Sal. She shared their grief, their shock, their loss, and now she would never be able to tell Norman just how much she had loved him.

'She doesn't understand,' Mary said tiredly, as Lizzie went out to do her daily shopping.

'I'm sure she does, Mary, maybe she's just, well, forgotten a bit.' Dee tried to sound comforting.

'She has forgotten. She's forgotten what it's like to be loved.'

'Mary, we really are sorry to come and ask you this—' Nancy didn't know how to go on, yet she had to. 'I don't know who else to turn to.'

'What's the matter, Nance?'

'I . . . I'm pregnant.'

Mary's eyes filled with concern. 'Oh, Nance, you fool. Is it Sean?'

Nancy nodded.

'She's written and told him but she doesn't know if he got her letter or even if he's . . . all right,' Dee said.

'I'm sorry, Nance, I really am.'

'Mary, I can't have it. I can't go through with it. You know what it was like for Monica Kerrigan. I'm desperate. Who is that woman that Madge went to? You told us about her.'

'You mean Ma Mulholland? Nancy, you're not serious!'

'Mary, I'm desperate!' Nancy was pleading now.

Mary could see she was. So, all Dee's talk about Sean not getting Nancy's letter was a lie. He didn't want to know. Oh, poor Nancy. 'She lives at number three Leyland Court, off Great Homer Street. But she's expensive, Nance.'

'How much?' Nancy asked.

'Six guineas.'

'That's extortionate!' Dee cried.

'I know, but she's clean and experienced. The cheaper ones aren't.'

'I'll find it. I'll get it from somewhere.'

Nancy considered it a small price to pay for her reputation and for the rest of her life.

Mary turned to Dee. 'Can't you change her mind?'

'I've tried. God knows I've tried.'

'It's . . . it can be dangerous, Nance.'

'I'll take that chance.'

Mary sighed heavily and Dee got to her feet. 'We'll see ourselves out, and I'm so sorry, Mary, about Norman.'

Dee had four guineas saved up. Ever since the day

they'd first come to Burlington Street and there had been nothing, she'd had a horror of being totally without money and had saved religiously. Nancy had two pounds and they borrowed the rest from Phil, who was working in the same office as Edward. Dee insisted on going with her to Ma Mulholland's the evening of the following Monday.

As they walked into the dark, dismal court Dee shuddered. 'You can still change your mind, Nancy,' she urged.

Nancy was shaking inside with fear; it wouldn't take much encouragement on Dee's part to make her turn and run for home. But she shook her head, not trusting herself to speak.

Dee rapped sharply on the door of number three and a small, fat woman opened the door. Her iron-grey hair was snatched back and she wore a clean white apron over her black skirt.

'Mrs Mulholland?' Dee asked.

'That's me, luv.'

'We were recommended . . . er told . . .' Dee faltered.

Nancy was so petrified she couldn't utter a word.

'Come on in the pair of you, quickly.'

The door was closed behind them and they followed the woman into the front room. A cotton lace curtain covered the window and was in need of washing, but there was no dust on the mantel shelf, or the small table and two ladder-backed chairs. The rugs on the floor were also clean but faded and threadbare, and Dee wondered what the woman spent her ill-gotten gains on.

'Right, which one of you is it? Or is it both of you?'

'It's me,' Nancy managed to answer, in a voice that was so low it was a whisper.

'I charge six guineas and I want it before—'

'We understand,' Dee interrupted curtly.

'How far gone are you?' Ma Mulholland scrutinized Nancy with dark, bead-like eyes.

'Three months.'

Dee fumbled in her pocket and drew out all the coins. 'There's six guineas there.'

Ma Mulholland counted it out slowly on to the table, then nodded to herself. 'Right.' She turned to Dee. 'You can stay here or you can come back for her later on.'

'I'll stay,' Dee answered determinedly. There was no way she was going to leave Nancy here and go home.

Ma Mulholland took Nancy's arm. 'You come upstairs with me, queen. I'll have a look at you, then I'll boil up some water and . . . other things.'

Panic gripped Nancy. She was rooted to the spot and began to tremble. Ma Mulholland had seen many girls like Nancy.

'Don't go getting all airyated, now. There's nothing to it. Just a couple of seconds pain, then a bit of a rest and you'll be right as rain. There's no sense ruining the rest of your life, is there?'

Nancy submitted to being led out of the room.

Dee, too, was shivering. Even though it was July the room felt damp and musty. She tried to pray, but that didn't work, and she couldn't reconcile praying with what Nancy was about to do, either. She went to the window and peered out, but there was nothing to be seen except the wall of the house opposite. Even in daylight these courts were dark and dismal. Someone was singing drunkenly in one of the houses. All the windows were open to catch any breath of air that may filter in.

She heard the heavy footsteps come down the stairs and wondered should she go and sit with Nancy. Any minute she expected to hear Nancy running down and out of the door. Eventually she heard Ma Mulholland going back up. She jammed her fingers in her ears and closed her eyes. She knew she wouldn't be able to stand it if Nancy began to scream. If she did then she would just race to her side and Dee knew that that was the last thing she should do. This was something Nancy had to do alone.

The time dragged. Dee began to count the seconds, wondering how long it would take. Eventually she lost count and when she at last found the courage to unblock her ears and open her eyes, the house was silent and Ma Mulholland was standing in the doorway, staring at her.

'That's it then. All over and done with. Give her a few minutes, then you can both go home.'

Dee felt her knees go weak with relief. 'Is she all right? Did she scream? I—'

'She did a bit, but they all do. I've told you, there's nothing to worry about.'

Dee sank down on one of the chairs and breathed deeply. It was all over. Soon they could go home and

Nancy could pick up the pieces of her life and make a new start.

When at last Nancy came downstairs, Dee was relieved. She was very pale and was still shaking, but she was walking. Dee put her arm around her. 'Let's go home, Nancy.'

Nancy leaned against her heavily. She felt weak and sick. There was a dull ache in her lower abdomen, but Ma Mulholland had said that was normal. The pain had been excruciating and she'd bitten her lip until it bled.

'Your lip is all swollen. We'll say you had a fall.'

'I bit it. The pain was awful, Dee. I think I might have fainted.'

Dee shuddered. 'It's over now. You'll be better in the morning, when you've had a good night's sleep. The first decent night's sleep you'll have had for ages.'

Nancy managed a weak smile.

'If you don't feel well tomorrow, take the day off. Your mother will understand.'

All Nancy wanted to do now was to get home and go to bed. To sleep and sleep. To block out the last couple of hours and what she'd done.

'What happened to you, girl?' Bridie asked upon seeing her daughter.

It was Dee who answered. 'She fell. There's a broken kerb at the end of the road. She hasn't broken anything, just cut her lip, and she's badly shaken up.'

'Sit there while I put a bit of iodine on your lip.' Bridie went into the scullery.

Nancy was feeling faint. 'I'll go straight up to bed, Mam, I think I must be bruised. I feel awful,' she called.

'I'll bring it up,' Bridie called after her.

Dee pushed the kettle onto the fire. 'I'll make her a cup of tea and I'll take the iodine up to her, save your legs.'

'You're a good girl, Dee. Always thoughtful, like your da.'

'Where is Father?' Dee suddenly noticed that her father and both boys were out.

'He's taken the lads for a sail over to Wallasey and back. It was a nice evening and he said they don't get enough fresh air, particularly Phil, being stuck in that office all day.' Bridie looked concerned, but Dee was too preoccupied to notice.

'He worries about Phil, Dee. He's sixteen; Mike and Tommy went and joined up at sixteen.'

'They'd never take Phil, he looks too young. He doesn't even look sixteen. You don't think he'd go and try to lie about his age?'

'I don't know. There are lads still doing it. Your da's worried. He doesn't want to let him out of his sight.'

Dee tried not to think about Phil, she would find time to talk to him later, once she knew that Nancy was over the trauma of her experience.

It was nearly dawn when Dee woke. She, too, had been exhausted and had slept heavily. It was Nancy crying in pain that had woken her. She raised herself on one elbow, rubbing the sleep from her eyes.

'Nancy, what's wrong? What is it?'

'The pain! Oh Dee, the pain is terrible and I'm bleeding.'

Dee jumped out of bed and quickly drew back the

curtains, letting in the first rays of the early morning sun. Rose slept on in the truckle bed in the other corner. Turning back the coverlet Dee cried out in horror. The sheet was bright red, it was soaked in blood and Nancy looked terrible – she was drawn and haggard, and her lips were blue. Dee began to scream, running from the room and down the stairs, half falling in her haste.

Edward appeared as she reached the lobby.

'Deirdre, what's the matter? It's only five o'clock.'

She clutched his arm. 'It's Nancy, she's bleeding! She's bleeding terribly! Oh, please, get Bridie. Quickly.'

He was dazed. 'Bleeding, Deirdre, what do you mean?'

But she had run past him, into the room.

Bridie was pulling her shawl over her nightdress.

'Come quickly! Nancy's bleeding all over the place! Oh, hurry!' Dee screamed.

Rose and the boys were now all in the lobby, but Edward took charge, ushering them into the kitchen as quickly as he could.

Bridie had never moved so quickly in all her life. But she, too, screamed aloud when she saw her daughter and the state of the bed.

'Get an ambulance! Get the scuffers to get an ambulance! Nance, for God's sake, Nance, what happened?' She bent over Nancy.

Nancy's eyes were glazed.

'She went to Ma Mulholland in Leyland Court. I went with her!' Dee blurted out.

The colour drained from Bridie's face. 'Oh, my God! Why didn't she tell me? Why didn't she say something? I'd never have let her go near that woman!' Bridie gathered Nancy in her arms and began to weep.

'She couldn't face the disgrace. She wrote to him but he never wrote back to her. I hate him! I hate Sean Doyle!' Dee, too, was sobbing.

Bridie steadied herself. 'Dee, you mustn't tell anyone that you went with her.'

'Why not?'

'Because they'll arrest you for aiding and abetting. You can't say anything, Dee, do you understand?'

Dee nodded.

The police arrived first. A middle-aged sergeant and a constable who looked even older. 'The ambulance is on its way, luv. Oh, God Almighty!' the Sergeant cried, catching sight of all the blood.

'Who did this to her?' he asked Dee. He'd seen the work of these back-street abortionists before, butchers he called them.

'I . . . I don't know. She . . . I woke up and found her.' Dee stammered; her confusion was real.

The tinny clanging of the ambulance bell sounded even louder than usual as it came down the empty street. Heads began to emerge from bedroom windows and a couple of early risers came to their doors.

Dee clung to the ambulance driver's arm. 'Will she be all right?'

'I can't tell you that, luv,' he answered as kindly as he could.

Bridie and Edward had dressed hurriedly.

'I want to go with her. Please, please let me go with her!' Dee begged.

'It's not allowed, luv, only her mam and dad.'

'I'm her stepfather,' Edward said quietly.

'Then just her mam then. Best if you stay here, sir, and see to the rest of them,' Sergeant Harris advised. 'Then perhaps we can try and find out who did that to her. Butchers they are, these bloody women. If we get her she'll be put away for good, I can promise you that.'

It had all happened so fast, and suddenly the room was empty. Dee stood alone, staring at the bed with the crimson sheets. 'Oh, Nancy! Nancy! I should have stopped you!' she cried.

Her cries brought Edward back into the room and Dee threw herself into his arms.

'It's my fault! It's my fault!' she sobbed.

'Hush, Deirdre, it's not your fault. I'm sure she'll be all right, once they get her to Stanley Hospital and stop the bleeding. She's young and healthy. Hush, Deirdre. She's going to be fine, and her mother is with her. You've no need to upset yourself like this.'

'But if I hadn't helped.'

'Hush! The police are still here. She'll be fine.'

His words made no difference to Dee, she just clung to him, sobbing. She felt so guilty and so helpless. If she could have gone with Nancy it wouldn't seem so bad.

This time it was Hilda Burgess who came to help out. Sal had too much grief to contend with, she'd said, when Rose had informed her of what had happened.

Hilda got Phil off to work and gave David a list of small tasks to do. Both were badly shaken. Hilda had put two and two together and was consumed with rage and pity. Pity for Nancy driven to take such a dire step, and rage at Sean who was obviously the father. Nancy was a decent girl. It was because she was decent that she hadn't been able to bear the disgrace; and that ungrateful, selfish young pig had left her to face it alone. She raged at herself, too; she should have realized what he was up to and put a stop to it. If she ever got her hands on him again, she'd kill him. She banged the big iron skillet down hard on the draining-board and wished it was Sean Doyle's head. And Frank had no small part in this. It was he who'd wanted the no-good Irish ingrate here in the first place.

Dee was still sobbing, her eyes swollen so much she could hardly see, her throat raw and her head aching, when, two hours later, Sergeant Harris came back. He spoke quietly to Edward, who immediately reached for his jacket, then turned towards Dee, biting his lip.

'I'll tell her, if you like,' Sergeant Harris offered.

Edward nodded.

There were times when he hated this bloody job, Sergeant Harris thought, when, as gently as he could, he told Dee that Nancy had died fifteen minutes ago.

Chapter Nineteen

———◆———

EVEN THE SKIES WERE weeping, Dee thought. A soft, warm drizzle had fallen steadily from sullen grey clouds all morning. It had soaked into the clothes of the mourners, but they hardly noticed it. She clung tightly to Philip's arm the whole of the time, fearing that if she released her grip she would sink to the ground, immobile and senseless. The cobbles under her feet were like dull pewter, and were slippery with rain. It was another reason for needing her brother's support.

Ahead of her walked Edward, bare-headed, with shoulders hunched, his arm around Bridie. She was unnaturally calm, but hugged Elizabeth to her and occasionally buried her face in the confused toddler's hair, as though she were actually breathing in comfort and strength from her small daughter. Elizabeth had her life ahead of her, while for Nancy there was only darkness, Dee thought brokenly.

The neighbours followed, huddled in a group, many

weeping openly, for Nancy had been such a gentle, pleasant girl that she was universally liked. At the rear of the cortège walked two uniformed policemen, Sergeant Harris and Constable Rodgers, their faces set in grim lines that betrayed the burning anger and frustration they felt. There had been no evidence, no witness to point the finger of blame at Mrs Mulholland, leaving her free to maim and possibly kill again, and they were powerless to stop her.

At the graveside Father Fitzpatrick bowed his head and began the *De Profundis*. The rain had seeped into his starched white cotton surplice and it was now limp, the black stole around his neck stained with damp patches. Dee fought down the sobs that again threatened to engulf her. She couldn't stand much more, she thought, as panic rose. It all had to end soon. It *had* to, or she'd break free and run. Run as far as she could from the open grave that gaped like a wound in the green skin of the earth. But even if she ran until she were twenty miles away and dropped from sheer exhaustion, she couldn't run from her conscience. One fact dominated all else in her mind. It was her fault that Nancy was now in the coffin being slowly lowered into the ground. She should have stopped her. She should have told Bridie or her father. If only . . . Oh, how often those words had hammered in her brain. If only she had acted differently, then no one would be here today.

Moist, sticky earth was being pressed into her hand, and looking up through her tears she saw her father's concerned face. She shook her head violently. 'I can't!' she choked.

Edward understood and, bending down, he picked a bright yellow buttercup from the grass at his feet and pressed it into Dee's hand. 'It's not much. It's really only a weed, but maybe . . . maybe she'd look on it as a real flower.'

Dee watched the little speck of brightness, like a fleeting beam of sunlight, fall from her fingers down into the darkness. She should have bought some flowers, she thought. Nancy should have had proper flowers to lie with her, not that poor little weed. She should have had violets – they'd always been her favourite. Weeds were second best, she thought tiredly, and poor Nancy had never had the best of anything in her life.

When the ordeal was finally over and everyone went back to the house in Burlington Street, Dee wanted to be on her own. She felt she couldn't bear the brave, polite but stilted conversations of their friends and neighbours, but it was impossible, it would be so rude and hurtful to them. So she made her way out to the back yard and sank down on the upturned dolly tub. With fingers that shook she withdrew the pins that anchored her hat and took it off, the straw sodden beneath her fingers.

'Dee, you've got to stop blaming yourself.'

Dee looked up to find Abbie Kerrigan standing beside her, a slim figure dressed entirely in black, making her skin look paler. Her blond hair, swept up in a loose roll beneath the wide black brim of her hat, looked like a halo.

'Oh, Abbie! It *is* my fault!'

Abbie reached out and took Dee's hand. 'Stop it! You're going to make yourself ill. You can't go on like this.'

'Abbie, if only I had told someone. Father, Bridie, Aunty Sal, anyone, they would have stopped her. I should have said something. I shouldn't have been so weak and let her swear me to secrecy.'

'You thought you were helping her; she'd have been at her wits' end if you'd given her away and she'd have been forced to have the baby. She would never have forgiven you. Her life would have been ruined.'

'Better that, Abbie, than to have no life at all now.' Sobs racked Dee again, her thin shoulders heaving. Abbie gathered her into her arms and held her tightly.

'Oh, Abbie, it all hurts so much! The worst part is that I can't even admit to going there with her, or having the satisfaction of seeing that woman locked up. If I could do that I'm sure it would help me.'

Abbie stroked the light brown hair gently. 'I know Dee. We all feel the same way. And did you see the policemen? They looked so – so beaten and sad.'

'I saw them and I wanted to go and tell them. I know I'd go to prison, but at least I would feel as though I would be doing some good and that I was being punished. I committed a crime too, Abbie. I went with her. I should be punished, and it would help if I were,' Dee sobbed.

'No it wouldn't, Dee. It wouldn't help anyone. Oh, it may help some other poor girl but not you, or Bridie or your dad, and it wouldn't bring Nancy back. You've got to stop tearing yourself apart. The one who should be punished is Sean Doyle. He's the one who needs locking up. I hope a shell lands on him and blows him straight to hell where he belongs.'

There was pure venom in Abbie's voice as she thought of her brothers lying dead in a foreign land and of Tommy badly hurt in a military hospital and Mike – God alone knew where he was or if he was all right.

Dee's sobs had begun to lessen and finally she raised a blotched and swollen face, found her handkerchief and wiped her eyes.

Abbie smiled. 'That's better.'

'I'm sorry, Abbie.'

'What for? Isn't that what friends are for: a shoulder to cry on when you need one?'

Dee began to twist her sodden handkerchief between her fingers as her thoughts settled back into the same repetitive train. 'If only I'd had some real training, I might have been able to do something for her. I might have been able to stop the bleeding at least until help came—'

Abbie looked thoughtful. 'Why don't you come back with me to Whalley, Dee? Nurses are desperately needed.' Something positive would take Dee's mind off things and she would also be far away from Burlington Street and all its painful memories, Abbie reasoned.

Dee grasped at the straw that Abbie was offering. 'I could, couldn't I?'

'Definitely. Bridie has Elizabeth and your dad, Phil has his mates and his work, David and Rose spend most of the time with our Bertie and Seb. You need to do something, Dee. Oh, I know it's going to be hard and as soon as we're trained we go out to Flanders, to the field hospitals, but at least you won't be here—' she didn't finish, she didn't want to remind Dee of the memories, so she left the words unsaid.

'When? When?'

Abbie became brisk and businesslike. 'Tomorrow. That's the end of my leave. I've done as much as I can for Mam; she's over the first shock, and she and our Joan seem to help each other. She's a tower of strength really is Mam. She's had to be, my da's not much use for anything at the best of times. You tell Bridie and your dad tonight, then get your things together and come up to Whalley with me.'

Dee managed a lopsided smile and nodded, but before she could speak, Chrissie Burgess appeared holding a cup of tea.

'Mam told me to bring you this, it's got plenty of sugar in it, so drink it all. Sugar is hard to get.'

Dee just nodded and it was Abbie who took the cup from Chrissie.

'Are you all right? Mam told me to ask.' Chrissie wanted to go home. She really hadn't wanted to come at all and she really didn't want to know how Dee was feeling.

'Of course she's all right. Well, as right as anyone could be after all that,' Abbie replied curtly for there was something about Chrissie that she'd never liked.

'Well, it's not my fault, so don't bite my head off. Anyway, Mam said what Nancy did was a crime and a mortal sin as well. She as good as murdered her baby and—'

The smashing of the cup and saucer on the flagstones coincided simultaneously with the sharp crack of Abbie's open hand as it met Chrissie's cheek. 'You little bitch! You wicked, cruel, heartless little bitch!' Abbie screamed at Chrissie.

Chrissie didn't cry out but stood, holding her hand against her smarting cheek, her eyes wide with shock.

Dee burst into tears.

Abbie's eyes flashed as she turned towards the door, determined to find Hilda and give her a piece of her mind, but Hilda was already standing in the doorway, her face scarlet, her mouth set in a tight line.

Chrissie had also seen her mother and had started to cry. 'Mam, Mam she belted me. Abbie Kerrigan belted me.'

In a second Hilda covered the few steps between herself and her daughter and, catching Chrissie roughly by the shoulder, gave her a hefty swipe across the side of the head. 'I'll swing for you yet! Get home you bad-minded little madam! Get home this minute before I give you a damned good hiding!'

Chrissie wrenched herself free and fled through the yard door and into the entry, realizing that this time she had gone too far and that there would be no mercy to be got from either of her parents and she probably would face a hiding when her da got in.

'Dee, I'm so sorry, I really am! She twisted it all. I never meant it to sound like that.'

Abbie was still furious. 'You must have said it in the first place. What a cruel, wicked thing to say about poor Nance!'

Hilda bit her lip and two spots of colour burned on her cheeks. 'What I said was, thank God Father Fitz got to the hospital in time to absolve Nancy and give her the last rites. What I said was thank God she didn't . . . die in sin: the church looks on it as murder.'

'We all know that, but did you really need to say it?' Abbie snapped.

Hilda had composed herself, at least outwardly. 'No, I don't suppose I did. It was a conversation with Frank, a private conversation—'

'But with that one earwigging at the door as usual,' Abbie interrupted.

'I'll deal with our Chrissie!' Hilda snapped back. The girl was angry, that she fully understood. Who wouldn't be, after the way Chrissie had misconstrued her words. Oh, she'd murder Chrissie for putting her in this position. 'I just came to say that people are starting to leave and that Dee had better come inside. Bridie's been asking for her.'

Abbie helped Dee to her feet. 'Tell her we're coming in and that Dee is coming back with me to train as a VAD nurse.'

Hilda pursed her lips but nodded slowly. 'It's probably for the best,' she agreed, but thought privately that Abbie Kerrigan was taking a lot upon herself these days.

Chrissie had been given a hiding and such a dressing down from her usually placid da, that she was rendered utterly speechless and had gone to her room chastened and sore. Frank had gone to open up the shop and after Hilda had covered her black mourning dress with an apron and had cleared away the tea dishes, she sat down at the table with a pen and writing paper. She had two letters to write. One to Sean Doyle and one to his Commanding Officer. She'd had a postcard from that no-good, heartless ingrate recently, so he was still alive and in one piece, although that was a fact she now regretted after the day's events. He must have known, she thought bitterly. Nancy had written to him. She knew that for a fact, for Bridie had told her that Dec had actually posted the second letter. He'd known and yet he'd done nothing, refused to face his responsibilities, and because of that a young trusting and innocent girl had been driven to despair and a terrible death. In her eyes, Sean Doyle had committed more sins than Nancy had ever done. True, she had said to Frank that it was murder, but she understood how desperate and distraught Nancy must have been to have sought out Ma Mulholland. There was only one other abortionist in the neighbourhood that she knew of, and she was so dirty and drunk most of the time that Nancy would never have gone near her. Two large tears slid down Hilda's cheeks and fell on the blank sheet of white paper. Oh, Chrissie was a terrible trial to her, but God forbid that she would ever have to endure what Bridie was now going through. To get a child reared was an achievement in itself, but then to lose her, and like that. It didn't bear dwelling on.

She was weary and heart-sore, for everywhere she turned there seemed to be grief and worry. She went to early mass every day and prayed for Michael and for all the other lads and their wives and mothers, but now she'd waste no time or prayers on Sean Doyle. She crumpled up the stained sheet of paper and straightened her shoulders determinedly. Oh, she intended to give him a piece of her mind. She would certainly make it clear that if he ever had the temerity to set foot in Burlington Street again, she personally would lead the lynch mob, for that's what he could expect if he ever came back. In more polite terms she would convey to his Commanding Officer what an unprincipled coward he had in his battalion and that everyone would be better off without Sean Doyle for he couldn't be trusted, he had no loyalty to anyone except himself. He hadn't really wanted to join up at all, it was only to save his face. In fact it would be of benefit to everyone, the British Army included, if Sean Doyle were to become another fatality on the casualty list. In fact, in this respect the Hun would be doing everyone a favour.

When she'd finished she sat back and sighed deeply, but she felt a little better. However, she doubted that the Hun would be so obliging. After all, as Frank often said, the devil looks after his own.

Dee had had a long talk with her father after everyone had gone and they had half-heartedly tidied up. Bridie was putting Elizabeth to bed.

'Isn't it a bit too soon to be making such decisions?' Edward asked gently.

'No. Abbie's right, Father. I need to do something, something useful. It may help to make up for what I did.'

'Deirdre, it wasn't your fault.'

Dee felt too drained to argue. 'I can't stay here, can't you understand that?'

Edward nodded slowly. The future looked gloomy on every front. The war seemed to be going badly, the casualties were horrendous and he was very worried about Phil, who was always talking about wanting to join up. The house would be strangely quiet without Nancy and now Deirdre, but he did understand. 'When do you plan to go?'

'Tomorrow. Abbie is going back in the morning and I said I'd go with her.'

'Isn't that very soon? Surely you could follow her in a day or two? I'm worried about Bridie, she's too quiet.'

Dee felt the first stirrings of emotions other than grief and guilt. Impatience and resentment that Edward should burden her with his anxiety. 'She doesn't need me, Father. She has you and Elizabeth, Phil and David and Rose.'

'I know, but they don't understand in the same way you do.'

The tears sprang to Dee's eyes. 'I have to go, I want to go. I need to go. I'll go mad if I stay here. I will!'

Edward knew it was hopeless. She was right. 'I'll tell Bridie,' he said, getting slowly to his feet.

Dee sighed with relief. 'I'll make a start on my packing. I think they provide the uniform, so I won't need much.'

Edward watched her as she went towards the stairs. He felt as though he'd lost her, and he wondered sadly when he would see her again after tomorrow.

Chapter Twenty

———✦———

DEE SOON BEGAN TO feel that she'd made the right decision. Her new life was a world away from Liverpool and Burlington Street. The small Lancashire town was surrounded by farmland, criss-crossed with dry stone walls, and it was possible to see the Pennines rising starkly towards the sky, forming a natural border between Lancashire and Yorkshire. Dee loved the ancient Cistercian abbey and the clear waters of the river Calder that bounded the ruins from which the monks had been driven four centuries ago. She found it comforting to sit in the quiet old church at the abbey gate, and often looked longingly at the row of pretty almshouses that faced the ruins. She would have loved to live in one. It would be somewhere of her own, a place of tranquillity where she could rest and heal her shattered spirit.

The work at the hospital was hard and demanding. Her first day had had all the characteristics of a nightmare. She had forgotten her 'sleeves', the half

sleeve elasticated at both ends, that replaced her
starched cuffs while she worked. She had been
reprimanded sharply and a pair had been found for her
in the drawer of a table in the kitchen.

Then there was Sister Elliott, a demon in nurse's
garb. Small, thin, efficient and with eyes like two pieces
of flint. Eyes that missed nothing.

Dee's first 'duty' had been to scrub the kitchen table,
and she'd just started when Sister Elliott had appeared
beside her.

'Is that your idea of scrubbing, Nurse Chatterton?'

Dee had become confused. 'Er, yes Sister.'

Sister had rolled up her sleeves, taken the brush and
had scrubbed a corner vigorously. 'Go with the grain of
the wood, Nurse, not against it, and put more effort
into it. This is a hospital, not a rest home.'

Dee had nodded as the scrubbing brush was thrust
back into her hands.

Her duties included the Sink Room, which she came
to loathe, after she'd got over her embarrassment.
Urinals and bedpans were stacked on shelves, along
with the linen bedpan covers. There was a large sink
and a flushing unit and also a big sack of 'tow'. A strong
smell of carbolic soap and Jeyes Fluid hung on the air.
She'd not known what 'tow' was and no one had
explained, so she'd asked Abbie.

'It's that hairy stuff – jute, I think it's called.'

'What do we use it for?'

'Well, when you take a bedpan you stuff the hollow
bit in the handle with tow.' Dee's forehead was
furrowed in a frown of concentration but Abbie could

see she was still mystified. 'It's to use instead of paper, to wipe them, you know – for toilet paper.'

Dee had blushed.

'Dee, you're going to see things and have to do things – well, you'll get used to it.'

Dee soon did, although she never really succeeded in covering her embarrassment.

Everything in the Sink Room had to be scrubbed: shelves, sinks, bowls and rubber sheets. As the weeks wore on she learned to use a thermometer, to give an enema, how to dress wounds, and *Taylor's Manual of Nursing* and *Black's Medical Dictionary* became her constant companions in her free time.

There was a strange porcelain figure with hooks all over it and a box containing the bits which fitted these hooks, shaped as a heart, liver and kidney, a box of bones, all labelled, and a skeleton, all of which constituted Sister Tutor's teaching aids. She learned about morphine and ether and Paraldehyde, which had a foul smell but which was used as a cure for the insomnia that plagued so many of the patients.

Nurses were never still. The work was relentless and she had no time to brood. She fell exhausted into her bed and dragged herself from sleep each morning. Even on the rare occasions that she was sitting, her hands were never idle. There were calico shrouds to be sewn, bandages to be rolled, the list was endless.

She had been pleased the day that Sister Elliott had actually praised her, telling her she worked well and had dedication, sound sense and was always calm –

qualities that were always applauded in a good nurse. It was high praise indeed, for Sister Elliott was a hard woman to please.

She and Abbie had become close, something they'd never really been in the past, and Dee found that Abbie was sensible, practical and yet sensitive. There was also a stubborn streak in her that made her work doggedly at the theoretical side of her training, for her education hadn't been of the best.

That November afternoon they had an hour's break for rest and they'd climbed the steep rise of ground known locally as Whalley Nab. It was a rare, crisp afternoon, the air already sharp with frost, the sky a very pale blue and streaked with fingers of blush rose from the cool, hazy sun. The clusters of trees on the river bank and around the church and the abbey gate, were bare and skeletal. The fine tracery of their branches was silhouetted clearly against the pale stones.

'You could almost believe that there wasn't a war on,' Abbie said as she leaned her back against the trunk of a tree and raised her face to the luminous sky.

'I love it here, it's beautiful. It has a sense of peace and stability and, well, history, I suppose,' Dee mused.

'I don't know much about history, I was never really interested in it at school, it seemed a waste of time. After all, everyone's dead, just like the monks that used to live down there.' Abbie inclined her head towards the ruins, silent and dappled in the sunlight.

'They say that the last abbot, Paslaw I think he was called, was hanged from up here when the abbey was sacked.'

Abbie shuddered. 'Oh, Dee, don't be so morbid!'

'There's a history of witchcraft as well. Over on Pendle Hill.' It was Dee's turn to shiver a little as she looked into the distance to where the dark bulk of Pendle Hill rose like a sleeping, hump-backed monster from the green pastures at its foot.

'That is definitely something I don't want to know anything about. For heaven's sake let's change the subject,' Abbie pleaded.

'Have you heard from Mike?'

Abbie nodded. 'He's fine. As fine as anyone can be over there. I wrote and told him about Nancy, and he was so upset. He said if he ever sees Sean Doyle he'll put a bayonet through his guts.'

Dee shuddered again. 'I had a letter from Father. He said things aren't too bad, but he is having to watch Phil like a hawk in case he goes and joins up.'

Abbie sighed. 'They're that desperate, they'll believe anyone.'

'Thank God Phil isn't tall, and he doesn't even look sixteen never mind eighteen. Father also said your mother is starting to get out and about again, but that Joan isn't looking well.'

'Poor Joan, she's got herself well and truly saddled with Terry's mam now, and she's always ailing, although half the time I'm sure it's all put on to get attention. She keeps going on and on about being a poor widow, but she forgets our Joan is, too. She's selfish, she doesn't think Joan should spend so much time with Mam. Of course she took it badly, Terry getting killed; he was all she had.'

They both fell silent, gazing out across the small town below, absorbed in their own thoughts until a figure came hurrying up the hill towards them. It was Tilly Beckett, who worked on the same ward.

'Oh, it's not time to go back yet, is it?' Abbie grumbled as the girl drew nearer.

Dee got to her feet as, red-faced and a little breathless, Tilly came within calling distance.

'You've to come back now!' Tilly shouted.

'What for?' Abbie called back, brushing bits of dead bracken from her skirt.

Dee's heart gave a sudden lurch. 'Oh, God, not more bad news, please,' she prayed.

Tilly had reached them. 'It's your brother, Abbie.'

Dee uttered a cry and clutched Abbie's arm. Her heart had plummeted like a stone. The colour drained from Abbie's face.

'Oh, not our Tommy too!'

'No! I mean yes, he's here! He's just arrived with the new batch of wounded. Come on, he can't wait to see you,' Tilly urged.

Abbie gave a cry of joy and broke into a run, and Dee picked up her long skirts and followed.

When she finally caught up with Abbie it was to see her with her arms around Tommy, who was sitting in a bath chair. He looked much thinner. Oh, so thin and pale and much, much older than the lad she'd last seen marching down Lime Street.

'Dee, it's great to see you. I didn't know you'd be here too. Come on, give us a hug.'

Dee was so relieved that she smiled down at him,

before holding him tightly for a few seconds. 'How is the leg?'

'Oh, it's great now. I'll be as right as rain in a week or two.'

Abbie was fussing around him, tucking the blanket gently over his legs. 'Oh, no, it won't. It's a bad fracture, I believe. You were lucky not to lose your leg.'

'Oh, get her! A proper little Florence Nightingale, ain't she?' Tommy laughed, but he was delighted to see them both. He was overjoyed to be home in 'Blighty', safe for a while at least, and with the added joy of being able to see Abbie and Dee every day.

'Now don't you go rushing to get back over there. You must take things easy,' Abbie urged.

Tommy's expression changed. 'No one in their right mind would want to go back there, never mind "rush" it.'

'Did you see anything of Mike before you left?' Abbie ventured.

'No. I didn't see him again after he helped get me on to the stretcher, but he'll be fine, Abbie, don't you worry. He'll keep his head down.'

'How can I not worry? You don't know what it was like when all those telegrams began arriving. They just kept on coming, hundreds of them, it was awful.'

'I know what it was like only too well, Abbie, luv,' Tommy said quietly, thinking of all his mates and of Norman, Ken and Terry. 'It was a bloody disaster.'

Dee decided it was time to change the subject. 'We'd better leave you to get settled. We're due back on duty and if we're late, Sister Elliott will be livid. I've never met anyone who can get mad so quickly,' she laughed, taking Abbie's arm. 'We'll all have plenty of time to catch up later,' she promised.

She thought she saw a look of relief in Tommy's eyes as she steered Abbie towards the door; perhaps he didn't want to talk about his experiences yet.

The medical care, fresh air, good food (albeit very plain) and peace all had a beneficial effect on Tommy. His leg was healing well the doctors told him, but it was the atmosphere, the peace and tranquillity of the place after the mayhem of the trenches, that had begun to heal his shattered nerves and spirit. He had stopped waking in the night yelling, drenched in sweat and shaking, but he was still often woken by the terror that invaded other men's dreams and held them in its grip.

Sal had made the long journey once, just before Christmas, accompanied by Pat, Bertie, Ginny, Seb and Rose Chatterton. The children had not been allowed inside the hospital, but Dee had begged ten minutes from Sister Elliott on the pretext that Rose was her sister, and had taken them all to the village shop. It was a much quieter, more subdued Sal, Tommy noticed, although he was overjoyed to see her. His da, too, looked more careworn and older, his once-thick dark hair now sparse and grey. They'd chatted on about mundane things, all afraid to mention sons and brothers who wouldn't be coming home. Tommy was determinedly cheerful and made light of the appalling hardships and danger of trench warfare, but when the goodbyes had been said and his parents had left to collect their brood who were waiting outside, he couldn't help but think of the days when they had all squabbled and laughed and sometimes cried together. And he was worried about his mam.

Dee came to sit with him when her shift was over. It was something she'd taken to doing, just as she'd often taken long walks on a Sunday with Jerry Harvey. It had helped Jerry to talk while she listened, and she used the same strategy with Tommy.

'Wasn't it good to see them all?' she said brightly as she sat in a chair next to him in the Day Room.

'Aye, it was. Pity they wouldn't let the kids in though. It's a long way to come and have to wait outside.'

'Oh, they didn't seem to mind too much. It was all an adventure to them, they'd never seen fields and sheep and cows before. They'd never been on a long train journey, either. Well, Rose had, but she couldn't remember it.'

'I never thought of it like that, Dee. But I'm worried about me mam, she's gone, well, quiet like.'

'She's had to change, Tommy. You can't cope with such loss and not change. I know that.'

'I suppose so.'

'She'll be just fine. She's still got the "tribe", as she calls them, to keep her occupied, although she really could do without our Rose as well.'

'Oh, she looks on Rosie as one of her own,' he managed a grin. 'Mind you, Rosie soon lost her "posh" accent that our Joan admired so much. Remember the fuss over Joan's wedding, and Rosie being the bridesmaid?'

Dee also grinned. 'Don't I just? Oh the tantrums we had when the dress had to go back.'

'It was like another world then, wasn't it Dee?'

She nodded.

'Sometimes, well, sometimes I feel so guilty. Guilty that I'm alive and only wounded, and not seriously either. I'll be able to walk again, work again. So many of my mates—'

'Hush. Don't dwell on it,' Dee interrupted. 'I often feel guilty, too,' she added.

Tommy was surprised. 'What about?'

She picked at the hem of her stained apron. 'About Nancy. I'm alive, too. I've got a life ahead of me, she hasn't.'

Cautiously Tommy reached out and took her hand. 'Stop it, Dee. Even if you'd refused, she'd have gone, she was in such a state you wouldn't have talked her out of it.'

Dee gave a wry smile. 'Abbie might have done, though.'

'She might, she's a great girl, our Abbie. I'm dead proud of her.'

'I never realized how practical and good she is. It was her idea that I join the VAD; she even brought me here. I couldn't have coped without her. She knew exactly what I needed.'

'She's like Mam, is Abbie. Or how Mam used to be.'

'Aunty Sal hasn't changed that much, Tommy. She'll bounce back again. She's a survivor.'

'I know, but she's had a rotten life really. There was never much money and we were always wanting and needing things, and me da was always boozing. Then there was our Monica's disgrace, and now losing Ken and Norm.'

'But she's got Joan and Abbie and you to be proud of. And Monica too, now that all turned out well in the end.'

'I just hope our Abbie gets more from life – she deserves it. I hope nothing bloody well happens to Mike Burgess.'

'So do I.'

Tommy realized he was still holding Dee's hand, but she hadn't withdrawn it or commented on it and it was comforting to just sit and talk. He wished he was more educated, then they could discuss things in more detail. 'The doc tells me I should be able to walk almost without a limp eventually.'

'Oh, that's great!'

'I'm doing really well with the crutches now, it's just a matter of getting used to them. They might even let me go home for a bit, when I can walk with a stick.'

Dee sighed, there had been another reason why she'd come to sit with him tonight and she'd been putting it off. 'I won't be here to see that, Tommy,' she said quietly.

'Why not?'

She raised her head and looked directly into his eyes. 'Because Abbie and I are going to the front in January. We're going to a field hospital at Flers.'

'Oh.' Tommy swallowed hard, trying not to think of the appalling conditions in the field hospitals where the nurses and doctors wore tin hats like the troops, and often worked against a background of shell and rifle fire.

Dee squeezed his hand. 'Abbie said she couldn't face telling you, so I promised I would do it. She said she was a coward, but I told her not to be stupid.'

'It's no picnic over there, Dee. It . . . it will change you. It changes everyone. Oh, I haven't got the words, I'm not educated like you, but you seem to become – someone else.'

'We've all been told what to expect. We've had long lectures and photographs on it, but after all, it's what we joined for. We didn't expect to stay here at home in comfort.'

Tommy seemed unable to speak.

'Don't worry about us, we'll manage, and we're of far more use over there than here.'

He at last managed a grin. 'It's just that I'll miss you both. The place won't seem the same without our Abbie bossing me and you fussing over me.'

Dee laughed. 'I don't fuss, do I?'

'Not really, but I'll miss sitting here and talking to you, Dee. You're very easy to talk to,' he said, suddenly shy.

'It goes with the job,' she laughed.

'I know you won't have much time, Dee, but will you write to me?'

'Of course I will.'

'I know I only wrote you a couple of letters, and my writing is rotten, but I'll write more often, I promise. I know how much letters mean when you're over there.'

Dee rose reluctantly and placed a hand on his

shoulder. 'You're going home soon Tommy, you've that to look forward to.'

Tommy released her hand and hoisted himself to his feet with the aid of the crutches. 'I'd better keep at it then, keep walking. Come on, I'll escort you to the door. Will you tell our Abbie to come and see me before you go?'

'I won't need to.'

'Remind her just the same,' Tommy urged, as he watched her walk down the corridor, wishing he had the guts to tell her how he felt about her. Each time he'd tried to muster the courage he just seemed to clam up. He couldn't find the right words, he was so clumsy. There were ways of doing these things – he'd just mess it up and make a fool of himself. He was so afraid she would laugh at him or reject his advances with that quiet, aloof manner that he'd witnessed a couple of times when she'd been angry. He couldn't stand that. No, better to say nothing; that way, there would be no humiliating rejection.

'Dee!' he called and she turned around. 'Dee, take care of yourself.'

She smiled. 'I will, Tommy. I will.'

They were given a day's leave to go home and see their families, but Abbie wasn't looking forward to it and her steps got slower as she walked down Burlington Street.

'I wish they'd sent us straight off; it's going to be hard seeing the look on Mam's face. I know what she'll be thinking.'

'Tell them quickly and simply and then say how safe it is, how far back from the front line the hospitals are,' Dee advised.

'I'll tell them how well our Tommy's doing and that he'll be allowed home soon; that will cheer them up and take their minds off me. Call for me, Dee, on the way back and we'll go and see Jerry.'

Dee gave her an encouraging smile and a gentle push and watched Abbie take a deep breath and walk through the Kerrigans' ever-open door.

Bridie greeted Dee with pleased surprise and Dee took off her coat and hung it up. Elizabeth gave a shriek of joy and hurled herself bodily at Dee.

'You didn't tell us you were coming! I wanted you to come home, Dee. I wanted it ever so much.'

Dee hugged her. 'I know you did, but I couldn't. Well, I'm home now and we're going to have a wonderful night together, I promise. Now let me sit down and talk to your mother.'

Dee disentangled herself and Elizabeth went off to inform her friends of the news.

'Don't you look just great,' Bridie said, openly admiring the lilac-and-white check dress with the small white collar and cuffs, the stiff white apron that had a red cross sewn on the bib front, and the starched, short, scarf-like cap that covered Dee's hair.

Dee kissed her on the cheek. 'We're only home for a few hours. I couldn't bring myself to tell Elizabeth that. We're off to France tomorrow.'

'You're a brave girl, Dee,' Bridie said proudly as she filled the kettle.

Dee busied herself with the cups. 'No I'm not. I'm terrified.'

'What of, the guns?'

'No, strangely enough. It's just that I'm afraid that I won't be able to cope.'

Bridie set the kettle on the hob and then laid her hands on Dee's shoulders. 'Dee, you've coped with far worse things in your life. Losing everything and coming to Liverpool. Losing your mam – and our Nance.'

Dee bowed her head at the mention of Nancy, yet she sensed in Bridie a calm acceptance.

'I'll never get over it, not properly. I know that time heals, I've known grief before, and Edward is so kind— But that's enough of that. Let's not ruin your few hours at home. I tell you what, take Elizabeth down to Hilda's and get some cakes or biscuits. We'll have a bit of a celebration tea, and she'll be glad to see you.'

Hilda was serving Lizzie Simcock and they both smiled broadly as Dee and Elizabeth entered the shop.

'Dee, don't you look very professional! I take it they've let you come home before they pack you off over there?' Hilda said.

Dee nodded at Hilda. 'That's right. How are you Mrs Simcock? How's Mary?'

'Oh, she's still working in munitions and earning a small fortune, not that I see much of it.' Lizzie sniffed, her features returning to their usual sour expression. There had been more rows over Mary's wages than she'd had hot dinners. 'She's always dressing herself up and going out. Soon got over poor Norman Kerrigan.

Oh, she'll always be flighty will that one. I don't know where I went wrong.'

'Is there anyone special?' Dee asked, more to stop Lizzie from launching into a lengthy diatribe about Mary's faults, although she was glad to hear that Mary seemed to have overcome her grief.

'Oh, no, although there's not much to choose from these days.' Lizzie shook her head sadly.

'Have you heard from Mike?' Dee asked Hilda.

'Michael is fine, the last I heard anyway, thank God. I'll serve you first, Lizzie won't mind. Not that I've got much to offer you, those damned U-boats are crippling everyone.'

'Then I suppose it's too much to ask have you any biscuits or cake?'

'Oh, I think I can manage a bit of both, for a special occasion.'

'Elizabeth will choose.' Dee smiled down at the child, whose fair curls were tied up with a ribbon in a style that reminded her of her own hair when she'd been seven, except that her hair had been straight.

Lizzie grimaced disapprovingly. 'Oh, aye, she'll choose. Spoiled rotten she is.'

'Well, there's more money around these days. Things aren't as bad as they used to be, money-wise at least,' Hilda remarked.

Dee turned as the shop bell clanged and Hannah Harvey entered. 'Hello, Hannah.'

'Dee, I hardly recognized you,' Hannah said in her die-away tone.

'How is Jerry?'

Hannah's expression changed and Dee thought she looked very guarded. 'Oh, he has his good days and his bad days.'

Hilda was weighing out biscuits but, catching Dee's eye, shook her head.

'We were going to call and see him.'

'Oh . . . er . . .' Hannah seemed lost for words.

'Is it not a good day, Hannah?' Dee pressed.

'No. Not really, he's very down.' Hannah couldn't bring herself to say to Dee that she would be shocked by the change in Jerry, that the disease was twisting his spine, causing his back to hunch. 'I wish, I wish I could join the VAD.' The words came out in a rush.

Hilda's eyebrows shot up. 'You, Hannah?'

'Yes me, Mrs Burgess. I'm old enough and I'd like to do my bit, but, well . . . I'm needed at home. Mam would find it hard without me.'

Hilda said nothing, thinking it was the longest speech she'd ever heard Hannah make.

'Will you tell Jerry that I was asking after him and that Abbie was too? We'll try and write.'

'There, that will be threepence,' Hilda said briskly.

'Can I have a toffee apple?' Elizabeth interrupted, tugging at Dee's skirt.

'No, you can't. Don't be greedy, miss!' Hilda retorted.

'You'll get all sticky and then your mother will be cross with me,' Dee laughed.

'Please, Dee?' Elizabeth cajoled, eager as always to sense and exploit Dee's fondness for her.

'Oh, all right, seeing as I'm going away.'

Hilda shook her head and Lizzie tutted as the sticky confection was handed over. Hilda waved away the coins Dee held out. 'Keep it, Dee, now off you go, girl, take care of yourself and God bless you.'

As the shop bell tinkled Hilda sighed. 'It's a terrible world we live in, Hannah, when our young lasses have to go to such places now, risking their lives and being forced to see things no girl should ever have to see.'

Hannah looked after Dee wistfully; even with all the danger and the horror, she was sure it couldn't be much worse than home and what she had to put up with.

Hilda was serving Lizzie and both women were too wrapped up in their own thoughts to see the look of utter despair in Hannah Harvey's eyes.

Chapter Twenty-One

———◆———

MARCH. MARCH. MARCH. THE word beat repetitively in Sean's mind. All they ever seemed to do was bloody well march. That, or wait shivering in the trenches or sweltering under a burning sun, plagued by flies – flies that lived and bred on the bodies of dead men. They all waited for the sudden death that rained down from artillery and machine guns. For the thousandth time he wished he'd never set foot in this blasted country. Never let himself be coerced into joining up. He should have stuck it out, no matter how many white feathers or taunts he'd received. Better all that than being here. There was no glory, or what there had been of it – a couple of march pasts – had been short-lived. All the illusions had been shattered as soon as they'd disembarked and had begun the long journey to the front. They were the reserve battalion, but that hadn't stopped their ranks being decimated. They were cannon-fodder like everyone else.

Ahead of him stretched lines of men in khaki. Not

straight ranks marching with shoulders back and heads high, but weary men; dispirited and disillusioned men. The poplars that lined the road in double banks had once been straight and stately, their leaves rustling in the wind, now they were blasted and twisted; the battle for Sanctuary Wood had seen to that. The battle for Pitkem Ridge was behind them, and, if he lived to be a hundred, he would never forget it.

They had been given targets, objectives, the Blue Line, the Black Line, the Green Line, bloody stupid names he'd thought. The Black Line actually crossed the Menin Road, and it was a nightmare of noise, confusion and carnage. They'd come up against a large area of uncut wire, but finally someone had managed to find a gap – a gap that was to be fatal for so many, for as fast as they'd tried to push through, they'd been cut down, like targets at a shooting gallery.

There had even been talk that some of the men, led by a Second Lieutenant Graham, had been killed by fire from a British tank. No one ever seemed to get it right. No one seemed to know what the hell they were doing. Forwards and backwards they went, like a human yo-yo. Gaining, losing and regaining land that was nothing more than a blood-soaked quagmire. Moving up the line was virtually impossible. Men had drowned in the glutinous slime. It was certain death if you strayed off the track: the weight of your pack dragged you down.

The straps of his pack, rifle and gas mask cut into his shoulders and added to his discomfort. How much further did they have to go along this pitted, rain-sodden track before they reached the assembly trenches? How many more hours before they could rest? He turned and looked backwards through the drizzle. The landscape was grey, totally without colour. Not a blade of grass, not a leaf. Nothing but the grey mud and deep, water-filled craters. It was like the surface of the moon, but with, here and there, a shattered tree or the remains of a building, nothing more than a fallen pile of stones. Now there was nothing recognizable, no houses, barns, churches or even hedgerows broke the flat plane of the horizon. Then a flash of bright colour caught his attention and he narrowed his eyes and focused on a group of men standing on a slight incline by the roadside. 'Who the hell are they?' he asked of no one in particular.

'Who?' the man beside him asked half-heartedly.

'That lot, over there. Officers they are. Would you look at the bloody cut of them! Clean as a whistle they are. All gold braid and red epaulettes. Not a spot of dirt or bloody mud on them.'

His comrade became interested and suddenly straightened his shoulders and held his head up. 'Smarten yourself up, lad,' he hissed.

'What the hell for?'

Sean's gaze rested on the group and he felt anger begin to burn inside him. Oh, it was just great for them to stand and stare at them. The poor, stupid eejits, and loyal to a man. Why should he show any sign of military correctness? Soft beds, good food, warm fires and safety were commodities that would be provided for them. Well, this wasn't *his* war. It wasn't *his* King or *his* bloody country.

He'd given them nearly two years of his life, and that was long enough. Two years and some of the most savage fighting – and with barely a scratch – it was a miracle, but his luck couldn't hold out for ever. One day soon his number would be up and that would be that. He should have been with Connolly, Pearce and Clarke and the others who'd risen in arms in Dublin at Easter last year. They'd fought and died for freedom for Ireland and, if he had to die at all, it would be better to have done so for the country he'd been born in. He kept his thoughts to himself as they passed on, but he'd made a firm decision.

By the time they had reached the assembly trenches it had begun to rain heavily and the already sodden ground was a morass, a quagmire of sucking, treacherous mud. They stood knee-deep in water, leaning against the dripping walls of the trench. Waterproof capes that only half covered them were pulled up around their ears, but the rain still trickled down their necks. He couldn't feel his feet but maybe that was a blessing, he thought as anger and resentment deepened. At the first opportunity he was getting out. He was going to get as far away from all this as was humanly possible. Just how he was going to achieve this he didn't know, but he'd find a way. Oh, he'd find a bloody way out or die trying.

'Have you heard anything from that girl of yours lately, Mick?'

Sean's thoughts were interrupted by 'Chalky' White. A tall, thin, country lad from Ormskirk.

'My name's Sean, can't you remember that for

Christ's sake and no I haven't heard from her or anyone for months!' he snapped.

'Don't bite my bleeding head off, I was only trying to cheer you up.'

'I don't want cheering up. What the hell is there to be so bloody cheerful about?'

Chalky shrugged and turned away, seeking more amiable company. He was an optimist by nature, although these days he was sorely pressed to keep his spirits up.

His words had reminded Sean of Nancy and those memories he wanted to forget. He'd never been good at letters, but he'd replied to all hers. He'd even looked forward to them until *that* one had arrived. He could still feel the sense of shock when he'd read that she was pregnant. Panic had swept over him. She couldn't be. She just couldn't be, he'd thought. It wasn't his. It was someone else's, had been his next line of reasoning, but that hadn't worked. He knew Nancy was faithful to him.

He'd waited, hoping another letter would come telling him it was all a mistake. When the letter did arrive it had only confirmed his fears and, bad though things were here, he'd had no intention of marrying her. He'd never even considered it before the war started. If he came through this nightmare in one piece it wasn't to tie himself down with Nancy and a horde of kids. He'd almost been tempted to reply to her second, pleading letter, but he'd restrained himself. What did she expect him to do anyway? Up and leave and go home and marry her? She'd be all right in the end.

Look at Monica Kerrigan. Nancy wouldn't become a nun, at least he didn't think so, but she'd go to a convent and when it was all over she'd go home and in a while it would all be forgotten. He wasn't going to admit to anything.

Then had come Hilda's letter and a terrible shock. Nancy was dead – at the hands of an abortionist – and Hilda blamed him. She made no bones about it, nor about how he would be treated if he ever went back to Burlington Street. Why had Nancy done such a thing? He'd felt a pang of guilt. Maybe he should have written, but how was he to know she would go and try to get rid of it? Then there had been that very unpleasant interview with Captain Moorfield. He'd been furious that Hilda had written to the man, and he'd managed to lie about it all and blacken Nancy's name into the bargain. He'd sworn she'd slept with half the street. He wondered what else Hilda had put in her letter, and in a way he'd been glad when Moorfield had been killed, for he'd often seen the man looking at him speculatively. He dug his hands deeper into his pockets and tried to get comfortable. He desperately needed to sleep, on his feet if need be. He didn't want to be reminded about Nancy or Hilda Burgess or anyone from Burlington Street. He'd spent months trying to forget them all.

The artillery barrage started early next morning and went on all day until early evening. They had had no sleep, for supplies had been moved up even before the cannonade began. At half-past six the whistles shrilled and the attack began. Sean gritted his teeth; this was the last time he'd jump to their command. As he stumbled over the parapet of the trench, Lyddite shrapnel burst all around him, lighting the darkening sky with yellow flashes. Men beside him just disappeared. Bits of bone and flesh rained from the sky and adhered to his uniform.

As darkness fell, it became apparent that the attack had degenerated into a complete shambles. Those men who had not fallen in the first two waves had realized that the advance was useless and had started to fall back, colliding and merging with those behind still trying to press forward. The entire mêlée was being cut down ruthlessly by the murderous machine gun fire from the enemy trenches.

He jumped into a shell crater and tried to think. Ahead of him a shell burst, sending a shower of earth high into the sky, tossing the body of a soldier, already dead, his legs missing, to land a few inches away from him. Sean fell to his knees with exhaustion and horror. No one even seemed to know where the German front line was. Men fell screaming, or were simply blown to pieces, and many had been taken prisoner; he supposed they were the fortunate ones. Even Captain Laird had been captured, and he had the payroll. The bloody fool had wandered into enemy lines. If there was such a place as hell, then this was certainly as close to it as he would want to come. He'd had enough. They could keep their bloody war. Now was his chance. He wouldn't be missed in such total chaos, or they'd think he'd been captured. All he had to do was keep clear of the Hun. If he could manage to get behind the British front line, or what passed for it, he could crawl away in the darkness. He'd make his way back towards the road, although he'd keep off it. He'd crawl alongside it and somehow he'd get away.

He'd managed to reach the road and was, he hoped, heading north, away from the guns, the screams and the infernal pandemonium. Then as he gingerly raised his head there was a blinding flash of light and he felt himself being lifted bodily from the ground and hurled into a black chasm.

He came to twice. The first time he saw the faint, pale outline of the sun above him in the sky and then it was night again and the moon shed a watery light over him and there was silence, such a peaceful, blissful silence that he drifted off again.

Dee worked feverishly. In the time she'd been at Number 23 General Camp Hospital at Zillebeke, she'd never known a slack moment. There were always wounded men to treat. Men with major wounds, minor wounds, infections, diseases. There was always a steady stream, but when she'd heard the artillery barrage begin in earnest she'd known that the flow would become a tide.

She hated the sustained bombardment, it stretched her already taut nerves further, and she tried not to think about the flood of casualties that would come in when it ceased. She knew it was done to cut the barbed wire and hopefully save lives. It made everyone tense, and tempers were frayed. It had gone on for so long and the number of dead and wounded was so enormous that it defied belief.

There was never much time to think about home. She scribbled a few lines as often as she could, and she still wrote to Tommy. His letters, though, were infrequent, for he was back in action and the mails in France were spasmodic, depending on the lines of communication. There was very little time to eat, sleep or to wash and yet they all tried to keep up certain standards. She had long ago abandoned the stiff white apron, cuffs and cap. Over her dress she wore an army greatcoat, on her head a tin hat.

There were times when she felt a burning, helpless rage at the blind stupidity of all men on both sides: those who led and those who followed, those who commanded and those who obeyed. Then there were times when her heart was almost broken with the pity of it all. Most of the time she was just tired. Sleep was snatched and often broken. Even when she was relieved of her duties for a week and sent back to a billet in St Eloi and had the luxuries of hot baths and a proper bed, her sleep was troubled. During her first day under fire she'd been violently sick and then thoroughly ashamed of her behaviour, until Sister Chapman had told her that she had fainted the first time she'd had to deal with the great tide of horrendous casualties.

It was impossible to believe that these men had been young, healthy soldiers. They were like bundles, labelled and wrapped in dirty, blood-stained khaki. Field dressings, sometimes twelve hours old, sodden with blood and caked in filth, adhered to terrible wounds. She'd worked beside doctors and experienced, qualified nurses, picking fragments of bone from gaping wounds, cleaning the oozing yellow pus from torn flesh, helping to lift men with mangled, mutilated limbs from stretchers stiff with drying blood and dirt. With lips firmly pressed together, she'd handed instruments for amputation to doctors covered, like herself, in blood, dirt and the stinking, putrid matter of infected wounds.

When she had time to think, she realized that of all the torment, pity and agony she felt for these men, it was the humiliation of those labels that affected her most. In the horrendous conditions of the Field Dressing Stations, to which some men had even crawled and hobbled, the cards were necessary. On them had been scrawled a vague description of the wound. The words head, shoulder, stomach, leg, were written down with the soldier's name and unit, then the card was slipped into a waxed envelope and tied with string through a button-hole. It wasn't right, she thought bitterly. It reduced men to things of no importance. A parcel, an object, a word written on a piece of card. It robbed them totally of any dignity they had left.

Abbie was on a different shift, but often, when the whole shift system was abandoned because of incoming wounded, they worked side by side and they usually spent some time together when they had leave.

'Are you ready, Nurse Chatterton?' Sister Chapman's voice broke into Dee's reverie.

'As ready as I can be, Sister. If only we had more beds, more blankets, more dressings.'

'We have sufficient to begin with, and supplies are on the way. It takes time, Nurse, you should know that by now. The weather doesn't help much either.'

Dee agreed silently, although there wasn't much to choose between days and nights of rain, or days and nights of frost and sleet. She always seemed to be cold. She knew that the sun did shine here. It had blazed down during the summer and she'd cursed it, for the flies had been insufferable. Now she longed to feel its warmth on her tired and aching back.

She was on her knees, dressing the wound of a young soldier who'd been shot in the chest. He sat against the wall, half turned towards her. At first she'd only seen the small hole in his chest and had quickly cleaned it and covered it with a pad of lint, but his breath was still coming in gurgling, bubbling gasps and she knew something was wrong. Gently she turned him towards her and then groaned. In his back was a hole she could have fitted her fist into. The lung was torn and collapsed. She reached for a long swab and packed it into the hole, then bandaged it tightly. It was all she could do until a doctor could see to it properly. Her hands and apron were covered in blood and it smeared her face, for she'd wiped away the perspiration from her forehead with the back of one hand. She got to her feet and turned to the nearest doctor.

'Shrapnel wounds in the shoulder and leg, and maybe some internal injuries, and he's half frozen. God knows how long he was lying out there!' he barked.

All around her men were being brought in on stretchers and their cries and curses filled the close-packed room, but she was staring down in horror at the face of the soldier the doctor was already working on. She uttered a cry of shock, her hand going to her mouth.

'What in God's name is the matter, Nurse?' The harassed doctor barked the question at her.

'I'm sorry, sir. I can't . . . I know this man and I can't help him.'

'Don't be a bloody fool, girl. This is no time for hysterics! You're not green, you're a veteran for God's sake!'

Dee clenched her hands tightly together. She must appear to be calm. 'I'm not hysterical, sir. I'm perfectly calm, but this man – helped to kill my stepsister.'

The doctor stared at her and then nodded curtly. 'Get someone else, but be quick about it. You can explain yourself later.'

Thankfully Dee turned away and caught the arm of Tilly Beckett who was cutting away the blood-soaked sleeve of an equally stained jacket on the soldier in the next bed. 'Tilly, swap with me, please? It's all right, I've got permission. I'll explain later. I'll take over here.' She was thankful that Tilly didn't argue but immediately went to help with Sean Doyle's wounds.

When at last she got a few minutes to rest, Dee went outside into the bitingly cold night. The stars looked huge in the inky black sky and there was a milky white rim around the moon that foretold a heavy frost. Only now could she give way to her emotions, and as exhaustion and anger swept over her she began to tremble. She hated him. As much as she had it in her nature to hate anyone, she hated Sean Doyle.

All the memories came flooding back to tear at her heart. Nancy – the laughing, carefree young girl – the night they'd gone for a ride on the ferry, after Bridie and Father had been married. Nancy, who had shared her revulsion at the shock of Bridie's pregnancy and her delight when Elizabeth had actually been born and had changed their lives for the better. Nancy, who had stuck by Sean loyally when he'd refused to join the army and Nancy, so proud of him the day he'd marched to Lime Street Station, following in the steps of Norman and Ken Kerrigan and Tommy and Mike. Nancy, her face drawn, her eyes haunted as she'd waited for a reply to her letters, a reply that never came. And Nancy, so drained of blood and dying on that terrible, terrible morning. And he was responsible for that. He'd killed Nancy almost as surely as if he'd cut the child from her and left her to die. She was unaware that the tears were pouring down her cheeks or that she was shaking uncontrollably.

'He deserves to die. He doesn't deserve any help, help that could have been given to someone else.' She said the words aloud, oblivious that she'd done so. Nancy had been so dear to her, surely it was only right that she take revenge, for Nancy's sake.

She turned and walked slowly back into the ward that was quiet now and in semi-darkness, the oil lamps giving out a soft, warm glow. She walked quietly between the beds, so utterly calm, so icily cold. Then she saw him, his face turned from her and in shadow. He doesn't deserve to live, she told herself over and over again as her hand reached out to grasp a scalpel that lay on the instrument tray on the night table. The nurse on duty was sitting at the far end of the room, engrossed in writing a letter for the young soldier whose head was swathed in bandages. He'd make no sound. She would be quick and quiet. She knew enough about anatomy now not to make it messy. She had no thought for the consequences, only that this was something she must do. Her fingers closed around the thin cold steel instrument, but then she hesitated. A small voice whispered in her head, a half-remembered verse from the Bible: 'Vengeance is mine, saith the Lord.' She silenced it. She wouldn't listen to it. This was for Nancy.

'Don't do it, Dee. He's not worth it,' Abbie said softly, her fingers covering Dee's as she firmly prised the scalpel from Dee's hand.

'Abbie – he killed her!'

'I know, but he's not worth your being hanged for his murder. Your life is too precious to waste on him, Dee. With any luck he'll die without our help. I heard them say he's lost a lot of blood. Come away. Leave him.' Gently Abbie placed her arm around Dee's shoulder and led her out. Then she held her as Dee sobbed hysterically against her shoulder. And Abbie cried, too. For Nancy, for her brothers and for all the boys she'd nursed who had died, but there was not a single tear for Sean Doyle.

Chapter Twenty-Two

———— ◆ ————

THROUGH THE WINDOW JERRY watched the dark clouds that scudded across the March sky in a long, undulating ribbon. They were like a murky grey river threading its way between dreary, wintry fields. The sight depressed him, but these days he was always depressed and often exhausted. The disease was exacting a heavy toll. Now his spine was becoming bent and he walked like an old man. Not that he could walk very far.

Everyone was at the front, even Dee and Abbie, for the casualties were so high. Despite that, and everything he'd heard and read in the newspapers, he would have swapped with Mike and Tommy and even Sean Doyle any day. Hannah had told him about her encounter with Dee in the shop, before Dee had gone to France. Hannah had been so impressed and envious of Dee, for he knew that his sister wanted to be a nurse, too. He couldn't blame her, it would be an escape from this house. Hannah had been so good to him. She even risked Da's anger and got him a half bottle of whisky occasionally from Red. It was all that kept him going when things got too bad. They'd told him at the hospital that they might have to amputate his arm, but then they changed their minds and he was grateful. It hadn't really shocked him, for it seemed as though he was impervious now to all traumas.

'How is it now, luv?' Winnie asked, putting another cushion behind his back, knowing from experience that she would receive perhaps only a grunt in response to her question.

'It's all right, Mam.'

Winnie busied herself setting the table; Abe would be in soon and he liked his meal to be ready. The room was spotless, as usual. The range was black-leaded, the brasses gleaming in the firelight. The floor had been scrubbed and the rag rugs were clean, as were the cushions and curtains.

'Mam, do you think Da would let our Hannah join the VAD?' Jerry asked suddenly.

Winnie was startled. 'The VAD, like Dee Chatterton and Abbie Kerrigan? Why would she want to do that?'

'Oh, Mam, can't you see it's her only chance to escape from all this . . . and me. I know it upsets her terribly me being like this.'

Winnie was shocked. 'Jerry, don't talk like that. You know your sister is very fond of you and what does she want to escape from?'

'She's always been kept in. She was never allowed out in the street to play with the other kids. Now he won't even let her go out to work. He says she's got to nurse me. It's not normal, Mam, and it's not fair. She's had no life at all. Why does he do it? Oh, I know he's fond of her, but sometimes I wonder if he's trying to keep her from talking to people. But why?'

'Jerry, stop all this nonsense. Your da wouldn't approve of Hannah going away to be a nurse.'

Jerry's temper rose, something that happened frequently now. 'I'm sick of hearing that word, Mam. He doesn't approve of anything. I don't know why he doesn't just become a hermit, then he wouldn't have to mix with anyone tainted by the things he doesn't approve of.'

'Jerry, don't talk about your da like that, please. He's a good man.'

'Oh, aye, when the mood takes him, but he's not been generous or kind to us. He keeps you short of money. You have to beg him for anything extra. He's never been interested in me. He's never cared what I thought, what I wanted. Hannah and me have never been able to turn to him for help or comfort. We're all just chattels, Mam.'

Winnie went on with her work. 'We're all souls to be saved, Jerry.'

'Saved from what? We're never given the chance to do anything. Look at the way he has always belted us. Other kids got hidings, but nothing like what we got or never so often. And he hits you, Mam, I know that. You try so hard to hide it from us, but we know, Hannah and I.'

'He never means it, Jerry, and he is always so sorry

afterwards. He spends hours down on his knees begging forgiveness, beating his breast. He really believes that there is a demon inside him at times, sent to torment him.' Lately she'd wondered about Abe's sanity for, as Jerry's condition worsened, so Abe's violence increased, followed by the black, remorseful moods.

Jerry didn't reply but had decided that he had nothing to lose. He was going to try to get Hannah her chance of freedom, the chance of a normal life, if working in the middle of a battlefield could be called normal.

Abe had had a bad day. The river had been rough, with a force eight blowing in from the estuary, and time and again the tug's bow line had almost snapped as the *Aquitania*'s stern had swung out into the river. It had taken hours to get her into the sheltered water of the Canada dock, where her cargo of wounded men could be taken off. He was wet and chilled to the bone.

Jerry wanted nothing to eat, he ate very little these days for he had no appetite. He decided not to beat about the bush. 'Da, will you give your consent to Hannah joining the Voluntary Aid Detachment?'

Hannah dropped her fork and it clattered noisily on her plate. Winnie's eyes widened with shock and fear at the suddenness of Jerry's demand, and she tried to catch her son's eye.

Abe glared around at his family. 'Is this something you've all been plotting behind my back?' he demanded.

'No, Da. I . . . never said . . . anything . . .' Hannah's denials faltered.

'She didn't, but it's something she desperately wants to do,' Jerry pressed.

Winnie at last caught his eye and shot him a warning look, but Jerry ignored it. He wasn't afraid of his da now, for what was there to fear? He was facing far worse prospects than his da's anger. He was determined that Hannah was going to get her wish.

'She isn't going. It's not fitting for her to see men in such conditions.'

Jerry's temper flared. 'What do you mean "in such conditions"? Men wounded, dying and needing all the help they can get. You're no Christian for all your bible thumping! You're no good Samaritan, because you'd pass by, and you're making Hannah pass by, too!'

'Don't you dare to quote the holy book at me. She'll be forced to see men undressed! She'll see and do things no chaste girl—'

'Don't be such a bloody hypocrite!' Jerry interrupted. 'It's all a show with you, you're an out-and-out hypocrite. You rant at us to "love thy neighbour" when all you ever really think about is yourself. *Your* rules and regulations. What *you* want. What *you* say. When have you ever "turned the other cheek"? All you do is belt us, and you hit Mam, too. She's tried to hide it but I'm not stupid. She's terrified of you and so is our Hannah. Well, you're not going to keep our Hannah here. She's going.'

Abe's face had gone a deep, ugly shade of puce, and uttering a bellow like a wounded bull, he sprang to his feet, sending his chair tumbling backwards.

Winnie and Hannah cowered together. In an instant

Abe had moved around the table. Jerry had also risen, his face scarlet, his body shaking with a fury the like of which he'd never experienced before.

'She's going! She's getting out of this hell-hole, she's put up with enough from you!' Jerry yelled.

Abe lashed out and the blow sent Jerry reeling across the room. Pain exploded in his jaw and a red mist swam before his eyes. He shook his head to clear his vision, and when he could focus his gaze alighted on the heavy brass poker on the hearth nearby. He staggered to his feet, the weakness of his ailing body forgotten as strength flooded through him, accompanied by wave after wave of anger. With his good arm he raised the poker and swung it in an arc. Both Winnie and Hannah began to scream as the poker smashed Abe's collarbone. Jerry had been aiming at his father's head but had missed. Abe roared in pain, but with a huge effort Jerry had raised the poker again.

'Mam! Mam! Stop him, he'll kill Da! Stop him Mam!' Hannah screamed.

Winnie knew she was powerless, so, snatching up her shawl, she ran from the room. Her hair had come loose from its pins, and her shawl flapped about her as she wrenched open the shop door. 'Hilda! Hilda! For God's sake come quickly. It's Jerry—'

Hilda was momentarily stunned by Winnie's appearance, and it was Frank who took Winnie's arm.

'Winnie, what's the matter? What's going on?'

'Come quickly, please, Jerry's going to kill Abe! He's got the poker! He's like a madman! Oh, God, please, hurry!'

Hilda immediately ran into the back and returned, dragging a mystified and protesting Chrissie behind her. The shop door stood wide open and Frank had already gone, racing down the street with Winnie a few steps behind him.

'You stay here! I'm going up to the Harveys and don't you dare follow me!' Hilda instructed Chrissie.

When Hilda arrived, out of breath and red-faced, she was shocked to the core. Furniture had been overturned. Dishes lay smashed to smithereens on the floor. Hannah was standing clutching the overmantel, and she was shaking and crying. Abe was lying half across the table with blood pouring from the side of his head; Hilda could see he was badly hurt. Jerry was slumped in the rocker, the poker discarded, his shirt spattered with blood. His face was grey and haggard and his eyes dulled with pain.

'He'll have to go to hospital,' Frank had quickly pulled himself together and had examined Abe's head. 'He needs an ambulance. Hannah, go and get the police.'

'No!' Winnie cried. 'No, they'll take Jerry away!'

Frank couldn't argue with her and Jerry looked gravely ill himself. 'Go for Doctor Wallace then, Hannah, and tell him to hurry!'

Hannah gathered her wits and fled.

'What happened, Winnie? Why did he do it?' Frank asked, as Hilda eased Winnie into a chair.

'It was all over Hannah wanting to join the VAD. Oh, Hilda, it was terrible! Abe refused and then Jerry

began to yell at him and Abe hit him, and . . . then—'
Winnie dissolved into tears of shock.

Hilda looked at Frank, who shook his head with
disbelief. What had possessed Jerry and – more to the
point – where had he got the strength? He looked as
though he couldn't raise his arm, never mind a poker.
In fact he looked as bad as Abe did. God, what a mess!
Jerry had obviously been provoked beyond endurance,
and as for Abe – well, Frank couldn't understand a man
who proclaimed to all and sundry the teachings of the
Bible and then struck his own son who was obviously
not long for this world. He'd never liked Abe Harvey.
He was a cruel, despotic man and he'd always thought
his religious rantings bordered on lunacy.

Hilda had done what she could to comfort Winnie,
and Frank had cleaned up some of the mess before the
doctor arrived. Abe's face was deathly white, his left
arm hung loosely at his side. Jerry was sitting
motionless in the chair; he hadn't said a word.

Doctor Wallace was also very shocked at such
violence in what he had always considered to be one of
the better homes, the more refined families in his
practice. He examined Abe while Frank relayed to him
the circumstances that had caused such an explosion of
violence.

Doctor Wallace shook his head. 'You should have
sent someone straight to the hospital for the
ambulance. It might be too late now.'

Winnie uttered a scream.

'Oh, dear God, you don't mean . . .?' Hilda voiced
Winnie's thoughts.

'I'm afraid so. I think he's going to die. I'm sorry.'

'Jerry! Jerry!' Winnie choked.

'The lad is ill, and was driven beyond the bounds of restraint, from what you've told me,' the doctor replied.

'They won't take that into consideration, doctor, you know that,' Frank said gravely.

'I know, and sometimes it's barbaric, but it's the law. If Mr Harvey dies they'll exact the maximum penalty.'

Frank looked at Jerry with pity. Jail would kill him before the hangman's noose.

Doctor Wallace had left a sedative for Jerry, Winnie and Hannah, but both Winnie and Hannah had refused to take it. Winnie went with Abe to Stanley Hospital and returned two hours later, with the police.

Hilda had stayed, but as soon as she saw Winnie she went and put her arms around the distraught woman. 'Oh, Winnie, luv, I'm sorry. I'm so sorry.'

Hannah had got Jerry to bed and had taken him a cup of tea and the laudanum. 'Drink this up and get some sleep. I know you did it for me.' Hannah bit her lip, thinking it was all her fault. He'd done it for her. He'd done it so she could escape from this house, from fear and beatings.

'You've got to get out of this house, Hannah, and have a normal life. You'll both be rid of him now,' Jerry had said tiredly.

'Stop it! Stop it, Jerry!' Hannah had pleaded.

'There's nothing much they can do to me, Hannah. Hang me, lock me up, it doesn't matter now. I've not got much longer.'

She'd burst into tears and gripped his hand until he'd fallen asleep. She'd sobbed quietly until Sergeant Harris had come into the room, when she'd realized that Da must be dead.

The sergeant had said nothing, but had looked closely at Jerry and had then gone back downstairs.

'I'll have to leave a man here. He'll wait until . . .'

Winnie looked up with red and swollen eyes. 'You're going to take him, aren't you?'

'I'll have to Mrs Harvey, it's my job, it's the law. I'm sorry. There's been enough heartache in this street already, and I'm truly sorry.'

Both Dee and Abbie had studiously avoided Sean. They had made their position clear to Sister Chapman, who managed to rearrange her rotas, but they were relieved when he left for England. They were both due for home leave next month, and it couldn't come quickly enough, Dee thought. She often tried to picture home, but she'd been away so long and things had changed so much that it was difficult.

'An English spring, it's hard to imagine, isn't it? Green trees, green grass, flowers, houses and churches without walls missing or great gaping holes in the roof,' she said to Abbie.

'And no mud or the smell of blood, dirt and the stink of gangrene.'

'No lice or fleas,' Dee interrupted scratching. They all fought a constant battle against vermin.

'The only trouble is, will we want to come back to all this?' Abbie gestured with her hand to encompass the wasteland that stretched before them as they sat on the porch of the hospital building. The air was still chilly, but it was clean air, better than the stench inside, as Dee had said.

Dee's gaze rested on the long column of soldiers who were filing past. There were young, fresh faces amongst them, but most of them had the weary look of battle hardiness, and a few were limping. 'Here's the next lot. Like sheep to the slaughter.'

'That's just what they are, Dee. Oh, God, is it never going to end? Will they only stop when they've run out of men on both sides? Will it only end when there's no one left fit to fight? Oh, I'm sorry, Dee, I broke the rule.'

There was an unwritten, unspoken rule that they never gave way to such thoughts, but seeing those men had cracked Abbie's resolve. So many of them would be back here soon, maimed and horribly mutilated, that it wasn't hard to let her anger override her self-control.

Dee was getting to her feet, her face screwed up in a frown.

'What's the matter?' Abbie was also on her feet as a soldier broke ranks.

'It's Tommy. I'm sure it's Tommy.'

Abbie's heart turned over as she saw that Dee was right. It only seemed like last week when she'd left him in Whalley, and yet it was two years ago.

They both hugged him. 'I didn't expect to see you here,' Abbie said.

'I knew *you* were here. As we've pushed on, you've moved up with us. We've been at Arras, but now we're needed for the push to Mons. You both look great.'

'Apart from being asleep on our feet and having forgotten what a normal life is like,' Dee answered, smiling warmly at Tommy. She was so happy to see him.

'We had Sean Doyle here. He was wounded in the leg and shoulder, and nearly died of the cold and loss of blood,' Abbie informed him.

Tommy's face changed. 'It would have been better for everyone if he had bloody well died. Is he still here?'

'No, he's gone.' It was Dee who answered.

'Where?'

'He's gone home.'

'If he has the nerve to set foot in Burlington Street he'll be lynched,' Tommy said grimly.

'Oh, let's not waste time on him. Have you heard from everyone?'

'I got a letter from our Joan yesterday. It took two weeks to get here. I'm worried about Mam, Abbie, and so is Joan. She's not well, but she won't admit it.'

'Well, I'll be home soon, I'll sort her out,' Abbie promised.

The conversation was brought to a halt by a sergeant major bellowing for Tommy to get back in line.

'It's my two sisters, Sarge!' Tommy yelled back, winking roguishly at Dee, who grinned back at him.

'Then give them a kiss and get fell-in. Sisters, my foot!' came the terse command.

Tommy hugged them both again, his arms tightening around Dee, holding her close to him. He wished he could stay longer, talk to her, see her smile, but it was not to be. He gave her a quick peck on the cheek and then reluctantly rejoined the line, waving cheerfully.

'Take care of yourself. Abbie and I won't be here to patch you up if you get in a mess!' Dee called, managing a smile. He looked so tired and drawn, and she was afraid for him.

Abbie said nothing, her arms clasped around her as though hugging herself, thinking of Dee's words about sheep and slaughter.

Dee's thoughts were running along the same lines and she prayed he'd be all right. His letters hinted that his affection for her was growing and when he'd put his arms around her she'd longed to hold him tightly and tell him how she really felt about him. Now she might never get the chance, she might never see him again.

Chapter Twenty-Three

———◆———

SEAN WAS READY TO leave. What few possessions he had were parcelled up in brown paper and tied with string. He'd been at Staveleigh Hospital in Blackburn for nearly two months but now he'd swapped hospital 'blues' for khaki. To all intents and purposes he was returning to the front, but his plans were very different to those mapped out by the military. He hadn't suffered the agonies of torn flesh and muscles, the giddy weakness and lethargy from lack of blood and shredded nerves from battle fatigue, only to go back and have it all happen again. Compared to others around him in the hospital, he'd led a charmed life, but he wasn't going to push his luck any further.

He was going to brave Hilda's wrath and everyone else's too, because there were things he'd left in Burlington Street that he now needed. He needed his civilian clothes, and he desperately needed the money he'd stashed behind a loose brick above the fireplace in the bedroom. Packed into a small Fry's Cocoa tin, it was, to protect it from the heat if ever the fire was lit, which in all his time there it never had been, and from Hilda's prying eyes. He had twenty-five pounds in that tin. Five large white notes. Money he'd saved and money he'd made selling the things he'd managed to get out of the docks, before he'd joined up. It was money that would give him a fresh start in Dublin, for he was going home. He could lose himself in Dublin, or go down into the country, to Kerry or Waterford, if he had to.

'Goodbye, Sean. Take good care of yourself, we don't want to see you back here.' Sister Thomas smiled at him with genuine concern. He'd been a model patient and he had a light-hearted, cheerful way about him that made everyone like him.

'Ah, they'll have to be quick to catch me again, Sister.'

'I'm sure they will, you're a fast one all right, Sean Doyle,' Nurse O'Leary laughed.

She was a pretty young thing, Sean thought, giving her a peck on the cheek. A Mayo girl who should be working on that farm in the West she'd told him all about, not here waiting hand and foot on men who didn't appreciate it half the time. Still, there were plenty of girls as pretty as Sheila O'Leary in Dublin. He waved cheerily to them all as the omnibus pulled out of the hospital drive.

Once he had boarded the train he settled back in his seat, his mind full of plans and memories. When he'd finally regained consciousness he'd been in a field hospital. He'd been in agony with the white-hot pain in his shoulder and leg, and he was so cold his teeth chattered noisily. Just as he'd come round in the field hospital, he'd thought he'd caught a glimpse of Dee Chatterton. He told himself then that he was mistaken, he was hallucinating. It was the pain and the shock. The nurse had worn a tin hat that covered her hair and a long army greatcoat. It could have been anyone, someone who resembled Dee. But he knew she was in France, as was Abbie Kerrigan. In fact he'd thought he'd seen them both. It had been at night, and he'd woken to see them standing at the foot of his bed, staring coldly at him, but he'd convinced himself that it had been a dream.

Then he'd seen her again, only from a distance, but he was certain this time. He'd kept a low profile, for he had no wish to speak to her or Abbie Kerrigan. It hadn't been difficult, for his injuries allowed him to do nothing much else. The realization had caused him a sleepless night.

He'd been glad that they didn't appear to be on his ward, but he sensed that he had been discussed at length. The sister in charge was unmoved by his wit and flattery, in fact, sometimes she was openly hostile.

'Save your blarney for those foolish enough to believe you!' she'd once snapped after he'd paid her a compliment. Oh, he was certain that Dee and Abbie between them had bent her ear more than just a little. When he'd been well enough he'd been taken to the coast and had boarded a boat crammed with other casualties and had arrived in Dover at the end of June. That was when his plans had really been formulated.

He barely glanced at the fields of ripening crops that swayed gently in the warm breeze. As the train drew further south, he didn't really notice the towns with their blackened buildings and tall mill chimneys that poured out thick, dark smoke, polluting the clean moorland air. The towns were surrounded by moors: a few minutes' walk from those dark cavernous mills and you were in wide-open spaces full of sunlight and the sounds and smells of summer.

He'd given enough of his life and his blood for this country, he was going home to Ireland, which was where he belonged. But he wasn't going back to the slums of Dublin. Oh, no. He had seen other people enjoying the better things of life. He'd rent some nice rooms in a good area of the city and then see what work there was available for a soldier invalided out of the British Army. That was the tale he would tell anyone who asked, although somehow he didn't think people would be terribly interested. Half the city was in ruins after the Easter Rising, when a naval gunboat had sailed up the Liffey and blasted many fine buildings into piles of rubble.

It was late afternoon before the train pulled into Lime Street, and he glanced around at the familiar buildings before catching a tram to Scotland Road and alighted at the top of Burlington Street. He took a deep breath. This wasn't going to be easy, and he could well face physical harm, but he had to have his money even if he got half killed in the attempt. All he had to do was brazen it out for an hour or so, give the performance of his life and then he'd be away – for ever.

Strangely, he met no one as he walked down the street, a fact he was thankful for. 'Be grateful for small mercies, Sean me boyo,' he thought to himself, although he noticed a few curtains twitching.

'I'll be with you in a minute!' Hilda called from the back room, hearing the shop bell clang tinnily. She came through carrying a sack half full of potatoes that fell with a heavy thud as she caught sight of him. 'What the hell are you doing here? How you've got the bloody cheek, the brass-faced nerve—'

Sean forced himself to smile at her. 'Aunty Hilda, now that's no way to greet me, I must say.'

Hilda was beside herself with rage. 'Don't you Aunty Hilda me, meladdo! You're not welcome here, in fact I'd get gone before the whole street is up and you get torn limb from limb!' she shouted, not caring if the whole street heard her, in fact, wishing someone would.

'What's wrong? What's all this yelling in aid of? Didn't you get my letters?' he blustered back.

'What letters? Didn't you get my letter?'

'I've not had a word from anyone for years. Two long years it's been. How do you think I felt when the other lads got mail! I've been wounded, been near to death. I've been in a field hospital and then a hospital in Blackburn, and that's the God's own truth. And not a line from anyone; you all deserted me when I needed you most,' he lied stoutly.

Hilda was still on the offensive, she knew him of old. 'Then you must have seen Dee and Abbie Kerrigan, if you were wounded.'

'I didn't. There are hundreds of field hospitals all

over France.' He prayed that neither Dee nor Abbie had written home saying they had seen him.

Hilda knew that was true, and she was feeling less sure of herself. 'So . . . so you don't know about . . . about Nancy?'

This was going to be the hardest part of all, he thought grimly. On the next few seconds hung his entire credibility and the chance to get his money. She could call Frank and he could be physically removed from the premises and then he could kiss goodbye to his twenty-five pounds.

'What about Nancy? She's a fine one. She's thrown me over for someone else, hasn't she? Maybe even married, and she didn't even have the guts to let me know. That hurt me, Aunty Hilda, it really did. Not a word of comfort for a lad fighting for King and Country.'

Hilda wished heartily that Frank were back from the docks where he went every afternoon to see what was available from spilled or damaged cargoes. Anything to put on half-empty shelves. She didn't know whether to believe Sean. He looked so crestfallen but was it all just an act?

'Nancy's dead,' she said flatly. 'She was expecting your child and she got no replies to her letters to you, so she . . . she went to Ma Mulholland. She died in Stanley Hospital next day. The twenty-fifth of June, nineteen sixteen it was.'

Sean covered his face with his hands, unsure how credible his performance would appear to Hilda's sharp eyes. 'Ah, God, poor Nance. Poor, poor Nance,' he cried through his fingers. He meant some of it, just a little. Nancy was only a memory now, but he had been fond of her and it was a horrible way for a girl to die, but he'd seen a thousand infinitely more cruel ways of dying. He sat down on the chair Hilda always kept in the shop for her older, less agile customers. He sensed she was weakening and rubbed his arm across his face. 'It's all the fault of the bloody posts! Desperate they are. She should have got my letters, I should have got hers and yours, but you don't know what it's like over there, Aunty Hilda.'

'I manage to get letters from our Michael, so it can't be that bad.'

He looked up at her with what he hoped was sincerity. 'Our mails were always bad, I swear it. I got nothing and many of the other lads had nothing either. The only things that seemed to be on time were the bloody Dispatches and sometimes even they got lost.'

Hilda was still not totally convinced, but she motioned him towards the back room. 'Maybe you'd better go and see Bridie.'

That was something he had no intention of doing. 'I've no time. I've to be away again, back to the front. I just came to see you, that's all. You're all the family I've got.'

'Frank has gone to the docks but he should be back any minute and Chrissie's working at the Post Office in Victoria Street. Her shift finished at four, she's been there since before eight o'clock this morning.' Hilda really didn't want him to be here when anyone came home. Instinctively she felt uneasy about him. She just wanted to be rid of him.

'How's Jerry?' Sean asked to change the subject. 'I've often thought of the poor lad and wondered how he was going on.'

'He's in Walton Jail, in the hospital there.'

Sean was stunned. 'Jaysus, what did he do?'

'He killed his father, not that I blame him. Abe Harvey was mad: a religious lunatic and a cruel, violent man. He pushed Jerry too far and then hit him. He hit a poor lad crippled with consumption. Jerry snapped and hit Abe with the poker. Poor Winnie, it's been terrible for her with the newspapers and the police and the courts.'

'Poor bloody Jerry,' Sean said and his sincerity was not feigned. He'd liked Jerry Harvey and had often echoed Hilda's remarks about Abe being a madman. Abe Harvey was no loss to anyone. 'What will they do to him?'

Hilda's shoulders seemed to slump. 'He'll hang, if he doesn't die first. It would be a blessing if he did, for Winnie and Hannah. I have heard that it's got to his lungs and he's now coughing blood.'

Sean was truly shocked. Poor inoffensive, brow-beaten Jerry. He hoped his end would be more merciful than dangling from the end of a rope.

'I'll just go up and get my bits and pieces and then I'll be off. Will you give my regards to Mrs Harvey and tell her – well, tell her I'm sorry for her trouble.'

It was nearly over now, he thought, as he packed his few clothes in the cardboard suitcase he'd brought with him all those years ago. He loosened the bits of plaster from around the brick with his penknife and sighed with relief. It was still there, his passport to the future. He emptied the tin, pocketed the money and then replaced the brick. Now he could leave and it would be without a backward glance.

As he came downstairs Frank was standing in the shop doorway.

'What the bloody hell are you doing here?'

'I've been trying to tell you,' Hilda said impatiently.

'You lily-livered bastard!' Frank yelled, anger consuming him as he thought of Nancy.

'I didn't know! By God and all His holy saints, I didn't know about Nancy!' Sean yelled, backing away, trying to put as much space as possible between himself and Frank. Just when everything had been going so well, why did Frank have to walk in now? He'd never seen him so furious.

'You bloody liar!'

'I'm not. I loved Nancy. I'm heartbroken. I never got her letters. It was the post, I thought she'd found someone else.' He had side-stepped Frank and had almost reached the door and his money was safely in his pocket.

'Stop bloody lying, you never loved anyone except yourself.' Frank lunged at him. 'A viper, that's what you are, the way you wormed yourself into everyone's affections. We took you in, we believed you. Saint Patrick might have got rid of all the snakes in Ireland, but God he missed one – you!'

Sean's hand was on the handle of the door and he

was about to wrench it open and run, but it was opened from the other side, pushing him backwards.

Lizzie Simcock and Harry O'Brien stood staring at him.

'God Almighty!' Lizzie cried.

'It's the devil himself, because no one else would have the bloody gall,' Harry said with menace in his voice.

Sean felt trapped.

Suddenly Hilda darted forward and pushed him bodily through the door. 'Get out! Get out of here and don't ever come back!' she yelled.

Sean needed no second telling. He ran and didn't stop until he reached the top of the street. Then he leaned back against a wall, panting. That was it. It was all over and he was away clear. He was going back to the station, but not Lime Street, to Exchange, and it wasn't to catch a train.

'What did you do that for? Harry and me were going to give him a hiding!' Frank demanded.

'To save you from being arrested, he's not worth it, Frank. Let him go.'

'He was asking for it, coming back here with his bloody lies.' Frank was still livid.

'What lies? What did the bugger say?' Harry asked.

'He said he didn't know about Nancy or the baby. Said he never got any letters from her. He blamed it on the post,' Hilda answered.

'You see, all bloody lies. The posts aren't that bad. Does he think we came over on the last boat?' Frank slammed the door shut.

'He deserved a good belting,' Harry growled.

'He had a cheek to even think of coming back here,' Lizzie said acidly, yet wondering why Hilda hadn't instantly thrown him out. 'What did he want?'

'He said he came to see us and to get his bits and pieces.'

'He should be tarred and feathered! By God, I wish I'd been here when he arrived.' Frank was banging the scales around on the counter top.

'Well, he won't be back and good riddance!' Hilda snapped.

'I hope there's a bullet over there with his name on it. Why is it that all the rotten ones seem to survive while the good blokes get killed and crippled?'

'Because the devil looks after his own, Lizzie, that's why,' Hilda retorted. 'Now let's forget all about him. What can I get you?'

Chrissie walked along Dale Street with two of the other girls. She knew she was lucky to work in the Post Office instead of in munitions, but she still grumbled about having to be up so early. It was Polly's birthday so they were going to Lyons Tea Rooms for something to eat, although things were so scarce now that they wouldn't have much choice. She glanced across the road and caught sight of someone she thought she recognized.

'Hang on a minute, I think I know that lad.'

'What lad?' Polly asked impatiently.

'Him, on the other side of the road by the corner of Moorfields.'

'That soldier? The good-looking one with the suitcase?' Polly asked.

Chrissie's eyes gleamed malevolently. 'Yes, it *is* him. It's Sean Doyle. I told you he used to live with us.'

'Isn't he the one that got that poor girl into trouble?' Ellen Woods enquired, peering across the road.

Chrissie nodded. 'I wonder what he's turned up for? I bet he hasn't been back to our house—'

'Oh, come on, Chrissie, I'm starving and if we dawdle along like this, they'll 'ave nothing left to eat,' Polly complained.

'You go on, I'll catch you up.'

'Why?'

'I'm going to follow him. I know him, and he's up to no good.'

Polly was annoyed. 'Suit yourself, Chrissie Burgess, but don't blame me if there's nothing left.'

'Don't get all airyated, I won't be long.'

Chrissie crossed the road, threading her way through the traffic and she stayed behind Sean all the way up Moorfields, occasionally stopping to glance in a shop window when his pace slowed. She'd find out what he was up to and then wouldn't she have something to tell Mam. He was carrying that old case, so he had been home. She wondered what it contained.

She found out after he had disappeared into the gents' toilet and re-emerged wearing not his uniform but his civilian clothes: his best suit, shirt and hat, no less. She turned away and pretended to be studying the clock as he crossed the station concourse, but slowly she turned around and watched as he opened a left

luggage box, pushed the case which obviously contained his uniform inside, and locked the door. Her
eyes were riveted on him and she saw him slip the key
into his pocket. As she left the station she was momentarily confused as to what to do. Go on to Lyons, or
follow him. It was only early, it would be light for hours
yet and she couldn't follow him all night. She decided
to see where he went first and then she'd join her
friends.

There was a strong, cooling breeze at the Pierhead
that ruffled her hair and tugged at her hat. Maybe he
was going to board the ferry, in which case she wasn't
going to pursue him. But he walked along the Strand,
past the Landing Stage and suddenly she knew what he
intended to do. He was going to buy a ticket for the
midnight boat to Dublin. That was where he was
headed, the ticket office of the Dublin ferry. She turned
away and retraced her steps, deep in thought. He was
deserting, and in time of war that was treason; if he was
caught he would be shot. Should she tell Mam and
Dad? It was only what he deserved after what he did to
poor Nancy Butterworth, although for some strange
reason Chrissie felt it would be better to say nothing.
She'd learned to keep her own counsel on a lot of
things these days – well, since after the hiding she'd got
after Nancy's funeral. No, she wouldn't tell. She wasn't
going to embroil herself with Sean Doyle and his
treachery, it could lead to all kinds of trouble. She
straightened her hat and headed back towards Dale
Street and the Tea Rooms.

*

Abbie couldn't wait to get home. Anxiety drove her, but to her surprise the relief nurse was her own sister, Monica, or Sister Mary Magdalene as she was now called. Sal had always said the name was a good choice, considering Monica's previous faults.

'I didn't think your order were nursing nuns?' Abbie said.

'That's not a very civil way to greet me, is it? We're not a Nursing Order, not really, apart from midwifery, but every pair of hands is needed now. "As ye sow, so shall ye reap."'

Abbie wondered what on earth she meant, but didn't ask. She looked at the calm unlined face of her twin and marvelled that this was really the hoyden of a sister who had caused so much trouble. 'Well, I'm glad to see you. Have you got something else to wear instead of that habit? You'll get filthy and there's no time to be washing and starching things.' Abbie's gaze went over the stiff white collar and the starched, winged wimple that covered Monica's head.

'I have another habit, but if I can't keep them clean, well, it's no use thinking like that. The Lord will see to things.'

Abbie raised her eyes to the ceiling, thinking that Sister Mary Magdalene was a sanctimonious half-wit if that was going to be her attitude to nursing war-wounded soldiers. In fact, the old Monica that she remembered would have coped far better, although she assumed that her sister would have been given some training.

'I'm glad I saw you, in fact I asked for you. I went

home for a few hours before I left England and Mam didn't look at all well, although she won't admit it.' Sister Mary Magdalene tucked her hands into the wide sleeves of her grey woollen habit.

Abbie frowned. 'I know, our Tommy told me Joan is worried. He's up there, you may well see him.' Abbie jerked her head in the general direction of the trenches. 'I hope he won't get hurt again.'

'I'll pray for him and for Jerry Harvey.'

'How is Jerry? Did you see him?'

Sister Mary Magdalene looked startled, 'Me? How could I see him? He's in jail.'

'What?' Abbie almost screamed the word.

Sister Mary Magdalene pursed her lips and sighed and then went on to inform her twin of Jerry's plight.

Abbie was very upset but the news from home got worse.

'There was quite a commotion going on at Burgess's shop, too.'

'Why?'

'Mike Burgess has been wounded and Hilda was in a terrible state.'

Abbie's heart dropped like a stone and she grasped Monica's shoulder. 'Oh, not again! Oh, dear Lord, not again! How badly? Did anyone know how badly?'

'Apparently a wound in the shoulder again, so Mr Burgess told me.'

After that Abbie could hardly wait to take her leave of Monica and pack her things. Jerry's plight was forgotten, all she had wanted to do was to get home, to see Hilda, find out everything.

*

So great was her haste to get home that she insisted that she and Dee take a cab from Lime Street. They were both silent as they rode through the familiar streets, both wondering what awaited them. Abbie went straight to the shop.

'Abbie, luv, it's great to see you,' Frank greeted her warmly. He was on his own and things had been quiet, as they were most days now, there being very little to sell.

'Oh, how is Mike? How badly hurt is he? I saw Sister Mary Magdalene, I mean our Monica, and she told me and I couldn't wait to get home, I haven't even been to see Mam yet!' Abbie was near to tears.

'Hold on, Abbie. He's not badly hurt. A bit of shrapnel in his shoulder and a graze to his forehead. His tin hat saved him – he's coming home.'

Abbie felt weak with relief. 'Oh, thank God!'

Frank had shouted to Hilda, who had come through and stood staring at Abbie speculatively. The girl looked tired and much older than her twenty-two years, but that was only to be expected with what she'd been through. Grudgingly Hilda had to admire her.

'How long are you home for then?' she asked.

'Three weeks, and I really need it. Dee is home, too. Will . . . will Mike be home soon?'

Frank smiled at her. 'Oh, he'll be home before you have to go back, Abbie, don't worry about that.'

Abbie's step was lighter as she walked the remaining distance home. The kitchen was as untidy as ever but there was no sign of anyone. 'Mam! Mam I'm home.

It's me, Abbie!' she called, She heard the boards creak upstairs and went to the foot of the stairs. 'Mam, it's me, Abbie. Are you all right?'

There was no answer so she went up. Sal was in bed propped up with pillows. The bedding was clean and the room was very tidy.

'Mam, what's wrong?'

Sal held out her arms. 'Oh, I've to take things easy, an' our Joan's been carrying on so much that I gave in and came to bed. Me, taking to me bed! She's a right little tartar when she wants to be is that one. Let me look at you, girl.'

Abbie was nearly smothered in Sal's embrace, but when her mother released her she sat on the bed and scrutinized Sal's face. 'What's been the matter? Our Monica said you didn't look well and Tommy had a letter from Joan—'

'Oh, it's nothing. Just a bit of trouble with me ticker, Doctor Wallace said. The trouble is, he said it to our Joan, an' all this is her fault, me being stuck up here, like. And she never stops tidying up or scrubbing and polishing. It wears me out just watching her.'

Abbie took Sal's hand and felt for the pulse, her brow furrowed in a frown of concentration.

Sal drew her hand away irritably. 'Ah stop all that, I'm not at death's door yet.'

'You will be if you don't do as you're told. I'm going to see Doctor Wallace when I've unpacked. I'm going to get to the bottom of all this and then I'm going to see our Joan.' Her expression softened. 'Oh, Mam, I've looked forward so much to coming home. I've missed you, I've missed all of you.' The tears sparkled on her lashes. Was this all a dream or was she really home, away from the fighting and the mud and the blood?

'Come on and give your owld mam a hug! I've been out of me mind with worry over the lot of you. Tommy, Monica, you – and our Bertie is nearly old enough now for the army.'

As Abbie embraced her mother she thought sadly that the war had other casualties. The women who waited and worried at home, and quite obviously that worry was responsible for so much distress that it caused illness. It was no wonder her mam's heart was bad, all her life she'd had more than her fair share of worry.

'I heard that Mike has been wounded,' Sal said, allowing Abbie to fuss over her and settle her more comfortably.

'Not too badly, he should be home soon.'

Sal managed a smile. 'How long is it since you two have seen each other?'

'Oh, three years, three months, two weeks and four days.'

Sal laughed. 'And you still love him?'

'Mam, how can you ask such a thing? Of course I do.'

'Then marry him, girl, and quickly. Snatch a bit of happiness. Our Joan did. She says her memories are what keep her going.'

Abbie nodded slowly. 'I've to wait to be asked yet, Mam, and even though she's not as bad as she used to be, his mam won't be very pleased if he does ask me.'

'Ah, stop that. Hilda's been through it the way we all have. This war has changed her as well.'

'It's changed everyone, Mam. God I wish it were all over, I really do.'

'I'll say Amen to that, luv, but if he asks, you tell him yes and get round to the church as fast as you can.'

Chapter Twenty-Four

———◆———

A WEEK LATER ABBIE WAS waiting on Lime Street Station with Hilda, Frank and Chrissie.

Emily O'Brien had agreed to hold the fort in the shop for an hour or two. Mike was coming home with other wounded men, and the army had commandeered a whole carriage for them; they were to be accompanied by nurses. They were all to be allowed home to recover, for the hospitals were so overcrowded now that only men who needed specialist care or who had no families to nurse them were being taken in.

Abbie could hardly contain her excitement and longing. She'd had a few moments of panic. Would he still really love her? Had she changed? Was she old and lined? After all, she was older than he was. She'd gazed critically at her reflection in the mirror on the wall of the bedroom she shared with Ginny. Oh, would he still think her attractive? Three years was a long time and he would have met other girls, other nurses, and French girls, some of whom were as bold as brass.

She'd worn her best clothes and had taken extra care with her hair, but now she was a mass of jangled nerves, and butterflies were dancing in the pit of her stomach.

'Will he be in a bath chair?' Chrissie asked.

Abbie bit back the sarcastic reply that had sprung to her lips. 'I shouldn't think so. They are only for those who can't walk or who are very weak.'

They all peered into the crowds that were spilling from the platform, but it was Frank who saw him first amongst the group of soldiers being shepherded towards the barrier by nurses. He pushed his way forward and took his son's good hand. 'Welcome home, lad! By God, it's good to see you!'

Mike grinned. Home. Home was like being on another planet after what he'd left. He was instantly surrounded by Hilda and Chrissie, both crying and exclaiming and fussing. Then he caught sight of Abbie, standing a pace behind his mam. His eyes lit up and his face split in a wide smile. 'Abbie! Oh, Abbie!'

Careless of what Hilda thought of her, and throwing all propriety to the winds, Abbie threw her arms around his neck, carefully avoiding the wounded shoulder. And then he was kissing her and holding her tightly.

'Oh, Abbie! Abbie! I've missed you so much!'

'I know. I've missed you, too, Mike. It's been so long, and letters aren't the same.' She drew away, brushing the tears from her lashes, a little bashful and embarrassed now under Hilda's gaze; but Frank was smiling broadly. Even Chrissie looked pleased. Mike held her hand tightly, but smiled and laughed with sheer delight.

'Chrissie, you've grown up. You're a smasher! I would hardly have recognized you.'

Chrissie simpered and pretended to be coy.

'She's only seventeen, our Michael, don't go giving her airs and graces, she's vain enough as it is,' Hilda chided gently. She was determined to keep him home for as long as was humanly possible. He was all skin and bone and the lines of suffering and hardship showed on his face. He was still only a boy, she thought, he was only twenty.

'Let's get back home and we can have a good natter and bring everyone up-to-date with all the news.' Frank ushered the little group towards the exit and they spilled out into the sunlight that bathed Lime Street.

'I'd forgotten how much I loved these dirty old buildings,' Mike laughed, his gaze sweeping across St George's Hall to the portico of the Library and Art Gallery. He was remembering the day they'd all marched along here to the strains of 'Dolly Gray'. He looked down at Abbie and knew that she was remembering too.

'Will we get a taxicab, Da?' Chrissie piped up eagerly, breaking the spell of those memories.

Frank was about to agree until Hilda interrupted sharply.

'No we won't, it's a shocking waste of money. We'll get the tram like everyone else is doing.'

Hilda had surpassed herself. With great ingenuity, hard bargaining and downright brow-beating she had managed to obtain enough food to put on a spread the like of which hadn't been seen in Burlington Street for years.

'Mam, where did you get all this, it's a feast!' Mike cried.

'Never you mind, just sit down and eat. Things are a bit easier now the ships sail in convoys and the Navy is getting to grips with those damned U-boats. Eat, you look like a bag of bones.'

No one needed any further encouragement.

Abbie had been reluctant to leave, but at last she said she should really get back and see to her mam. She touched Mike's face gently with her hand and reached up and kissed him as he let her out the back way. 'Will I see you later?'

'You bet. I've had no time to talk to you properly. Will you come back here?'

'Yes, it's still like a madhouse down there when everyone's at home,' she laughed.

'It won't be much better here, Mam will have half the street in to see me. Maybe we'll take a walk, or a ride on the ferry. I've missed that dirty old river so much.'

'I'd like that, but only if you feel up to it. You mustn't tire yourself out.'

'I won't, besides I can rest all day tomorrow; she'll probably tie me to the bed. Come back about seven.'

Abbie nodded and smiled. She knew she would be counting every minute from now until seven o'clock, and her feet seemed to have wings as she skipped her way home.

She'd managed to cajole seventeen-year-old Ginny into lending her a new, white, ruffled blouse. She'd searched all the drawers and had found some blue ribbon, which she'd ironed and used to re-trim her straw boater hat. With her dark blue skirt she thought she looked very smart.

'Don't go getting that blouse all messed up. I've only worn it once an' it cost half a week's wages,' Ginny instructed.

'I won't, I promise. Anyway, you earn a fortune in that factory, so stop moaning!' Abbie had replied good-naturedly.

When she walked into the shop it was obvious from Hilda's expression that she thought the outing was sheer madness.

'I promise I'll have him back early and I won't let him go doing anything daft. I am a nurse and he really should be resting,' Abbie said in what she hoped was her most brisk and capable tone. She had emphasized the word 'nurse' too.

'That's just what I told him. It's an early night in his own comfortable bed, not gallivanting on the ferry, that's what he should be doing.' And with his family, Hilda had almost added, but she had intercepted a warning look from Frank.

'Mam, you'll have weeks to mollycoddle me,' Mike laughed as they left.

It was a fine night. The breeze was warm and the river looked calm and sluggish under the misty, blue-grey sky of the summer evening. The *Egremont* was moored at the Landing Stage and they bought their tickets and climbed up to the open deck, where they managed to find a corner that was not crowded.

Mike placed his good arm around Abbie's shoulders and drew her to him, gazing out over the waterfront that was so much a part of him and which he had often feared he would never see again. 'Oh, it's good to be home, Abbie, and you look as pretty as a picture.'

Abbie smiled up at him. 'I was worried that you'd think I was old and plain.'

'You could never be called plain, Abbie. I haven't even got a photograph of you, but I kept remembering you the way you looked at Mam's party. You looked beautiful in that lilac-coloured dress. I fell in love with you that night and I carried that picture of you all through—'

Abbie placed her hand against his cheek. 'Don't! Don't spoil it by thinking about all that's happened. I sometimes feel it's all been a bad dream and I'll wake up back at home, but I know it isn't and I try not to dwell on it. Dee and I have a rule about it.'

'Abbie, I know you're needed over there, but sometimes I wish you were back here, safe and sound.'

Abbie tried to be cheerful. 'Oh, it's not too bad. We're well away from the front line.'

'Near enough for you all to have to wear tin hats like soldiers.'

'Who told you that?' she asked sharply.

'No one. I've seen the nurses out there, don't forget. Abbie, won't you even think about staying at home now? You've done your bit. Your mam needs you; my mam told me she's not well.'

Abbie sighed. 'She's got our Joan and Ginny to look

after her and Joan is sensible, even if Ginny's not. I'm more useful in France, Mike.'

He didn't press her, but he sensed that she'd have liked to stay at home. But Abbie was loyal and conscientious. 'How long is your leave?'

'Oh, I've another two weeks yet. Plenty of time,' she smiled, the soft river breeze ruffling the tendrils of blond hair that had escaped from beneath her hat.

Two weeks. Two short weeks, Mike thought, and then they'd be parted again, and for God only knew how long.

'Abbie, you know I love you. It was that and thoughts of you that kept me going, kept me sane. I'll have to talk to Dad and Mam, but ... but will you marry me, Abbie? Before ... before you have to go back, before I lose you again. I love you, Abbie, and I need you, and we deserve some time together. We deserve some happiness, we've waited so long.'

Her heart leapt. The blood raced through her veins like wine, and tears of pure joy sparkled on her lashes. 'Oh, Mike, of course I will! We've waited long enough.'

He kissed her long and passionately, to the amusement and envy of the other passengers, to whom they were totally oblivious.

'I can't offer you much Abbie, I don't know if I'll even—'

She silenced the words with the tips of her fingers. 'Don't even think like that! I don't need or expect anything – after all, we've never had much in our house,' she laughed ruefully. 'All I want is you.'

'Maybe we could get somewhere of our own, a

couple of rooms. I don't expect you'll want to live with Mam.'

That was a prospect Abbie didn't relish. 'You'd better talk to them before we go making plans. I'm twenty-two, so even if Da did object, there's nothing he can do about it; but he won't, he'll be made up. They all will, but you'll need your da's consent.'

Mike drew her head down onto his shoulder. He'd have no problems with his da, but Mam was going to be difficult. He'd talk her round though, he wasn't a kid any more, not after four years of war, and he'd tell her so.

Frank readily gave his consent, but it took a bit of time and a lot of coaxing and reasoning on Frank's part before Hilda finally accepted the decision, not that it really rested with her. It was Frank's consent that counted, as he tactfully reminded her.

'She's a good girl, Hilda. She's kind and practical and loyal. She'll make him a good wife and God knows they deserve a bit of happiness together.'

'I just keep thinking of that ... well, what if she turns out like Sal?'

'What's wrong with Sal Kerrigan?'

'Oh, you know what I mean, Frank, you're just being perverse.'

'Whatever else Sal is, she's been a good wife and mother, and not only to her own kids. Rosie Chatterton has been brought up by Sal.'

'Exactly. She was a little lady when she first came here.'

'Hilda, don't be such a bloody snob! You're getting as bad as Maggie Rooney.'

Hilda didn't reply, thinking that at least her arch rival had high standards, something Sal Kerrigan for all her generosity didn't have.

Abbie and Mike called on Dee together to tell her the good news and ask her to stand for Abbie. The wedding was to be rushed through by Father Fitz with a special dispensation from the Archbishop, something unheard of before the war.

Dee was overjoyed and embraced them both. 'Oh, I'm so glad for you. I really am! We haven't had a good wedding around here since your Joan got married.'

'Talking of which, will you be my chief bridesmaid?'

'What about Joan and Ginny? Don't forget poor Ginny has been done out of being a bridesmaid once before, and by our Rose.'

'Oh, I'm having Ginny as well, and our Joan's not bothered. She said she's having no one call her a matron of honour or anything else. She's offered to cut down one of her dresses for Ginny because there won't be time to get anything made. Chrissie will have to sort herself out.'

'Oh, don't worry about Chrissie. Mam will take care of her!' Mike laughed, although he knew there was no love lost between his sister and his future wife. Bridie bustled into the kitchen, laden with washing. She looked a little older, a little stouter Abbie thought, but still the same cheerful Bridie.

'What's this then, a deputation?' Bridie laughed.

'We're going to get married, Mrs Chatterton, and we want Dee to be chief bridesmaid.'

'Well, isn't that a nice surprise? The best of luck to you both and if you're as happy as I've been with Edward, you'll be doing well. When is it to be, then?'

'As soon as we can get things arranged. You know these two are due back in two weeks.'

Bridie looked a little shocked. 'You're never going back there, Abbie? A married woman's place is at home.'

'Things have changed—' Dee interrupted.

'Besides, I haven't got a home of my own.'

Bridie thought it best not to ask what was wrong with Hilda's house, or even Sal's. It was the way most young couples started out.

'When we get ourselves sorted out, we'll get a couple of nice rooms,' Mike added.

'Aye, that will be best all around, I think,' Bridie agreed. 'Dee, will you be a love and go and collect Elizabeth from school for me while I get the tea started? It's your da's night out with his office pals and he likes to be ready early.'

'We'd better be off too,' Abbie said. 'Will I send Rosie home when she gets in?'

'If you would, luv. Your mam's got enough on her plate without her as well. Has she heard from Tommy lately?'

'No, but I expect there will be a letter soon,' Abbie said bravely, smiling up at Mike. If only she had Tommy home safe and sound, then her wedding day would be perfect, but unless there was a miracle they would have to get by without him.

*

There was no miracle but there was a letter. Tommy had no idea about the wedding, but it was enough to know that he was still unhurt, Abbie thought thankfully as she did her hair before the dressing-table mirror in Joan's bedroom. Joan had insisted that she spend the night with her and Terry's mother who was now almost an invalid.

'You need a good night's sleep and then some peace and quiet to get ready in the morning, and you won't get either if you stay here,' Joan had insisted. 'Look at the state of the place. Da's so untidy, and as for our Ginny, not a thought in her empty head except dolling herself up and going out. That one won't soil her hands. She's not skivvying for Da or Bertie and Seb or Rosie Chatterton, so she keeps saying. No, you'll come home with me.' So Abbie had gone, despite all Pat's complaints and Sal's pleas that it was traditional for the bride to spend her last night at home.

'And since when has tradition ever been taken into consideration in this house, Mam?' Joan had commented acidly. Sal had glared at her eldest daughter, but knew she was no match for Joan these days.

'You've always been so good to me, Joan,' Abbie said, gazing fondly at her sister and mentor.

'Aye, well I remember what a madhouse it was the morning I got married. Da still had a hangover and Ken and Norm weren't much better. You kids were acting up something awful and Mam was yelling at everyone and still had her hair in curling papers at half past nine. I want it to be different for you because . . .

well, there's fewer of us now than there used to be,' Joan added sadly.

The neat, deep pink two-piece looked smart, especially with Joan's good frilled blouse underneath, Abbie thought. The hat she'd bought herself, but Dee had trimmed it with pink ribbon and two huge, black, artificial roses, unpicked from Bridie's best hat, which she'd sworn faithfully to replace the next day. There had been so much discussion and argument over what Ginny and Chrissie would wear that in the end Hilda had spurned Joan's offers and taken them both into town. The result was two identical lilac-sprigged muslin dresses and two wide-brimmed, light straw hats, trimmed with lilac ribbons. All of which could be worn again for best and were thus practical, once the fancy trimmings had been removed, Hilda explained to Sal.

'Pat will give you the money for our Ginny's on Friday,' Sal promised.

'Fine, but she's earning, Sal, she should chip in. I wasn't having it end up a rag-bag affair, just because it was so short notice. There's some around here always ready to make snotty remarks,' Hilda sniffed, thinking of Maggie Rooney.

'Er from the greengrocer's, you mean?'

'Exactly.'

'Our Abbie's a bit upset about not having a long white frock and a veil.' Sal had for once escaped Joan's watchful eye and was sipping her tea from one of Hilda's best china cups. 'She'd set her heart on it, so she told me.'

'What's she complaining about? Your Joan didn't have all that finery and she looked very elegant.'

'I know, but well, I suppose she thought that when she got wed things would be different.'

'Oh, they're different all right. They couldn't get much more different.'

'You know what I mean, Hilda. She's got a lovely costume and a very smart hat, which brings me to—'

Hilda sighed before interrupting. 'Your hat. Will that nice mustard one of mine with the feathers suit you, Sal?'

'It will go a treat with me brown dress. I'll say this for you Hilda Burgess, you're generous to a fault when folk need things.'

Gratified, Hilda smiled. 'Well, we've been through a lot together, Sal, over the years. How are you feeling, anyway? Has the doctor given you any instructions?'

Sal rolled her eyes towards the ceiling. 'Oh, aye. A list as long as me arm. No drinking, no unnecessary exertions as he calls it, and most of all no anxiety. Isn't that a bloody laugh? I don't know a woman in this street who isn't riddled with anxiety.'

'You'll have to try not to worry, Sal, about anything or anyone, at least until the wedding is over.'

'I'll try, but I can't help wishing she wasn't going back. I wish she'd stay here.'

'I wish the damned war was over and done with, it's gone on too long, far too long. But there's no sense in getting morbid.' Hilda got to her feet and went to fetch the hat.

The church was quite full, which surprised Abbie,

but pleased her as well. There were her own relations and Mike's, and all the Chattertons were there, and Lizzie Simcock and Mary, the O'Briens and even Hannah Harvey. The sight of Hannah really startled her, for none of the Harveys had ever been known to go within a hundred yards of a Catholic Church, let alone go inside one. Hannah had a defiant look on her face, so she assumed that the religious fanaticism that had prevailed in the Harveys' house when Abe had been alive had now gone by the board. She thought briefly and sadly of poor Jerry who was so desperately ill in Walton Jail.

When she caught sight of Mike looking so handsome and proud in his uniform it didn't matter that she had no long white dress, no veil, no garland of orange blossom in her hair. The look he gave her told her she didn't need all that. She was beautiful in his eyes and she always would be. Her smile was radiant as she handed Dee her small posy of flowers and prepared to become Mrs Michael Burgess, all thoughts of war and suffering banished.

Tears sparkled on Dee's lashes. Abbie looked so lovely, and she was so fortunate. Dee wished Nancy were here; she had always loved a good wedding. She hoped that Nancy was, perhaps, looking down on them and that she was happy, wherever she was. A small pang of envy stabbed at her heart. Would she ever look like Abbie? Would anyone ever love her? Then came the memory of Tommy Kerrigan's hugs, the quick squeeze of her hand when she'd sat with him in the hospital at Whalley, his fleeting kiss on the day he'd been marching past the hospital, and his affectionate letters. All of which she'd kept. She felt herself blushing. She was being stupid, reading too much into a few friendly gestures and endearing, amusing letters from a lad she'd known for years.

She knew she was plain, with her straight mousey hair, and her spectacles and she was too thin, she had no ample curves. She was probably destined to become the spinster aunt to her brothers' children and eventually Elizabeth's and Rose's, for they were both pretty. She'd probably stay in nursing even when the war was over. It was something she was good at, and she might even end up as a matron. No, there seemed no prospect of marriage for her. Tommy didn't love her in that way. She felt lonely and depressed as she dragged her thoughts back to the present and realized that the ceremony was over. Abbie Kerrigan was now Abbie Burgess.

Chapter Twenty-Five

Tthought, as she eased her cramped limbs and aching back down onto the battered sofa that served a double purpose in the tiny Rest Room. Sometimes it was used as a bed; it wasn't unusual to come in and see an exhausted nurse lying full stretch, still fully dressed.

All through the summer and early autumn the fighting had gone on. General Haig's troops were once more pushing forward to the Hindenberg Line, so at least there were some successes, but more names had been added to the long list of battlefields: L'Épinette, Le Cateau, Ruemont. The cost of the capture of those places was still too high, and as the army moved forward, so the field hospitals did too.

It was only six weeks to Christmas, so someone had remarked, and Dee wondered if she would spend another Christmas away from home. It certainly looked like it. It was Abbie she felt sorry for, though, not herself. It was Abbie's first Christmas as Mike's wife and she would spend it here, not with her husband, in the midst of her family, at home where they all should be. Abbie and Mike had had very little time together, really only those few days' honeymoon in a guest house in Llandudno. Abbie had returned to France and Mike had eventually been sent back to the front line, despite all Hilda's complaints and declarations that he was still unfit.

She took Tommy's latest letter from her skirt pocket and scanned the lines again. His writing was bad and his spelling dreadful, but he was amusing. He wrote as he spoke and she could almost hear his voice. Tommy was one of life's optimists, and she was his friend, but that's all it was, she told herself sternly. It was friend-ship, and she shouldn't expect more. She was someone he could talk to, someone who really understood what they were all going through. Someone who knew how things were going at home, too, and they had their own private little jokes and sorrows. They were two souls adrift in a dark and lonely world. But in her heart she wished he did love her. She could see Abbie's happiness daily, even though she was separated from Mike, and she longed to feel the same way. Resolutely she pushed the thoughts to the back of her mind.

His letters had been such a comfort to her when her father had written and told her that Jerry Harvey had died.

'At least he cheated the hangman, Deirdre,' Edward had written.

'That is such a comfort to poor Winnie,' was how

Bridie had put it in the postscript she always added to her husband's letters.

'Poor Jerry, I can't help thinking that if he'd had a decent father, a better home life, he might have lived longer,' Dee had written to Tommy.

'For how much longer? And would it have been worth it, Dee?' Tommy had replied.

Sal was now confined to bed. She'd had two mild strokes, and Joan and Doctor Wallace were both adamant that she rest. Dee smiled to herself. 'You can lead a horse to water but you can't make it bloody well drink!' Sal had apparently told Joan, according to Tommy's letters. Sal insisted on running the household and keeping up with all the neighbourhood gossip from the large, cast-iron bed she still shared with Pat. Everyone trooped upstairs to see her, to talk to her, to ask for advice. Joan constantly complained that the house was as bad as Lime Street Station and with about as much privacy, and it wasn't doing her mam any good. But Sal loved it all. She was never happier than when she was surrounded by her kids and their friends and most of their relations too.

'Nurse Chatterton, there's someone here asking for you. He won't let anyone else tend him, he's being most obstinate,' Sister Chapman called through the open door, obviously annoyed.

'Who is it?' Dee got to her feet.

'A Private Kerrigan, Thomas Kerrigan.'

Dee's heart turned over. 'Oh, he's not been wounded again!'

'It happens often, Nurse, you should know that.

Kindly tell him not to be so choosy in future, my nurses need their rest!' Sister rejoined.

Dee quickly went to the receiving area where Tommy was sitting on the floor. His face was smoke-blackened and he was holding one hand to his chest. He grimaced comically when he saw her.

'Oh, Tommy! Now what have you been doing, apart from putting Sister in a bad mood?' she joked to cover her confusion. 'At least it's nothing too serious. I'm sure you only do this to annoy me. Let me have a look.' It was so good to see him again and she felt the blood rush to her cheeks.

'It's a bit messy. I caught the tail end of a burst of Lewis gun fire. Ouch!' His face twisted with real pain as Dee gently and expertly examined his swollen and bloodied fingers.

'That one is definitely broken and maybe this one too. You'll have to see the doctor. I'll clean the blood and dirt off. Hold still, I won't hurt you. How did you get here?'

'I walked. There were two other lads with me, they've only got cuts and bruises. I thought they were Yanks at first, everyone's so bloody mixed up together now. They got dead narked because they're Canadians. You all sound the same to me, I said, but that didn't go down well either. Mind you, we'd got really pally by the time we arrived here.'

'Trust you to say the wrong thing Tommy Kerrigan, and your geography leaves a lot to be desired.'

'There's rumours that it will all be over soon, Dee. That's why I really came all the way back to see you. I could have managed with these, I'd have just got them strapped up.'

Dee sat back on her heels and shook her head in disbelief. 'Really? How soon?'

'Tomorrow morning at eleven o'clock.'

She was stunned, it was too much to hope for. 'That can't be true, Tommy! We would have heard something before now.'

'Not necessarily, the brass hats have never enlightened us before about anything. "Ours not to reason why", like that poet feller wrote, you know, what's-his-name?'

'Tennyson,' she replied absent-mindedly. 'Oh, Tommy, I want to believe it, but I'm afraid to. It's so sudden, so unreal, and if it's not true—'

'I know, Dee. Somehow it seems as though there should be a sort of slow winding down, it's been going on so long, but that's what I've heard and that's what I came to tell you.'

'You walked all that way to tell me. Oh, that was good of you, Tommy!'

'You'd never have forgiven me if you'd found out I knew and hadn't told you.'

'I'm not that bad, am I?'

'Oh, gerroff, Dee.'

Tommy's suppressed excitement was infectious and as she caught sight of Sister Chapman, Dee called her over. 'Sister, have you heard anything about the war being over tomorrow?' It seemed so utterly unbelievable that Dee uttered the last word almost *sotto voce*.

'I'd heard a whisper, but nothing definite, and I

hardly dared to believe it, so I said nothing. Better not to raise false hopes, that would be too cruel, but I suppose it's a rumour that can't be suppressed.' She looked directly at Tommy who stared back unflinchingly.

Dee couldn't sleep that night and neither could Tommy, despite the throbbing of his hand. Nor were there many in the entire hospital who slept, for the two Canadian soldiers who'd come in with Tommy had also voiced the news. Dee and Tommy talked all night, about every topic they could think of. Many points of view were exchanged and argued over to pass the long hours that they both hoped and prayed would be the last night of the war, yet neither of them felt they could broach the subject of their relationship.

Now that the end seemed to be in sight, Tommy felt as though he had nothing at all to offer her. He was still the ignorant thicko he'd always been. Take the uniform away and what was there? Nothing. He didn't amount to much even in the uniform, while she was a trained nurse and a good one. She was so bright that he was sure she could have been a doctor if her da had had the money for her training.

Dee felt comforted by his presence, and yet it disturbed her. The way he was treating her only seemed to confirm the fact that he looked on her as a friend or a sister. They laughed, reminisced and argued a bit too, but there was nothing endearing, no special smile, no attempt to reach out for her. They didn't even hold hands.

By the time the first dull streaks of the grey

November dawn broke across the sky, the air was electric. The tension was almost tangible as everyone waited, counting the minutes, then the hours, all hoping, some praying aloud. At one minute past eleven, on the eleventh day of the eleventh month, Captain Frazer-Jones, their Chief Medical Officer, told them it was over.

Laughing and crying at the same time, Dee threw herself into Tommy's arms, while shouts and cries of delight and joy resounded throughout the entire building.

'We can go home, Tommy! We can go home! Back to warm rooms, beds, sleep, good food and safety! Oh, we'll never hear the sound of the big guns again.'

'Nor the rattle of the bloody machine guns, nor the stink of cordite! Peace, Dee, it's peace at last!' and with his good arm around her waist he swung her off her feet and twirled her round until they were both dizzy. And then the thoughts of Norman and Ken and all the other lads sobered him. He released her and shook his head. 'What was it all for, Dee? In the name of God, what was it all about?'

'Oh, don't think like that, Tommy please. Don't talk like that, not now, not yet. Let's just enjoy ourselves for a minute. It's over! Thank God, it's really over!' Dee unashamedly dashed away her tears with the back of her hand.

There were thanksgiving services and private parties as the boys and men began to arrive home, although the official celebrations were not to be held until the following year. There were many homes where there were no celebrations, for there were too many families who had lost husbands, fathers, sons and brothers. A whole generation had been wiped out and many were starting to ask why.

There was a communal party at Sal's house, despite the protests of Hilda that she had more room and more dishes, in fact more of everything.

'I've got our Tommy and Abbie home, you've only got your Mike,' Sal insisted. 'Thanks be to God, though,' she had added and had ignored the fact that Abbie was now officially part of Hilda's family too – something Hilda and Joan pointed out in these arguments. But Sal was not going to be moved.

Mary and Marty Maguire, with whom she'd been walking out since he'd been invalided out of the Navy, had been laughing and joking with them. Mary even had an engagement ring set with tiny diamond chippings.

'So, it's official then?' Tommy said.

Mary smiled up at Marty. 'Oh, yes.'

Dee hugged her. 'Oh, I'm so glad for you, Mary.'

Mary smiled. There had been a time when she'd thought she'd never get over Norman Kerrigan, but for once her mam had been right. She was young, and time was a great healer. Of course, Marty wasn't Norman, but she didn't want to be an old maid or a bitter, lonely woman like her mam. There would be plenty of spinsters in the years to come, Lizzie had prophesied, so many of the young men had died. Mary had viewed with horror the prospect of spending the rest of her life at home with Lizzie.

'It's a bit like the old days, isn't it?' Dee laughed as she and Tommy sat on the stairs, one of the few vacant places to sit. Sal's bed had been moved down into the parlour by Tommy, Mike and Pat, who'd sworn it had 'done his back in', and that he was too old for such goings-on. Sal was now lording it over everyone in a pink crocheted bed jacket and matching bedspread that Abbie had bought for her.

'Not quite, Dee. There's too many faces missing, but Mo Cowley's playing hasn't got much better though,' Tommy finished, wincing as Mo thundered his way discordantly through his repertoire on the much abused Presbytery piano.

Abbie and Mike joined them. 'Nothing like a good old-fashioned "do" is there, with Mo in fine form?' Mike joked, giving his wife a quick peck.

'Have you two found anywhere to live yet?' Dee had to shout over the noise.

Thankfully Mo decided to take a short break for liquid refreshment.

'We've been looking, we definitely want to have our own place by Christmas,' Abbie replied firmly, raising one eyebrow which Dee knew meant that she was not finding it easy living with Hilda.

'I'd almost forgotten about Christmas,' Tommy said.

'How could you forget about Christmas?' Abbie cried. 'It's the first one we've had at home for years.'

'I didn't mean I'd forgotten, not really forgotten—'

'You mean you'd not really thought about it,' Dee helped out.

Mo crashed into 'Nelly Dean'.

'God, I can't stand this racket for much longer, you can hardly hear yourself speak.' Mike got to his feet, pulling Abbie up with him.

'Where are you off to then?' Tommy asked.

'To the Pierhead, are you coming?'

'For the ferry?' Tommy questioned eagerly.

'It's freezing out there!' Abbie complained, wishing she and Mike had a place to go to alone.

'No it's not. I think it's a great idea and we won't be missed for a couple of hours,' Tommy urged.

'What about Mary?' Dee asked.

'Oh, leave her, she's wrapped around Marty Maguire like tinsel on a Christmas tree, I don't think she'd appreciate us interrupting and dragging her off for a boat ride,' Tommy laughed, thinking that somehow over the years Mary had drifted away from the group, probably because she'd chosen to stay at home and work in munitions.

Dee went off to hunt out coats and shawls, dragging Abbie with her.

It was a bitterly cold night, but no one really seemed to mind. 'A quick bracing walk around the deck will do us all good,' Mike urged.

'If that's your idea of a good time, Mike Burgess, then you and I are about to have our first row,' Abbie protested. 'I get him to myself for the first time in days and all he wants to do is walk!' Abbie's laughing remarks were directed at Dee.

Dee understood instantly. 'Oh, go on the pair of you. You don't want us tagging along, you want to be on your own.' She gave them both a little shove and she and Tommy watched them stroll towards the stern, arms around each other.

They walked towards the bow, unconsciously putting as much distance between themselves and Abbie and Mike as possible.

'I can't say I envy her, living with Hilda,' Tommy said, leaning against the rail. The deck was deserted, everyone was down in the saloon out of the cold.

'At least Hilda seems to have accepted her.' Dee watched the lights at the Pierhead grow smaller and fainter as the ferry ploughed its way towards Birkenhead.

'But for how long? Mam says two women into one kitchen don't go. There'll be a row soon, she says.'

'She's probably right, but you heard Abbie; they'll get a place of their own.'

'Well, I hope so. It's not that easy.'

They both fell silent as they watched the bow cut through the dark water, leaving a white wave shimmering faintly in the translucent light of the moon. Just above the surface of the river hung a thin, wispy mist.

'Do you remember the night we all came down here for a sail?' Dee said quietly. 'Abbie and Mike, you and me and Mary and . . . Nancy and . . .'

'That bastard Sean Doyle! I'm sorry, Dee, for my language.'

'That's all right, I feel the same way. I don't ever want to see him again, I don't care if he's alive or dead. But I'll always remember what Nancy said that night, about the mist. Poor Nance,' she sighed. 'I suppose in a way she really is better off. If he'd been forced to marry her he would have given her a terrible life. He'd probably have left her in the end, with a couple of children, too.'

'You could look at it that way I suppose.'

There was a silence again before Tommy spoke hesitantly. 'What will you do now, Dee?'

She shrugged. 'I don't know. I've not made any plans. I suppose I'll go on nursing; it's all I'm trained for, and besides, they really don't need me at home. They've managed for so long without me. Rose is nine and Elizabeth's at school. I'd just be in the way. What about you, is it back to the docks?'

Tommy shook his head. Now was the time to voice his plans. 'You remember the lads I told you I walked to the hospital with, the day before the Armistice?'

'The Canadians?'

'Aye, well, we talked all the way and they told me about Canada. They told me I should go out there. Emigrate. It's a good life, they said. There's plenty of land, plenty of work. Tad, the one who I really got on well with, lives in a place called Grimsby.'

'That's in Lincolnshire, or is it Yorkshire?' Dee interrupted, her spirits tumbling. He was going away and she suddenly felt desolate.

'This one isn't, it's about seventy miles from a city called Toronto. It's right on the edge of a lake that's as big as the whole of Wales. Can you believe that, Dee?'

'It's called Lake Ontario.'

'Aye, that's what he called it. Well, his dad has a farm, a fruit farm. He gave me his address and I wrote to him.'

'But you don't know anything about farming or fruit, you're a city lad born and bred.'

Tommy grinned at her, but the grin was forced to cover his apprehension. 'There's always a first time. I could learn. I've learned to do a lot of things I never even dreamed I could do.'

'Have you told your mother yet?'

Tommy looked perplexed. 'No, you're the first one I've told.'

Dee didn't know what to say next, she felt thoroughly miserable and dejected. She swallowed hard, but the lump in her throat got bigger. 'Well, I suppose if you've made up your mind—'

Tommy took a deep breath. 'I haven't, yet. Dee, I . . . I want to ask you something.'

'What?' she replied without much interest. She was thinking how much she'd miss him.

'Will you come with me, Dee?' Tommy blurted out.

She was momentarily stunned. 'What? Go with you to Canada? But . . . what for?'

Tommy ducked his head, blushing furiously, thinking maybe he'd really made a bad mistake in just coming out with it like that, but he'd made up his mind and worked up the courage. He'd remembered the way she'd thrown her arms around his neck when they'd heard the war was over and that had given him a glimmer of hope. Maybe he'd been wrong but he'd hoped and now, well, he had to carry on now he'd started, or she'd think him a real fool. His hands were trembling and his throat felt dry.

'To grow fruit with me, as my wife, Dee. I . . . I'm very fond of you. I really am!'

Dee tried to speak but no words came out. Oh, she'd been such a fool! She'd been so blind; if only she'd have given him some indication, then the last days of the war could have been so different. A tide of pure happiness surged through her, then, stupidly, tears began to slip down her cheeks. It *was* more than just friendship. Maybe in time he'd even love her or maybe he did now and he was too shy to say so.

'You said yourself they don't need you at home, Dee,' Tommy urged, encouraged by her silence. At least she hadn't rejected him out of hand, or worse, laughed at him. No, her eyes were full of tears and she looked . . . overcome.

Dee found her voice at last. 'They don't need me and I'll come with you because I . . . I think I love you Tommy Kerrigan.'

'Oh, Dee, I love you too! I've loved you ever since the day you came to Liverpool!' Tommy cried before he took her in his arms and kissed her, while the mist floated gently up from the Mersey.